Sharon Kendrick once [...] competition by describing her ideal date: being flown to an exotic island by a gorgeous and powerful man. Little did she realise that she'd just wandered into her dream job! Today she writes for Mills & Boon, and her books feature often stubborn but always to-die-for heroes and the women who bring them to their knees. She believes that the best books are those you never want to end. Just like life…

Kim Lawrence lives on a farm in Anglesey with her university lecturer husband, assorted pets who arrived as strays and never left, and sometimes one or both of her boomerang sons. When she's not writing she loves to be outdoors gardening, or walking on one of the beaches for which the island is famous— along with being the place where Prince William and Catherine made their first home!

THE HOUSEKEEPER'S ONE-NIGHT BABY

SHARON KENDRICK

HER FORBIDDEN AWAKENING IN GREECE

KIM LAWRENCE

MILLS & BOON

First published in Great Britain 2023
by Mills & Boon, an imprint of HarperCollins*Publishers* Ltd,
1 London Bridge Street, London, SE1 9GF

www.harpercollins.co.uk

HarperCollins*Publishers*, Macken House, 39/40 Mayor Street Upper,
Dublin 1, D01 C9W8, Ireland

The Housekeeper's One-Night Baby © 2023 Sharon Kendrick

Her Forbidden Awakening in Greece © 2023 Kim Lawrence

ISBN: 978-0-263-30690-3

08/23

THE HOUSEKEEPER'S ONE-NIGHT BABY

SHARON KENDRICK

MILLS & BOON

This book is in memory of my adorable cousin,
Jennifer Shepherd.

She introduced me to music,
had the most demure yet mischievous smile,
and was such an enduring inspiration.

Not just to me and all her other cousins,
but especially to her three amazing children:

Denise, Roli and Danni.

PROLOGUE

'LEAVING?' LIZZIE'S FINGERS tightened around the phone and a pebble of fear hit the pit of her stomach as she listened to her employer's words. 'I... I don't understand.'

'It's quite simple, Lizzie.' Sylvie's cut-crystal accent slowed as if she were talking to someone very stupid. 'The house is going to have to be sold. There's someone coming to look at it next week, as it happens. That's the beginning and the end of it, I'm afraid.'

'But...' Lizzie's words tailed off as the fear inside her grew heavier.

There were things she wanted to say but she didn't know how, because she wasn't the sort of person who was confident about logical argument—especially with employers. She knew her boundaries. She was good at dusting and cleaning, and painting pictures of animals—dogs, preferably. She'd been brought up never to question the person who was paying your cheque, because security was all-important.

But Sylvie *hadn't* paid her, had she? Lizzie had been subsisting on what remained of her savings for months. Meanwhile her boss had been vague in that charming way the upper classes had—of making you feel as if you should be grateful for what seemed like their friendship. Only it wasn't *really* friendship. A friend would never leave you high and dry with barely any warning. A friend would never take advantage of you without a second thought. She sucked in a deep breath.

So tell her. Make her realise what this means to you.

'But that means I won't have anywhere to live,' she objected quietly.

Sylvie injected a note of faux understanding into her plummy voice. 'I realise that,' she said consolingly. 'But you're a hard worker, Lizzie. You're bound to find a job with accommodation, just like you did with me. And I'll write you a glowing reference, you can be sure of that. There's really nothing to worry about.'

Lizzie swallowed. This next bit was harder, because her mother had always taught her that talking about money was vulgar. But what price vulgarity if the cupboards were bare? 'But you owe me money,' she croaked, her cheeks flushing hotly. 'I haven't had anything for over three months now.'

'Yes. Bit of a cashflow problem, I'm afraid. Look, I'm not going to promise something I can't deliver, Lizzie—so how about you have a good hunt around the house and take anything you want, in lieu of payment? None of the antiques, obviously—but you'll find plenty of last season's clothes, which I won't be wearing again. You could flog them on the Internet and make yourself a small fortune—isn't that what people do these days? Listen, darling, I have to go—there's a car waiting. I just want to say thanks for everything, and could you make sure the house is super-tidy for next Wednesday? Someone called Niccolò Macario is coming to buy it, hopefully. Some super-hot Italian billionaire, apparently.' Sylvie gave a throaty laugh. 'What a pity I won't be there.'

CHAPTER ONE

HE HAD HIRED a sleek silver sports car for his stay in England, but, having driven it to the centre of the tiny Cotswolds village, Niccolò decided to park next to the duck pond and then walk the last couple of miles. He was feeling wired. More wired than usual. His nerves were jangled. His heart was racing and his lips were dry. He tried not to give it too much thought. Thinking never helped anything and he should be used to this reaction by now. It always happened on this day. Every year, without fail. A pulse thudded at his temple. Without. Fail.

His footsteps slowed to a halt in front of the imposing house and he looked around, trying to appreciate the beauty of his surroundings as the sun beat down on his head. The ancient building which rose into the cloudless sky was the colour of honey and cream. The grounds were lush and beautiful. Heavy roses scented the air with their rich perfume and bees buzzed happily in among the colourful flowerbeds. It was the most idyllic of scenes. Rural England at her finest.

He glanced around and his eyes narrowed, because the beauty was an illusion, like so much else in life. It had an unkempt air about it—like a woman who woke up with last night's mascara clinging to her eyes. If you looked closely you could see the peeling paint and scarred window panes. The inevitable creep of weeds not quite disguised by the vibrant hues of the abundant flowers.

His gaze flicked across to the glitter of an ornamental pool and a ragged sigh erupted from somewhere deep in his lungs. The ache in his heart was always at its most intense in the summer—the bright sunlight mocking the darkness which invaded his soul—the loss and guilt as potent as ever, even after all these years. He felt dead inside. As if someone had taken a blowtorch and blasted everything away, leaving him with nothing but a vast emptiness and a sense of futility.

That was why he chose an annual hands-on project like this to supplement an already busy life—a diversion to capture his attention, as well as adding to his considerable fortune. Buying a potentially valuable property took him back to when he'd first started, when he had been hungry to succeed. He didn't need the money any more, but work was a useful focus for his restless spirit. His lips tightened. It could blot out most things if you let it.

He glanced down at his watch and walked towards the door. The agent from the real estate office was supposed to be meeting him here, though there was no sign of his car. Maybe he had walked, too. As he pressed the doorbell, Niccolò thought about what he'd been told about the property. The owner was a wealthy socialite, apparently, and desperate to sell. He gave a calculating smile. Indiscreet of the agent to let that slip, but always good to know from a negotiating standpoint.

He heard the sound of echoing footsteps from inside the house and then the heavy oak door was pulled open and a woman stood there, framed by the darkness of the interior. A strange wraith of a woman with hair the colour of a faded Halloween pumpkin and translucent skin which was dusted with freckles. She wore a gown of rich green silk, which clung to the luscious outline of her body, and her bare arms were strong. The dress, its hem brushing the stone floor, was completely inappropriate for daytime wear—yet somehow it seemed fitting that such a glorious creature would inhabit a residence as old and historic as this.

Her full lips parted as if in shock and Niccolò felt the unexpected punch of desire as he gazed at her. It was powerful and it was potent. The heavy beat of his heart. The tantalising ache of his groin. He wanted to reach out and touch her, to see if her skin could possibly be as soft as it looked and then to trace the outline of her lips with the pad of his thumb and make them tremble. His mouth was dry as he shook his head, in an attempt to bat away his wayward thoughts. Since when had he started hitting on a total stranger? Didn't women always hit on *him*?

He cleared his throat but that did little to quell the tightening sensation in his chest. 'Niccolò Macario,' he explained succinctly, elevating his eyebrows in question, when still she said nothing. 'I believe you're expecting me?'

Lizzie gazed back at the powerful, black-haired figure who was standing in front of her and all the things she'd been trained to say, like: *Good morning, sir. May I help you?* or, *I believe you've come to view the house, sir?* were stubbornly refusing to leave her lips. Her head was spinning and she couldn't move. Literally couldn't speak. She felt disorientated and bewildered. Because…because…

Could this man possibly be *real*?

She blinked at him in disbelief.

It wasn't just that he was exceptionally tall or exceptionally muscular, with ruffled hair as dark as the wing of a crow. Or that her unwilling attention was drawn by his immaculately cut trousers to the powerful thrust of his legs, just as the rippling silk shirt directed her gaze to his honed torso. It wasn't even the glittering jet gaze, or sexy accent—both of which were making goosebumps shiver over her arms. No, it was the way he was looking at her, those hard eyes narrowed and curious. As if he'd just seen something he hadn't been expecting. Something worth looking at. Normally Lizzie would have glanced behind her to check if his attention had been caught by someone else, which of course it would have been.

Except that she knew herself to be alone.

Alone in a grand house which had been her home, but not for much longer, wearing an outrageously expensive dress belonging to her boss, which was gliding over her flesh like a second skin.

As instructed, she'd spent the morning going through Sylvie's wardrobe—trying to work out the potential value of the various outfits and balancing it against the unpaid wages she was owed. Most of the garments had been badly treated—the odd cigarette burn and red-wine stain making them unwearable—but this one had stood out like a beacon. It was a fantasy dress, the sort of thing she wouldn't usually have dreamed of wearing, even if she'd been able to afford it. She always dressed practically and comfortably, both of which suited her humble position in life and her tendency to shrink into the shadows. But something had compelled Lizzie to throw caution to the wind and slither into it, after first removing her bra so that the silky fabric wouldn't reveal any lumps or bumps.

She swallowed. It was the most exquisite thing she had ever worn. It made her feel different and was obviously making her *look* different, too. Why else was a man like Niccolò Macario seemingly transfixed by her, when usually she barely merited a second glance from members of the opposite sex?

'You *are* expecting me?' he repeated, slight impatience tinging his tone as he glanced over her shoulder. 'Is the estate agent here?'

'No. Not yet.' Her people-pleasing tendency asserted itself and she shot him a sympathetic look. 'He should have been.'

'Yes, he should,' he agreed coldly.

'Maybe he's been delayed.'

'Maybe,' he conceded, the careless flick of his hand indicating that already he was bored with discussions about the agent, before he frowned again. 'But you *are* still selling your house?'

'Oh, yes. Yes, of course,' she replied hastily and was

about to enlighten him that it wasn't actually *her* house and she was just the housekeeper, when something stopped her. He had obviously made the incorrect assumption about her status because she was dressed in this glorious emerald concoction, made by one of the world's leading designers. He certainly wouldn't have asked the same question if she'd been clad in the unflattering grey uniform Sylvie had always insisted she wear—'I think it's better when the staff dress like staff, Lizzie. Everyone likes to know where they stand'—or the sturdy black brogues her boss favoured.

'I'm not actually the owner,' she said reluctantly.

'Oh?'

She met the ebony gleam of his eyes and didn't know what made her say it. Was it because she was enjoying being looked at like a woman for once, rather than some drudge of a servant? Being treated as a human being with thoughts and feelings of her own—rather than as a piece of old furniture you could put your feet on.

'I'm…erm…house-sitting,' she blurted out. Which to some extent was true. She certainly wasn't being *paid* to be here, was she? She was poor and would soon be homeless, but right now she wasn't coming across that way, not judging by the way this man was still regarding her—with unmistakable admiration glittering from his beautiful ebony eyes. And suddenly Lizzie found herself wanting to play the game a little longer. To be a woman in an expensive dress without any scary fears about the future. Why shouldn't she act as if she were this man's equal, even if she knew very well she wasn't? 'But I know the property extremely well. I could show you round, if you wanted.' She hesitated. 'Or you go along to the drawing room and wait for the agent in there.'

'I could. But I haven't much time, I need to be back in London this evening.' His voice became matter-of-fact again and Lizzie wondered if she had imagined the ruthless expression which briefly hardened his strong features.

'Right,' she said uncertainly.

'And so I'm happy for you to show me around instead,' he continued, before fixing her with a quizzical smile. 'Unless you have something else you'd rather be doing?'

The impact of that smile was devastating and Lizzie's heart performed a rapid somersault. But that couldn't have been a serious question. Surely he must be aware that most women would have moved heaven and earth to spend time with him. She certainly would. Hell, yes. It wasn't every day that a man like this tumbled into your orbit.

And even though a small voice was warning against being dazzled by all his charisma, she shut her mind to it. She was perfectly qualified to give him a guided tour and hadn't lied about knowing the historic house. Sometimes she thought she knew the place better than Sylvie and, in truth, was miserable at the thought of having to leave. Over the years, Lizzie had made a point of learning about every precious room and artefact as she carefully polished and preserved them, and wasn't this an opportunity to put her knowledge to some good use? To step out of her self-made shadow and shine for once, before she stepped away from the historic splendour for ever?

'No, I haven't got anything else I'd rather be doing,' she said candidly. 'In fact, I happen to have the whole day to myself.'

'Lucky me,' he said softly.

'Erm.' She cleared her throat. 'Please. Come in.'

'*Grazie.*'

She watched as he inclined his jet-dark head and entered the property and as he passed she could detect the warm scent of bergamot and spice and something else. Something which seemed at odds with his sophisticated appearance. Was she detecting pheromones and a raw and fundamental sex appeal? Suddenly Lizzie wondered if she had bitten off more than she could chew and just as suddenly realised that she *didn't care.*

'L-let's start here, shall we?' she said, hastily beginning to recount the facts about the house which she'd learnt so assiduously. But that wasn't really surprising since she had grown to love Ermecott Manor, almost as if it were her own. 'This is the Great Hall, which was built in the mid-seventeenth century, although the stained-glass windows didn't appear until nearly seventy years later.' She gestured upwards towards the windows—some of which were unfortunately cracked. But the sudden movement caused her unfettered breasts to wobble beneath the delicate silk, reminding her that she was *still wearing Sylvie's dress* and she must look like a complete idiot. Was that why Niccolò Macario gave a short intake of breath, as if someone had suddenly robbed the room of oxygen?

'I'd better go and change into something more suitable,' she said quickly.

Dark eyes met hers. 'Why would you do that?'

'Isn't it obvious?' She gave a nervous laugh. 'It's an evening dress.'

'It is also a very beautiful dress, which makes you blend into these ancient surroundings perfectly,' he commented sagely. 'Certainly better than a pair of jeans, which I'm guessing would be your chosen alternative.'

To her horror, Lizzie started blushing at what *sounded* like a compliment, though she didn't exactly have a lot of experience of those either. She hadn't been out with anyone since Dan, who used to delight in putting her down, for reasons best known to himself. Why she had tolerated it for so long was another matter and more to do with her own lack of self-esteem than any magnificent trait possessed by her ex-boyfriend.

Resisting the desire to fan her face and draw attention to her hot cheeks, Lizzie glanced down at the emerald silk which was pooling luxuriously by her feet. No point in enlightening him that she hardly ever wore jeans because she considered her bottom too big, but neither did she want to go upstairs and risk breaking the spell he seemed to have cast over her. She wanted to hang onto this delicious feeling and revel in every second of it, like someone getting into a deep bubble bath at the end of a long day. Lifting her head, she met his ebony gaze and prayed the estate agent wouldn't suddenly ring on the front door.

'You really think it's okay?' she questioned naively.

'I really do,' he replied gravely.

Their gazes met and she couldn't seem to look away and neither, it seemed, could he. She'd never stared at anyone like that before—nor had the feeling that to do so was perfectly okay. It was as if he were exerting some silent and unknown power over her—making her long for things which had always eluded her before.

Her frigidity had been one of Dan's main complaints. *'You're like a block of ice, Lizzie.'* Well, she certainly wasn't feeling like a block of ice now. Her blood was burning through her veins and she could feel her breasts swelling to what felt like twice their normal size, their tips becoming painful little bullets which were pushing against the slippery silk of her gown. Did he notice that? Was that why his body had grown unmistakably tense?

She could feel the silken rush of heat low in her core and she turned away, terrified he would somehow guess the crazy thoughts which were crowding her mind. 'In that case, why don't we get on with the tour?' Her voice was artificially bright as she pointed an unsteady finger down towards one of the corridors leading off the Great Hall. 'We can do the ground floor first.'

'Perfetto,' he said, his brief smile almost making her want to weep because he looked so beautiful.

Niccolò followed the bright-haired woman through the shadowed rooms, forcing himself to concentrate on the panelled walls and worn flagstones and the jewel-coloured light spilling through the stained-glass windows. He looked around with a connoisseur's eye and thought how beautiful the bare bones of the house were, and how much better it would look if some money were lavished on it.

'This is the room where the original family chose to eat,' his red-headed guide informed him chattily. 'It gave them a little privacy, away from the watchful eyes of their servants.'

'*Sì*, the ever-watchful eyes of servants,' he observed. 'Though in a house this size it would be impossible not to have them around.'

'Yes, staff can be a bit of a double-edged sword, can't they?' she said, a slightly acid note entering her voice. 'A bit like a trip to the dentist. You know you have to endure them, you just wish you didn't have to.'

Her sharp interjection gave him the excuse he needed to study her again, but he didn't stop to wonder what had motivated it because he was so captivated by the eyes which were gazing up at him. They really were the most extraordinary colour—as green as fresh pistachios and fringed by lashes the same colour as her hair. Her bare lips were curiously inviting and he found himself staring at them for a second longer than was necessary. Was that the reason why—to his unexpected delight—she actually *blushed*?

As if she had revealed too much of herself she turned her back on him, and now he was presented with the equally delectable sway of her buttocks, green silk gleaming enticingly as it moved over the fleshy globes. The pale red hair reached almost to her waist and he wondered how it might feel to run his fingers through the heavy strands. His heart was pounding and suddenly Niccolò felt alive. The bleakness which was clogging his heart seemed to have been granted a temporary amnesty by the sudden urgent needs of his body and he wanted to taste her. To cover those soft lips with his own. Yet the sting of desire was coupled with confusion—because he couldn't recall such a fierce and indiscriminate hunger beyond his teenage years, when his behaviour had been governed by the unstoppable flood of hormones. His mouth hardened. And look what had happened as a result of that.

'Are you looking at this as a family home?' she questioned.

Her words burst the bubble of painful thoughts and he narrowed his eyes in question.

'If…if you decide to buy, I mean,' she added briskly. 'There are…there are lots of good local schools nearby.'

Niccolò knew exactly what she was doing. Trying to establish whether or not he was single. It happened. In fact, it happened a lot of the time. A clumsy query prompted by a fruitless search for the outline of a wedding ring, or the image of a smiling baby on the home screen of his phone. The thought of that made his heart twist and he wanted to recoil with all the hurt which was still inside him, but years of self-discipline enabled him to stem his reaction with a brief tightening of his hands.

'No, I don't have any family,' he clipped out. 'And that situation isn't going to change.'

'Right,' she said.

He knew he'd given her more information than was needed and wondered what had prompted his uncharacteristic disclosure. Was it to make her understand what kind of man he really was? To warn her that, while he acknowledged the powerful and unusual chemistry which was simmering between them, he wasn't looking for a wife to grace this elegant abode. Or anywhere else. 'If you must know, I'm looking for a property to develop in southern England.'

'Develop?' The word triggered an instant reaction and she was staring at him as if he had just proposed conducting a sacrificial rite beneath the beamed ceilings of the ancient building. 'You can't do that!' she blustered indignantly.

'Why not?'

'Because this is a Grade I listed property and there are strict rules concerning what you can and can't do with it.'

'What do you imagine I want to do with it?' he demanded sarcastically. 'Build a three-storey extension on the side and put in an underground swimming pool?'

'I don't know—you tell me!' she flared back, as if he had touched a raw nerve. 'We have far too many people coming to this part of the world, flashing their cash and trying to…'

'Trying to what?' he questioned as her words tailed away.

She shook her head, as if she had said too much. 'It doesn't matter.'

'No, tell me. I'm curious.' And he was, despite the fact that people rarely spoke to him with such insulting candour.

She shrugged and, in the subdued lighting, the

dark green straps of her dress shimmered. 'To change things.'

'And you don't like change?'

'Does anyone?' She seemed to remember that she was supposed to be helping sell her friend's house and shrugged. 'Well, I don't mind the changes we're in control of.'

Was there any such thing? Niccolò wondered. He thought of his dead sister. Of his mother. And the father who had never bothered to hide his contempt for him after the accident. He thought of a simple decision which could have changed the whole course of everybody's lives, his own included—and how the nightmare would never have happened. But nobody could rewrite the past—no matter how much they wanted to, he reminded himself bitterly. It was the present which should be concerning him.

'I'm not planning a major assault on a much-loved landmark building. I'm not totally without taste or sensitivity,' he said quietly, because he wanted to wipe that melancholic expression from her face.

'What are you planning to do with it, then?' she ventured curiously, before adding, 'If you buy it, that is.'

He curved her a smile. 'Why don't you have dinner with me tonight and I'll tell you?'

Lizzie blinked at him, not sure if she'd heard him correctly. Was he actually asking her *out*? On a *date*? 'You want to have dinner with me?'

'Is that such a wild proposition?'

Well, of course it was. Things like that didn't happen to women like her. She wondered what might have happened next if the shrill ring of the doorbell hadn't echoed through the house and they both froze, as if stunned by the sound of the outside world.

'It's the agent,' she whispered, peering out through the window to see a familiar figure.

'Don't answer it,' he whispered back.

'He's…he's got a key. He'll let himself in.'

'So let's hide,' he suggested silkily. 'And maybe he'll go away.'

There was a heartbeat of a pause while Lizzie weighed up the wisdom of such an action. No way should they be hiding away, like a couple of kids. Niccolò Macario shouldn't be suggesting it and she certainly shouldn't be colluding with it. But she knew what would happen the moment the agent walked in. He would see her—not clad in her habitual frumpy grey dress and sensible shoes, but shimmying around in one of Sylvie's more expensive cast-offs.

And it wasn't just his expression she was dreading—one of disbelief, quickly followed by suspicion, and a faint concern that she'd lost her marbles, or was in the process of stealing something. No, it would be the way he would behave which she couldn't face. With that slightly patronising air which was so hard to take sometimes. Because it didn't matter how liberal or nice people considered themselves to be, they always treated domestic staff differently. Sometimes they were a little *too* friendly, sometimes they were aloof, but one thing was for sure, they were never *normal*. They probably didn't even realise they were doing it, but it always made her feel small. Like a second-class citizen.

And she didn't want to feel that way in front of Niccolò Macario. She wanted to carry on pretending they were equals, with him looking at her with undisguised pleasure in his black eyes. With her revelling in the thought that he had actually asked her to have dinner with him and she still hadn't told him yes, or no.

'Okay,' she said breathlessly. 'Follow me.' Scarcely able to believe what she was doing, she walked towards a small broom cupboard at the far end of the corridor and stepped inside, clicking on the low-wattage bulb, which brought only a meagre element of light to the cramped space. Her throat dried as Niccolò followed her and the quiet click of the door closed them off from the world, muffling the sound of the agent's voice as he called out her name.

'Lizzie!' And then again, louder this time. *'Lizzie!'*

But Lizzie didn't answer. She just stood there, not moving, barely breathing—though her heart was beating so loudly she was certain Niccolò must be able to hear it.

'This is ridiculous,' she whispered, at one point.

'So what if it is?' He gave a short laugh. 'Isn't the very substance of life ridiculous?'

She couldn't think of an answer to that cynical query, because that was the moment the agent chose to pass right by the cupboard and Lizzie held her breath, her skin turning to goosebumps as she met the dark glitter of Niccolò's mocking stare.

It was very small in here, she thought. Much too confined for two people to be able to stand there and avoid touching. But that was what it felt like they were doing, even though they weren't actually *touching*. It was as if they were in a bubble, all of their own. He was close enough for her to be able to detect his body heat, and be acutely aware of his breathing. Close enough for him to see her erect nipples, outlined boldly against the emerald silk, and she couldn't seem to shift the inappropriate thought that she wanted him to stroke them. She wanted that very badly and that kind of raw hunger and urgent need had never happened to her before.

She didn't know how long they stood there, while the hapless agent continued to call her name. Only that the tension seemed to increase with every second which passed—especially when she heard the faint vibrating sound of Niccolò's phone, coming from his pocket. She saw his eyes widen but he didn't move and she prayed the agent wouldn't have super-sensitive hearing and come charging back down the corridor. She imagined him opening the door and finding them and, if that were the case, what on earth would they *say*?

But there was nothing except the sound of retreating footsteps and after a while the front door slammed and the sound of an accelerating car informed her that they were alone once more.

Their gazes met. The tension broke and they burst out laughing, at exactly the same time. It was a heady rush of pure adrenaline. A unique moment of shared communication, acknowledging their complicity. But when the laughter died away, the tension was back, only this time it was different. It was so powerful it was almost tangible. It was all-consuming—but most of all, it was physical. Her senses were on fire. She ached with a desire and heat which was drenching her core. She felt dizzy with the sensation—helpless yet energised, all at the same time.

'Now what?' he questioned softly.

Lizzie wasn't experienced enough to know what he meant yet somehow she knew exactly what he meant. She ought to move. Open the door and let some daylight in. Say something bright and superficial which would make everything seem normal again.

But she didn't move.

Didn't speak.

She just waited for something she knew shouldn't be happening, which she wanted. So much. Because the weirdest thing was that somehow she felt *connected* to this man. As if this meeting was in some way predestined and everything was exactly as it should be. Was it the dress which was making her feel so decadent? The sensation of cool silk coating her skin like honey and making her feel like a real woman for once, instead of a common skivvy? Or was it that Niccolò Macario was the most gorgeous man she'd ever met and she felt as if she were in the middle of some amazing dream, with all kinds of possibilities?

Life had been tough for Lizzie. She'd grown up with more responsibilities than most of her peers. She'd learned to put everyone else first and place her own needs last, but for once she wanted to do something for herself. Something incredible. Just for the hell of it. A dinner date was a stretch too far. She'd feel far too self-conscious in a posh restaurant and he would quickly discover she wasn't who he thought she was. And then he would be disappointed.

But right here was perfect for what she wanted right now.

Feeling a bit like Cinderella, she gazed up into the ebony glitter of his eyes.

Kiss me, she prayed silently. *Just kiss me.*

CHAPTER TWO

THE WOMAN HE now knew to be Lizzie was breathtakingly close and Niccolò knew he needed to get out of this damned broom cupboard before it was too late and he did something he regretted. His heart pounded. But she wanted him to kiss her. There was no mistake about that. Her eyes were wide and dark with longing and the sexual hunger radiating from her curvy body was instantly apparent. She looked sweet and desirable.

He shook his head, trying to hammer some logic into his befuddled brain, because he was responsible for the position in which he now found himself. He had made an impetuous suggestion and, to his surprise, the redhead had agreed to it. Yet he didn't *do* impetuous and he'd never had sex with a stranger before—a prospect which was becoming more likely with every passing second. It wasn't even something he'd ever considered—and he certainly wouldn't have chosen this most unlikely of settings, with a feather duster dangling inconveniently nearby and some sort of mop and bucket in the corner.

Yet something nebulous drew him to the curvy little guide. Something which transcended her pale green eyes and translucent skin. He had laughed uninhibitedly with her as they'd hidden from the hapless agent, and that was rare for a man known to be sombre. It had felt like the most potent of aphrodisiacs. Like a fierce light flooding his darkened soul. That it should have happened on this, the worst day of his calendar year, made it even more significant. Did that explain the exquisite hardness in his groin and the pulsing slug of his blood? His heart was beating erratically as he stared down into her face, a fast-dwindling sense of rationality silently imploring her to warn him off. 'I want to kiss you,' he said unevenly.

There was a pause while he waited for an outrage he knew deep down wouldn't materialise. Yet part of him had wanted her to refuse him, because it would be far simpler to beat a hasty retreat. To go back to his hotel room and blot out the rest of the day with a glass, or three of whisky. But no, she tilted her face upwards so that her soft lips were a mere breath away.

'Well, that's handy, because I want you to kiss me,' she whispered.

'Are you sure?' His voice was deliberately hard. 'You should be careful what you wish for, *cara*.'

'Why?'

Did she realise that the near innocence of her question was completely at odds with the blatant sensuality of the foxy dress she was wearing? Or perhaps she was aware that men were turned on by apparent contradictions and was capitalising on that. 'Because once we start kissing you're going to want to have sex with me,' he drawled. 'And you need to decide if that's really such a good idea.'

Her lashes lowered to shade her widened eyes, but her expression was composed when they fluttered open again, as if she had just given herself a silent pep talk. 'You're very sure of yourself, aren't you?'

'With women?' He shrugged. 'Always.'

He wanted her to rail against him for his perceived arrogance—when all he was doing was stating a fact—but she didn't. There wasn't a trace of recrimination on her freckled face. Instead, her lips were parting in as blatant an invitation as he'd ever seen and the glint of hunger in her eyes was unmistakable as she swayed towards him.

And now it was too late for caution or warning, because his own needs had taken over and he was kissing her and she was kissing him back with a fervour which took his breath away. And her lips tasted incredible. *Incredible.* Niccolò gave a small groan. *Madre di Dio.* Like honey and silk.

Her hair felt like silk too, and he ran his fingers through the luxuriant strands as he'd wanted to do from the first moment he'd seen her. Cupping her face, he deepened the kiss until she was moaning with soft abandon, her hands clutching at his shoulders—and that was all the leverage he needed. He brought her even closer so that her breasts were pressing into him, the hardened tips jutting provocatively against his chest and he closed his eyes as spears of desire made his groin grow rocky. He thought about unzipping himself and plunging deep inside her molten heat and he almost gasped aloud with the anticipation of that.

Still, he offered her another chance to call a halt to this madness as he dragged his lips away from hers. 'If you want to change your mind,' he managed unsteadily, 'now might be the moment.'

'No,' she whispered, shaking her head so that her bright hair glimmered in the dim light. 'I don't.'

His throat tightened and relief rushed over him as he caressed a thrusting nipple between his finger and his thumb.

'So. Are you going to take me upstairs?' he questioned silkily as she squirmed with pleasure.

Lizzie struggled to steady her breath as she met the glitter in Niccolò's eyes. Her heart was beating faster than she could ever remember, her body was on fire with need but she was afraid to move—terrified that the journey between this tiny alcove and the bedroom would destroy the magic they had created.

Because what if he changed his mind on the way? What if she did? That would obviously be the most sensible option, but right now she didn't want to feel sensible. She felt almost...*wild*—and that wasn't like her at all. But she had played safe all her life and where had it got her? Stony broke and soon to be homeless, that was where. What did she have to lose? She had always been a good girl but suddenly she wanted to be bad. Really, really bad. Surely that wasn't such a major crime.

'Upstairs? It's a bit of a trek.' Rising up on tiptoes, she trailed her lips over the darkened rasp of his jaw and her throaty response came out of its own accord, as if she were the type of woman who whispered flirtatious questions to strange men every day of the week. 'Is that what you want?'

His breath was shuddering as he took her hand and placed it over his heart, its fierce thunder easily matching her own. She could see tension tautening his strong features as he bit the words out, his Italian accent suddenly very pronounced. 'What do you *think* I want, Lizzie?'

She hoped he wasn't hoping for a coherent answer because she couldn't give one. Couldn't do anything except gasp out her undisguised pleasure as he brushed his hand slowly over her swollen breast and the nipple peaked against his palm. He made a low murmur of appreciation but his hand did not stop to linger and Lizzie closed her eyes with expectation as he skimmed his fingers over her hips and began to ruck up the silken dress.

'Oh,' she gasped as a questing forefinger found her bare leg and tiptoed up her inner thigh, only he took so long about it that she thought she was going to lose her mind. At last it reached her panties and she heard him mutter something appreciative as he encountered the moist heat, which must have seared against him. She gave a little cry as he edged the damp fabric aside and touched her aroused flesh and she was scarcely aware of the feather duster brushing against her bare shoulders as she leaned back against the wall, while he began to strum her with sweet precision. And then things got heated. The pleasure was building and building, sweet and intense. She couldn't stop it, even if she wanted to. She bit her lip. And sweet heaven—how could she ever want to stop something like this?

'Niccolò,' she crooned restlessly.

'Tell me,' he coaxed, fractionally increasing the pressure.

But she couldn't answer. All she could do was cry out as she started to orgasm, her body bucking helplessly beneath his finger, and he smothered her lips with his own and kissed her. And only when she had quietened and the spasms had faded did he draw away from her. In the dim light, he brushed her hair away from her face and she could detect her musky scent on his fingertips. His gaze was jet-dark and piercing as it sliced into her and his breathing was quickened, but it was hard to tell from his expression what was going on in his head.

'I want to be inside you, Lizzie,' he said silkily. 'I want that very much. But not in here, with a damned broom sticking into my back. Do you want to take me upstairs now?'

His tone was as calm and as logical as if he were putting a proposition to a debating society—making it sound as if she had some sort of choice in the matter when she felt as if she would go mad if he didn't possess her completely. She wondered how he could be so *controlled* when her blood was practically at boiling point. She wondered again what he was thinking but she sensed she would never know.

It made sense to move but where did she take him? Not up to her room, that was for sure. If he thought the broom cupboard was claustrophobic, he'd get a shock when he saw her tiny eaves room at the very top of the house, with its single bed and sloping ceiling. She wouldn't use Sylvie's room for obvious reasons—she didn't want to look at her boss's haughty portrait staring down at her as she lay on the bed with Niccolò. She thought about the Red Room—which was the best of all the guest rooms and a little bit decadent, as its name suggested. And since she was the one responsible for keeping it clean and tidy—what did it matter if they mussed it up a little?

'Okay,' she said huskily. 'Come with me.'

Slowly, she ascended the dark wooden staircase, trying not to focus too deeply on what she was about to do. She pushed open the door into a room resplendent with heavy red velvet and satin. There were swags and fringes and thick golden brocade and as Niccolò followed her inside, she remembered the time one of Sylvie's drunken guests had proclaimed that it looked like a bordello. Did it?

She watched him walk over to the window and look out at the overgrown gardens and suddenly she remembered that he was here as a prospective buyer and her thoughts shot off on an unexpected trajectory. What if he *did* buy it? Would he need a housekeeper? And if so had she just destroyed her chances of getting the job by letting him bring her to orgasm in the broom cupboard?

But that mass of crazy possibilities dissolved when he crossed the room and took her in his arms again, staring down into her face with an unfathomable expression before he dipped his head, so that his warm breath fanned her lips.

'Now,' he murmured. 'Where were we?'

Her head tipped back and suddenly she was shy and out of her depth. Wasn't she supposed to be a frigid virgin? she wondered dazedly. 'I... I can't remember.'

'Then perhaps I'd better remind you.'

He started with a kiss, then slowly trailed his lips all the way down her neck, until his tongue reached her cleavage and Lizzie gave a little moan of pleasure as he traced a moist line between her breasts. With a low and unsteady laugh, he unzipped her dress and it slithered to the ground in a whisper of heavy silk as he took a step back to look at her. But oddly, Lizzie didn't feel in the least bit self-conscious as she stood in front of him, wearing nothing but her panties.

Was that because his dark gaze was sweeping over her body with blatant admiration, or because she felt as if she were on the brink of something extraordinary? As if everything which had happened in her world up until now had happened for a reason. And this was the reason. Him. This man with whom she felt a powerful connection which was more than just physical. She was aware of helping unbutton his shirt with fingers which were unusually shaky, and that he was having some difficulty sliding the zip of his trousers down. Maybe that should have daunted her, but it didn't because, unexpectedly, he told her she was beautiful as he kicked away his handmade leather shoes and, even though she knew she wasn't, he actually made her *believe* it.

And nothing could have prepared her for the joy of being naked in his arms once they were lying on the bed together, as if that were a perfectly normal thing to do. Or revelling in the silken texture of his warm skin against hers. The contrast of the hard planes and sinews of his body against the softness of her own was nothing short of intoxicating.

She grew bolder by the second, her fingers beginning to explore him—edging over his chest and down over his hard belly. But when she tentatively tiptoed towards his groin, he said something fervent in Italian and shook his dark head, reaching for a small packet on the bedside table, which he must have put there, unnoticed by her. But then his face hardened, and he tilted her chin so that their gazes were on a collision course.

'It is not too late,' he ground out.

'T-too late for what?' she echoed unsteadily.

'To call a halt to this madness.' His lips twisted in an odd kind of smile. 'For that is what it is.'

He might as well have held up a written warning, but Lizzie paid his words no heed. How could she? She'd read about the point of no return plenty of times, where foreplay had gone too far to be able to stop. Another wave of longing rippled through her. This must be it.

'No,' she said, through lips so swollen with his kiss that the words sounded slurred. 'I don't want to stop. Unless...' She forced herself to say it. 'Unless you do.'

He growled with what sounded like anticipation. 'What do you think, Lizzie?' He buried his lips in her hair as he moved on top of her, all muscle and skin and warm weight. 'Oh Lizzie,' he whispered. And then he was inside her. With one thrust he filled her with his hardness and she cried out, mostly in wonder that something could be so intimate. She could feel her body expanding to accommodate him—and after that initial pierce of pain it felt nothing short of amazing. She was briefly aware of him growing still inside her, but she was too intent on her own needs to pay it any attention.

'Please,' she whimpered instinctively.

'Please what?' he husked.

'M-more.'

He gave another growl as he began to move again and she angled her hips to meet his powerful thrust—slow and provocative at first until it increased in urgency. The tension inside her began to build as wild excitement gripped her, and this time she knew what to expect. She felt his big body shudder in time with hers and Lizzie was overcome by a feeling of utter contentment as he gave a shout of something which sounded shaken, and exultant.

In that dreamy state, she must have fallen asleep because she was woken by the unwelcome sensation of him withdrawing from her body, though already he was hard again. She opened her eyes to object to find herself confronted by a searing black gaze and apprehension spiked at her skin like needles. It wasn't exactly a *hostile* look, but it wasn't what she was expecting. What *was* she expecting? That he would slowly raise her fingertips to his lips and tell her he'd just found the woman of his dreams?

Before, his expression had been filled with passion and appreciation—but now... Now he was surveying her with an expression she couldn't work out.

'Niccolò?' she questioned uncertainly.

Niccolò raked his long fingers back through the disarray of his thick hair, trying to make some sense of what had just happened. He'd just had sex with a stranger. A virgin. A sweet, tight, passionate virgin. 'That was *not* what I was expecting,' he husked, his heart still racing as he stared at her, in all her ruffled beauty, as she lay outlined against a pillow of scarlet and golden brocade. 'Why the hell didn't you say something?'

'You mean…' the tiny tip of a very pink tongue touched the edges of her lips '…that you were the first?'

He gave a short laugh. 'What else would I mean?'

'You didn't…' Her voice faltered. 'You didn't like it?'

His eyes narrowed. He didn't *think* she was being disingenuous, but with women you could never be sure. 'You know damned well I did,' he bit out, before expelling a heavy sigh. 'But you shouldn't have wasted your innocence on a man like me.'

She was regarding him with bewilderment. 'Wasted it?'

Did she really need him to spell it out for her? 'If you've waited this long, then you should have chosen a man with whom you want to have a relationship— and that man isn't going to be me, *cara.*'

There was a pause, but she didn't take the hint. 'You're saying you don't have relationships?'

He shook his head. Not with women who had eyes he could drown in. Who kissed him as if they'd never been kissed before. Who could make him forget his pain and his grief but leave something in its place which made him uneasy. 'Not with people who live on the other side of the world.' He gave her an apologetic smile. 'Nothing personal. I just don't have the time.'

'Okay. Well, thanks for being straight with me. I… appreciate it.' She sat up straight and began to slide her legs towards the edge of the bed and, although he could see it was an effort, she slanted him the sweetest smile. 'I guess there's nothing more to be said.'

Was it her generosity which made his mind race—a generosity he probably didn't deserve? Or just the realisation that she was taking him at his word and preparing to leave and, as she stood up, all he could see was the rosy tightness of her nipples and the pale triangle of fire at the juncture of her thighs? And suddenly his thinking brain was no longer functioning efficiently as the rush of blood was diverted towards the more elemental requirements of his body.

'Or we could spend the rest of the night together,' he said slowly.

She turned her head, her green gaze clashing with his. 'Haven't you got to be back in London tonight?' Clearly not making it easy for him.

'Yes, I was going to a business dinner, but I can make my excuses. I want to make love to you again,' he told her softly. 'There are so many things I would like to do to you, which I think you would enjoy. But I meant what I said.' He paused and said the words very deliberately, just so there could be no misunderstanding. 'No strings. No expectations. What do you say to that, Lizzie?'

Her lashes had lowered and her cheeks had grown very pink and at that moment she looked every inch the virgin she had been until very recently. He wondered if she would respond with outrage. He wondered, achingly, whether she would prove to be the exception of every other woman he'd ever known and refuse him. But when she looked up he could see the answer written in the sensual softening of her features.

'I say yes,' she whispered shyly. 'I'd like that very much.'

CHAPTER THREE

Six months later

LIZZIE WAS BENDING over the ironing board, pressing what felt like her hundredth shirt of the day when she heard the sound of the doorbell and she sighed. Sometimes the steep steps leading up from the basement of the grand house to the front door made her feel as if she were scaling Mount Everest. She got so very tired these days, yet sleep was increasingly hard to come by—such were the downsides of her condition. But she mustn't concentrate on the negatives, she reminded herself firmly. She needed to remember her gratitude list. Her pregnancy was progressing extremely well and she was lucky to have a job, in the circumstances.

But her mental list had petered out as she reached the entrance hall, her footfall noiseless on the silken Persian rug. She wondered who was calling at this time in the morning. Her boss was out but even if she'd been at home, Lizzie doubted whether any of her friends would have just dropped by to say hello. Spontaneity wasn't a word she associated with the upper classes.

It was cold up here, because the heating was kept

off during the day while she was working and Lizzie shivered as she opened the front door. But the blast of cold air in wasn't responsible for the sudden icing of her skin, or the frozen horror of her reaction as her shocked gaze alighted on Niccolò Macario standing on the doorstep, blocking out most of the light behind him, his features set and forbidding.

Last time she'd seen him it had been summer, when the sun had transformed him into a glowing golden god—whereas today he was outlined in stark shades of monochrome, against the bare landscape of winter. Her heart raced. Actually, that wasn't strictly true. The last time she'd seen him he had only recently been thrusting deep inside her and she had slithered back into Sylvie's—now very rumpled—green dress. And if he'd wondered why she hadn't thrown on a dressing gown, or a pair of jeans to see him off the premises, he hadn't asked and she hadn't been required to tell him that her clothes were all upstairs in the box room, not the fancy scarlet guest room. But then, they hadn't asked each other any questions, had they? They'd been too busy exploring each other's bodies as the clock had ticked the night away into a sleepless morning.

She dragged in an unsteady breath as she stared at him. For a long while she'd wondered how she could have behaved in such an impetuous way, with a man she barely knew. It had been hard not to beat herself up about it but as she looked at him now her error of judgement became a lot more understandable. He was, she thought, her throat drying to dust, still the most magnificent man she'd ever laid eyes on.

She had fallen for him big time but, clearly, he hadn't felt the same way about her and a whole night together hadn't changed his determination that there would be no strings, or expectations. But she wouldn't have been human if she hadn't held out a little hope that he might change his mind. She'd wondered if she might bump into him again and, if she did, whether that overpowering chemistry would lead them straight back to the bedroom. Another no-hoper, because the Jacobean mansion had sold a few weeks later—but not to him. Ermecott Manor had been bought by a family from Scotland who had brought their own housekeeper with them, leaving her looking for a job. That she had found one in the circumstances had been something of a miracle. And the question which was looming large was how had Niccolò found *her*, especially as she was now living in London? And why, when he had gone out of his way to avoid her?

She looked him directly in the eye, trying to make him focus on her face and not her body—though instinct told her this was a pointless exercise.

'Good morning, Niccolò,' she said calmly, somehow managing to keep the tell-tale waver of emotion from her voice. 'I must say, this is a surprise.'

'I imagine it must be,' he replied. 'You took some tracking down, *cara*.' There was a pause, while his black eyes narrowed. 'And you seem to have no presence at all on the Internet.'

'You're right, I haven't,' she agreed. She wasn't registered on any of the social media channels. She didn't post carefully filtered photographs of herself online, desperate for other people's approval. She didn't have the time, even if she'd ever had the inclination. She drew in a deep breath. 'Anyway, surely that's irrelevant. What are you doing here?'

'Isn't it obvious?' At last his gaze swept over her, from head to toe, his lips hardening as it returned to linger on the curve of her belly, which was pushing against the checked beige tabard, which was her latest housekeeper uniform. 'And surely it's a little late in the day for maidenly blushing.'

She wanted to slam the door in his face, but she knew she couldn't do that and not just because his expression was so flinty. She wasn't an unreasonable person and she hoped that, when the chips were down, neither was he. She couldn't hold his behaviour against him just because he hadn't wanted to see her again. And hadn't this brand-new life growing inside her given her the kind of self-belief and courage she'd never had before? Wasn't she a much stronger woman now there was someone else to consider?

So find out what he wants and then decide how you're going to deal with it.

She would take him downstairs into the basement and after he'd finished saying his piece, he could slip out of the kitchen door and nobody would even know he'd been here. She opened the door wider.

'Come in,' she said. 'Though you'll have to be quick. My boss will be back soon.'

Niccolò didn't answer. He didn't trust himself to say another word as he stepped in and shut the door behind him, still reeling from the sight of her, which was affecting him in ways he couldn't begin to understand. In silence he followed her down a flight of stairs, into the lavish subterranean basement kitchen. But it was cold in here, he thought critically, and found himself wondering if she was warm enough.

She turned round and once again he was shocked by her appearance. Not just because her dark-ringed eyes suggested chronic tiredness—though the bright hair piled on top of her head looked thicker than he remembered—but because of the very obvious signs of her pregnancy. It was strange. You could know something to be a fact, but it wasn't until you were actually confronted with the evidence that you really started to believe it was true. And this was true all right. His throat grew dry as he scanned her abdomen, for beneath the ugly garment she wore he could see the unmistakable sign of a bump.

His child.

A child he had never wanted.

Pain speared at his heart. And guilt. That ever-present sense of guilt. And something else, too. Something he didn't recognise. Something he didn't want to recognise. 'You're pregnant,' he observed raggedly.

'Six months,' she offered.

'Yet I have only just found out. Why the hell didn't you contact me?'

'Are you kidding?' she questioned. 'I tried! So many times. Soon after the second pregnancy test came back positive and I knew it was really happening, I set out to get in touch with you, but I encountered a setback every step of the way. I had no alternative other than to try to contact you through your company, which meant I was always onto a loser.'

'What are you talking about?' he clipped out.

'Think about it,' she accused. 'You're a very powerful man, Niccolò and you have a very protective ring of staff surrounding you. You're a billionaire and I'm just a humble working girl. Gaining access to you was a bit like someone trying to get their hands on the Crown Jewels. That's why I ended up writing you that letter and sending it by snail mail.'

'Which I have only just received!' he exploded, pulling a crumpled sheet of paper from the pocket of his overcoat and waving it in front of her. 'And you're no longer living at the address on the letter, hence the difficulty in finding you.'

'Maybe you need to speak to your team of assistants about relaxing their draconian methods of protecting you,' she suggested, before biting her lip. 'If you recall, we didn't even exchange phone numbers, which was another complicating factor, otherwise I could have tried you at home or texted you, or *something*.'

'I thought we'd decided that was for the best.'

'Well, you decided that,' she argued.

'Because what happened that day was a crazy aberration between two people living on opposite sides of the world!'

'Yes, of course there were practical reasons why we weren't going to see each other again, but they weren't the only ones, were they?' Her gaze sliced through him, as pale as new leaves. 'Do you remember what you said to me, or shall I remind you? *"No strings. No expectations."* Those were your exact words, weren't they, Niccolò—or has pregnancy scrambled my brain so much that I can no longer rely on my own memory?'

'I was trying to do you a favour,' he said harshly. 'I didn't want you building up any unrealistic romantic dreams about me.'

'I was hardly likely to do that. A broom cupboard is hardly the most romantic of settings.' She gave a short laugh. 'I mean, we're not exactly talking Romeo and Juliet here, are we?'

'You wanted it,' he said softly.

There was a pause as her cheeks flushed and when she spoke, her voice was so low he could barely hear it. 'You're saying you didn't?'

He shook his head before biting out the words reluctantly. 'Of course I did.' He wondered how she would react if he told her that the desire he'd felt for her had been off the scale. That he'd never felt anything like that before in his life. Wild. Hungry. Out of control. Hadn't that realisation been a bigger incentive to make him resist the temptation to see her again than the perceived incompatibility of their two lifestyles? And that had been when he'd thought she was a rich socialite, not a woman actually working in the house. He gave a heavy sigh. 'If you'd told me you were a virgin, you wouldn't have seen me for dust.'

'I didn't get the chance, did I? We didn't exactly do a lot of talking.'

He could hear the tremble of something in her voice. Was it anger or was it hurt? 'No,' he said, at last. 'We didn't.'

'Oh, well. At least we know where we stand now. It's hardly ground-breaking stuff. I'm having a baby. On my own. Don't worry about it. It's been happening since the beginning of time and women have dealt with it, just as I am. So...' She tilted her chin up with a fierce gesture of pride and a bright strand of hair came tumbling down to lie against one freckled cheek. 'Was there anything else?'

Niccolò shook his head with frustration. Was she playing games? Did she really think that, having tracked her down, he was going to walk out of her life again and act as if nothing had happened? 'You think I'm just going to renege on my responsibilities?' he demanded roughly. 'That I would leave the mother of my child to continue working as a servant?'

'There's nothing wrong with being a housekeeper,' she defended hotly. 'Certainly nothing to be ashamed of.'

'No?' His voice grew silky. 'So why, I wonder, did you keep that rather significant fact hidden from me?'

Lizzie chewed on her lip as she wondered how to answer him. If their passionate liaison had continued a bit longer—she might have confided that she had enjoyed being someone else for once. A woman able to make a gorgeous man regard her with hunger and passion in his eyes, rather than being treated as invisible, or part of the furniture. A woman who had felt like a gorgeous man's equal for once. But if she told him that *now*, wouldn't it indicate that her self-esteem had been at an all-time low? Which wouldn't do much for her morale. It would make her appear weak and she needed to be strong, for all kinds of reasons—but mostly for the sake of her baby.

'I didn't tell you any lies,' she said.

'No, you didn't. But you let me think—'

'What? That I was posh? That I was rich? Why, are those the only sort of women you have sex with, Niccolò?'

'I hadn't had sex for over a year before that afternoon,' he gritted back.

Lizzie wasn't sure why this unexpected confidence gave her a huge rush of pleasure, only that it did. It slugged through her veins like honey and made her feel as if she were lying in a warm bath. But that type of reaction was dangerous. It belonged to someone attempting to read too much into a situation which Niccolò Macario clearly regretted.

'You made an assumption about who I really was, based on my appearance,' she said coolly. 'I'd tried on one of Sylvie's designer dresses because she owed me money and didn't have it. She told me I could sell some of the pieces online and that's what I was planning to do. So instead of being in my frumpy old grey dress, I was wearing designer for the first time in my life. You obviously thought I was someone completely different when I opened the door, and I was having far too much fun to correct you.'

'I see. And were you aware of *my* identity?' he questioned, with equal cool. 'Before I arrived?'

'Well, yes. Of course I was. Sylvie told me you were expected and the estate agent had already rung me up that morning'. She stared at him, unsure of where the conversation was heading until the inference behind his drawled question become insultingly clear. 'Hang on a minute. You don't think… You don't think I *planned* this? That I targeted you and had sex with you and gave you my virginity because you happen to be one of the richest men in the world?' She blinked. 'Maybe that I was even trying to get myself pregnant, so I'd have a meal ticket for the rest of my life?'

'I don't know. Were you? You might have been looking for the richest possible baby-father.' He shrugged. 'These things happen. Read the newspapers if you don't believe me.'

He didn't even have the grace to look apologetic, Lizzie thought furiously. And even though what he said might be true, it hurt like crazy that he considered her capable of such a thing. Though maybe she only had herself to blame. If she'd gone out to dinner with him first, would he have thought more of her? *Stop it*, she urged herself. You don't have to wear the mantle of blame just because you let passion run away with you for the first time in your life.

But at least he had done her a favour, by revealing his true colours. During weak, scary moments—often in the middle of the night when she had felt so lonely and vulnerable—she had sometimes found her thoughts straying to him. To the jet-black gleam of his eyes and the way he had made her feel when he'd held her in his arms and kissed her. That night he had made her feel safe as well as desired—particularly when they had shared a bath together and he had lathered her breasts with soap and washed her clean. That had seemed almost as intimate as having sex with him, and those kinds of memories inevitably prompted the occasional fantasy—which usually involved Niccolò turning up unannounced and telling her that letting her go had been the biggest mistake of his life.

Well, the first part of her fantasy had come true— but the ending couldn't have been more different. Or more cruel. It seemed he was here to do nothing but mock her and hold her to account. *So get rid of him before your defences crumble and you dissolve into a mess of snotty tears in front of him.* That *wouldn't* be a good lasting memory.

'I'm afraid you credit me with far more deviousness than I'm capable of,' she remarked. 'And since your wealth obviously makes you so mistrustful of other people's motives, then I feel sorry for you.'

'You?' he echoed incredulously. 'Feel sorry for *me*?'

'Oh, dear.' She tilted her head to one side. 'You don't think a humble housekeeper has the right to feel sympathy for such a powerful man as yourself?'

His jaw clenched. 'I'm not getting into a debate about status. This is just wasting time.'

'I agree,' she said airily. 'And since I've got a stack of shirts waiting which aren't going to iron themselves, why don't you let me get on?'

'Lizzie!' he flared, exasperatedly.

And that was her undoing. Hearing her name on his lips again brought back all kinds of erotic memories. Hadn't he whispered it just before he'd entered her— even if the word had frozen in his throat once he had broken through her tightness? Hadn't he murmured it again when they'd been in the bath together—and then later, when she'd served him up her trademark soufflé omelette, which had been the best he'd ever eaten, he had confided on a note of surprise. She felt her heart tighten and her voice was husky. 'My boss will be back any minute and it's better she doesn't find you here.'

His voice grew hard and steely. 'Does she know the identity of your child's father?'

'I haven't been using your name as a badge of honour, if that's what you think.' Her gaze slid to the shiny face of the bronze kitchen wall clock and she felt the quick thump of fear, because the last thing she wanted was to be discovered alone with the powerful billionaire. Imagine all the questions she'd have to answer.

How did you say you met him?

You were wearing your boss's *dress*?

'I think you've said everything you need to say,' she added quickly. 'So you'd better go.'

'But that's where you're wrong, Lizzie. I haven't even begun.' His tone was deceptively soft, because his black eyes were capturing her like a dangerous snare. 'And since you've made it clear we can't talk here, I suggest you meet me for lunch.'

But it wasn't a suggestion, it was more of a command. The words of a man used to getting his own way. And although prolonging this torture of seeing him again was the last thing Lizzie wanted, what could she do but agree? He *was* technically the baby's father—she could hardly pretend he didn't matter. But what exactly did he want from her, and why was her heart still racing? Was it because his power was so much greater than hers and she was nervous how he might choose to use it, or because she remained achingly aware of his physical presence, no matter how much she might wish otherwise? He was a difficult man to ignore. Raw energy radiated from his muscular body. His raven hair gleamed in the pale, wintry light which filtered in through the basement window. His eyes looked like glittering jet, set in the luminescence of his olive skin.

'Oh, very well,' she said, trying to convey a reluctance she didn't feel. 'If you insist. There's a café at the end of the road, just inside the park entrance. I'll see you in there, as close to two o'clock as I can manage.'

He nodded but his next words surprised her.

'Just make sure you put a sweater on first, will you?' he said gruffly. 'It's cold outside.'

He turned away and Lizzie was glad because her eyes had started pricking with the hint of tears, and she bit down on her lip. She didn't want him to be *kind* to her. She wasn't sure she could cope with that. Much better he be judgemental and disapproving. At least that would help keep her feelings in check.

Shutting the door behind him, she leaned against it and closed her eyes.

She'd already had her head turned by a black-eyed man with a killer kiss and dangerous smile and look what had happened.

Her fingers strayed to the curve of her belly and lingered there.

From now on, she needed to be on her guard.

CHAPTER FOUR

THE GLASSHOUSE CAFÉ sat within a grove of leafless winter trees and Niccolò positioned himself directly in front of the park gates, so that he would see Lizzie when she finally appeared.

If she appeared.

He glanced again at his watch, because it was easier to concentrate on logistics rather than the tumult of unfamiliar emotions he was doing his best to block. Was it possible that the petite housekeeper had stood him up? It was already a quarter off three and never had he waited so long for someone to arrive. His mouth hardened. Especially not a woman. It went with the territory of being a billionaire. Everyone was always punctual—in fact, people invariably arrived too early. They waited for him and hung onto his every word and jostled for his attention. It meant he never had to try very hard socially—others were always more than willing to do the work for him. But Lizzie hadn't reacted that way. He remembered the accusations she had flung at him and frowned. Had his wealth really made him so remote and inaccessible that the mother of his child had been unable to get an appointment to see him?

The mother of his child.

The phrase was cloaked with an intimacy which set his teeth on edge. It made his heart ache with hard-wired pain. It made the mantle of guilt even heavier.

His thoughts were interrupted by the sight of Lizzie, walking through a giant wrought-iron arch towards the café, tiny and instantly recognisable, her hair banner-bright against the gunmetal-grey of the sky. As she pushed open the door and approached his table he noticed that her thin overcoat barely fastened over the curve of her belly and a fierce rush of something he didn't recognise made him want to fix that. To swathe her in layers of cashmere and remove that pinched and suspicious expression from her face.

She spotted him instantly but didn't smile or nod in recognition. As he rose to his feet to greet her all he could see was wariness cloaking her features and making her regard him with undisguised suspicion.

'Hi,' she said, and as she removed the thin coat and hung it on the back of the chair, he ran his gaze over her critically.

She had changed out of the ugly tabard into a dress of sturdy brown corduroy, which must have been chosen solely for its accommodatingly shape, rather than any attempt to look pretty. Yet despite her pallor and tired eyes, there was something intangibly appealing about her, which made Niccolò's pulse unexpectedly quicken. Was it the spill of pale red hair which pregnancy had made extra thick and glossy—or the extraordinary colour of her pistachio eyes, which made it so hard to tear his gaze away from her face? He found himself wondering what she might look like if she took a little care with her appearance.

'Sit down. Please,' he said—and, to his astonishment, found himself moving round the table to pull out a chair for her, as if he were an accommodating waiter.

'Thank you.'

Her narrow shoulders brushed against his fingertips as she slid into her seat and as Niccolò felt the jolt of instant physical connection he felt a lump invade his throat. So, that aspect of their relationship hadn't altered, he acknowledged unwillingly— uncertain whether to be intrigued or alarmed. Their physical chemistry remained as white-hot as ever. His voice was thick as he resumed his place and offered her a menu. 'What will you have to eat?'

'Nothing, thanks. Just herbal tea for me.'

He frowned. 'Have you had lunch already?'

'No,' she admitted, chewing the inside of her mouth.

'Then why are you so late?'

Lizzie hesitated. She didn't want to come over as some sort of victim, but that was how it would sound if she explained that Lady Cameron had needed a silk shirt ironed before she went out to play bridge that afternoon. Didn't matter that she was supposed to have been off duty. Or that there were dozens of similar items hanging neatly pressed in her employer's ginormous walk-in wardrobe. It had to be *that* one—and no, Lizzie couldn't possibly go off to meet her 'friend' until the task had been completed.

'I needed to finish up some work,' she said vaguely.

'You need to eat—especially in your condition.'

She glared at him as some of the stresses and strains of the past few months came bubbling up out of nowhere, though maybe that wasn't so surprising. Because if she couldn't vent her indignation to the man who'd actually put her in this position, who else *could* she sound off to? 'What is it about pregnancy which suddenly makes the whole world an expert on my welfare?' she demanded. 'I *should* be eating and I *should* be resting. Well, I'll be the one to decide what I should be doing, if it's all the same to you.'

'So you're not hungry?'

Unfortunately, her stomach chose that very moment to give a loud and very distracting rumble. Was it the mention of food which provoked it, or the tantalising waft of soup as a waitress carried a piled tray past their table?

'A bit,' she admitted reluctantly.

An expression of satisfaction flickered over his face, before it was replaced with one of resolution. 'I thought so,' he said, lifting his hand.

It was weird sitting back and watching him take charge—and equally weird to have someone taking care of *her*, for a change. With consummate ease Niccolò soon had two waitresses fussing around him and the chef himself bringing a basket of warm bread from the kitchen—which was something of an achievement for a place where the views were wonderful but the service usually atrocious.

Before too long, Lizzie was sitting in front of a steaming bowl of vegetable soup, accompanied by bread, a chunk of cheese and a sprig of juicy purple grapes. And then hunger took over and blotted out every other consideration. With a hungry moan, she started eating and for a couple of minutes forgot where she was and why she was there. She even forgot who was sitting opposite her, watching like a hawk as she scooped up the delicious broth, finally sitting back with a sigh of satisfaction as her spoon clattered into the empty bowl.

'Better?' he questioned softly.

'I suppose so,' she said grudgingly.

His lips curved into a smile, which managed to look triumphant and supremely sexy at the same time. And she didn't want him to smile like that. She didn't want him to smile at all, because it was making her heart thump in a way which wouldn't do her any good.

'So.' The smile had vanished and his gaze was boring into her, suddenly hard and cold and calculating. 'We need to discuss the future,' he said, pushing away his tiny espresso cup.

Lizzie was interested to know what he meant by the word 'we', but couldn't think of a way of asking which wouldn't make her come over as needy. So she didn't say anything, just continued to regard him in silence.

'Do you have parents who are ready to embrace their roles as grandparents?' he enquired tightly. 'Siblings who are eager to be uncles and aunts, perhaps?'

Lizzie shook her head. If he was hoping for a huge and supportive family network which would pick up his share of parental responsibility, he had picked the wrong woman. 'My mum and dad are both dead.'

'You're very young to be an orphan,' he said and

the unexpectedness of this observation made Lizzie disclose stuff she hadn't been planning on telling him.

'My father died when I was a baby and my mother wasn't…she wasn't in the best health, so I had to spend a lot of time looking after her and that's the reason why my schooling was so sporadic. I don't have any siblings,' she rushed on, realising that any more sympathy might make her vulnerable and she couldn't afford to be any more vulnerable than she already was. And then, because he was the father of her baby and she realised she knew practically nothing about him either, curiosity got the better of her. 'What about you?'

She was unprepared for the tautening of his striking features, or the way his eyes suddenly became hard and bleak and empty. 'This isn't about me,' he snapped. 'It's about you. And the baby. And it seems you have nobody to support you—'

'I don't need anybody to support me.'

'No?' His eyes narrowed. 'So how are you intending to manage after the birth?'

It was a mantra Lizzie had repeated to herself many times over the past few months, mostly in an attempt to believe it. 'It will be fine. Society is a lot more accommodating than it used to be. My boss knows. Obviously.' With a self-conscious shrug, she glanced down at her bump. 'She says I can carry on working for her. She's even prepared to let me carry on living there during my maternity leave—in return for a few light housework duties when the baby's asleep.'

'"A few light housework duties"?' he echoed, his voice hardening. 'What's that supposed to mean?'

'It's pretty obvious what it means, Niccolò. It's called housework. That's my job. Cooking. Ironing. Cleaning. Washing floors. Scrubbing loos. I expect there are people who take care of that side of your life for you and you probably don't even notice they're doing it. Am I right?' She met his obdurate stare and knew she needed to be strong. To keep at bay this overwhelming urge to reach out and touch him. To test if he was real, or just some gorgeous figment of her imagination. 'Anyway, it's nothing to do with you.'

'Are you serious?' He studied her closely for a moment, then nodded. 'Yes, I can see you are. This has everything to do with me—and you're missing the point, Lizzie.'

'The point being what?' Defensively, she crossed her arms over her chest and as his gaze was drawn to the frumpy bodice of her thrift-shop dress, she found herself wishing she'd been able to buy some pretty maternity clothes. With what? The paltry stash she was trying to save before the baby was born, for a 'rainy day'? For a dress she'd only be able to wear for a few short months? And surely she didn't think that whatever she wore would have made the slightest bit of difference. He had walked away from her. He didn't want her. 'Are you trying to tell me you care what happens to this baby?'

'Why else do you think I'm here?' he questioned coolly.

Lizzie was glad she was sitting down, not sure she'd heard him properly. Yes, that had once been her fantasy, on that terrifying morning when she'd done two tests in quick succession and had allowed herself the wistful image of Niccolò Macario cradling his newborn. But that had been before she'd come up against all the roadblocks he'd put between them, ensuring she couldn't contact him, and the realisation that he'd never intended to see her again. She could cope with that—of course she could. The idea that a man like him had been attracted to her in the first place had always been difficult to get her head round. Yet now he was implying...what?

'I can't believe you want to be a father,' she croaked.

'You're right, I don't. Or rather, I never intended to be one. Fatherhood was never part of my game plan,' he added grimly. 'But since it seems I have no choice in the matter, I don't intend to turn my back on my responsibilities.'

'You mean...that you're offering financial help?' she questioned cautiously, because she couldn't think what else he meant.

'Is that what you'd like?'

She blinked at him. 'Erm—'

'New house? Nanny? Would that work?' he continued silkily.

'That's very...kind of you,' she said, though she was so busy wondering whether she'd want anyone else—like a nanny—being hands-on with her baby, that she wasn't really taking in his words.

'Perhaps you'd like a new car, too?'

This was taking generosity to a ridiculous level, she thought—when his sardonic expression informed her exactly what he was trying to do. Making out she was a greedy woman with her eye on the main chance! Just like earlier when he'd implied she'd only had sex with him because she'd known he was so rich. What must life be like if you were as cynical as Niccolò Macario? she wondered scornfully. So play him at his own game. 'Oh, yes, please,' she breathed, injecting her voice with an acquisitive note. 'And plenty of shiny baubles, too. Diamonds would be best. Rare, glittering diamonds which I could sell on the open market.'

There was a split second of a pause while he seemed to be taking her demands seriously and then, to her surprise and, yes, her consternation, he tipped his head back and started to laugh. It was, hands down, the sexiest laugh she had ever witnessed and Lizzie couldn't stop herself from reacting to it. She felt a distracting tug of heat. She felt her tummy tightening and gave silent thanks that her pinafore dress was bulky enough to conceal the unwanted hardening of her nipples as she shifted awkwardly on her chair.

'Ah, *cara*,' he murmured. 'Your ability to inject a little humour into this unwanted situation will go some way towards making it a little more...' He seemed to have some difficulty selecting the next word. 'Agreeable,' he concluded eventually.

Lizzie regarded him suspiciously. 'I'm still not sure what you're getting at.'

'Think about it.'

'Sorry. No can do. I'm pregnant and my head's gone to mush. Some people call it "baby brain", though others think that's very rude.'

'Then let me spell it out for you so that there can be

no misunderstanding.' There was a pause. 'You cannot carry on in your current role, working in that house.'

'Why not?'

He placed his hands flat on the wooden table and, annoyingly, Lizzie found her attention drawn to his long fingers, remembering how they'd whispered over her trembling thighs, before bringing her to that noisy orgasm in the broom cupboard. Her cheeks flushed, first with embarrassment and then with self-directed fury. Why was she thinking about that *now*, when she had successfully erased all such erotic memories for weeks?

'Why not?' he repeated thoughtfully. 'Well, I'm no expert, but you aren't exactly glowing, as pregnant woman are supposed to.'

'Oh, dear. I'm so sorry to have fallen short of your exacting standards. If you'd given me a bit more notice, I might have had time to apply some blusher!'

'I have also discovered a couple of things about your employer,' he continued, 'who doesn't have a fantastic reputation when it comes to keeping staff. Now, I'm no lawyer but I do employ a lot of people and I know it's against the law to ask a woman to work during her maternity leave.'

'But she's giving me a room and board!'

'So what happens if she kicks you out because she doesn't like the sound of a crying baby? And within a few months, the baby will be crawling. How will you do your job then?'

'Then I'd have to look for another job. Obviously.'

'What? Going from door to door with a squalling infant in your arms?'

'I hate to disillusion you, Niccolò, but most people go through employment agencies these days.'

He shook his head. 'I'm afraid this is all very unsatisfactory.' He leaned back in his chair. 'And I cannot allow it to happen.'

'Excuse me?' she squeaked. Lizzie tried to sound outraged but that masterful note in his voice was unexpectedly comforting, and although some previously unknown aspect of her character was making her want to bask beneath all the implied power which backed up his statement, she forced herself to see sense. 'I don't know which century you imagine we're living in, Niccolò, but you can't just come barging into my life, demanding your rights!'

'But you aren't going to deny that I do *have* rights, as the father?'

This really wasn't what she had expected. She wanted to be fair and she wanted to be logical, but now she felt confused. 'Are you sure you want to claim them?' She stared at him frustratedly. 'Aren't I just a woman you had some regrettable sex with? A one-night stand which has resulted in consequences neither of us could have foreseen? I would have thought you'd be happy about me giving you a let-out clause.'

Niccolò flexed and unflexed his fingers but it made no difference to the tension which was tightening his body. He couldn't deny that her words were accurate. He had come here today, not because he'd *wanted* to, but because he'd been driven by a sense of duty he couldn't ignore. He had imagined she would fall in a grateful heap at his feet. That she would be charmed and relieved at his offer to take her out to lunch and would have sat there, waiting eagerly to see what he had to offer.

But she had done none of these things and her attitude had taken him by surprise. She'd made it clear that she considered their relationship to be firmly in the past, and was prepared to bring up their baby without his assistance. Her fierce independence should have allowed him to walk away, his guilt assuaged by giving her a generous settlement which would keep her and the baby comfortable for the rest of their lives. But guilt was hardwired into his nature. And it seemed that it had not been assuaged at all. Why else would he feel such a strong sense of concern for her welfare, and a reluctance to let her go it alone?

'You look tired and overworked, and I cannot allow that to continue.'

'So what are you going to do? Wave a magic wand?'

He studied her for a moment in silence.

'You're going to have to come to New York.'

She frowned. 'I don't understand.'

'That's where I'm based.'

'Right.' Calmly, she took a sip of water. 'But I'm still not with you.'

'You must come and live with me.'

Now he had a reaction. She sat up straight, her soft lips falling open.

'*Live* with you?'

He wondered why he had put it so baldly—without nuance—knowing the tendency of women to read too much into a few simple words. 'Not *with* me,' he clarified abruptly. 'I'm offering you temporary shelter, that's all. A holiday, if you like. I will provide warmth, food and a generous expense account—as well as the finest medical care in the country—while you decide what you want to do.'

'No expense spared for the baby, you mean?' she questioned quietly.

'Why not?' he drawled, on familiar territory now, as the conversation shifted into financial negotiation. 'I'm a wealthy man, with no dependants. Until now. I have more than enough for my charities to benefit from my fortune, so why would I leave out my own flesh and blood?' He leaned forward across the table, his voice low. 'Don't you realise I'm in a position to offer this child the best of everything?'

Except love, thought Lizzie desperately. All the money in the world couldn't buy that. She looked into his face, but as her gaze rested on the sculpted slash of his features, she could see nothing but coldness and calculation in his eyes. Every instinct she possessed was urging her to reject his proposal. Quickly she corrected herself. No. This definitely wasn't a *proposal*. This was an expedient offer from a powerful man whose motives were unclear.

Unlike hers.

Over the last few months, she had thought of this baby as hers and hers alone. She had become territorial about the new life growing inside her, which had allowed her to feel as if she was in control. If she accepted Niccolò's offer, surely that control would slip away. He was already talking about their child as an acquisition—an heir to inherit some of his vast fortune. Where would that leave her? Penniless Lizzie Bailey, without a qualification to her name? Would he try to edge her out—to dazzle their offspring with all the things she could never provide?

She wanted to push back the chair and run out of the café and pretend this conversation had never happened. But that would be the action of a coward and something her conscience wouldn't allow.

Stop thinking about yourself.

Could she honestly deny their child this golden opportunity, just because her pride had been hurt and the man who had made her pregnant didn't want her?

She couldn't keep the stab of hope from her voice. 'Are you saying you want to be a proper father to this baby?'

'No, I'm not.' There was a pause. 'That's the last thing I want,' he said. 'Neither you nor this child deserve a man like me in your life, Lizzie. But I'm prepared to finance your future and give you time to think about what that future might be.'

'Why are you being so kind to me?'

'Not kind,' he corrected. 'I don't do kind. Let's just say it's a kind of thank you, for not having gone to the papers telling them how I'd deserted you. Possibly armed with a few naked photos you might have taken while I was asleep. It would have made a juicy story, don't you think? *Niccolò Macario dumps his baby-mama!*'

'Are you always this cynical?'

'Always,' he agreed acidly. 'I find that experience has made me that way.'

Lizzie stared into the hard glitter of his eyes. He was painting a harsh picture of what sort of a man he really was. He'd told her with brutal honesty that he didn't want a baby, but would support her financially. So far, so fair. But there was one thing he hadn't mentioned. The thing which had got them into this situation in the first place. The old Lizzie wouldn't have dreamed of bringing up such an intimate subject, but that innocent creature was part of the past. For her sake, and for her baby's sake—there was nothing to be gained from being coy.

'What about…sex?' she questioned.

'Sex?' he repeated, elevating his brows. 'Surely you're not *propositioning* me, Lizzie?'

'Of course I'm not!' she declared furiously. 'I just thought…'

'What? That I'm trying to lure you to the States because I want to pick up where we left off that crazy afternoon?' He gave a bitter laugh. 'Then let me assure you that your fears are unfounded, *cara*. I'm not that desperate.'

'Desperate?' she repeated furiously.

'You think I am turned on by a woman who looks at me as if I am the devil incarnate, even though she might be right? Believe me when I tell you that I have no intention of installing you in my bedroom, Lizzie. I prefer my women a little less prickly and a little less pregnant.' He gave a soft laugh. 'You will be quite safe from me.'

Safe? Suddenly, Lizzie didn't feel in the least bit safe, because even when he was being angry he was devastatingly attractive. He still made her want to sidle up close to him and present her lips to be kissed. Her breasts still ached to be touched by him. He represented danger on so many levels, yet she couldn't deny being tempted by his offer. The constant nag of worry about not having enough money would be removed in a stroke—and what was the worst that could happen? She could come back to England any time she liked—he was hardly going to keep her prisoner in New York, was he? But he needed to understand that the impetuous creature who had fallen into his arms that day hadn't been the real Lizzie Bailey. The real Lizzie was careful and responsible and weighed things up. She was decent and honest and didn't let people down.

'I'd like some time to think about it,' she said stiffly. 'I can't just leave my boss in the lurch. I'll need to give her notice.'

He shrugged, seemingly unimpressed by this demonstration of conscientiousness, withdrawing a thick cream card from his wallet and sliding it across the table. 'Suit yourself. Here are my details. My plane leaves tomorrow. Let me know if you're going to be on it. Do you want a lift somewhere now?'

'No, thanks. I'll walk.'

It was a relief to get away from the distracting gleam of his eyes and walk back across the park, even though the cold wind was biting viciously into her cheeks and penetrating her inadequate coat. She had intended to speak to her boss when she returned from her bridge lesson, but Lady Cameron cut her short by demanding Lizzie bone and cook three chickens for an impromptu dinner party she was giving that evening.

Lizzie's heart plummeted. 'But I'm supposed to be off duty—'

'And?' A pointed glance swivelled to her belly. 'Aren't you lucky to have a job at all?'

Insecurity won out over any championing of employment rights and Lizzie nodded obediently, more out of habit than anything else. In the basement kitchen, she stood shivering with her hands deep in icy water and entrails, trying not to retch, and somehow managed to produce and serve a three-course supper, and tidy up afterwards. But despite a fatigue which seeped deep into her bones, her night was restless. As the pale gleam of the winter morning crept in through the thin curtains, she suddenly sat bolt upright in bed and looked around the attic room as if she were seeing it for the first time.

What was she *doing*? First Sylvie and now Lady Cameron—both of them treating her like dirt. She had told herself she needed to be strong from here on in, mostly for her baby's sake. So how many more times was she going to allow herself to be exploited by unscrupulous employers before she came to her senses?

After showering beneath a meagre trickle of water in the poky bathroom, she packed all her possessions into a single suitcase, took out her phone and punched out the number Niccolò had given her. The irony didn't escape her when he answered. All those fruitless attempts to contact him in the early days of her pregnancy, when she had come up against an impenetrable wall of security. But now? Now he picked up on the second ring, his velvety tones making a complicated series of reactions sizzle over her skin.

'Lizzie?'

'I'd like to come to New York. If the offer's still on.'

'When?'

She drew in a deep breath. 'You said your plane was leaving today.'

There was a pause and when he spoke his voice was silky. 'What changed your mind?'

Lizzie stared out of the tiny attic window at the bare treetops silhouetted against the pewter sky. She didn't want to tell him about the tiny ray of hope which had flickered into her heart in the middle of the night, because that was ill founded and sentimental and he wouldn't want to hear it. It might even be enough to make him change his mind and, suddenly, that was a prospect she couldn't bear to contemplate.

'Well, I haven't exactly been inundated with attractive offers,' she confided, as carelessly as she could. 'So it seemed a bit short-sighted to turn it down.'

'Bene.' He didn't bother to hide his satisfaction. 'I will send a car for you.'

CHAPTER FIVE

'I DON'T UNDERSTAND.' Her voice sounded bewildered. 'Why are we in a hotel?'

Their whistlestop tour concluded, Niccolò watched the tiny redhead slowly circumnavigate the vast reception area of his suite of rooms. As she walked over to one of the floor-to-ceiling windows and stared at the skyscraper view outside, he thought how small she seemed in these vast surroundings, and how vulnerable. When she turned to face him her eyes were wide, as if she was having difficulty adjusting to her new reality. That made two of them, he thought grimly, wondering whether he had taken leave of his senses when he had blurted out his offer to her back in London. 'Because this is where I live.'

As she shook her head, her pale red hair shimmered. 'You live in a hotel? Who *does* that?'

Words seemed to fail her as her gaze alighted on a glass coffee table on which stood a stack of rare books. She had removed her coat to reveal a dress which appeared to have been fashioned from a pair of old drapes and was slightly too small for her, so that it clung to her fecund curves. The new shape of her body was glaringly apparent in a way he hadn't really noticed back in England. The heavy breasts. The slightly widened hips. When she did that unconscious thing of fluttering her fingers against her belly, she seemed the embodiment of fertility. She was pregnant. Lushly and terrifyingly pregnant.

And he had made her that way.

She stuck out like a sore thumb in the sleek bachelor world he inhabited. The crew on his private jet had been unable to conceal their surprise when she'd arrived at the airfield, emerging from the limousine carrying nothing but a battered suitcase and wearing that thin coat straining over her bump. The hotel staff clearly thought the same—though Niccolò had glowered when he'd noticed one of the bellboys staring at her askance, before sending the hapless individual away without a tip.

Yet, for a man who always travelled solo, Lizzie Bailey had proved to be an undemanding companion during the flight from London to New York. There had been no mindless chatter, at which women excelled. Even the barrage of questions which he assumed that she of all people had the right to ask hadn't materialised. She had spotted one of the large bedrooms on board and—after establishing that, yes, of course she was allowed to use it—had shut herself away for much of the flight.

As they'd flown over the Atlantic, Niccolò kept glancing towards a door which had remained firmly closed. Like all powerful men, he was attracted to the things which seemed unavailable. Annoyingly, he'd found himself wondering whether she was sleeping naked and how that might look, then reminded himself that sex was a complication he definitely didn't need.

She hadn't emerged until shortly before landing, and despite his determination to subdue his desire, he had found himself focussing reluctantly on the bareness of her lips, fighting back a desire to take her in his arms and taste their honeyed softness again.

Yet now, seeing her rounded body silhouetted against the glittering Manhattan skyline, that desire had been replaced by incredulity, and yes, dread. Her presence was driving home the realisation that he had placed himself at the centre in a situation he'd always gone out of his way to avoid. His heart began to hammer painfully against his ribcage. Wouldn't a new baby bring back all the memories he'd worked so hard to suppress, haunting him with guilt and grief all over again?

He must not let it. He must compartmentalise—which he was good at—and put things in perspective. He had offered Lizzie Bailey nothing but a temporary refuge and once she realised the true extent of the funds he was willing to put at her disposal she would doubtless wish to return to her own country and cash in on them. To make a fresh start for herself and find a husband who was capable of giving her the affection she undoubtedly craved. He gave a small nod of satisfaction. People lived complicated lives these days—why should theirs be any different? Every dilemma had a solution if you searched for it hard enough.

'You don't approve of the accommodation?' he hazarded sarcastically. 'It is a little too cramped perhaps?'

'Ha-ha. Very funny. I can't believe there are actually...' she did a rapid calculation on her fingers '... six rooms! Six!'

Drawing in a deep breath, she redirected her verdant gaze at him and Niccolò was irritated by the corresponding ripple of pleasure that gave him.

'You could probably live in a palace if you wanted to,' she persisted. 'So why here?'

He shrugged. His usual response to a question he'd been asked countless times was that he owned the hotel, which was true. But flippancy seemed inappropriate in Lizzie's case and to talk about his many assets might be interpreted as boastful. She was pregnant with his child and somehow that uneasy realisation filled him with a responsibility to answer her questions honestly, and to expect the same honesty in return. Anything else would be a waste of his valuable time.

'I like to keep my life simple and this allows me to do so,' he explained. 'I have all my needs catered to, with the minimum amount of involvement or effort on my part. Things are brought to me at the push of a button. There are constantly changing staff, whose names I never need bother learning.' He shrugged as his gaze flickered over to the panoramic wall of windows. 'As well as having one of the best views in the city—it suits me.'

'Yes, I get all that,' she said slowly. 'It just doesn't feel much like home, that's all.'

'That's intentional. Because I'm not looking for a home, Lizzie. My life is nomadic. I travel a great deal. I have a plane on permanent standby. I don't stay anywhere for very long. I don't have any emotional connections to places, the way that other people do.'

'Yet when you came to Ermecott Manor, you seemed to love it,' she observed.

'Let's not go overboard. Love isn't a word which tends to feature in my vocabulary.' He gave a short laugh. 'I liked it well enough.'

Her gaze grew thoughtful, as if she was storing away this nugget of information for future use—which was exactly what he intended she do.

'Yet you didn't put in an offer, did you?'

'No,' he agreed. 'I didn't.'

'Why was that?'

'Mmm?' he questioned distractedly because the sky-scrapers outside the window were spangling her face with shafts of light, giving her skin a jewel-like luminance.

'You didn't think the house had potential?' she persisted.

'Oh, it had plenty of potential. It was one of the best properties of its kind to come on the market all year, and I thought very seriously about buying it.'

'But you changed your mind.' She glanced down and began to fiddle with the snug skirt of her floral dress, as if reluctant to meet his eye and when she lifted her face again, her cheeks were flushed. 'Did…did what happened with me influence your decision?'

Niccolò's eyes narrowed, surprised she'd had the guts to ask the question and risk the rejection she must have known was coming. But wasn't it better she realised exactly where she stood? If he explained it to her in stark shades of black and white, so there could be no grey areas of misunderstanding? 'In a sense, yes. It would have been difficult if we kept running into one another.'

'In case I formed an unwanted attachment towards you?'

'That was always a consideration,' he conceded.

'Because you're so irresistible?' She gave a short laugh. 'Because women find it so hard to forget you once you've had sex with them?'

Unapologetically, he shrugged. 'So they tell me.'

'That's the most big-headed thing I've ever heard!'

If she'd been a little more experienced he might have replied with mocking innuendo but no matter how he answered, he wasn't going to deny the truth. He was an excellent lover. He knew that. He prided himself on giving pleasure, as well as receiving it. But women often mistook good sex for something different, because they were programmed to search for something deeper and he was programmed to avoid exactly that. Occasionally he embarked on a relationship, but it was nearly always brief and he was always strangely relieved when it ended and he could feel free once more. He knew his limitations. He was too complicated and emotionally repressed for any kind of romantic partnership. Too damaged for anything permanent. That was the reason he only ever had liaisons with women who knew the score. Who regarded sex as an enjoyable pastime, not as some kind of audition to become his wife.

He'd thought Lizzie Bailey was cast from the same mould—with her foxy green dress and inviting eyes. Yet her unexpected innocence and sweet fervour had placed her in a category of her own, which had thrown him at the time. He'd spoken the truth when he'd said he wouldn't have gone near her if he'd known she was a virgin—though deep down he wondered whether he would have been strong enough to resist the allure she had radiated that day. His heart had been raw and aching on the anniversary of the deaths. He had been filled with sorrow and regret. Deep in emotional pain, she had been exactly what he needed at that time. A transient and sensual balm for his troubled soul and nothing more.

The night which had followed had been sensational. Her lack of experience had meant that everything they'd done had been new to her and she had been the most delightful of students, eager to learn what pleased him and shyly discovering what gave *her* pleasure. The intensity of her many orgasms had been matched by his own—a mind-blowing amount—even by his standards.

But when he had woken next morning and seen her serene smile as she'd snuggled up to him, warning bells had sounded in his head. She had been too inviting. Too sweet and too soft. Her nipples like ripe cherries topping the creamy mounds of her breasts, he had wanted to lick her all over. He had wanted to thrust into her wet tightness again and again with a need which had threatened to devour him. But these days he was better equipped to recognise danger in its many forms, and these days he always heeded it. Ignoring the hard throb of an erection, he had forced himself to get out of bed and steel his heart against the confusion in her green eyes. He hadn't wanted to get to know her better, because there was no point. He hadn't wanted to hurt her.

'It just seemed less complicated to walk away,' he concluded heavily.

'So what made you walk back?'

There was a pause. 'Guilt,' he said eventually. 'And duty. Nothing more.'

'Wow. You don't pull any punches, do you?'

'I don't lead women on. Not even in your case. Especially in your case, Lizzie. You are carrying my child and because of that I owe you the truth. It's better you understand that I'm not planning to play happy families any time soon.' His mouth hardened. 'And I'm certainly not the man of your dreams.'

'Oh, I really don't need you to tell me that, Niccolò,' she said. 'I'd sort of worked that out for myself.'

Something about the quiet dignity of her response made him feel uncomfortable and, suddenly, he needed to get away. He glanced at his watch as if it were a lifeline. 'Look, I have a number of work calls I need to make before dinner, so why don't you—?'

'Make myself at home?' she interjected sarcastically.

'Meet me back here at seven,' he said, refusing to rise to the sudden fire in her eyes. To show her that he was in control, even if at that precise moment he didn't feel it. 'We can either eat dinner in the hotel restaurant or have something prepared here. Up to you.'

Lizzie hesitated. She didn't want to walk into a posh hotel restaurant in her cheap clothes, but the thought of sitting at either end of a table which could comfortably have seated ten in Niccolò's private dining room filled her with horror. There had been too many high-end new experiences to contend with today and she figured she had just about reached her limit.

'If you want something fancy, then please go ahead without me. I certainly don't mind if you want to go out on your own,' she said. 'I'd be perfectly happy staying in with a sandwich.'

His lips curved into a reluctant smile. 'I think the chef could just about run to that.'

'I'm perfectly capable of making it myself.'

'I'm sure you are.' There was a pause. 'But the staff get a little proprietorial about the kitchen. Perhaps you can relate to that?'

'Are you trying to reinforce my servant status?' she demanded.

'Not at all.' He held up his palms in mock appeal. 'I was simply being factual.'

His contrition seemed genuine but Lizzie didn't trust herself to say another word as she left the room and made her way to the accommodation he'd pointed out to her a few minutes ago. It was difficult to take in just how arrogant he could be. All that stuff about women finding him irresistible—what an ego!

But you found him irresistible, didn't you? taunted the voice of her conscience. *You let him have sex with you within an hour of meeting.*

She had gasped out her disbelieving pleasure in a broom-cupboard and then led him upstairs to bed. She had behaved in a way she hadn't thought herself capable of and the worst thing was that she didn't seem to have moved on from that position.

She shut her bedroom door, barely registering the

enormous room or clever lighting, which made the whole place glow like a carefully staged department-store window. The expensive furniture in the adjoining sitting room was equally wasted on her because all she could see was the bed, looming up like a great monolith. The biggest bed she had ever seen. The snowy linen seemed to mock her and she found herself wondering why she had come here, and what she'd thought might happen. The practical aspects of accepting Niccolò's offer had made perfect sense but she saw now that she had been naïve about the emotional ones. Had she imagined she would suddenly acquire a miraculous immunity to his sizzling sex appeal? Or that he might override his terse assurance that he wouldn't be inviting her to share his bedroom? Because, given the current way she was feeling, she would find that very difficult to turn down.

It had never even occurred to her that she would react like this, even though she'd read plenty of books full of advice for pregnant women. They'd said that sexual desire was perfectly normal when you were expecting a baby, but she'd thought that had been aimed at prospective parents who were in a loving and committed relationship. Living with a man who had gone out of his way to cut you out of his life should have been enough to have killed her desire for him stone-dead. But nobody could predict what would happen until you were actually in the situation yourself. And the truth was that she still wanted him. Despite his overriding arrogance and egotism, deep down she wanted him to sweep her into his arms and make her tremble again.

How stupid was that?

Very stupid indeed.

Clicking open her case, she stared at her paints and brushes and thought how long it had been since she'd had a chance to use them, but her pregnancy had pushed all thoughts of painting dogs out of her mind. After she'd placed them neatly on the dressing table, she surveyed the remaining contents of her suitcase with a gloomy eye. It was disconcerting how out of place she felt in these luxurious surroundings, in the thrift-store outfits she'd accumulated. Like a muddy boot dropped onto a white carpet. Everything was sparkly clean and she felt dingy and faded in comparison. Scooting off to the en-suite bathroom, she turned on the taps and squirted in some geranium-scented oil before stripping off her clothes.

Unfortunately, her reflection bounced back at her from every available wall as she waited for the giant tub to fill. It was the first time she'd viewed her naked pregnant body in a full-length mirror—there had only been a tiny one in her attic room at Lady Cameron's—and Lizzie was unable to hold back her instinctive flinch when she saw herself. Her petite frame was dominated by the curve of her belly, making her limbs look positively scrawny in comparison. Her breasts were big and swollen—the nipples two large, dark rosy discs—and surely her hips were far curvier than they used to be. It was a sobering vision to witness the physicality of her condition and see how much she had changed.

How shocked Niccolò Macario must have been to see her like this when he'd turned up the other day.

He'd only had sex with her because she'd been dressed like a toff and had been giving him the green light in her borrowed designer dress. It had been a moment of madness and one which he clearly regretted.

But he was doing the right thing by her, wasn't he? He had offered her shelter. He had flown her to America on his private jet and installed her in a penthouse suite which probably cost more per month than most people paid for their accommodation in an entire year. He'd made an offer it would have been insane to turn down, but she needed to keep it real. She had been right to ask the difficult questions, even if the answers had been difficult to hear. And that was what she must continue to do. To confront the truth, no matter how painful.

Gingerly, she lowered her heavy body into the scented water and spent ages soaking in it, and for the first time in a long time, she felt properly relaxed. Afterwards, she blow-dried her newly washed hair and wondered what she should wear for dinner. Not that there was a lot of choice. But though second-hand maternity clothes were often frumpy, at least they never got worn much. The dress she pulled out was floaty and black with tiny gold stars embroidered over it. Best of all—it looked almost new. And although she convinced herself that there was no need to make an effort with a man who had stated emphatically that he no longer found her attractive, she still had *some* feminine pride. So she buffed up her ancient boots, then brushed her hair until it gleamed.

When she walked into the main reception room Niccolò was talking on the phone, his back to her, and for a moment she stared at him, her gaze drinking him in. Against the bright skyscraper backdrop he looked so tall and muscular and his black hair was ruffled—as if he'd been running frantic fingers through it. Yet despite all his wealth and power, which should have made him comfortable in such sumptuous surroundings, there was a strange restlessness about him. She was reminded of an animal she'd once seen at the zoo, before the laws had been changed. A snow leopard, pacing a too-small compound—all that untapped energy failing to cover a deep, underlying sense of sorrow. A caged beast behaving in that way was understandable, but what gave Niccolò Macario such a tangible aura of melancholy? she wondered.

He must have heard her because he turned and his reaction drove every concerned thought straight from her mind as he stared at her, the phone still clamped to his ear. She had tried to dress up to make herself look pretty but it seemed she had fallen at the first hurdle. He was diplomatic enough to try to conceal it, but Lizzie couldn't miss the flare of disbelief which sparked from his narrowed eyes. And suddenly she saw herself as he must see her. A pregnant woman in a cheap, second-hand dress with a pair of old boots which had been polished to within an inch of their life.

Suddenly, he seemed to remember that he was still in the middle of a phone call, because he started speaking. 'I'll have to get back to you, Donna. Yeah. Sure. I will.'

And in a funny sort of way, Lizzie wondered whether she should be grateful to Donna for bringing her to her senses. Whoever Donna was. His latest lover? Why not? He might have been celibate for a year before he'd ravished her in the broom cupboard—maybe that had been why—but there was no reason why he hadn't started putting himself out there again, making up for lost time. And if that was the case, that was one more thing she needed to accept. And she would do it.

She could do anything she set out to do.

'Hi,' she said briskly. 'Hope I'm not late.'

'No, you're not late.' He raised his dark brows. 'Find everything you needed?'

'Put it this way, I certainly won't be making any complaints to the management,' she said with a feeble attempt at humour, but he didn't raise a smile.

'Shall we go and sit down? We need to talk.'

It was another cool command. He pointed to one of the sofas—a long, low affair, sprinkled with velvet cushions which looked squashy and inviting and Lizzie sank down on it, grateful to take the weight off legs which had become suddenly unsteady. But then he sat down beside her and any sense of stability quickly deserted her.

She wondered if he knew how he was making her feel, just by being this close. Was he aware that her nipples were tightening and all she could think about was the way his tongue had explored their puckered flesh until she had yelped with pleasure? And then the way he had continued to lick his way down over her belly until—shockingly and deliciously—he had reached her thighs, which had parted so eagerly, as if having his face between her legs were the most natural thing in the world. But she didn't want to remember that. She didn't want erotic recall to play tricks with her mind and make her grow flushed and restless. It was inappropriate and it was dangerous, too.

'So.' She turned her head to fix him with a questioning look. 'What are we going to talk about? The sandwich filling on tonight's menu?'

'Practicalities,' he said succinctly.

Of course. 'Such as?'

He shrugged. 'You need to think about how you're going to spend your days while you're here. Obviously, you will see an obstetrician. There's someone at Lenox Hill Hospital who's been highly recommended, which the wives of several of my friends have used. I can arrange to have someone drive you to the medical centre. My assistant is currently dealing with that.' He leaned back, tousled locks of blue-black hair brushing against the collar of his silk shirt. 'But I run a very big company and work long hours, so I'm afraid I won't be around much during the day.'

'Oh, I think I can just about cope with your absence, Niccolò,' she commented wryly. 'I've managed for all these years on my own. Actually.' She hesitated, as she thought about the exotically named tubes which were lined up beneath the mirror on her dressing table. 'I've brought my paints with me.'

His eyes narrowed. 'You're an artist?'

Suddenly Lizzie felt shy about accepting this particular accolade, as if the only thing she'd been good at was going to come over as pretty feeble in his high-octane world. 'Only a very amateur one,' she said quickly. 'I've never been to art school. But I enjoy dabbling.'

'What do you paint?'

'Portraits, mostly. Dog portraits,' she elaborated, in response to the sudden elevation of his brows.

'Dog portraits?' he elucidated slowly.

'There's no need to look like that. It's a growing trend for people to want a picture of their beloved pooch to keep for posterity. I like to meet the dog to get a sense of them but mostly work from photos. A bundle of fur curled up in a basket, or bounding across a field, chasing a ball.'

'Fascinating,' he said faintly, lifting a hand to stem her flow, as his interest in the painting of animals had now been exhausted. 'But we really ought to concentrate on what you're going to do in the evenings, while you're here.'

'I'm quite happy to read or watch telly.'

'I'm sure you are.' His cell phone started to ring but he switched it to silent. 'I have a busy diary, especially at this time of year. I receive lots of invitations and I see no reason why you shouldn't come along with me. Much better than staying home alone all the time, don't you think?'

Lizzie chewed on her lip, wondering if she could cope with accompanying him to glitzy events. But he did have a point. Wouldn't she drive herself mad if she was left staring at the walls, like a thrift-store princess in a gilded tower? 'Okay,' she said casually. 'I can probably cope with being your plus one.'

'Please don't feel you have to overdose on gratitude.'

'Don't worry, I won't.'

His gaze raked over her. 'You'll need some new clothes—'

'Nice, but not necessary,' she said tightly. 'I've got enough to see me through. Honestly. You've already been more than generous.'

'Poor but proud is an undeniably attractive combination in a woman, Lizzie,' he mused, his lips curving as he leaned towards her, as if to emphasise the point. 'Particularly when the sentiment appears genuine.'

Lizzie held her breath and her heart pounded. He was so *close*. So ridiculously and deliciously close.

His black eyes gleamed as he readjusted his position. 'But in this case, I'm afraid it will work against you. This is a wealthy city and the people I mix with are wealthier than most. If you don't look as if you fit in, you will feel even more of an outsider than you probably already do.'

'Wow.' She tried to lash out with sarcasm, aware that she really *had* wanted him to kiss her. 'You really *are* selling New York to me.'

'There's something else, too.' His eyes narrowed as he studied her. 'You're pregnant and you're living in my hotel suite.' There was a pause. 'And since I'm a man who is notoriously averse to sharing his space… people are bound to speculate.'

'And you're worried they're going to work it out for themselves?'

'I don't think you'd need to be a genius to make the obvious connection, do you? Which is why I think we should pre-empt the inevitable gossip and put it out there that it is…' there was a pause '…my child.'

Lizzie told herself that the possessive-sounding phrase didn't actually *mean* anything, but that wasn't true because it meant something to her, and she prayed her face didn't give anything away as she attempted to quash the sudden fierce aching in her heart. Just as she tried to block out the unhelpful image which his words had produced. Of a tiny black-haired baby, nestling against the bare chest of his daddy, just like in those fantasies she used to have about him before she'd taught herself they were too dangerous. She wondered what sort of father he might make, and wasn't there part of her which longed to find out? But he had never wanted a baby, she reminded herself.

He spelled that out for you in cruel, but helpfully candid words—he doesn't want to play happy families.

With an effort, she dragged her thoughts back to what he was saying. 'And then what?' she persisted, continuing on her mission to stick to the facts—no matter how painful. 'How are you planning to cope with the inevitable questions which will arise?'

'Why should there be any questions? We'll have told them everything they need to know.'

At this, she actually laughed. 'I think that's a bit naïve, Niccolò.'

Ebony eyes bored into her. '*You* are accusing *me* of naivety?'

She shrugged. 'People—especially women—will be desperate to hear the details about how we met and why you're about to become a father after all this time—especially since you're a self-confessed commitment-phobe. So, do we tell them it was a hook-up which started in the broom cupboard, or pretend our liaison lasted longer than a single night?'

His eyes narrowed into obsidian shards. 'Neither,' he answered silkily. 'If pressed, we say it was a short-lived affair which was over almost before it began and we are handling the outcome like two mature adults.' His lips pressed together in a cynical smile. 'A story is easy to kill with the truth.'

And the truth could kill, too, Lizzie thought, her heart clenching. It could destroy her foolish little hopes with a single, well-aimed blow. *It was over almost before it began.* His words, not hers. And they hurt. Why did they hurt so much?

'Fine,' she said flatly.

'There are already a couple of things in the diary. A drinks party next week,' he said. 'That's what Donna was ringing about.'

'Who's Donna?'

'A friend.'

It was a word which carried a wealth of meaning—especially when you were pregnant and feeling ultra-sensitive—but the arrival of the chef bearing a large platter terminated the conversation. Which was probably a good thing. Much better to find out about Donna when she wasn't suffering from jet lag and was feeling more resilient. She lurched towards the pile of delicious-looking sandwiches. When it wasn't such an effort to pretend she didn't care if he was having a relationship with someone else.

Or to hide how badly she wanted him to kiss her.

CHAPTER SIX

LIZZIE'S NIGHT WAS punctuated with hot dreams of Niccolò kissing her, alternated with visions of giant silver sandwich platters and she woke late and slightly disorientated next morning, not quite sure where she was. She turned her head this way and that. Beside the bed was a remote control and one click made the blinds float silently upwards, like the curtain rising in a theatre. And there—in all its brash and glittering splendour—was the backdrop of the Manhattan skyline. She really *was* here. In the heart of New York. In a vast but slightly sterile hotel suite, in a hotel owned by the father of her child.

She spent a few minutes stretching expansively in the enormous bed, before making her way to the luxurious bathroom and experimenting with the different settings on the taps. Who knew that having a shower could be so complicated? After dressing in a pair of dungarees and a sweater, she set off in search of breakfast, but everything remained spookily quiet until she was startled by the sight of a smiling woman who appeared at the far end of the corridor, her white uniform making her look like a friendly ghost.

'Good morning!' she said cheerfully. 'I'm Kaylie. And you're Lizzie, right?'

'That's right. Good morning.' Lizzie's smile was bright but she was finding it hard to know how to react in this particular situation. She was there as a guest but deep down she felt more kinship with the maid who was walking towards her. What was the other woman thinking? she wondered. That it was bizarre to have this strange pregnant woman turning up out of no-where, and installing herself in a separate bedroom in the billionaire's hotel suite? She swallowed, trying to reclaim some sense of identity. 'Erm… I wonder if you could point me in the direction of the kitchen? I was thinking I might make myself some breakfast.'

'Oh, don't you worry about that,' said Kaylie, with an airy wave of her hand. 'I'll bring you whatever you fancy. How about eggs—any way you like? Or some pancakes? Chef does a mean pancake.'

'Pancakes would be great,' said Lizzie, feeling about twelve. Except that nobody had ever clucked around her like this, had they? Her mother had spent a lot of time in bed with her 'nerves', like a character from a Victorian novel. Treats had been in very short supply and they'd come either courtesy of schoolfriends, or hard won by Lizzie herself.

'Go and sit yourself down in the dining room and I'll bring it through,' said Kaylie. 'There's a letter in there waiting for you.'

Lizzie made her way into the dining room, which she'd rejected as too formal last night, so goodness only knew how it would feel this morning. But it was strange how your mood could lift in the cold, clear light of day. The room was hung with stunning oil paintings and there was a vase of flowers at the centre of the polished table, which were filling the room with the most delicate and delicious scent. And there, propped up against the crystal bowl of creamy roses was an envelope with distinctive black handwriting on the front, which Lizzie instinctively recognised as belonging to Niccolò.

She was right. The script was bold and slashing, the words succinct. But, despite the maid's description, it certainly wasn't long enough to qualify as a letter.

Lois, my assistant, will ring you after breakfast. Ask her for anything you need. N

There was no affection or softness in the brief message. But perhaps she should embrace his lack of guile, rather than despair of it. He wasn't pretending to feel anything for her, was he? He wasn't saying things he didn't mean, which meant he was fundamentally honest. Surely that would help curtail her foolish tendency to build fanciful dreams around him.

She ate the pancakes, which were delicious, and drank copious amounts of jasmine tea, and was just piling up her crockery when Kaylie appeared in the doorway, a telephone in her hand. Shaking her head in mock reprimand at Lizzie's attempts to clear up, she handed her the phone.

'Hello,' said Lizzie brightly, feeling the annoying sink of her heart when she heard a female voice she didn't recognise.

'Lizzie? This is Lois Kenton, Nic's assistant. He asked me to ring once you'd finished breakfast.'

'How do you know that? Do you have X-ray vision or something?' asked Lizzie, only half joking.

'No. Kaylie buzzed me over once you were done.' The other woman's voice was kind. 'I hope you're settling in okay?'

'Yes, it's...' Lizzie looked up, wondering now if there were spy cameras hidden in the ceiling '...very luxurious,' she finished truthfully.

'I'm glad. If there's anything you need, just holler. I've made an appointment at Lenox Hill Hospital tomorrow morning at eleven. Dr Campbell is one of the country's finest obstetricians and he comes highly recommended. I hope that's okay? One of my assistants, along with a car, will call to collect you at ten—because there will be paperwork to complete.'

'Th-thanks,' Lizzie said, feeling slightly overwhelmed by all this smooth efficiency.

'I also understand that you're looking to update your wardrobe and we can help you with that, too.'

Lizzie started to bristle defensively until she reminded herself that Lois was only relaying what she'd been told by her boss. *Don't shoot the messenger.* 'I think I'll take a rain check on that one,' she said politely, until something occurred to her. 'Lois. I don't know if you can help, but I need something to do while I'm here and I... Well, I paint portraits of dogs and maybe you could ask around. To see if anyone is interested. Oil on canvas—though I need to get hold of some canvasses.'

'I can sort that out for you. And, as it happens, I know someone who would be very interested,' said Lois. 'Me!'

'Really?'

'Really.'

'What have you got?'

'A bichon frise! Called Blanche.'

'Oh! Lucky you. I love that breed. Could you get a few photos of her to me? And maybe a favourite toy. Doesn't matter if it's all chewed up, or has a bit missing. Just something particular to her, so that of all the bichon frises in the world, it could only be Blanche.'

'Sure,' said Lois. 'I'll bring something in and give it to Nic to pass on to you.'

The dog-friendly conversation continued in this vein for a couple more minutes, until finally Lizzie hung up, delighted to have got her first commission. And Lois had been very sweet, there was no denying that. She hadn't asked her any intrusive questions, had she? Perhaps this experience wasn't going to be the ordeal she'd anticipated. She just needed to get real. To accept Niccolò for the man he was, not the dream lover she wanted him to be.

But a couple of hours spent in the high-rise suite were enough to have her pacing the rooms restlessly. Didn't seem to matter how spacious the suite was—bottom line was that she was stuck at the very top of a steel and concrete box and she felt trapped. It seemed her fears of being stuck in a gilded tower weren't far off the mark. She tried watching TV, but, despite the biggest screen she had ever seen, she couldn't find anything she wanted to watch, and flicking through the channels made her even more restless.

She was used to being outside in her down time, and although the sky beyond the tall buildings was the colour of dark steel, Lizzie felt a sudden desire to be out in the fresh air, away from the carefully controlled temperature of the hotel suite. This might not be a *real* holiday, but this was the first time she hadn't worked in years, so why not make the most of it? She keyed in the Wi-Fi code on her phone, studied the map to see that Central Park was conveniently close and consulted the temperature. Cold. Very cold. She added a cardigan before putting on her coat, though the extra layer meant there was an even bigger gap at the front. Then she wound a scarf around her neck and set off for a walk, running into Kaylie in the entrance hall, who was arranging a burst of amber roses in a tall vase.

The maid's expression was one of unfeigned alarm as she took in Lizzie's state of dress.

'You're planning on going out somewhere?'

'Only for a walk,' said Lizzie, with a smile. 'It's such a beautiful day.' This was patently untrue, but didn't they always say beauty was in the eye of the beholder?

'But you don't know the city,' objected Kaylie.

'I soon will!'

Kaylie frowned. 'You don't want me to call one of Mr Macario's assistants?'

'No, honestly. I'll be fine. I wonder, is there a key I could take?'

The penthouse elevator was empty as Lizzie rode downstairs, but the foyer was full of the kind of people who looked as though they'd wandered straight out of Central Casting, all sharing the same common denominator of extreme wealth. Two towering men with the physique of basketball stars. Several beautifully dressed children who looked bored out of their skulls as they waited for their mother outside the hotel boutique. Hard-faced middle-aged men with their impossibly beautiful trophy wives. It was hard to feel comfortable as she walked across the lobby.

Was she imagining the glances being slanted in her direction, and the unmistakable sense of surprise which followed? No, of course she wasn't. Places like this were all about pecking order and it was obvious to anyone that she was right at the bottom of the pile. But Lizzie brushed off her insecurities as she stepped out onto the busy sidewalk, the cold air hitting her like a blade and so bitter that she almost turned back and might have done, if it didn't involve walking back through the foyer and risking looking like a fool. Besides, the thought of kicking her heels in that sterile suite didn't exactly appeal.

The car-crammed streets were busy, the air filled with the sound of a cacophony of horns—but seeing the yellow taxis gave her an almost childlike thrill of pleasure. The pavements were busy, too, and everyone looked so purposeful and confident. Everyone in a hurry.

With the aid of her phone she found Central Park without too much trouble and soon was walking the paths and hugging her coat around her as she looked around. It was a place which was so familiar from various films that she felt as if she knew it well. Such a beautiful space to have within the heart of the bustling metropolis, she thought as she glimpsed the distant shimmer of water. The trees were bare and, although they had their own kind of beauty, she thought how stunning the place would look in springtime and that thought stabbed at her heart. By spring, she would have a baby—and who knew what state her relationship with Niccolò would be in by then? Not that you could call it a relationship in any conventional sense of the word, which meant that normal rules didn't apply. What if they'd stopped speaking by springtime, if he'd cut her and the baby out of his life?

This gloomy progression of thoughts had preoccupied her so much that she hadn't been paying attention to where she was going. At some point she must have left the main path to go off at a tangent and she quickly realised she didn't have a clue where she was. Retracing her steps only made it worse and her instinct was to stop a passer-by and to ask for directions—but she wasn't sure if it was her wild eyes or slightly scruffy appearance which made all the people she asked shake their heads and walk on. Maybe they were tourists themselves, she thought forgivingly, or maybe they didn't speak English.

She mustn't panic but she *was* panicking, especially as the odd flake of snow had started fluttering down from the pewter clouds, and she wondered what the chances were of getting totally stranded. What if the city was blanketed in a whiteout—did that kind of thing happen in New York, as well as in ski resorts?

If only she were the kind of person who could read a compass—but what good would that do her when she didn't have one and wasn't sure which direction the hotel was in? Her heart had started racing and, inside her thin gloves, her fingers were beginning to feel like sticks of ice. Should she ring Niccolò? But how could she describe where she was when she didn't even know herself?

Her footsteps speeded up as she looked around, but she wasn't sure if she'd been in this bit before. That big bush looked familiar, but she couldn't be certain. She thought she heard a sound behind her and tried to reassure herself that no, of *course* she wasn't being followed—but that she shouldn't look round, just in case she was. And then, like her worst nightmare, she felt a hand on her shoulder and she sucked in a shudder of air. The hand spun her round, and she was about to scream when she found herself looking into a pair of familiar black eyes.

A pair of very angry black eyes.

His mouth was set in a furious line and a muscle was working furiously at his temple.

'Niccolò!' she gasped, instinctively reaching out to clutch his broad shoulders and she didn't think she'd ever been more pleased to see anyone in her life. He felt so warm and strong and safe that for a moment she just clung to him, like the proverbial limpet on the rock. He didn't say a single word for at least thirty seconds, but when he did his words sliced through the air like daggers.

'What…the…hell…' he snapped '…do you think you're up to, Lizzie?'

'What d-does it look like I'm up to? Is it such a terrible crime?' she demanded, her voice rising with slight hysteria. 'Can't I take a walk in the park when it suits me, or does my pregnancy somehow preclude me doing *that*, too?'

She saw him flinch at the P-word, but the anger still hadn't left his eyes.

His fingers dug into her upper arms. 'I thought—'
He swallowed the next word as if it had been poison.
'You thought what?'

'I thought I'd lost you!' he raged.

Taken aback by this unexpected blaze of emotion,
Lizzie stared at him.

'Anything could have happened to you!' he continued. 'You're all alone in a strange city!'

'So are thousands of other people!'

'But not anyone as gauche and as woefully under-
dressed as you,' he gritted out, his gaze raking down
over her coat, which was gaping wide open. 'I mean,
come on—what the hell are you wearing, Lizzie?'

At least now she was on familiar ground and his
caustic words gave Lizzie the strength to try and push
him away and reassert her independence. But her balled
fists felt puny against the muscular wall of his chest,
and wasn't the truth that she liked being this close to
him? Didn't she want to sink right into him and absorb
all that strength and power?

'What does it look like? This is my winter coat,'
she mumbled. 'Why don't you just go away if you're
ashamed to be seen with me? Just because I c-can't
compete with your f-fancy cashmere coat!' she said,
her teeth beginning to chatter.

'This isn't about competition,' he negated. 'And it's
nothing to do with me being ashamed of being seen
with you.'

'Then, why…?' Her words died away as she stared
at him. 'Niccolò! What are you doing?'

'Isn't it obvious?' he snapped, dislodging her hands

and removing his dark overcoat, which he placed over her shoulders before starting to button it up. 'I'm trying to make you warm.'

She wanted to protest at this unexpected display of chivalry because he was standing there wearing nothing but a lightweight charcoal suit but, oh, the sensation of warmth from the all-enveloping coat felt like heaven and it smelt of him. 'You must be fr-freezing,' she breathed, choking a little as a gust of wind whipped a strand of hair straight into her mouth.

'Shh…' Niccolò found himself pulling the errant lock away from the cold tremble of her lips and smoothing it back into the thick fall of her hair. 'Don't worry about it. My car is waiting over there. Come on. We're going.'

And wasn't the craziest thing of all that he wanted to put his lips where her hair had been and pull her into his arms and stand there kissing her, as if they'd been a couple of teenagers at the end of a first date? But he resisted the desire to touch her in any way, other than the protective arm he placed around her shoulder as he began to guide her along the path towards his limousine. He waited until she was ensconced beneath a rug on the back seat and he had turned the heating up, and the flakes of snow had begun to melt on her pale red hair, before giving voice to his concerns, careful to temper the full force of his anger and his fear.

'You can't just disappear like that in future, Lizzie,' he observed flatly. 'Without telling anyone where you're going.'

'I didn't think. I'm sorry. I certainly didn't mean to

worry anyone.' She bit her lip but her green eyes were fixed on him. 'How did you find me?'

'I sent some of my staff to look for you.'

Her contrition of a few moments ago seemed to be forgotten, her voice rising with indignation as she glared at him.

'You sent some staff to *look* for me? I mean, what *is* it with you, Niccolò?' she demanded, not bothering to moderate her own anger, he noted wryly.

'Do you get off on spying on your housemates for no reason?' she continued furiously.

He leaned back to study the infinitely fascinating definition of her lips as they pursed together in exasperation. 'Point one, you are the first "housemate" I've ever had,' he drawled. 'And if this kind of behaviour is anything to go by—you're likely to be the last.'

'Oh, yeah?' She elevated her brows. 'And point two is…?'

But her spiky challenge had altered the atmosphere and suddenly everything had changed. He felt a new kind of tension creep in and suddenly Niccolò felt close to helpless, because she looked so tiny and so alluring that all he wanted to do was to crawl underneath that rug with her.

She stared back at him, her eyes darkening, her lips parting, and the desire which fizzled through the air was off the scale. She wanted him to kiss her. He would have bet his entire fortune on that. And he wanted that, too. Hell, yes. He could never remember feeling such an overwhelming desire to kiss someone—except maybe in that damned broom cupboard. But even as his groin grew hard, he reminded himself that to act on his feelings would have consequences and he mustn't allow the needs of his body to tip them into an ill-judged relationship. He would end up hurting her and she, of all people, did not deserve to be hurt.

And neither did he. He thought about how he'd felt as he had run through the icy park to find her, logic deserting him as he'd imagined something bad happening to her. And he couldn't live with that. Not again.

He fixed her with a challenging look. 'Point two is that if I hadn't turned up when I did, you might very well have caught pneumonia.'

'Isn't that a little melodramatic?'

'Maybe. But it doesn't change the fact that you need new clothes,' he added. 'Clothes which are weather-appropriate and which actually fit you.' He knitted his brows together. 'So why don't you stop posturing about some pointless principle and make yourself an appointment at Saks?'

There was silence for a moment while she absorbed this and then she pulled a face. 'And what if I told you that it wasn't just some *pointless principle*?'

He met her gaze. 'Go on.'

'You seem to make out that just because you're offering to buy me a brand-new wardrobe, I should be falling over myself to thank you. Why? Is that what usually happens?'

'I've never bought a woman clothes before,' he snapped.

'Presumably because the women you usually mix with can afford to buy their own swish clothes, and that's okay. I understand why you're doing it, Niccolò and I don't deny that it's with all the best intentions, but I grew up with...'

'Grew up with what?' he said, curious in spite of himself as her words tailed away.

'My mother never really worked and we lived on benefits. Handouts from the state,' she filled in, as the American model was probably different. 'We did that because we had to, because she never tried to get herself a job, and she was okay with that. But it's not how I wanted to live my life and since she died and I've been on my own, I've never taken a penny from anyone.' She tilted her chin. 'I may not have had the most lucrative jobs in the world, but I've always paid my own way.'

'Which puts us at a bit of an *impasse*, doesn't it?' he observed slowly.

'I know. I can't even cook you meals to pay you back because you have a famous chef do that and I can't make beds or dust the suite, because I think it would put Kaylie's and all the other maids' noses out of joint. But...' her eyes narrowed consideringly '... I could do your portrait.'

'If you think I'm sitting still while you paint me, Lizzie Bailey, then you're deluded,' he told her softly.

'I usually do animals, but I think I could make an exception for you. Although come to think of it...' She tipped her head to one side and narrowed her eyes consideringly. 'Hmm. Yes. Definitely. I can see a distinct resemblance to an angry bear.'

And to Niccolò's surprise, he started laughing.

CHAPTER SEVEN

NICCOLÒ DROPPED HIS briefcase on the floor more loudly than he intended, the sudden rush of air causing the roses in a nearby vase to shiver. With impatient fingers, he began to unbutton his jacket, throwing it down on a chair with his usual attention to sartorial detail forgotten. He'd had yet another frustrating day at the office for reasons which were as inexplicable as they were irritating—and it was all down to her.

Lizzie.

Lizzie Bailey.

A freckled face swam into his mind as it had been doing on occasions too numerous to count. Pale green eyes and glowing skin. A pair of soft, rosy lips crying out to be kissed. He shook his head, but the image refused to budge and he scowled. Total preoccupation with his unexpected houseguest was now his new normal and he didn't like it. He didn't like it one bit.

For days, he had uncharacteristically found himself glazing over during meetings at his company headquarters, in a way which had produced vague flutterings of surprise from his staff. Instead of focussing on the latest stratospheric profits of Macario Industries and finding new ways to increase them, which was what he was extremely good at—his attention had been dominated by one Lizzie Bailey.

He had tried too many times to analyse her allure—and this was the confusing thing, because he had dated women far more conventionally beautiful than her. But then, he'd never lived with a woman before and had perhaps underestimated the potency of proximity. He had deliberately placed her off limits, yet was discovering that the forbidden had a power all of its own. She was feisty and she was vulnerable—an undeniably distracting combination, made all the more affecting because he sensed it wasn't contrived. And then there was her air of stubborn independence. Her reluctance to accept any of his considerable wealth, despite being as poor as a church mouse.

But there were other things about her which were equally perplexing. How come she was so uncannily good at reading his mood—sensing whether he wanted to talk at breakfast time, or remain silent? Was that rooted in her experience of working as a housekeeper? But she isn't your employee, he reminded himself frustratedly. She was your lover—briefly—but not any more.

And wasn't that something else which was driving him crazy? Those vivid memories of how good it had been between them?

A muscle began to work at his temple. He had tried to deny, ignore, dismiss and subdue his desire for her—but nothing seemed to work. Punishing early-morning sessions at the gym had proved useless. Long hours at his desk didn't help. He felt as if he had temporarily ceded control to the tiny redhead, and since he was a man for whom control was key, this was disturbing. He'd even considered eradicating the pervasive memories of her curving body by taking another lover—although obviously, he would be very discreet about it. But although other women were always coming onto him and there was an abundance of suitable candidates from which to choose, he found the idea of having sex with anyone else abhorrent.

His mouth hardened.

He wanted her, and only her—despite the combative dialogue which sparked between them, like iron on flint.

He balled his hands into two exasperated fists.

There were a million reasons why he should be content to keep the pregnant housekeeper at arm's length, but when he sought to reassure himself by analysing them—they seemed meaningless.

And while he had been giving less than one hundred per cent at the office, Lizzie had been settling into her new life in Manhattan, according to various members of his staff who she seemed to have charmed into total compliance. Mostly, she had been visiting the city's art galleries, along with a guide she had grudgingly agreed to tolerate after the Central Park incident, and a security detail he'd arranged to keep an eye on her from a discreet distance.

Calculatingly, he had tried staying away from her as much as possible and had even stopped turning off his phone while eating dinner, which meant he was often able to distract himself with work calls instead of looking into her amazing eyes. But tonight he was taking her to a party and, weirdly, he was looking forward to it. It felt like a date when it most emphatically was not a date.

According to Lois, his assistant, Lizzie had finally capitulated and spent the day shopping at Saks, leaving the acquisition of a new wardrobe right up to the wire. He frowned. And that was another thing. He hadn't realised that Lois owned a dog and that Lizzie had started painting it, setting herself up in a box room within the apartment and making the whole place smell of oil paint. It was an entirely new—and unwanted—pattern for his usually frosty aide to arrive at the office bearing a clutch of photos featuring some tiny piece of fluff called Blanche and asking him if he could pass them on to Lizzie. He wasn't at all comfortable about his home life spilling over into his office life—but what could he do?

The hotel suite was quiet, which he liked, and the main reception area was empty, which he also liked. He gave a heavy sigh. It was at moments like this that he could almost imagine he'd got his old life back, and was just about to pour himself a restorative glass of whisky when Lizzie walked into the salon and Niccolò almost dropped the tumbler. He tried to scramble his thoughts into some kind of coherence because of *course* he recognised her—a pregnant red-head was hardly going to slip beneath anyone's radar—but he wasn't expecting such a visceral response to her dramatically altered appearance.

Gone were the ugly, shapeless clothes. She wore a fitted dress of ivory lace, which complemented her colouring and glowing skin. Her shiny hair had been styled into a fall of sleek waves which cascaded over her breasts and, quickly, he averted his gaze from their luscious swell. Reluctantly, his eyes strayed to her stomach and it was hard not to stare, because no longer was her condition concealed beneath a swag of shapeless material. Instead, in the close-fitting gown, her pregnant shape seemed almost to be *celebrated*. And wasn't there something daunting about that? His heart gave a powerful punch because he didn't like that feeling. So he focussed instead on her face... What had changed in her face? Niccolò regarded her suspiciously.

'Are you wearing make-up?'

She blinked, apparently surprised by his question— though he couldn't fail to notice the gleam of something unfamiliar in her green eyes, which looked a little like triumph.

'Just a touch. A little mascara. A brush of lip gloss,' she said, before slanting him a look of challenge. 'Why? Is that not allowed?'

'Of course it's allowed.' He reached for the carafe of Scotch, then thought better of it. 'You just look... different. That's all.'

'I thought that was the whole idea?'

'Yes, I know, but...'

Lizzie hid a smile as, for once, the powerful billionaire was lost for words. She might not have had much experience of men but even she could tell he was impressed by her appearance. More than impressed. For a moment she'd thought his eyes were going to pop out of his head when she'd walked into the room. And although that realisation gave her pleasure, it was superseded by an irritation that he was obviously so shallow. What did her mother used to say? *Fine feathers make a fine bird.*

He wasn't interested in the real her, she reminded herself. Only the dressed-up-doll version. First of all in the borrowed dress and now wearing a brand new maternity wardrobe accompanied by a series of jaw-dropping price tags, bought from a shop so dazzling that many times during that afternoon she'd wanted to pinch herself to check she wasn't dreaming.

But the dream was soon to become reality, because tonight Niccolò was taking her to some fancy cocktail party and although he had assured her that the Livingstones were 'good people'—whatever that meant—she was terrified of having to go out and face his inner circle. Galleries and hospital trips accompanied by one of his many staff were one thing. This felt very different.

'Remind me again why I'm going?' she said.

'Didn't we agree that it might make your time here more enjoyable?'

'Did we?'

'I'd hate people to think I was channelling Mr Rochester by locking you in the metaphorical attic,' he drawled. 'So why don't you leave me in peace and let me go and get dressed?'

Lizzie wanted to ask if he could please stop speaking to her in that voice, because the lazy intonation was doing dangerous things to her pulse rate. She preferred it when he was clipped and precise. When he was trying to avoid her. He was doing that for a good reason and she needed to heed it. She needed to stop melting whenever he was around and remind herself that he was unknowable and remote, and that was deliberate.

But he hadn't been so unknowable in the park the other day, had he—when he had found her wandering around in the snow? His face had been raw and savage, filled with a powerful emotion she didn't recognise. The usual gleam of his black eyes had been replaced by a bleakness which had chilled her to the bone and made her want to reach out to him. She had wanted to ask him what had caused it, but his jaw had been so set and forbidding that she hadn't dared.

In fact, she had contemplated the wisdom of accepting tonight's invitation at all, wondering if she was getting in deeper than she should by involving herself in his life like this. For someone like him, this was probably nothing but a mildly amusing exercise. He was powerful enough and wealthy enough not to care if he created something of a society scandal—in fact, it might even enhance his playboy reputation. Bringing a pregnant ex to a party was a pretty audacious move in anyone's books and it would probably serve her better if she refused to go.

But how would that come over? She couldn't hide herself away for the rest of her life, could she? Their night of passion might have been ill judged, but it had still been the most wonderful thing which had ever happened to her. Niccolò had made her feel things she hadn't thought possible. And yes, he'd done a runner afterwards and she had become pregnant as a result, which wouldn't have been on anyone's wish list, least of all hers. But from the first moment of discovering she was having a baby, Lizzie had been in a state of wonderment.

She thought about the lovely fatherly doctor she'd seen at the plush clinic on the Upper East Side earlier that day who'd told her she was doing just fine—more than fine, she was positively *blooming*. He might have been a bit surprised but had passed no judgement when she'd explained that the father didn't want to be involved in any way, other than paying her medical expenses. She wondered what he'd say if he knew that Niccolò hadn't asked her a single question about the baby. She'd thought natural curiosity would lead him to enquire about the sex of their child, at least. But no. She wasn't even sure if he knew her due date. He didn't want to know because he didn't care, she reminded herself fiercely—and she was going to have to deal with that. She was going to love this baby enough for both of them. And she could. She would.

Climbing into the back of a chauffeur-driven limousine, Lizzie thought how incredible her new clothes felt. There was something to be said for the sensual feel of natural fibres against your skin. She'd bought new underwear, too—which she hadn't realised she needed, until the rather bossy woman in the lingerie department had informed her just how much her measurements had changed. Now, thanks to the delicately supportive bra, her breasts were pert rather than bouncy—something which hadn't escaped Niccolò's attention either—judging by the searing look he had subjected her to, before quickly averting his gaze. Her breasts had tightened and she'd felt a rush of pure lust in response. Did he realise that? Was he aware that he could reduce her to a quiver of need, with just a single smoky glance—or did all women react to him in that way?

The party was being held in a place called Tribeca, in a sprawling penthouse apartment at the top of an impressive old building, and from the moment Lizzie walked in, she was dazzled—because it was like being inside a giant snowball. Everything appeared to be white. White carpets. White sofas. A man in a snowy jacket was playing on a white baby grand piano. Against this stark backdrop, the guests stood out with dramatic elegance—the men in dark tuxedoes, and beautifully dressed women perching effortlessly on precariously high heels, their precious jewellery sparkling beneath the lights.

'Don't tense up,' instructed Niccolò softly.

'That's okay for you to say. You do this sort of thing all the time. I don't.'

'Would it help to tell you that you look amazing?'

She wanted to say it wasn't about how she looked, it was how she *felt*—which was totally out of her depth. But she wasn't going to flag up any more insecurities, especially not at a moment like this. 'Very kind of you to say so,' she answered.

'It's not kindness, Lizzie,' he said softly. 'It's the truth.'

'Don't be nice to me, Niccolò. It throws me off-balance.'

'Very funny.'

'I thought so.'

Everyone turned to look when they walked in. Of course they did. When you were a servant you noticed everything and Lizzie still thought of herself as essentially, a servant. She could see the women's gazes flick assessingly from Niccolò to her and then back again. What were they thinking? That they were a mismatched pair? Normally she would have agreed with them, but she was still glowing from his words of praise.

She scanned the room. There was a man with horn-rimmed glasses she'd definitely seen on a chat show back in England and, in a far corner of the penthouse, a leggy model with a Cleopatra hairstyle—surrounded by a clutch of adoring men. A woman in a shimmering gold cocktail dress and a mane of matching hair came gliding over to greet them. 'Nic!' she murmured, her smile brushing each of his chiselled cheeks as she leaned forward to kiss him. 'So good to see you.'

'Donna!' he responded, with a smile Lizzie had never seen him use before. 'I'd like you to meet Lizzie. Lizzie—this is Donna, our host.'

So *this* was Donna! His 'friend'—with all the possible permutations which that word carried. Lizzie gulped. She was so gorgeous, and so thin. And calling him Nic sounded incredibly intimate, didn't it? As if she knew him really well. She probably did. After all, *Lizzie* was the only person in the room who knew practically nothing about him, despite the fact that she was carrying his baby. Why hadn't she bothered to interrogate him and discover a few facts about the father of her child before they ventured out like this in public? It could be an emotional minefield if she was interrogated by any of the guests and betrayed how little she knew about him. She tried her best not to feel intimidated but it wasn't easy because Donna was everything she wasn't. Classy and rich and confident. And nice. Really nice. This is the sort of woman Niccolò should be with, not me, she thought desperately. Until she reminded herself that he wasn't actually *with* her, either. Oh, why had she come?

'Pleased to meet you,' she said stiltedly.

'Oh, I *love* your accent!' purred Donna. 'And the colour of your hair is adorable! What will you have to drink, Lizzie?'

'Erm—'

'How about some soda?' prompted Niccolò.

'I'll have someone bring some over.' Donna smiled, a quick flick of her fingers bringing a handsome waiter gliding towards them. 'By the way—Jackson Black is here, Nic, but not for long. There's a big vote coming up and I know he's desperate to speak to you before he goes back to Washington.'

'Yeah.' Niccolò turned to scan the room before redirecting his gaze towards Lizzie. 'Would you mind? I need to talk a little shop. I won't be long.'

'No. I don't mind,' Lizzie ventured gamely, wondering if his departing squeeze of her arm was entirely necessary as he moved away. Because all it did was to remind her how little he'd touched her since he had reappeared in her life. She sighed. With him it had definitely been a case of feast or famine. She didn't think there was a centimetre of her skin he hadn't explored on the night she'd conceived his child—and since then nothing other than his dramatic intervention in the park.

And wasn't it insane how such a fleeting contact could make her react like this—making her dissolve from the outside in? Didn't it make her think about his hard body, next to hers? In hers. The way she'd husked out her satisfaction as he had been pulsing out his seed.

Her breath dried in her throat. *Why was she having such x-rated thoughts in the middle of this civilised social setting?*

With an effort, she tore her eyes away from his rugged profile to discover Donna regarding her with thoughtful eyes and she cobbled together a smile, aware that her cheeks had grown very pink.

'So, how are you finding New York, Lizzie?'

'I love it. It's so buzzy, and the service is great. Of course, it's still all very new to me,' she answered politely. 'I haven't been here long.'

'And this is your first trip, I believe?'

Lizzie nodded. *Say something. Don't just stand there like a lemon.* 'I was supposed to come here on a road trip,' she said truthfully. 'But then I split up with my boyfriend and it got cancelled.'

Donna nodded, her cool blue gaze directed towards her bump—and perhaps it was Lizzie's disclosure about her past which made her come out with a confidence of her own.

'I have to tell you, we were all pretty surprised

when we heard about you, and the baby.' The glamorous blonde gave a soft laugh. 'So if you hear the sound of shattering—it's just the sound of a million female hearts being broken all over the city! Oh, please don't look like that, dear. Most of us are very happy that Nic has found somebody at last, we really are. He's been on his own for a long time, though not from the want of women trying to pin him down.' She slanted a complicit smile. 'Anyways, I mustn't keep you all to myself. Come and meet Matt, my husband.'

A completely inappropriate sense of relief washed over Lizzie, which briefly eclipsed her confusion that Donna seemed to be labouring under the illusion that she and Niccolò were a couple. 'Your...husband?' she managed, trying to distract herself, because now was not the time to fret about her hostess's words.

'Sure. We've been married nearly seven years now. Nic was our best man, actually.' Donna's eyes twinkled. 'His speech was outrageous.'

'Hmm. Somehow I don't find that difficult to believe,' said Lizzie and this time her smile was genuine.

'Come on over and say hello,' said Donna. 'There are lots of folk here who want to meet you.'

Lizzie followed her hostess through the vast, bleached room as Donna introduced her to a blur of guests, including her handsome husband, Matt—who it turned out had been to college with Niccolò, in Massachusetts. In a way she was grateful it was a cocktail party and the common language was mostly small talk. If a select bunch of them had been gathered around a dinner table she might have had a tougher time of it, mostly because she was aware of being an imposter—especially since Donna wasn't the only one who made the assumption that she and Niccolò were an item. How shocked they would be to discover the truth, she thought ruefully. To realise that he hadn't asked her a single question about the baby he had never wanted.

But now wasn't the time to enlighten every person she spoke to and risk embarrassing them both. She just concentrated on asking lots of questions, because people liked nothing better than to talk about themselves. She was deep in conversation with a professor of archaeology, who was showing her a photo of his dachshund, when Niccolò returned. His shadow seemed to consume her as he moved to her side, as if he were determined to dominate all her senses with his presence, leaving no room for anyone else. And he was succeeding, because nobody else in the room seemed to have any real substance any more. Suddenly it was all about him.

His raw, masculine scent.

The power of his muscular body.

Those carved, patrician features.

That mocking smile.

The breath died in her throat. No matter how much she tried to convince herself that it was over between them, that didn't stop her wanting him and right now, the feeling was as powerful as it had ever been. Did he notice the instinctive shiver rippling over her skin and realise what had caused it? Was that why his black eyes grew hard and a sudden tension seemed to have crept into the atmosphere?

'Let's go,' he said softly.

'Isn't it a little early?'

'No.'

She thought how comfortable he seemed giving orders and how sometimes he behaved as if she were a puppet, whose strings he was pulling. Was that how the party guests saw her? As some passive, previously unknown conquest who had turned up at the party like a tame incubator and left meekly when the powerful billionaire commanded her to do so. But she smiled her way past the doorman and waited until they were back in the limousine and driving through the thronging streets of Manhattan, before turning to him.

'What exactly did you tell Donna about me?'

He turned towards her but the only thing she could see in the passing city lights was the glitter of his narrowed eyes. 'The facts, of course. That I met you in England and that you're pregnant.'

'And?'

He frowned. 'And what?'

'You were supposed to say it had been a brief fling and we were handling it like adults.'

'I did.'

'So why was she making out we had some kind of future together? Like we were...' Her words stumbled, but she forced herself to say them. 'If not exactly love's young dream, then certainly some kind of item.'

'Was she?'

'Yes, she was! Like I'd pretty much broken every heart of the women in this city.'

'That part could be accurate,' he mused.

'Niccolò!'

He breathed out an impatient sigh. 'I guess it's human nature to see the things you want to see, and she and Matt have been mounting a campaign for years to find me the *right* woman. A *good* woman.'

'And I suppose I couldn't be further from that model, could I?' she retorted, aiming for brightness rather than bitterness as their limousine stopped in front of the hotel.

There was a pause before the chauffeur opened the car door. 'But there is no such woman, Lizzie,' he informed her softly. 'Not for a bastard like me.' His laugh was bitter as he guided her across the shiny lobby towards his private elevator. 'I just wish people would accept that.'

But despite the candour of his words, Niccolò's heart was hammering as the lift doors slid closed behind them, imprisoning them in this silent box, which was the last thing he needed. He'd spent the evening giving her space and that had been deliberate. He had tried to concentrate on what was being said to him, rather than watching her moving around the room, which had been his instinct. But now there was nowhere to look but at her and he couldn't seem to tear his eyes away.

Her hair was gleaming like fire beneath the overhead light and, in the pale lace dress, she looked soft and ripe and inviting. He could detect her scent—sharp as limes and sweet as blossom—and, vividly, it took him back to that night he'd spent in her arms. His blood thundered as he recalled the way she had given herself to him so fully. So completely and openly, and without condition. He remembered the exquisite feeling of tightness as he had broken through her hymen, and the sense of wonder in her voice when she had come that first time beneath his fingers.

He glanced up at the dial. Had time slowed, or something? They had now reached the fifteenth floor, with another eight to go and sweat had begun to bead his forehead, because this was claustrophobia with a spicy twist. Was she aware of the need which was pulsing through his body, and was it the same for her? Was that why she was staring at him like that—all startled green eyes, her freckles standing out like tiny stars beneath the harsh elevator lights?

'Lizzie,' he said urgently. That was all. But maybe his husky tone sparked something inside her because suddenly her lips were parting.

'Niccolò.' Their eyes locked. Her voice seemed almost slurred, though she'd drunk nothing stronger than water—and all he knew was that she sounded nothing like the innocent he had bedded back in the summer. Didn't look like her either, with that slumberous spark in her eyes and a soft smile curving her lips. Yet he didn't know how to be with her, even though his desire for her was off the scale. The rules were different. She was pregnant, for a start.

'Don't you know that you're driving me crazy?' he grated.

'In what way?' she enquired.

'Oh, no. You're not getting away with that, Lizzie. You're no longer qualified to play the innocent,' he told her heatedly. 'You know damned well what I mean. In every which way.'

'But you're the experienced one,' she pointed out, her calm logic fuelling the fire of his senses.

'What does that have to do with anything?' he growled.

'Well…' Her voice was soft. 'I have no idea what to do in a situation like this.'

'You know something?' He gave a short laugh. 'Neither do I.'

Niccolò wasn't sure which of them moved first, only that suddenly she was in his arms and he was smoothing back her hair and bending his head to kiss her, with an aching frustration building inside him which made him feel like a novice. That first touch was like wildfire—igniting all the pent-up hunger which had been building inside him for months—and he groaned as the tip of her tongue entered his mouth, because never had such a simple gesture felt so intensely erotic. Why was that? Because he could feel her fecund new shape pressing against him, terrifyingly unfamiliar to his usually experienced fingers?

Bitter thoughts attempted to assault his mind but his body's needs were greater than the painful tug of his memories. Their mouths still locked, he splayed his palms over her ripe breasts, luxuriating in their heavy firmness. He could feel the diamond tips of her nipples pushing hard against her lace dress and he wanted to peel it off and reveal her freckled flesh. He heard her groan as he deepened the kiss and now the scent of her cologne had been replaced by the far more evocative tang of feminine desire, obliterating any last vestiges of doubt in his mind. He wanted to ruck up her dress and feel her silken thighs. He wanted to touch her bud and feel it engorged with blood. But most of all, he wanted to be inside her again, with a wild and primitive hunger which took him by surprise. To fill her with his hardness. To hear her cry out his name, as she'd done before. To forget the world and all his memories.

He tore his lips away from hers as the elevator pinged to a halt and, although the doors opened, he stayed perfectly still and so did she. The tense silence punctured only by their laboured breathing, he dragged oxygen back into his lungs as he stared at her. 'I want you, Lizzie Bailey,' he said unsteadily.

'And I…well, I want you, too. I imagine that's pretty obvious.'

He gave a short laugh. 'Just a bit.' He could barely articulate his next words as the elevator doors closed again and still they hadn't got out. 'So, little Miss Redhead. What are we going to do about this?'

'This?'

'Do you want me to spell it out for you in words of one syllable?' he questioned huskily. 'Are we going to have sex, or not?'

Her cheeks grew even pinker, as if she were embarrassed by his choice of words, and that rush of colour made him realise exactly what he was asking of her. Suddenly, Niccolò was appalled at himself. Her sweet blush reminded him of her inexperience—not only around sex but, by definition, around men, too. It reminded him that he could offer her nothing but brief pleasure. No lasting commitment, nor even any lasting protection. Especially not protection. His heart twisted.

Why the hell was he coming onto her like this, despite all those stern pronouncements he'd made about staying away? Wouldn't he be putting her in danger if they ended up making out—and here, of all places? In the damned *elevator*? Had he learned nothing at all, or did he still excel at making disastrous choices?

Breaking away from her, he felt the wash of self-contempt. 'This is *not* going to happen,' he stated angrily. 'We are not a couple. We were never intended to be. And if we start having sex, the boundaries are going to be blurred even more. For you, especially. Do you understand what I'm saying, Lizzie?'

Lizzie met his heated gaze, her natural indignation that he should speak to her in that rather patronising way blotted out by a keen sense of curiosity. She wanted to know what he'd meant when he'd stated he was a bastard earlier, in that flat and empty voice. She wanted to know what had caused that terrible look of anguish to tauten his sculpted features a minute ago. But how could she ask him when everything was complicated by her physical reaction to him? The tension between them was stretched so tight she suspected it would take very little to snap it. One move from her and she suspected he would be kissing her again and making her melt helplessly beneath the seeking pressure of his lips. And that could end with only one conclusion.

With an effort she pulled herself together, because maybe he was right. Maybe it was better this way. Donna had implied that women had always thrown themselves at him and although Lizzie couldn't blame them, she didn't intend being one of their number.

'I understand perfectly, Niccolò,' she answered calmly. 'If you don't want to, then we won't. It's not a problem—in fact, it's probably the most sensible outcome, if I stop to think about it. But now, if you don't mind, I think it's time I went to bed. It's getting a little...*heated* in here.'

His face was a picture of frustration and disbelief as she turned away, but suddenly Lizzie felt empowered by her actions as the elevator doors slid open once more. It wasn't what she wanted, but it was the right thing to do—and sometimes that was the best you could hope for. She knew he was watching her as she walked along the seemingly endless corridor and only once she had closed her bedroom door behind her did she let out the breath she hadn't realised she had been holding.

She stared into one of the mirrors, noting the brightness of her eyes and her flushed complexion—but besides the signs of sexual desire, the tilt of her chin was resolute and she allowed herself a small smile of satisfaction. She might not have much money or prestige to her name, but at least she still had her pride.

CHAPTER EIGHT

LIZZIE GOT VERY little rest that night, despite telling herself that not sleeping with Niccolò had been the best possible outcome. She lay tossing and turning and trying not to think about the man just along the corridor, but her unconscious mind was refusing to play ball. Every time sleep beckoned, the Italian's gleaming gaze and sensual lips kept flashing up behind her closed eyelids. She wondered how she would be feeling this morning if they *had* ended up in bed together. She wouldn't be filled with this aching sense of frustration, that was for sure.

She stared out of the windows at the night-time sky, which never really got dark in New York. Coming to America had seemed like the only sensible choice when Niccolò had made his offer, but it had always been a move fraught with danger. And the biggest danger was the way she felt about him. Still. She swallowed. It was relatively easy not to think about someone in a romantic sense when all you were doing was sharing the occasional meal, surrounded by swarms of staff—all eager to gain the billionaire's approbation. Less easy when you'd been kissing passionately in the lift and come within a hair's breadth of going back to one of the many rooms for a taste of the intimacy she'd been craving.

Staring at her phone, she saw it was still only three a.m., and sighed. It didn't seem to matter how much she told herself she shouldn't want the Italian billionaire after everything which had happened between them. The truth was that she did.

But, lest she try to delude herself, *he* had been the one to call a halt to it—using brutal words calculated to wound. He couldn't have made it plainer how he felt. *He didn't want his baby and he didn't want her, either.* That was the bottom line—and continually putting herself in the line of temptation was surely counter-productive. Wasn't it time to stop obsessing about Niccolò Macario and start focussing on what was best for her and the baby? She pulled the duvet up to her chin and snuggled beneath it. She needed to start thinking about going back to England and what she was planning to do when she got there. And that was a conversation the two of them needed to have some time very soon.

Eventually, she drifted off into a fitful sleep and it was gone nine when she awoke to a room which was unnaturally bright and she looked out of the window to see snow falling and big white flakes swirling down past the skyscrapers. The Manhattan skyline resembled one of those miniature snow globes you sometimes saw in museum shops, though when Lizzie peered out of the window on her way to the bathroom, she noticed that all the snow had all melted by the time it hit the pavement.

Tying her hair up and wrapping a scarf around it, she

covered her dress with a smock she'd bought specially
for working. The painting of Blanche was taking shape
and she needed to finish it and give it to Lois before she
went home. But it was the other portrait she was working on—a black and white drawing of Niccolò—which
was infinitely more tempting. She'd never been so absorbed by one of her subjects before, her movements
rapid and insistent, as if the pencil which stroked its
way over the paper was a poor substitute for her finger.

She hurried along to the dining room, her appetite
huge this morning. There had only been canapés at
Donna and Matt's party and everyone knew they never
filled you up. But as she sat down, it was a bit of a
wake-up call to discover how quickly she had adapted
to her new role as a rich man's guest, rather than as a
person used to serving such a guest. It was remarkably
easy to get used to plonking herself in a chair and telling somebody else what she'd like to eat, and breakfast
had become her favourite meal. Often, Niccolò would
be draining the last of his coffee when she appeared at
the door of the dining room, his black hair still gleaming from the shower—sending out the erroneous illusion of intimacy and closeness.

But not today.

Today, the room was empty, save for Kaylie. How
stupid that his absence could make her heart sink, even
after everything he'd said to her last night.

Kaylie began to spoon out fresh fruit. 'Signor Macario left very early,' she announced. 'He said to tell
you he's going to Pennsylvania. Would you like eggs?'

'No, thank you. Fruit will be fine,' answered Lizzie,

shaking out her napkin and trying to do her blueberries and coconut whip justice, though she couldn't stop wondering why Niccolò had gone to Pennsylvania, or why he hadn't told her.

As soon as she'd finished eating she sought the distraction of work, in the small space she had made her own. She had been wrong when she'd counted six rooms in Niccolò's suite, because one morning she had stumbled across a box room—largely empty, except for a couple of suitcases. She had asked one of the porters to move them and reposition a desk there, so that it looked out over the city and was the loveliest workplace she had ever used. Best of all, it was north facing with a beautiful clear light and it wasn't long before she was lost in her growing portrait of the tiny white bichon frise.

After a lunchtime sandwich, she resumed painting, pleased with the shape it was taking, so deep in thought that she didn't hear the door open, or close again. She didn't hear anything until the sound of Niccolò's voice disturbed her.

'They told me I'd find you in here.'

She didn't turn round. She didn't dare. Her heart was hammering and her breathing had quickened and she didn't want him to see that. There was plenty she needed to say to him and she needed every bit of clarity and calmness she possessed in order to do so. 'Well, you've found me,' she remarked. 'I thought you were going to Pennsylvania.'

'I was. I rescheduled.'

'It wasn't important?'

'It can wait.'

'Right.' Still she didn't turn round, but now she could barely hold the paintbrush, her fingers were so clammy, and she knew she couldn't maintain this charade of polite conversation for much longer. 'Was there something in particular you wanted, Niccolò?'

He didn't answer, just walked across the bare floorboards to peer over her shoulder. Usually Lizzie hated it when people did that but her reaction was complicated by the fact that she liked him being this close to her.

'It's good,' he said steadily, his gaze flicking from canvas to photo. 'I've never met the dog, of course, but you seem to have created an uncanny likeness.'

'Thank you,' she said, wishing his praise didn't fill her with such a disproportionate amount of joy.

'You're welcome,' he said, but now his voice sounded strained. Different.

She turned round then, surprised to see the shadows beneath *his* eyes, as if sleep had eluded him, too. But she didn't comment on it, as she might have done if they were a real couple. Because they weren't, she reminded herself bitterly. Hadn't he drummed that into her over and over again?

Their relatively banal exchange was in danger of lulling her into a false state of security, but as she stared into the obsidian gleam of his eyes, Lizzie knew she couldn't let that happen.

So have the discussion now, she thought. *Don't wait for the 'right' moment, because there is no such thing. And don't use the image of a cute, fluffy dog to try to invoke some sort of emotion from this cold-hearted man because he doesn't seem capable of it.*

Rising from her chair, she rubbed her left hand in the small of her back and saw his eyes narrow.

'Are you okay?'

She wondered what he'd say if she mentioned that his baby was especially active today, whether that would elicit the kind of response she dreamed of. But she didn't enlighten him.

'I'm absolutely fine,' she said instead. 'But I'm thinking about going back to England sooner, rather than later.'

There was a pause.

'You said a month.'

'Did I?'

'You know you did,' he said heatedly.

'I don't remember signing a contract!'

She could see him dragging in a deep breath, as if she had taken him by surprise.

'Why?' he demanded. 'I mean, why now?'

'Isn't it obvious?' She stared at him. 'This isn't working, Niccolò, we both know that. I mean, it's working up to a point, but it's not ideal.'

'Is it because we didn't have sex last night?'

'No!' But his brutal candour cut through her defences. 'Well, maybe a bit. It's…' Be honest, she thought. Don't try to pretend to be someone else and then get trapped in a web of your own deceit. 'Staying here is doing my head in,' she admitted. 'It seemed like a good idea, back in England. I was tired and, yes, of course I was worried about the future, like anyone else in my position would be. And then you turned up like some knight in shining armour, and although you were grouchy you offered me a safe haven and a break from responsibility and it seemed too good an opportunity to miss. But that party last night was excruciating—'

'Every time I looked, you seemed to be enjoying yourself,' he mused.

Oh, you *stupid* man. 'I was. To an extent. They're a bunch of very interesting people, but I'm an imposter and nothing can take that away.'

'Yet Donna rang me up and wondered if we'd like to spend Thanksgiving with them.'

'Because it's *you* they want, not me,' she exploded. 'I'm not even your current piece of arm candy, am I, Niccolò? And I can't cope with the sustained curiosity which will arise if I continue to accompany you to these kinds of events. With me getting bigger with every day which passes while you...'

'While I what?' he prompted curiously as her words tailed off.

Was it so wrong to voice your worst fears? What did she have left to lose? 'I don't know,' she said slowly. 'I started thinking that maybe I'm providing some kind of hidden service in your life, which you haven't bothered telling me about.'

His eyebrows rose. 'Perhaps you'd care to elaborate?'

She shrugged. 'You've said many times that traditional family life isn't for you.'

'It isn't.'

'No. I realise that. But maybe there are some who don't quite believe you. You said yourself that people are guilty of believing what they want to believe. And what better way of discouraging any billionaire-hungry women intent on changing your mind than by parading your pregnant ex-lover and making it clear there is nothing between you? In one fell swoop you can demonstrate that your heir requirements have been satisfied, but your compartmentalised heart remains intact.'

There was silence for a moment before he spoke. 'Let me get this straight,' he said slowly, his silky voice edged with a frisson of danger. 'You're actually accusing me of using you as some sort of *prop* to help facilitate my reputation as a confirmed bachelor?'

Put like that, it *did* sound a bit harsh, but Lizzie's vexation was genuine. 'I don't know, do I? I don't know what you are or aren't capable of!' she howled. 'Because you never really talk to me, do you, Niccolò? Oh, you open your mouth and words come out—but I don't feel any closer to knowing you than when we spent that night together in the Cotswolds. And that's freaking me out. I don't want to give birth to the baby of a stranger. I want to be able to answer questions about you when our child asks. Because, believe me, he—or she—will ask about you one day.'

She paused long enough for him to enquire about the sex of their baby but—predictably—he didn't. 'I know that for a fact,' she added quietly, sucking in an unsteady breath, unable to stem her sudden stream of insecurity. 'When I was a little girl I was desperate to know more about my dad, but my mother was never able to tell me anything.'

'Why not?'

'Because after their one-night stand—yes, isn't it funny how history repeats itself?—she found out he was married and he said he would never leave his wife. She didn't even tell him she was having his baby and then, when she thought better of it…' Her words tailed off. 'I must have been about two months old at the time and I think she was depressed—she found out he'd been killed in a motorcycle accident. And that was the end of that,' she concluded bitterly. 'That's why I never knew my father and why I didn't want the same to happen to my own child.'

'Why didn't she—?'

'Why didn't she what?' Lizzie interrupted savagely. 'Go to his grieving young widow and inform her that her husband had been playing away? Lay herself open to rejection and censure—and for what? He was dead and he was never coming back.'

Niccolò nodded as he absorbed her words in silence, suddenly aware of what it must have taken for her to have tried so hard to find him, and now understanding why. He thought how unwittingly cruel he had been to her and wondered why she hadn't told him all this before.

Because you wouldn't have wanted her to. You always recoil when women try to tell you their life story, don't you?

'I'm sorry,' he said automatically.

But she shook her head, as if determined to show him that she was not a victim. 'It's not your fault. It's not anybody's fault. But this…this situation is all wrong and the longer it goes on, the more confusing it will be, for everyone. It's time I went home.'

Niccolò found himself thinking how brave she'd been but now he saw the disquiet on her face, as if the emotion of it had all become too much. And even though on one level he knew he was bad news for her, he found himself unable to move, lost in a fog of feelings he didn't understand. It was hard to think straight and even harder to know the right thing to do. Well, that wasn't strictly true. His head told him exactly what he ought to do, but his body was telling him something entirely different. And Lizzie wasn't helping matters any. Her green eyes had grown smoky and he'd seen enough women look at him that way to know she wanted him. But she had to be sure. His lips twisted. Even if he wasn't.

'If you want to go back to England, I'm not going to stop you.'

'I wasn't expecting you to.'

'But that doesn't change the way I feel.'

'Oh?'

He saw the flare of hope in her eyes and forced himself to quash it, because this was nothing to do with romance and everything to do with desire. 'I want to carry on where we left off last night.'

The silence which followed this admission seemed to stretch like a piece of elastic as the tension between them grew. He watched as her lashes lowered to conceal the flash of disappointment in her eyes, but when they fluttered open her gaze was dark and bold.

'So what's stopping you?' she asked quietly.

'How long have you got?' His laugh was short. 'Sense. Logic. Reason. The fact that nothing has changed. Not inside...' He slammed the flat of his hand against his chest, where his heart was. 'Here.'

Her pale green gaze clashed with his.

'I don't care,' Lizzie declared softly, because she didn't. It might be wrong—it was very definitely stupid—but there was only one thing she cared about right then and that was being in Niccolò's arms again. Because when he held her, he made her feel...*real*. And that was a very powerful feeling. She wanted him. She needed him—even if this was only ever going to be a bittersweet memory. Just do it, she thought, her desire spiked with hungry impatience.

But to her surprise he didn't. There was no demonstration of mind-blowing passion to make her instantly compliant and obliterate the remaining possibility of doubt. Instead his thumb traced a slow line down over her cheek and as he moved it away to examine it, she could see a small daub of silver paint on the whorled skin of his thumb-print.

'I was painting the little bell on Blanche's collar,' she babbled in an explanation he hadn't asked for and, surprisingly, he smiled.

'Let's go to bed,' he said softly, lacing her fingers in his.

CHAPTER NINE

IT FELT VERY grown-up and slightly scary to be led by Niccolò Macario through the echoing corridors of the vast suite. Any of the hotel staff could have seen them! But the place was silent and empty as they shut the door of his bedroom—and Lizzie got her first sight of a room which made her own look as if it would be better suited to a doll's house. Outside the snow was still falling—white and ethereal and swirling—while inside the solid antique furniture emphasised the fundamental masculinity of the room. Just as the man before her did. How supremely powerful he looked, in his custom-made suit, the pale silk of his shirt managing to make his hair appear even blacker than usual. Yet, for once, his hard edge of control seemed absent. She could tell he was trying hard to control his breathing, but the urgent glitter of his eyes was a dead giveaway, even to her.

'Come here,' he whispered, and Lizzie went straight into his waiting arms, lifting up her face as he drove his lips down on hers—and it wasn't until they were both out of breath that he drew away and looked down into her face, his eyes hot with hunger.

'Do you know how long I have been thinking about doing this to you?' he growled.

'How long?' she said breathlessly.

'Since I walked out of that door, back in the summer—there hasn't been a single day when I haven't fantasised about this.'

She was about to admit to the same such longings, but then he started kissing her again and the moment was lost.

She made an inadequate little gulp of protest as he picked her up and carried her over to the bed—the additional weight of her pregnancy not seeming to bother him at all. But his hands were gentler than Lizzie remembered as he began to remove her painting smock and the rest of her clothes, until she was left in nothing but her underwear. She should have been nervous, but nerves weren't getting a look-in, because wasn't there something incredibly flattering about the slight unsteadiness of his fingers as he whipped back the snowy counterpane and laid her down on his vast bed?

His hand reached behind to unfasten her new bra with its miracle underpinning and her breasts came tumbling out, bigger than he would have remembered them. For a moment he just stared at them, before bending his head to slowly kiss each peaking nipple, and Lizzie moaned beneath the lick of his tongue, turned on by the contrast of his tousled black head against her freckled skin. Next came her panties, slithered down over trembling thighs before he unceremoniously flicked those aside too. His black gaze raked over her with a burning intensity, but as it lingered briefly on the curve of her belly she saw his eyes cloud with something which looked like pain and instinctively, Lizzie shivered. Did he find the sight of her burgeoning body repulsive? Was he about to change his mind?

'Is something wrong?' she whispered.

But he shook his head, scooping up the discarded duvet and floating it down on top of her as if he couldn't wait to cover her up.

'You're cold,' he remarked matter-of-factly.

Lizzie thought about all the things she could say and knew one thing for sure. She might not get another chance to do this—so why waste it by playing games? She didn't feel cold. She felt strong and vital. She didn't want him swathing her in bubble wrap and treating her as if she were made of glass. She wanted him as man to her woman. As equals. Even if it were for one night only. Just like last time. 'I'm not,' she contradicted. 'Just excited.'

'Well, that's a coincidence because so am I.' He gave an unsteady laugh. 'And this has been a long time in the waiting.'

She watched as he began to undress, removing his clothes unselfconsciously, as if this was something he'd done many times before—which of course, he must have done. But Lizzie forced herself not to focus on the differences which existed between them. It didn't matter how many lovers he'd had before her. What mattered was being here now. With him. And he wasn't thinking of other women—not if that hungry expression on his face was anything to go by. He stepped out of the silken boxer shorts which had made no secret of his arousal, but seeing him completely naked drove home just how physically well endowed he was.

Did her face betray her flicker of apprehension? Was that why he came towards her, sitting on the edge of the bed while he stroked away the tumbled strands of her hair?

'Changing your mind is always a viable option, but sooner might be better than later,' he commented wryly.

As Lizzie shook her head, it occurred to her that he might actually *want* her to cancel this. Did he? Wouldn't that be more sensible for both of them, in the long run? Well, too bad. If that was really what he wanted then he was going to have to do the ejecting because she couldn't move. She didn't want to do anything except drink in all his strength and magnificence. 'That's not going to happen,' she whispered boldly, her hand trailing slowly over the rocky muscles of his arm.

'This is all new to me.' His words were urgent as he got into bed and pulled her into his arms. 'I've never had sex with a pregnant woman before.'

'I should hope not.' But it thrilled her to think this was something he'd never done before. That she was his first, just as he had been for her. She shivered as he began to touch her, featherlight fingertips whispering over her skin. With rapt preoccupation, he stroked her breasts, her hips, her thighs…though she noticed he steered well clear of her belly. 'You won't hurt me,' she whispered. 'Intercourse is allowed. At least, that's what the clinic told me.'

He drew back from her, his black eyes narrowed. 'You were asking the clinic about sex?' he demanded.

Lizzie knew he had no right to be so proprietorial, but that didn't stop her from basking in the possessive husk of his tone. 'It's all part of their general advice,' she said. 'The staff go out of their way to make you realise that having sex during pregnancy is perfectly normal and nothing to be frightened of.'

She waited for him to ask more. To ask the question she'd been longing for him to ask ever since he'd turned up on that cold winter's day in London. But he didn't and she felt the sudden twist of her heart. He didn't *want* to know about the sex of their child and either she accepted that, or she shouldn't be here. He lowered his head and began to kiss her and she wasn't sure if he'd done it to silence her, or reduce her to a state where she wasn't thinking properly. But it worked. He kissed her until she was mindless with longing. Her nipples prickled and her tummy tightened—a rush of pure heat flooding her as his hand reached between her legs.

'Oh,' she said faintly, as his finger flicked out a delicate rhythm and she lay star-fished against his mattress.

'Oh, what?' he whispered.

'I don't remember,' she whispered back.

She knew she was probably being too passive but she couldn't seem to stop herself. She couldn't even think straight as waves of sensation began to swamp her and soon she was convulsing around his questing finger and choking out little moans of satisfaction.

His lips against her hair, he cradled her in his arms and for a while she just lay there in warm silence while her senses slowed and righted themselves. And didn't some fragment of her mind wonder whether he had deliberately bombarded her with pleasure while demanding none for himself because it gave him back all the control and left her with none?

'I want to be inside you,' he said roughly, as if he had read her thoughts, and Lizzie was taken aback by just how relieved she felt.

'I want that too,' she said, almost shyly—which was slightly ironic in the circumstances. She was heavy with his child, for heaven's sake—and yet she was behaving like a virgin. But what happened next wasn't what she had been hoping for. His lips and his fingers were as dextrous as ever, but there was something almost *mechanical* about his actions as he gently turned her onto her side and began to play with her nipples from his position behind her. It was a turn-on most definitely, but it wasn't in the least bit emotional.

Yet still she reacted. She couldn't help herself. She could feel his muscular body pressing against her back. The unmistakable nudge of his erection butting against her bottom. The powerful, hair-roughened thighs so hard against her soft flesh. A slug of desire hit her as his fingers reacquainted themselves with her moist folds and he began to strum her until she was mindless with longing once more.

'Do you like it like this, Lizzie?' he murmured into her ear, as his finger feathered up and down over her slick skin. 'Does it feel okay?'

She knew exactly what he meant. He was solicitously enquiring about her welfare—and hadn't the nurse at the clinic explained that this kind of position worked especially well for pregnant women? How the hell did he know *that*? Had he been reading books on the subject, or was it simply intuition? But it wasn't what she had been longing for. She wanted him to turn her over so she could look at him. She wanted to watch his face as he entered her, because that seemed like the ultimate intimacy which her foolish heart was craving. She wanted to get close to him, in ways which were more than just physical.

But he didn't.

It seemed that while she was silently praying for one thing, he seemed intent on doing the exact opposite. And God forgive her, but her body didn't seem to care. She was in total thrall to him, opening her thighs so that he could make that first thrust, and she shuddered with ecstasy. She could feel him. Hear him. She grabbed hold of his hand and began to suck on his thumb so she could taste him, too. But she couldn't see him. And because sight was the only one of her senses not engaged, she clamped her eyelids closed. But in a funny sort of way the lack of visual stimulation added an extra layer to her enjoyment, because it made everything seem so intense. And anonymous. Was that what he was aiming for?

Hot and hard, he increased his rhythm and Lizzie was so caught up as she was taken on that delicious ride with him that suddenly nothing else existed. Nothing but intense pleasure and the tumult of sensation. She heard him moan and suddenly she was moaning, too—her body clenching around him as he jerked out his seed.

She lay there, lost in a daze as he absently kissed her bare shoulder. She must have fallen asleep and so did he, because when next she became aware of her surroundings, she was lying tangled in his arms. His breathing was slow and steady—his lashes two black arcs set in golden olive skin and, once she had stopped drinking in his sheer gorgeousness, Lizzie realised this was her opportunity. Because if he couldn't open up to her at a moment like this, then when could he?

'So…' She touched her fingers to the dark curve of his jaw. 'Are you going to tell me something about yourself now, Niccolò Macario?'

Thick lashes fluttered open to reveal the obsidian gleam of his black eyes, but the expression on his mouth was hard. 'Is that the price I must pay for what just happened?'

'Is that how you think the world works?' She blinked. 'That everything has a price?'

'Because it does. We both know that,' he said silkily. 'Just like everything happens for a reason. Cause and effect. It's simple.'

'Does that mean you're not going to answer my questions?'

'I would prefer not to. But if you insist, I won't evade them. Unless,' he murmured, running a slow finger from her neck to her cleavage, 'you can think of something else we could do other than talking.'

It was a deliberate attempt to distract her and he *still* hadn't gone anywhere near her bump. Lizzie wriggled away from him fractionally, even though the drift of his finger felt wonderfully enticing. 'I'm asking on behalf of our child,' she said firmly, and then spoke the words she had been rehearsing in her head for so long.

'You do realise I don't know anything about you? Not even where you were born.'

Niccolò stared into her flushed features and gave a heavy sigh, recognising that the time for prevarication was over, no matter how much he wished it was otherwise. Because he owed her this. He knew that. But that didn't make it any easier to say things he'd kept buried for nearly two decades. Secrets he'd never divulged to anyone. Not even the therapist one of his enlightened college tutors had insisted he see, although the association hadn't lasted beyond a few uncomfortable, silent sessions. Because hadn't he always guarded his past as if it were a caged and dangerous beast? He'd locked it away in a dark and inaccessible place, which nobody could get at.

'I was born in Turin.'

'Rich boy? Poor boy?' she questioned succinctly, stretching out her legs so that her bare thigh brushed against his. 'A somewhere in between boy?'

'My father was one of Italy's most successful industrialists,' he clipped back. 'I grew up in one of the wealthiest suburbs of the city, with a summer home on the Amalfi coast, and was afforded every privilege a young boy could possibly want. Does that answer your question?'

'Some of them. I've got plenty of others. How about brothers and sisters?'

It was a natural question but his instinct was to deflect it. To provide the stock response he'd cultivated years ago, which would terminate the subject and make it clear that pursuing it would be crossing a forbidden line. But her thigh was still touching his and her silken hair was trailing over his arm and she felt little short of…amazing. As she lay there, her expression ridiculously trusting, Niccolò realised he had put himself in a honey trap of his own making. How could he possibly short-change the mother of his child when she was looking at him like that, even though the truth would change the way she looked at him for ever?

'For a long while it was just me,' he said slowly. 'My parents tried very hard to have another child. In fact, it dominated pretty much every facet of their lives—and mine. They'd almost given up hope, and then my…' How could his voice still falter like this, even after all these years? 'My sister was born.'

'How old were you?'

'Fourteen.'

'That must have been…difficult.'

It was a perceptive remark but she spoke matter-of-factly, and in a way her lack of emotion was making it easy for him to continue. 'Yeah. Overnight, my life changed. My parents were completely obsessed with Rosina but how could they not be, when…' His voice shook as pain ripped through his heart. 'When she was such a beautiful little girl.'

'You must have loved her very much,' she said, into the brittle silence which followed.

'I killed her.'

Her face blanched but she didn't leap from the bed and stare at him in horror and disbelief. Hadn't part of him hoped she might? So that the sweet look of trust would be wiped from her face, leaving him in peace to nurse his enduring guilt and his shame.

'Tell me,' she said simply.

That was all. A small, quiet query which somehow managed to pierce his heart, like a blade. Was that why it was so effective? So that suddenly the words were tumbling from his lips in a way which the highly paid therapist had never managed to achieve. The hand which had been resting in her hair clenched into a tight fist. 'Everything at home was about the baby,' he said hoarsely. 'And at school my classmates teased me relentlessly about the fact that my parents were still having sex.'

'And did you care?'

'I tried not to let it get to me.' He had cultivated a policy of not reacting. Of letting things bounce off him and showing the world he didn't give a toss. Until the day his insouciance had finally cracked. He remembered the temperature gauge creeping upwards. The slow whir of the air-conditioning. The creak of the old-fashioned lift.

'It was the summer holidays and it was unbearably hot in the city, but little Rosina didn't travel well, so we had been there for the entire school break.' He remembered feeling invisible. And bored. Nobody had been around. There had been nothing to do and no one to see. And then the invitation had landed on his mat—with all its bright and glimmering possibility.

'One of my schoolfriends invited me to his birthday party in the mountains. There would be people I hadn't seen all summer. Girls. One girl in particular. My parents refused to let me go.' It had seemed unjust to treat him like a child when he had been trying so hard to behave like a grown-up. He remembered the anger which had flared up inside him. 'So I sneaked out and hitchhiked there.' He paused. 'I lost my virginity that night and I lost track of time.'

'Oh,' she said, but he couldn't miss the crumpling of her face.

'My mother was going out of her mind with worry,' he continued, words firing from his mouth like bullets. 'My father was away on business and so she strapped Rosina in the car and set off up the mountains to come and get me. It was a clear night and visibility was good. There were no other cars around and my mother was a brilliant driver. But somehow...' His tone slowed. 'Somehow the car left the road and ended up in pieces on the ground, and by the time they found them, my mother and my sister were both...' The tightness in his chest was making it impossible for him to get the word out—but he had to. 'Dead.'

'Niccolò—'

'Don't,' he bit out. 'Don't say it.'

'You don't know what I was going to say.'

'Yes, I do. That it wasn't my fault. It was. If I hadn't gone to that party, it would never have happened. My mother and my sister wouldn't have died and my—'

She looked at him curiously as his words were severed. 'What?' she said softly. 'What?'

'Can't you see it doesn't matter, Lizzie?' he ground out bitterly. 'None of it matters. Not any more. It's done. Cause and effect, remember? End of story. I have to live with what I have done and it has informed my life ever since. It is why I am the man I am, and why I can never be the man for you. I am cold. I am cruel. So maybe you are right to go back to England and not spend a moment longer here than you need to. You need to find a man who can care for you. Who can love you in a way that I can never do. Who can protect you.'

'Niccolò—'

'No!' he negated furiously. 'I won't discuss it any more. There is no point.'

'Are you quite sure about that?'

He was taken off guard by the soft wash of understanding in her voice and even more by the way she rolled over to face him, so that her belly was touching his. That curved and alien shape he'd been trying so hard to avoid, even when he'd been making love to her. And then he felt it. Faint but unmistakable. Weak but immeasurably strong. The kick of a tiny limb. The tremble of new life. Their eyes met as an iron shackle was tightened around his heart and for a moment he couldn't speak. But what right did he have to this child, or any child?

'I'm very sure,' he said at last. 'I want to get my old life back. I never wanted to be a father. How many times do I have to tell you that, before you start believing me, Lizzie? I'll be doing you both a favour,' he added roughly.

'It doesn't feel that way right now.'

The hurt tone of her voice stabbed at his conscience and Niccolò could feel emotional chaos beckoning like an old enemy. She had been right to tell him she was leaving. Better to end this madness now and give them both some much-needed peace of mind. But somehow her arms had entwined themselves around his neck and she was clinging to him and—God help him—he was kissing her again and she was kissing him back. The sexiest, sweetest, yet most womanly kiss he could ever have imagined.

'Lizzie,' he said brokenly, against her lips.

'Shh…'

It seemed that his erstwhile virgin was now in control and required no interruption. She drew her mouth away from his, as if to concentrate fully on his body, and he wondered afterwards if her hands were stroking over his flesh like that because she wanted to demonstrate her power over him, which at that moment was considerable. But then he stopped caring. He was lost in the responses she was inciting. Powerless to do anything other than comply with her sweet ministrations. Maybe it was his body's need to block out the bitterness of his thoughts which made his physical reaction to her so instant and overwhelming.

'Lizzie,' he gasped as her fingertips skated across his sternum—making a slow, sensual foray over each hard nipple. He held his breath as the flat of her hand reached the bony jut of his hip and she brushed her palm tantalisingly over the rigid throb of his erection and then away again. 'Please,' he said at last, when she did it again and again, and he thought he could bear no more.

Her fingers encircled him, sliding up and down the rigid shaft to create a light, soft rhythm. Her movements were dextrous and sure and he felt his eyes flutter to a close, helpless to resist the coming storm. And when he was almost there, she wriggled down the bed, her long hair brushing against his groin. Gently, she clamped her mouth around him, that soft imprisonment sending him under. He gripped onto her silken shoulders as he felt the powerful spurt of his seed into her mouth and when the last spasm had died away, he opened his eyes to see her licking her lips, like a satisfied pussycat.

It was possibly the most erotic but certainly the most intimate thing which had ever happened to him, and probably why he pushed back against it and felt the urgent need to escape. He shoved aside the rumpled bedclothes and got out of bed, seeing her look of bewilderment and, yes, hurt, but he shut his mind to it. He didn't want to be distracted by her nakedness, or her growing sexual confidence, or to have to dodge a stream of soft sympathy he had no right to. He didn't want to feel a child he had never asked for kicking against him like that. Or to see the woman he had impregnated boldly swallowing his seed. It was too much. He felt as if he'd lost a layer of his skin and she had been instrumental in that loss. As if Lizzie Bailey had somehow clawed it away from him, leaving him raw and exposed.

Turning his back on her, he picked up his discarded shirt and pulled it roughly over his shoulders, thinking he'd use one of the other bathrooms, rather than prolong this unbearable intimacy. He tugged on his trousers and by the time he turned back to her, he had recovered himself. But his brief flirtation with the past was over. She was right. It was the future she needed to negotiate. A future without him—and the sooner that happened, the better. Should he wait until she was dressed, until tempers and passions had cooled? And how long would that be? What if it was another day? A week. Prolonging this sweet torture of wanting her while knowing he needed to push her away, for both their sakes?

Steeling his heart against the crumpling of her lips, he slanted her a gritty smile. 'We need to think about income.'

'Income?' she echoed.

'Don't look so horrified, Lizzie. I assume you're not going to turn down a reasonable settlement just because we're not together? I don't imagine you're going to make enough from your dog portraits to live on.'

'Don't you *dare* trash my work!'

'I'm not. I happen to think your work is great.' His voice gentled and he wished she wouldn't look at him that way. He wished she weren't flushed and vulnerable beneath the rumpled duvet. He wished for a lot of things, but they were never going to happen. His throat tightened. 'I'm just being practical, that's all.'

'Yes, I know you are,' she said, a note of bitterness entering her voice. 'Practicality is something you're good at, isn't it, Niccolò?'

'You're making it sound like a character flaw.'

'Because sometimes I think it is!' she snapped back.

'I will buy you somewhere to live—be assured of that,' he continued coolly. 'A house, or an apartment. Big or small. Whatever you like. It's yours. Just let my office know.'

'Yeah. Thanks.'

But her words sounded automatic. As if she was saying them because she had no choice, rather than acting like a woman who had just hit the jackpot. But the way she *felt* about his offer was nothing to do with him, he reminded himself grimly. He just needed to get his old life back. The welcome solitude of domestic isolation and the complete absence of emotional disruption. 'Oh, I nearly forgot.' He walked across the room to the jacket he'd slung on a chair and fished something out of the pocket. 'Lois asked me to give you this.'

She surveyed the frayed piece of fabric in his hand. 'What is it?'

'It's Blanche's favourite blanket,' he explained. 'Apparently, the dog originally belonged to Lois's neighbour, and she knitted it. And when the old lady died...' He shrugged and, infuriatingly, his voice had a slight crack to it. 'Lois took the animal in.'

This story, told to him by his obviously emotional assistant, had been yet another thing he hadn't needed to hear, and he blamed Lizzie for that, too. He didn't *want* that kind of interaction with members of his staff. He wanted his world to go back to normal. A world where Lois organised his meetings and fielded phone calls, not where she started fumbling for a crumpled-up tissue, her eyes filling with tears while she told him some sob-story about a dog. A world where he could start dating other women again who wouldn't niggle and get underneath his skin.

'You said you wanted something particular belonging to the animal to enhance your portrait, and this is it,' he finished on a growl as he dropped the ragged piece of fabric on the bed. 'I'll ask my office to arrange your flight back to England.'

She nodded, like a reluctant father of the bride,

forced to make an unwanted speech at a wedding. 'You know, despite everything you've said, you can always change your mind, Niccolò.'

'About us?'

'No, not about us. Don't worry—I'm getting that particular message loud and clear. About the baby. I will make it as easy as I can for you, if you decide that fatherhood is something you want to embrace. Even if...' She swallowed and assumed a bright smile. 'No matter who you bring with you,' she amended quickly. 'You will always be welcome in our child's life.'

Niccolò winced because, in a way, her quiet dignity made him feel even worse, if that were possible. But he wasn't going to promise something he could never deliver, so he just nodded his head.

'Oh, and I've left the drawing I did of you in your office.'

His eyes narrowed. She hadn't mentioned it again and he'd assumed she'd forgotten all about it. 'But I didn't give you any photographs to work from,' he objected.

'I know you didn't. I did it from...well, for once I did it from memory. I've wrapped it up in brown paper because I didn't think you'd want the staff gawping at it.'

Silently, he nodded, forcing himself to tear his eyes away from the rumpled bedclothes, which bore all the hallmarks of their incredible lovemaking, and then to retreat from his own room, as if Lizzie Bailey's pale green gaze and freckled proximity had the power to contaminate him. The power to make him feel stuff he just wanted to forget.

CHAPTER TEN

LIZZIE STARED OUT of the bus window, lost in thought as she waited for the stubborn sheep to stop blocking the mud-splattered country lane. It was strange really. She hugged her arms across her chest as raindrops trickled down the windows. When you were broke—particularly if you were going through a slightly dodgy time—you thought that having loads of money would be the silver bullet to solve all your problems.

She sighed.

How wrong could she have been?

Because it didn't feel like that at all.

She was no longer *poor* Lizzie, scrimping and saving with the ever-constant worry that her boss might not be able to cope with the sound of a crying baby and throw her out on the streets. She had been back in England for nearly a month and it seemed she was now rich Lizzie. Her bank manager had called to request a private meeting and she had been summoned into his office and offered a cup of tea *and* a biscuit, while the man had talked to her in almost reverential tones about her new 'portfolio'.

And that was the power of money, she guessed. After

a lifetime of terse communications about the state of her overdraft and wondering if she should cut up her credit card, she was now flavour of the month. Because while she'd been on the flight back from America, Niccolò Macario had deposited a vast sum of money into her account, his brief email informing her that if there were insufficient funds for her needs, she should speak to his office and ask for more.

Insufficient funds? Was he insane? Maybe if she was planning on putting in an offer on Windsor Castle, or if she fancied acquiring a fleet of expensive racehorses, then she might feel a tad stretched. But despite the ridiculous amount he had given her, Lizzie had been bitterly disappointed by the way he'd gone about it. It had all been so cold-blooded and compartmentalised. So hands-off and distant.

The stubborn sheep trundled into a nearby field and the bus began to move again. What had she expected? It seemed a bit churlish to rail against the billionaire's generosity, but it did feel as if he was paying her off. As if he was throwing a lot of money at her to keep her quiet.

But that was the kind of man he was.

He had told her there was no future for them, just before she'd made that ill-advised trip to his bedroom, and no amount of wishing otherwise was going to change that simple fact. Had she imagined that the amazing sex which had followed would be enough to change his mind? That he might miss her as much as she missed him? Because she did. She missed him with a pain which was almost physical.

She closed her eyes.

But he didn't want to be involved in her life in any way. That was the whole point of giving her a lump sum. She was free to do as she pleased. Free as a bird. Free from any involvement with the father of her child. And if that state of affairs wasn't to her liking, well, she would have to get used to it and, eventually, move on. She bit her lip, praying it happened sooner rather than later, because surely this constant aching in her heart was unsustainable.

Yet even though it was pointless, sometimes at night she couldn't stop herself remembering *his* pain. The unbearable bleakness on his face when he'd told her about the deaths of his mother and baby sister. The terrible weight of shame and guilt which had surrounded him had been almost palpable and she'd thought how alone he had seemed in that moment. Her heart had gone out to him, but the grim and unremitting expression on his face had warned her that he would not welcome her sympathy. But it had become instantly understandable why his behaviour had been so contradictory. Why he didn't want a family of his own, because he had experienced the indescribable anguish of a child's death.

Lizzie swallowed. Was that why he had been so protective of her? She remembered his face in the park when he had found her—raw and ravaged with pain, his words whipping through the icy air.

I thought I'd lost you.

And where had his father been during all the heartbreak he had suffered? He hadn't mentioned that. Not once. There were so many questions she hadn't asked him and would now never get the chance. So let it go, she told herself, as her hand rested on the curve of her baby bump. She wasn't doing herself or little Freddy any favours, lying awake obsessing about a man who didn't want her. A man who had suggested she go out and find someone else!

With no ties and a reasonable budget, she could afford to live pretty much anywhere she wanted, but the anonymity of a big city left her cold. Despite the bittersweet memories it invoked, she found herself drawn back to the Cotswolds, where she'd worked for longest as a housekeeper and which still felt like the closest thing she'd ever had to home. With no desire to move this side of Christmas, she started renting a cottage, joined a prenatal exercise class and met other mums-to-be. And even though she was the only person in the class without a partner, Lizzie convinced herself it didn't matter. Her mood brightened considerably when the teacher asked if she could possibly paint a portrait of her mother's Maine Coon and Lizzie cautiously agreed. She had never attempted painting a cat before, but she certainly wasn't going to turn down a commission.

On Christmas Eve, she did what she had been wanting to do ever since she'd got back, even though it went against her better judgement. She drove past Ermecott Manor, expecting to see a giant Christmas tree blazing outside the Jacobean mansion, but to her surprise, the house was in darkness. Perhaps the family who'd bought it had gone back to Scotland for the holidays. For a minute she just sat in the car staring at it, but then she started up the engine and set off again. Why was she choosing the most emotional night of the year to remind herself that this was where it had all started?

It was almost dusk by the time she arrived back at the cottage and Lizzie had just switched on a string of fairy lights and lit the fire, when she heard a knock on the door. She froze, her heart beginning to race like a train as she was filled with the senseless hope it might be Niccolò. But it wasn't. It was a driver from a local delivery company, struggling beneath the shape of a huge and cumbersome-looking package, which she hauled from the back of the van.

'Let me carry it in for you,' the woman said, after a cursory glance at Lizzie's extended belly.

'That's very kind of you. There isn't a lot of room, but over here would be lovely.'

After the woman had left, Lizzie unpacked the package with curious fingers, peeling back the cardboard wrapping to find an easel inside. For a moment, she just sat there and stared at it. It was handmade and very beautiful. The kind of thing she had always dreamed of owning. Running her hand over the smooth beech wood, she searched for the sender's name—though she knew there was only one person who would have sent something like this. And yes. There it was.

She picked up the note.

Hopefully you'll get a chance to use this before and after the baby is born. Niccolò

It was brief and typewritten, and for a moment she wondered if it was some kind of olive branch, until she forced herself to see sense. It had probably been suggested by Lois, and dictated by her. She mustn't start reading things into a simple message. When they'd parted in Manhattan they had agreed to be civil and courteous, and this was obviously a demonstration that he intended to keep his word. It was a very kind gesture and she would send him an equally brief and polite thank you note in return.

But Lizzie couldn't resist picking up the phone and telephoning him in America, her fingers trembling as the call connected too quickly to allow for a change of mind.

'Niccolò?'

'Lizzie.'

It was only weeks since she'd heard his voice but it seemed like a whole lifetime as his rich accent rippled over her skin like velvet. She closed her eyes. 'Thank you for the easel.'

'Do you like it?'

'It's…beautiful.' She hesitated as she studied her reflection in the mirror—the fecund woman who stared back—and imagined Niccolò in his sleek penthouse, with all the sleek people who comprised his friendship circle. 'I haven't bought you anything.'

'I wasn't expecting you to.'

'Because you're the man who has everything?'

There was a pause. 'So they say.'

She drew in a breath, the pleasure of talking to him again almost cancelled out by the pain. Because that's the reality, she thought bitterly. He might not have everything he needs, but he certainly has everything he wants.

'Anyway, there's the pencil drawing you did of me,' he continued.

'What did you think of it?'

'It was…interesting,' he concluded, without elaboration.

Wasn't interesting one of those polite words people used when they didn't like something? The silence stretched, and Lizzie thought about all the things they weren't saying. The conversation which was going on in her head, which was so different from the one which was actually happening. She wanted to ask why he'd sent her this Christmas present out of the blue and whether he recognised that it ran the risk of sending out the wrong sort of signals to a woman who was missing him so much. She wanted to ask if he missed her, and if he'd slept with anyone else since she'd been back. But she said none of these things, just wished him happy holidays, and then hung up.

But she dreamt about him that night and the dreams were uncomfortably vivid and Lizzie decided that a half-life of communication was only going to hold her back. He could make contact about the baby whenever it suited him, but she was never going to ring him again, not even if he sent her a diamond necklace.

On Christmas Day she pulled crackers, ate turkey and manufactured having the best time with the kind couple from the antenatal group who had invited her to share their lunch. And in the quiet days which followed, she worked hard on her painting of Fluffy, the Maine Coon—why *were* people so unoriginal when it came to naming their pets? she wondered.

Having an easel in the cottage was a real game-changer—even if it was always going to be associated with Niccolò. But at least painting had always been a distraction and never had she needed it quite as much as she did at the moment. Her brush dabbed rapidly against the canvas and Lizzie was so engrossed in getting Fluffy's eyes just right that initially she mistook the knock for the branches of the climbing rose being battered against the door by the howl of the winter wind. But when the knock was repeated, some second sense made her grow still and a trickle of excitement whisper down her back. Don't be so stupid, she thought as she opened the cottage door. Why would it be Niccolò?

But it *was* him. All dark virile power, his thick hair ruffled by the wind, the breadth of his shoulders emphasised by the dark cashmere coat he was wearing. Against the frosty, dusky day, he looked amazing—black eyes glittering like polished jet, in the sheen of golden olive skin. The impact of seeing him was so visceral that her breath dried in her throat, but she recognised that the powerful pull he exerted was more than simply sexual attraction.

Because this was the father of her baby. A bond had been forged between them which could never be broken. He had let her walk out of his life and told her he didn't want to be part of hers. But he was here, wasn't he? Lizzie's heart was filled with a rush of hope but she tried not to let it show, because it was tempered by fear. And wasn't her biggest fear that he might hurt her all over again, and she would just keep coming back for more?

So don't lay yourself open to it, she told herself. Protect yourself from this cold, sexy man who finds it easy to make expansive gestures. He can buy you houses and confuse the hell out of you by sending unexpected presents, but he doesn't want love.

And while it was all very well agreeing to be polite to one another—wasn't he bending the rules by turning up here without warning?

'Niccolò!' she exclaimed. 'Why didn't you tell me you were coming?'

Niccolò's eyes met hers and saw the unmistakable flicker of challenge flickering from their pale green depths. 'Perhaps I thought you might refuse to see me,' he said slowly.

'That would be extremely foolish, since you're the one who's financing my life,' she said flippantly. 'Don't they say you should never bite the hand that feeds you? I'm guessing that the easel was a sweetener?'

Niccolò flinched as her accusatory words washed over him. Was that how she saw him now—as her provider, but nothing else? And could he blame her if she did? 'I wonder, is this a conversation we should be having on the doorstep?'

'Well, there's nobody around to hear us so I'm not worried about that, but it *is* a cold day.' She shrugged. 'So I guess you'd better come in.'

She opened the door wider and he stepped inside and closed the door, though he noticed how quickly she moved away from him, as if any kind of contact was something to be avoided at all costs. Bending his head to avoid the low beams on the ceiling, he went to stand by the fire.

'If you sit down, I'll make you a cup of tea,' she said.

Niccolò gave a reluctant nod. He didn't want to sit down, and he didn't particularly want a cup of tea, for the English national beverage had never really appealed to him. In truth, all he wanted was to feast his eyes on her, but in her current spiky mood it might be best to humour her. He looked around, assessing the place Lizzie Bailey had chosen to make her home, taken aback by its modesty, though Lois—for the two women had continued to communicate—had informed him that Lizzie was renting something 'quirky'.

His eyes narrowed. She certainly hadn't decided to flash the cash he had given her, that was for sure. The cottage was homely, but small—though the room was alive with colour and warmth from the fire. Flickering light from the flames danced on the bare walls, splashing shades of coral and gold over the half-painted canvas of a rather terrifying-looking cat, which stood on the easel.

He could hear her crashing around in the kitchen, the noisy demonstration of domesticity worlds away from the carefully orchestrated mealtimes which had resumed in his hotel suite in Manhattan, and the irony of that didn't escape him. Because hadn't he discovered that the peace and quiet he had craved could suddenly feel like a vacuum? All the things he'd thought he was missing weren't everything they were cracked up to be, something which was being hammered home to him every second of every day. His lips twisted. Be careful what you wished for.

A few moments later she emerged from the kitchen carrying a loaded tray and he walked over to her.

'Here. Let me.'

'It's quite all right,' she said firmly. 'I'm perfectly capable of doing it myself. I'm not some clinging vine, Niccolò. How do you think I manage when you're not here? I don't need a man to lean on.'

Despite her spirited objections, Niccolò overrode her protests and took the tray from her, putting it down on the table. But neither of them sat. They just surveyed each other from opposite ends of the weathered surface—as if they were about to engage in a duel. Her expression was mulish as she stared at him, but this was the perfect vantage point from which to study her. She was wearing a paint-spattered smock, with a scarf wrapped round her head, so that stray strands of pale red hair were escaping from their confinement. Her cheeks were rounder since he'd last seen her and so was her belly. Had the removal of complications in her life—like him—contributed to her glowing appearance? Pregnancy suited her, he realised with a sudden ache as he thought how long it had been since he'd seen her in the flesh.

And it was nobody's fault but his own.

He had wanted Lizzie Bailey out of his life, never dreaming her absence could leave such a hole in his existence.

She pushed a plate towards him. 'Mince pies. Homemade.'

'I haven't come here to eat cake,' he growled.

'Well, they're not strictly cake, of course. These ones are made from orange pastry, filled with a spicy mixture of raisins and currants. I don't know if you're familiar with them in America but we…' And then she lifted the palms of her hands into the air before letting them fall helplessly to her sides. 'What am I *doing*? You turn up on my doorstep without so much as a phone call, and I start talking inanely about mince pies. What the hell is going on, Niccolò?'

He glanced at his watch. 'Before I answer your question, I'd like to take you for a drive.'

She narrowed her eyes suspiciously. 'Where?'

'If I told you, it would spoil the surprise.'

'But we are not a couple, Niccolò. And therefore, you shouldn't arrive on my doorstep like this, dangling surprises. It's not appropriate behaviour.'

'We haven't exactly been a model of appropriate behaviour from the get-go, have we?' he questioned drily. 'Please. Just come for a drive with me, Lizzie. Let's talk on neutral territory.'

'I didn't think there was anything left to say.' She stared at him defiantly but must have read the determination in his eyes, because she puffed out a sigh. 'Oh, very well. But I don't want to be long.'

He waited while she unwound the scarf from her hair, put a guard around the fire and slithered into the coat she'd bought in New York. But he had to subdue his fierce desire to button it up for her—recognising from the warning glint in her eyes that any such gesture would be unwelcome.

Outside, the wind was strong and icy as he led her towards the car.

'So. Where's the chauffeur today?' she questioned as he opened the passenger door for her.

'There is no chauffeur. I'm driving.'

'And are you any good?'

'What do you think, Lizzie?' he challenged softly and the way she bit her lip did something strange to his heart.

As he started the engine, neither of them spoke—but as they drove through the muddy lanes, he heard her give a sharp intake of breath and she turned to him.

'We're on the way to Ermecott Manor!'

He kept his eyes on the road ahead. 'Yep.'

'Why?'

'Why don't you wait and see?'

'I'm not sure I want to,' she moaned. 'I was up there the other day. They were away for Christmas but they're probably back by now, and I don't want to be spotted lurking around the place like the Ghost of Christmas Past.'

But as the car swished down the driveway, the ancient house was still in darkness, the pale winter light of dusk surrounding it like a halo. Niccolò stopped the vehicle and went round to open the passenger door, and she got out and stared up at the impressive old house.

'Why have you brought me here?' she whispered, the sting of emotion in her voice.

'Because I've bought it.'

'*Bought* it? What are you talking about?' She shook her head. 'It isn't for sale. Sylvie sold it to a family from Scotland. They own it.'

'Not any more they don't.' There was a pause. 'I made them an offer they couldn't refuse.'

'Are you for real, Niccolò?' she demanded. 'People don't say things like that outside gangster films.'

'But it's true,' he said unapologetically. 'So why don't you come inside?'

Lizzie hesitated, filled with confusion, unsure why Niccolò had purchased the ancient property, yet over-whelmed by a very human desire to revisit a house which had meant so much to her. She could see it first, and then ask him. 'Okay,' she agreed grudgingly. 'Why not?

Once inside, he pressed a master light switch and an instant glow illuminated the historic interior with a soft, apricot light. Lizzie scanned the immediate vicin-ity, reacquainting herself with all the nooks and cran-nies she knew so well. The bare bones of the beautiful structure remained intact. The carvings and moulded ceilings were just as she remembered them, as were the tiled floors and panelled hallways. But that air of faint neglect still existed and, of course, it was com-pletely empty.

And there was that stupid broom cupboard down the hallway. A lump constricted her throat as memo-ries of that sultry afternoon came flooding back. The feel of his fingers on her flesh and the taste of his lips. She could barely relate to the woman she had been then, who would behave so impetuously with a man she had only just met. Lizzie could feel herself flush-ing but now wasn't the time to be thinking about sex, or to remember how joyous and carefree everything had seemed on that golden afternoon when their child had been conceived. This was a different time, she told herself fiercely. And they were both in a different place.

Yet nothing had really changed in her feelings towards the man who had joined her in that crazy dance of passion, had it? She still felt the same potent pull of attraction—only now she knew him better, which complicated things even more. She actually *liked* him, even though she had tried very hard not to.

She turned to him, to find him studying her intently. 'Tell me why you've bought it,' she said.

'Because you love it. I remember you telling me so, that night we spent together here.'

Her hand crept up to her neck, as if to hide the pulse which was flaring so rapidly there. 'And what does that have to do with anything?' she questioned huskily.

He shrugged. 'I thought you might want to live here. Bring the baby up here. You'd have a generous budget to do up the place as you saw fit. I sensed how much you've always wanted to restore it, only you didn't have the necessary funds before.'

It was a gross distortion of her secret dreams but, no matter how painful it might prove to be, Lizzie knew she had to pick it apart. 'Just the two of us?' she verified. 'Me, and the baby?'

'Well, yes.' There was a pause. 'Unless you were prepared to consider an alternative scenario.'

'Go on.'

'I miss you, Lizzie,' he said. 'The apartment has felt empty without you, and I don't want you out of my life.'

'I see,' she said slowly, but she didn't, not really.

Because they were weasel words. A double negative, or something like that. He wasn't actually saying he wanted her *in* his life, was he? Just that he didn't want her out of it.

His mouth hardened as if he was disappointed by her understated response, and from his eyes glittered a strange, black light. 'We could even get married, if that's what you wanted,' he added harshly.

CHAPTER ELEVEN

As Lizzie froze with what looked like genuine horror, Niccolò found himself thinking it wasn't a particularly complimentary way to respond to a proposal he had spent his life vowing he was never going to make.

'Run that one past me again,' she said tightly.

'My lawyers think it would be a good idea. To get married.'

'Your lawyers think it would be a good idea to get married?'

'Is it really necessary to keep repeating everything I say?'

'I think it is. Just to check I haven't slipped into some parallel universe. Because this is surreal, Niccolò. In fact, it's beyond surreal.'

'But why?' he demanded. 'Isn't this what people used to do in the old days? They honoured their responsibilities, as I am prepared to honour mine. As my wife, you will be afforded status, income and security.' He paused. 'And, of course, inheritance would be a much tidier issue for this baby, if he or she is my legal heir.'

Niccolò waited for the inevitable rush into his arms, the tears mingled with shouts of laughter as she accepted his proposal. But the face she presented to him was not the one he had expected to see. It was a militant face. Her eyes were flashing green fire and her colour had become heightened so that two bright spots burned at the centre of her cheeks.

'*This* baby? Is that all you can say? All you can *ever* say!' she declared, flicking back a lock of pale red hair with an angry hand. 'When are you going to start thinking about *this baby* as a person, Niccolò, rather than a thing—or is that too big a stretch?'

He flinched. 'That isn't fair.'

'Isn't it? Think about it. Not once—not *once*—have you asked me whether it's a boy or a girl.'

His voice was quiet. 'Do you know?'

Her voice was equally quiet. 'Yes, I know.'

His body tensed. 'Tell me.' His eyes met hers. 'Please.'

'It's a son,' she said, at last, her jaw working. 'You're having a son, Niccolò.'

Niccolò felt his heart clench. 'A boy,' he said hoarsely.

'A boy,' she agreed, her eyes scanning his face as if searching for clues. 'I call him Freddy.'

'Freddy,' he echoed as an unexpectedly powerful rush of emotion flooded through him and Niccolò couldn't work out whether it was relief, or sorrow. Or both. He knew he owed her some reaction to what she had just told him, but he couldn't give one. He felt weighted to the place where he stood, as if he were made of marble instead of flesh. As if this were happening to someone else, not him.

'I guess you must feel as if you've hit the jackpot,' she continued quietly.

He stared at her uncomprehendingly. 'What are you talking about?'

She shrugged. 'Isn't marriage just a way of securing your legal heir? Of getting what you want.'

'You think this is all about *me*?' He shook his head, hurt and angered by her assumption. 'I just want to do my best for you and the child. I am prepared to have you inherit the majority of my estate on any terms you like, and marriage makes that a whole lot easier. You must believe that, Lizzie.'

But she shook her head as she walked away from him, as if she needed a safe distance from which to glare at him.

'Money, money, money, that's all you seem to care about,' she declared, beginning to pace up and down the ornate reception room. 'You're going to be a father—yet not once have you mentioned your own father. Why not?'

Niccolò swallowed, the heavy weight of pain turning his heart into a lump of stone. 'You know more about me than anyone else. Yet still you want more. Because this is what women do,' he said bitterly. 'They grasp and grasp and are never satisfied. Well, you've had as much from me as I'm prepared to give, Lizzie. This is the man I am. You've heard what my offer is. Take it or leave it. So...' He raised his brows. 'What's it to be?'

A long silence followed as he waited for her inevitable capitulation, knowing he mustn't appear smug or triumphant.

'Actually… I'll leave it.' She sucked in an unsteady breath and stared at him. 'I don't want to bring my child…our child…up in that kind of way. In a cold, empty marriage where certain subjects are off-limits just because you say so.'

He stared at her, at first in disbelief and then with suspicion. 'If this is your way of trying to negotiate, Lizzie, I can tell you now that it won't work.'

'It isn't,' she said simply. 'It's the way I feel. The answer is no.'

'Then there's nothing more to be said, is there?' he questioned, his voice cooling. 'If you wait while I turn off the lights and close up the house, I'll drop you back at your cottage.'

Lizzie felt numb yet emotional as she got back into Niccolò's car, trying to process the things which had been said. She had to bite down very hard on her lip to stop it from trembling—glad the darkness hid the rapid blinking of her eyes as she attempted to keep rogue tears at bay. But her heart was twisted with pain and hurt and disappointment. She felt as if they'd come so close. He'd bought the house of her dreams, which was a pretty thoughtful thing to do. And though his marriage proposal hadn't been the stuff of fantasy, it had been a start—a foundation to work on. If he'd taken just one more step… If he'd opened up a little and let her get closer… But he hadn't. When it had come to the crunch, he had retreated from her questions and turned back into an emotional iceberg, and she couldn't live like that. It wasn't fair. Not to any of them.

Neither of them spoke during the journey back

through the cold winter's night. She guessed there was nothing left to say. But when they reached the cottage, he insisted on opening the car door for her and seeing her safely up the path and Lizzie wanted to cry out—to *implore* him not to be so damned protective, because it was making her long for more of the same. But she was quickly brought back down to earth by his reluctance to set foot inside—as if the interior of her humble abode might contaminate him. She waited for him to mention Freddy, but he didn't do that either—and a fierce pride began to take shape inside her because she certainly wasn't going to *beg* him to talk about his unborn son. She suddenly pictured a future. A horribly realistic future, where the billionaire's occasional visits to see his unplanned offspring became more and more sporadic—until in the end they tapered off completely. She shivered.

'It's cold. Go inside,' he said roughly. 'And think about what you want to do. You can move in to Ermecott any time you like, but if you'd rather choose somewhere else to live, I will understand. Just let me, or my office, know.'

'I will.'

'Goodbye, Lizzie.'

'Goodbye.'

Niccolò turned away from her, steeling his heart against the sombre note in her voice, telling himself throughout the drive back to London that he had made the right decision—for all of them. He shook his head. She was ungrateful. Unrealistic. He couldn't give her what she wanted—and she wanted way too much.

He gave his car keys to the waiting valet. He would spend the night here at the hotel and have his plane made ready for his return flight to Manhattan in the morning. He would order dinner to be delivered to his suite and catch up on a little work, just as he always did.

But his gourmet meal remained untouched, and the figures on his computer screen were a meaningless blur. Night-time brought no relief either, for the hours were disturbed by images he couldn't seem to ignore. Of hair the colour of a faded Halloween pumpkin, and the softest lips he had ever kissed. Her sweet, virginal tightness. Her understanding. Angrily, he slammed his fist into the goose-down pillow, then turned to stare up at the ceiling as the pale glow of dawn crept in through the windows.

Better get used to it, he thought grimly, because this was his new normal.

He was free.

Unencumbered.

And he didn't like it.

He didn't like it one bit.

At breakfast time, the strongest coffee the Granchester hotel could offer didn't help, and his plate of eggs remained untouched. Several times he took out his phone to call his pilot, and several times he slid it back into his pocket. At a quarter after ten, he gave up the fight and retraced the drive he'd made last night, his mouth dry and his heart thumping as he stopped the car outside Lizzie's little cottage. He thumped on the door with his fist and when she answered, she didn't smile. She looked at him questioningly.

'I'd like to come in.'

'Sure. But I'm not sure we've got anything left to say to each other, Niccolò—particularly at the moment,' she responded calmly. 'So shall we just try and keep it amicable?'

His mouth grew even drier as he closed the door behind him and the pounding of his heart was almost deafening. The fire was unlit and the room was chilly and suddenly he knew there was no time for prevarication. 'You want to know why I've never talked about my father?' he demanded hoarsely. 'Because I don't know anything about him. Not any more. We haven't spoken for nearly twenty years,' he continued, dragging in a ragged breath, which burned his throat even more.

She had grown very still as she stood in front of him, her green eyes still burning with questions. Close enough for him to touch, but never had she seemed so distant.

'Not since the morning after the accident, when he told me that if I hadn't been so selfish then my mother and my sister would still be alive. That his child—his *favourite* child—wouldn't be lying in a satin-lined casket, surrounded by white roses.' His bitter laugh was edged with self-contempt. 'And that he wished above all else I could take her place.'

He could see her swallowing, her neck working convulsively as she tried to work out what to say, and suddenly all that distance was gone as her face grew soft. 'People often say things they don't mean in the heat of the moment, Niccolò.'

'But he *did* mean it. Every word,' he emphasised

harshly. 'And since I wished for exactly the same fate, I accepted those words and his anger as my due. And that was the last time we spoke. He sent me away, to the home of my maternal grandmother.'

She seemed to absorb this. 'And what was that like?'

Now it was harder to speak. Harder to articulate words without his voice breaking. 'She lived in Tuscany. So you could say it was the perfect opportunity to discover one of the most beautiful regions of Italy.'

'What was it *like*, Niccolò?' she persisted quietly.

The pain of remembering twisted at his heart. Was that the reason why he had refused to think about it all these years? 'My grandmother adored her daughter and her granddaughter,' he said slowly. 'And she was obviously influenced by my father's version of the accident.' He swallowed. 'Like him, she held me responsible for their deaths and perhaps that was understandable.'

'And was she...cruel?'

'No, no. She fed me and provided a roof over my head and made sure I never missed school.' He paused. 'But she found it difficult to talk to me, without...censure, which was why I left Italy just as soon as I could and have never returned.'

Her green eyes had grown narrow. 'And did your father never try to reconcile with you?'

'Never. But in many ways, I was relieved. Too much water had flowed under that particular bridge and sometimes there is no way back from something like that.' He shook his head. 'You think I wanted to put myself—and him—through all that pain again?'

Lizzie bit her lip as his words died away and the expression on his face was almost too much to bear. But she *had* to bear it. To share it. If they were to have any chance together, she couldn't let him suffer alone any more. And why else had he turned up this morning, if he wasn't still holding out for some kind of future for them? But, oh, hell. It was worse than she could ever have imagined. No wonder he had such problems with trust and relating to women, if his grandmother had subjected him to such a cold and silent punishment.

He had told her early on that love didn't feature in his vocabulary and now she could understand why. He was convinced he didn't know *how* to love, she realised, because nobody had ever shown him. His formative years had shaped him. A boy neglected by his parents as they sought to increase the size of their family. A father who could not live with the consequences of how that had impacted on their son's behaviour. And a grandmother who had been unable to see beyond her own grief to help the teenager who had been hurting so badly. No wonder Niccolò had become the man he had. No wonder he had pushed emotion away.

But surely he was underestimating himself. He might not be comfortable using the words, but at times he had *behaved* like a man who knew the true meaning of love. The question was—would he allow himself to believe it? Could she show him?

She *had* to show him. She had grown up without a father and many times had felt the absence of his presence. Why subject their baby to the same fate, if there was a chance it could be different?

But she wasn't just thinking as a mother, she realised. She was thinking as a woman, too. She wanted this man so much. This clever and complicated man who made her feel things she hadn't thought possible. Was there any way he could ever open up his heart and let her inside?

'I think your grandmother and your father were both hurting very badly,' she said slowly. 'And because of that, they lashed out at you and behaved in a way they shouldn't have done, and which made it much worse. But that's...' She drew in an unsteady breath. 'That's all in the past, Niccolò. It's the future we've got to think about now. So I'm going to start by saying that I really do appreciate you buying Ermecott for me.'

She hesitated as she met the granite of his features and she wondered if she'd imagined the faint flicker of relief in his eyes—as if she'd granted him a reprieve by sticking to practicalities. 'But don't you understand that, without you, it's just bricks and mortar?' she continued softly. 'It might as well be a shoebox on the side of the motorway, for all the appeal it would have. It would only be having you there with us which would make it into a real home.'

He gave a swift shake of his head. 'But I can't give you what you want. What you deserve. I can't give you love, Lizzie.'

'Are you quite sure about that?' she asked him. 'You see, I think you already have. You didn't want a baby— you were so, so clear about that. But despite all those reservations, you came to find me when you found out I was pregnant, and you scooped me up and gave me a place to stay, didn't you? You guarded and protected me in New York, and even though at times I thought it was a bit over the top, secretly, I absolutely loved it.

'Remember that day you rushed to find me in the snow? When you...' Her voice wobbled a little. 'When you took off your own coat and put it on my back and buttoned it up, and it felt like the most caring thing anyone had ever done for me. Well, actually—it was. You've supported me and continue to support me. You've tried to do your best by me and the baby, but you haven't told me any lies along the way. You might not think you're capable of love, Niccolò Macario, but I do. Love is not what you say, but what you do, and I'm prepared to hang around long enough for you to recognise that.'

She swallowed. 'And just in case you should be in any doubt of my feelings for you, I'm putting it on the record that I love you. I love you so much.'

Total silence followed these words and Niccolò knew he should say something in response, but... He shook his head, for the change taking place in his heart and his head was so seismic that for a moment he couldn't think. All he could do was feel. He stared at her. At the softness of her lips and her eyes as the truth of their situation came slamming home—and what a truth it was. She didn't want his money, but she wanted his baby. And she wanted him. Him. The man beneath all the trappings.

She was the purest, sweetest thing which had happened to him in a lifetime spent trying to bury his pain by papering it over with money and 'success'. But Lizzie had seen beyond that. She'd looked inside him and seen him, and she loved him. His heart stabbed with pain and joy and recognition, because wasn't it time to tell her his final secret? To reveal the mind-blowing impact she'd had on him from the get-go?

'You know something?' he said huskily. 'The day we met was the anniversary of my mother and my sister's deaths.' He paused to allow the brief sting of tears to pass. 'A day I always reserved for something to distract me and keep me busy. A day of guilt and pain, which inevitably ended with a whisky bottle and the beckon of oblivion. But not this year. You opened the door and looked at me with those big green eyes, and I...' How could he explain what had happened—a famously uptight, high-profile man having sex with a total stranger in a broom cupboard? Didn't the country of his birth have an expression for the love at first sight he had experienced in that moment?

'*Un colpo di fulmine.* I was hit by the thunderbolt,' he explained simply. 'And I've never really recovered from that.' He cleared his throat, and suddenly the words were coming thick and fast. 'But that's good, because I don't want to. I just want to spend the rest of my life with you, Lizzie Bailey. I would prefer to marry you and make you my wife, but if you refuse— then I will accept it. But be certain of one thing. That I will spend the rest of my life trying to change your mind.' He stared at her for a long moment, revelling in the sensation of anticipation and desire heating his blood. 'Now come here,' he said.

'No. You come here.'

'Is this a battle of wills?' he challenged softly.

She gave a lazy and speculative smile, as all her new-found sexual confidence reasserted itself. 'Maybe.'

He crossed the floor to take her in his arms, touching her face and hair and then the curve of his unborn child with trembling fingers, as if he couldn't quite believe she—or the baby—were real. His lips brushed against hers and suddenly he could taste the salt of tears and he couldn't work out if they were hers or his, and only when the kiss had ended did he wipe them away. 'I love you,' he said unsteadily, his fingers tangling with the pliant silk of her fiery hair. 'Even though you drew the most unflattering portrait of me.'

'I knew you didn't like it.'

'Actually, it was very useful. It made me think—do I really look as forbidding as that?'

She tilted her head to one side. 'Only some of the time. But not at this precise moment, that's for sure.'

He gave up on conversation then and pulled her closer still, his heart kicking in his chest as his baby kicked beneath her breast.

EPILOGUE

'IS HE ASLEEP?'

Niccolò's gaze travelled across the room to the window seat to where his wife sat, bathed in a pool of gold from the nearby lamp. Her green dress matched her eyes and the giant Christmas tree framed in the window as she finished tying a scarlet ribbon around a present. Behind her, thick snow was falling and the newly white grounds of the Jacobean mansion appeared silvery bright in the moonlight. If it looked like a perfect scene, that was because it was, he thought with a sense of satisfaction. Upstairs lay their beloved son, now almost five years old, clutching a toy puppy called Pesto.

Lizzie looked up and smiled, her hair falling over her shoulder. 'Is he asleep?'

'Like a cherub,' he affirmed as he walked across the room towards her. 'I told him Babbo Natale would not come to visit children unless they were fast asleep.'

'That's what I said earlier, but he wouldn't listen to me. He's such a Daddy's boy.' She gave a contented sigh. 'And did you tell him that tomorrow we can build a snowman?'

'Yes, my love, we can build a snowman,' he answered indulgently, sinking down onto the window seat beside her, because didn't all parents live out their longings through their children? He put his hand on her knee. 'So, what would you like to do now?'

'Oh, I don't know,' she murmured as she pushed the present aside. 'I'm open to all suggestions.'

'Well...' Slowly, he stroked his finger over one silk-covered thigh. 'We could go and drink a glass of champagne before dinner.'

'We could. But there's something much more important we need to do first.'

He knew exactly what she meant, even before she clambered on top of him and wrapped her arms around his neck. She bent her head and kissed him—long and slow and deep—and when the kiss was over, she gazed at him, those incredible green eyes dark with longing and as dazed as they always were whenever they got this close and personal.

'Will it always be this good?' he asked her, his voice suddenly urgent.

'Always,' she affirmed, just as fiercely.

Lizzie hugged him tightly as she felt the powerful beat of his heart against hers, basking in the beauty of her life, because wasn't that what Christmas was all about? About counting your blessings...

It was hard to believe how far they had journeyed and how good it was. The logistics of their new life had taken quite a bit of planning and Niccolò had delegated a stack of stuff to his second-in-command, to concentrate on setting up a new branch of his business in England. It was why they had put extending their little family on hold for the time being, while they got used to their baby and, of course, each other. But they crossed 'the pond' whenever they could, and whenever they were in the States, they stayed in their new house in Westchester, close to Donna and Matt, after Lizzie insisted on moving from the sterile hotel suite, which had never really felt like home.

But it was here—their beautiful house in the Cotswolds—which had claimed both their hearts. They had renovated Ermecott together, moving into the restored manor house shortly after the birth of Federico—a lusty nine-pounder who was the spit of his handsome father. And, yes, there had been a tiny part of her which had worried that Niccolò would find it difficult to get used to fatherhood—a fear dispelled the moment the cord had been severed and her husband had cradled his newborn against his chest, his eyes bright with tears. Lizzie had met his gaze, and she had cried, too.

Her animal portraits had continued to sell to friends, and friends of friends, but it had been Lizzie's impromptu painting of an adorable mutt from the nearby dogs' home which had changed the trajectory of her life. The picture had been used in a national campaign to make people aware of the pitfalls of buying a pet without thinking it through and the animal's liquid brown eyes, wonky whiskers and slightly anxious-looking mouth had touched a chord with the public. After repeated requests, Lizzie had turned him into a cartoon and these days one of the country's biggest-selling newspapers ran a weekly strip about Pesto, the mongrel. She'd even agreed to help market a slew of dog-related products, the proceeds of which all went to charity. Apart from anything else, it was refreshing to find a pet with an original name!

Somehow, she had found the career she'd always wanted and was so grateful for that, but her priorities were always her son, and her husband—the two true lights of her life. She and Niccolò had married in Manhattan when Federico had been six months old, and honeymooned in Italy, because she'd never been there and had longed to see the land of his birth. They had been staying in the Cinque Terre when she had persuaded him to go and visit his father, who Lizzie had discovered was still alive.

'Why should I?' Niccolò had demanded, his face darkening. 'He won't have anything to say to me, and I certainly won't have anything to say to him.'

But Lizzie had been resolute as she'd watched that old pain clawing at the features of the man she loved. 'It's the courageous thing to do, to confront your demons,' she had insisted quietly. 'To give you the chance to lay them to rest.'

It wasn't what either of them had been expecting. Niccolò's father had lain dying, a broken shell of a man, his cloudy eyes full of tears as he'd touched the face of the young grandson he would never see again. He had spoken in Italian, his words tremulous and faint—but Lizzie hadn't needed to be a linguist to realise how much he'd regretted the past and the way he had behaved towards his son.

Her thoughts cleared as she looked into the jet gleam of Niccolò's eyes.

'Thank you,' he said simply.

'For what?'

'For being the most wonderful mother and wife. For showing me love and how to love. For...' He shook his head, for once seeming uncharacteristically lost for words. 'I love you, Lizzie Macario,' he growled. 'I love you more than words could ever say.'

'And I love you, too. More than you will ever know.' Her throat was thick with emotion as she touched her fingers to the shadowed rasp of his jaw. 'So, we could drink that champagne now, or...'

'Or?' he echoed softly.

'We could start trying for another baby.' She savoured the moment as she met his narrowed gaze.

'You think?' he said huskily.

'Yes. Oh, yes, my darling. I've been thinking it for a while now. And I think you have, too.'

For a long moment he just held her, very tightly, and said something in Italian against her hair, his voice choked with raw emotion. And then he led her from the window seat to the flame-warm rug in front of the fire, a speculative smile curving his lips as, slowly, he began to unbutton her dress.

* * * * *

HER FORBIDDEN
AWAKENING
IN GREECE

KIM LAWRENCE

MILLS & BOON

CHAPTER ONE

THE MOMENT HE stepped out of the soundproofed sanctuary of his office Zac was hit by the nerve-shredding racket; the small window of silence had lulled him into a false sense of security. 'Theos!' he gritted under his breath.

It was unrelenting. How could anything so small make this much noise? he wondered as the scene of the recent handover floated through his head. There had been no noise then, the silence broken only by the voice of the woman holding the impossibly small bundle. The woman from child services had offered the child to him and Zac, who relished challenges, had frozen, his arms at his sides—a challenge too far.

The nanny had stepped into the breach, and the moment had passed. He doubted if anyone had noticed, but he had, his first test and he had failed. All he had got was a view of a mop of dark hair against the blanket the baby was bundled up in. Did he resemble his father or mother…? Zac didn't know. He hadn't entered the nursery yet…delaying the inevitable, he knew, but his feelings, his *anger*, were still raw, and what would his presence achieve?

He was determined the child, Declan, would lack nothing growing up, except of course a mother and father.

Before it could settle over him he pushed the bleakness away. His energy was better spent on dealing with the present—which involved inconsolable crying and sleep deprivation. In retrospect the nanny's advice to dispense with the services of the night nurse after two nights had been proved both optimistic and premature, given the fact the baby had not stopped crying since.

Despite her assurances that the infant was not ill and this situation was *normal*, Zac had opted for a second opinion. The paediatrician of worldwide renown recommended by Zac's own physician had backed her up after his house call—turned out if there was enough cash involved *everybody* did house calls.

The medic's patronising attitude had set Zac's teeth on edge, but then experts who dumbed down always irritated him. An irritation that faded into insignificance when compared with this constant racket.

If the last few days had taught him anything it was that any effort to tune out the auditory assault of a six-week-old child who, in truth, had every right to sound unhappy, given his start in life, was pointless.

Not running away, more walking calmly, he told himself as he strode towards the blonde wood door and his private lift that gave access to the top-floor penthouse he occupied when in London.

His route through the normally soothing open-plan shades of white gleaming space involved a few detours to avoid the signs of the extra member of the household. The live-in nanny had looked at him blankly when he had pointed out the overspill of items from the nursery, then laughed and said cheerfully, 'Wait until he's walking.' As though she thought he was joking.

He hadn't been, and to be fair she appeared to have

made an effort, or one of the other staff had. Even so the overspill included a stack of freshly laundered baby clothes on his favourite leather swivel chair, and rings on the previously spotless surface of a low glass-topped table. He stepped over a damp towel on the floor and clenched his teeth while trying and failing to tune out the nails-digging-into-a-chalkboard wail that had stepped up another painful ear-shattering decibel.

Zac liked order in all things. His life was compartmentalised, business and private, there was no messy overspill between the two, which was one of the more minor reasons he had decided never to have children of his own. This had not changed despite the fact one of the guest suites had been turned into a nursery and an en suite room for a nanny. This child did not carry his flawed DNA so, even with him as a parent, he had a chance.

Zac liked space and, while the London penthouse did not compare in size to his other homes, the ten-thousand-plus square footage of the minimalist apartment at a prestigious address was large enough to accommodate this inconvenience—at least on paper.

It had quickly become obvious that the reality was very different. Reality was something he was struggling with at the moment.

He still hadn't got his head around the fact that Liam and his young wife were gone. It seemed surreal, and he was too busy dealing with the practicalities of being a guardian to a newborn to even think about grieving. It was all he could do to keep his anger in check.

Such a bloody waste.

If Liam had known the unspeakable, utterly impossible would happen, that he and his sweet, bubbly wife Emma wouldn't be around to care for their son, he might have made a less sentimental and more practical decision when choosing a guardian for their first and, as it turned out, *only* child, than his friend.

But Liam always had been ruled by his heart. The first time Zac had seen him, a student like himself, Liam had been emptying his pockets to fill the charity collection tin that other students entering the union bar were pretending not to notice. Zac had stepped in when he'd found Liam counting out coins and coming up short to pay for his beer—he'd grinned and toasted Zac, calling him his guardian angel.

They had still been students when Liam had become Zac's very first employee after Zac had spotted a gap in the market and had bought his first property to lease out to well-heeled students with no cash-flow problems.

Later, when Liam had started his own IT firm, Zac had been his first customer, not because Zac was anyone's guardian angel, but because Liam had been the best at what he did. Sentiment and business did not mix and if this pragmatic approach meant people called him ruthless, he could live with it. In fact his reputation for playing hard ball frequently worked in his favour.

There had certainly been no guardian angel watching over Liam and Emma when the driver of an articulated truck had had a heart attack and swerved across the central reservation.

The entire family gone…though actually not. Their premature baby had been deemed not ready to come home from the hospital with his mother, or he too would have been snuffed out.

Zac was feet away from escaping through the door, running through the pros and cons of moving into a hotel until the baby stopped crying and trying not to replay those grim words—*Wait until he's walking*—when he caught the gaudy display in the periphery of his vision. He could ignore a lot, but there were limits!

He opened his mouth to call only to find the man who ran his domestic life and much else besides already standing at his elbow. If Zac had believed in such things, he would have said the guy was psychic, but what he did believe in was efficiency. And Arthur, ex-military, might have gained a few inches round the middle since he'd left the service, but he had not lost any of his military bearing or his unflappable problem-solving genius.

'A moment, boss.'

Zac was distracted from his justifiable outrage when the older man proceeded to remove earplugs from his ears.

'Now why didn't I think of that? You're a genius.'

The older man gave a modest smile that tugged at the scar on his cheek but looked less than his normal buoyant self once exposed to the noise. 'A problem?'

'What are these?' Zac's finger stabbing expressed his disgust.

'Birthday cards. Many happy returns, boss.'

Zac had actually forgotten it was his birthday, and hadn't celebrated one since he was eighteen, but his extended family refused to believe this and every year the envelopes continued to arrive. The surprise parties and dinner invitations, which usually involved balloons, drunken speeches and the inevitable *suitable* woman. Zac made a point of having a full diary the days either side of his birthday, or rather Arthur did.

'Are you trying to be funny?'

'No, trying to make light of a tense situation,' the other

man responded, wincing slightly as another bellow permeated the room.

Zac shared his pain.

'The maid is new. She thought she was showing initiative,' he continued drily. 'I have removed the banner from the library, and the balloons your sister...?' He paused, brow crinkling.

'It doesn't matter which one,' Zac cut back quickly. The list of possibilities was long.

Sometimes it seemed endless. He found himself comparing himself to Liam, who had had no living relatives. Zac had them in abundance, he didn't lack sisters, and when you added the nieces and nephews, he sometimes struggled to match the child with the right parent. The entire tribe seemed to live in each other's pockets, and tried to pull Zac into their social circle, which had got larger as the years progressed.

His youngest half-sister was ten and his oldest stepsister twenty-nine. The oldest and several in between had children of their own from within marriages and outside. There were the partners that brought their own offspring from previous relationships: they had one divorce, one remarriage and several reconciliations between them... also a handful of affairs.

Zac steered clear of the soap opera that was their lives, not because he did not *care* for his family—he did—but they were incapable of recognising boundaries any more than a puppy was. They shared everything and he, and his inability to reciprocate, hurt them. Both sides of the equation benefited from an emotional distance.

The idea of introducing any woman who shared his bed to his family was his nightmare scenario. Bed-sharing suited Zac very well. He'd tried to explain to his family that he had no desire for a partner to share his life with but they insisted that he'd change his mind once he found the right person.

His mother had found the right person in Kairos, his stepfather, and look how well that had ended. Too young to recall the details, he remembered the yelling and rows and then, worse somehow, the utter total silence as they had moved on to the indifference phase, not an experience he ever intended to enjoy. So, yes, he was looking out for the right person so that he could cross the street to avoid her.

He was willing to concede there *were* happy marriages, but it would seem getting to that point involved kissing a lot of frogs and paying divorce lawyers through the nose.

After his parents' eventual amicable divorce after wedded disharmony, Zac's stepfather, Kairos, went on to have what was, or at least *appeared* to be, a very happy marriage and four children with his second wife. The way the volatile pair argued sometimes made him wonder if those children, who, unlike himself, were all biologically Kairos's own, were the reason the marriage had lasted.

Not that Kairos had ever treated his cuckoo in the nest any differently, but Zac always *knew* he was different—the consciousness of *how* different never left him. He had been taking a step back, keeping himself apart, all his life rather than maintain a pretence of being an integral part of this happy family.

It was an open secret, the world knew that Kairos was not his biological father, and occasionally the media speculation about who his actual father was would surface. Would some enterprising investigative journalist one day follow the breadcrumbs to the juicy truth?

He was prepared, but he knew that his mother was not. The face she presented to the world gave no hint of her vulnerability. Escaping his father to save him had been the actions of a brave woman, a proud woman. If the history became known people would see her as a victim and Zac knew that was her worst nightmare.

The full story was known only to Kairos, Zac and his mother, so no one outside realised just how generous Kairos had been in treating Zac as his own. To take on any man's child was a big thing, but the child of a father like his...that took a great man, which his stepfather was.

The Greek shipping line billionaire had been even-handed with all his children, or, as his biological children put it, mean and miserly to the people he should care for most. That was their reaction to the news that their father's intention was to leave his fortune to various charities. They would not starve but they would have to make their own way in the world as he had.

Zac took the view that it was Kairos's money, and what he did with it was his business. In a way it had been a relief. He didn't want to take any more from the generous man and no golden spoon meant no expectation, no restrictions. As there were no footsteps to follow, he could be himself, and, unlike his stepsiblings, Zac had a hunger for success.

Strictly speaking, Zac was meant to spend an equal time with both parents as he grew up, but in reality he hadn't. His mother's next three husbands had not considered his presence a plus, and Zac could see where they were coming from! Zac had hit six feet at thirteen and carried on growing. If you added his physical six feet of teenage angst to his fiercely protective attitude towards his mother, he could not have been a relaxing presence.

The situation had meant he'd actually spent more time with Kairos, who moved between Greece, London and the Norwegian home that they euphemistically referred to as a cabin. The amount of time he spent with his mother and the children she had with each of her husbands was limited.

Seven half-and stepsiblings, the number of nephews and nieces growing yearly, and all of them, even those that could not write yet, sent him birthday and Christmas cards.

'Sorry, this noise is—' He took a deep breath. Even miracle-maker Arthur couldn't make a baby stop crying—could *anyone* stop this baby crying?

When the older man didn't meet his eyes, and cleared his throat, Zac knew it could not be good news. 'About the noise, boss…'

'Yes, I know, I'll speak to the nanny again…'

'The nanny has handed in her notice, a family situation apparently.'

Zac closed his eyes and counted slowly to ten…a pointless exercise as ten thousand would not solve this problem. For the first time in his life Zac could not see beyond the problem or even a way around.

Liam was gone.

'Sir?'

Zac shook his head to free himself of the statement that still didn't make sense. The funeral hadn't made it seem any more real, but it was real.

Zac had broken a leg once playing soccer and walked off the pitch. Pain was something to be conquered, but this pain was different, this pain was visceral.

After all his hard work, Liam had been living the dream, *his* dream, the IT business he'd built from scratch, the beautiful, sweet wife and the child he'd longed for, and it had all been snatched away.

And people still believed in happy endings? Continued to look for love when falling in love seemed to mean massive disillusionment or loss.

The last time he had spoken to Liam, his friend had been going to the hospital to pick up Emma.

'I told you I'd marry her, didn't I, Zac, when she walked into that bar?'

'You did indeed, and I laughed.' Because only fools and Liam believed in love at first sight.

'Em laughed too. She thought I was insane…' he had reminisced, his voice warm as he'd spoken of his wife. 'Emma doesn't want to come home without the baby, but they just need to keep your godson in a few more days. You will, won't you, be godfather, Zac?'

A card, one of the garish home-made variety, fluttered to the floor. He bent and picked it up, crushing it in his hand as he did so, pushing away the sound of his friend's voice and wondering if the time would come when he would be unable to recall it.

A bleakness settled over him as he shoved the crumpled card into his trouser pocket before gesturing to the rest. 'Just bin them, will you?'

'Certainly. The nanny…?'

'Get in touch with the agency…no, I'll do it.' It would be some compensation to let them know how low his level of satisfaction with them was.

In the underground garage, Zac had just got behind the wheel of his sleek designer car when his phone rang. He glanced at the screen ID and switched the engine back off before putting the phone on speaker.

'Have I caught you at a bad time?'

'No, it's fine, Marco.' Liam had been his first employee and Marco had been his first well…*very* well-heeled tenant back in their uni days, the only two friendships forged back then to survive the transition from student life to the real world.

'Sorry I couldn't get to the funeral. Kate—'

'Liam would have understood,' Zac cut in immediately.

Crown Prince Marco Zanetti got straight to the point, a characteristic that Zac had always approved of in the other man.

'I need your help, Zac. I know you have a lot on your plate at the moment with the baby… How is it going?'

'Work in progress.'

'If you can't or don't feel able, just say.'

'Don't worry, I will,' Zac promised drily, knowing full well that, had the situation been reversed, the Crown Prince of the island kingdom of Renzoi would do anything for him, no questions asked. Zac had few close friends, and now one less.

'So how can I help?'

Marco told him and Zac heard him out before responding.

'So Kate was adopted?' An image of his friend's beautiful new red-headed bride flashed into his head. 'She never knew she had a twin?' That must have been quite a discovery to make, he mused.

'*Identical* twin. When the marriage broke up she stayed with the father and Kate went with her mother.'

'What did they do, pull straws?' He was no father, not in the real sense, but for Zac the idea of parents dividing up a family as though they were a record collection was incomprehensible.

'I asked myself the same thing,' Marco admitted, his voice hard as he added, 'The records I have seen suggest the mother was desperate to keep both girls, but the father threatened a custody battle. The bastard admitted, boasted during our last conversation that he split them to punish their mother, told her he'd get both, prove her unfit.'

Zac swore, adding. 'But surely he wouldn't have stood a chance!'

'Probably not but she knew how convincing he can be and could she risk losing both babies? Awful choice to make.'

'She died?'

'And he refused to take Kate back—seems she was always sniffing and crying—his words.'

Though ironically that rejection turned out to be lucky for Kate—her adoptive family are the real deal. She had a good childhood.'

'He sounds a charmer,' Zac observed sardonically, thinking there were a lot out there, including his own father.

'The guy is…' The expletive down the line drew a nod of agreement from Zac. 'He is no longer in the picture.'

Zac approved of the cold implacability in his friend's voice. Maybe Marco had not changed that much.

'So you're saying Kate wants to find her sister and you want me to locate her.' Zac's dark brows drew into a puzzled line above his deep-set dark eyes. Marco had resources at his command that few could match. He could only assume that the prince was outsourcing the search to avoid information leaks within the palace.

'Contacting her or not is Kate's call and we—or at least

I—know where she is…and on paper there is nothing to suggest that she is…that she…' He hesitated.

Zak helped the other man out. 'Is like the father?' The subject of tainted genes, and the circuitous nurture versus nature debate, was one he was no stranger to, having spent his formative years watching for signs of inherited weakness, for his own tainted genes surfacing, until he'd latterly found some sort of closure.

If he was a monster in waiting, the chances were he would not notice the signs and, even if he did, what would he do about it? He was what he was, his philosophical attitude stopped short of risking passing his flawed genes on to his own children.

'The debacle with her birth father upset Kate a lot and I don't want anything like that happening again. This pregnancy is not an easy one. I just want to double-check before I give Kate the details.'

'So you want me to check her out…and what…?' Realisation hit and Zac's brow smoothed. 'Ah, you want me to pay her off if there's an issue?' Zac speculated, seeing the logic of this plan. With him acting as Marco's proxy, the other man would have deniability and clean hands if his wife found out.

'Pay her off? No, Zac, I don't want you to pay her off!'

Shock followed by outrage resounded down the line, which seemed a pretty irrational response to what was an obvious and expedient solution to this problem. The Marco he had known would have recognised this too. Marriage had changed his royal friend.

Did marriage change every man? Zac did not intend to personally test his theory.

'I don't lie to Kate.'

Except by omission, thought Zac.

'Our relationship is based on honesty.'

The fact that Marco obviously believed what he was saying deepened the cynical grooves around Zac's mouth. Some marriages worked, but *honest*…? Even marriages that were considered successful, like that of his stepfather and his beautiful, charming second wife, had their share of half-truths and compromise.

'I just want Kate to know what to expect this time, to be prepared, no nasty surprises. She's going to be mad as hell with me for waiting until after the birth,' he admitted with a laugh. 'But her blood pressure is troubling the… You don't want to know this, do you?'

Zac, who really didn't, said nothing.

'I'm prepared to take the flak if it's about keeping Kate and the baby safe.'

'If there were skeletons that your team didn't—'

'I'm not asking you to dig for dirt,' the prince shot back, and Zac could hear the frown in his voice. 'I've got dossiers but they can't tell the whole story. The father didn't have a record, he just conned his way through life. Some of that might have rubbed off on his child…'

Zac could see why Marco had decided that it was all about nurture—to take the opposing view that DNA was responsible would mean that his wife was tainted too.

'My stepfather is a saint, it didn't rub off on me, Marco.'

'Oh, you have your moments. I know that you were the anonymous investor who bailed Liam out in the early days when he could have gone under.'

A spasm of impatience quivered across Zac's mobile lips. 'That was Liam and I knew he'd succeed. There was no risk or altruism involved.'

'Don't worry, I won't tell anyone you have a heart.'

Zac didn't hide his impatience. 'Look, Marco, I don't really see what I can find out, short of dating her, that—'

The lightness vanished from Marco's voice, leaving it cold as ice as he shot back, 'I do *not* want you to date her, Zac, you're the last man in the world that I would... That would be a game-changer for me, do you hear what I am saying?' Marco asked, drawing a very firm verbal red line in the sand.

Zac took no offence from the tone, and saw no point defending his reputation or pointing out that he had his faults, but he was no heartbreaker. He had never dated a woman who wanted more than sex, or a partner for an event, frequently both.

He wouldn't want someone like him to date a sister-in-law of his either.

'Fair enough. So what do you want me to do?'

'I want to know if she is *genuine*, that her character is... It just so happens that you are actually in the perfect position to *observe* her, Zac.'

Zac smiled a little to himself at the *'observe'* that carried the heavy message: *Look, don't touch.* Marco need not have worried. There were enough women out there without pursuing one who came with complications. 'I don't quite see how.'

'She works for you.'

The pen that Zac had been rotating through his long fingers during the conversation slipped to the car's carpeted floor. 'You sure about that?' Redheads did stand out, so if they were identical he would have remembered a twin of Kate Zanetti.

'Yes, she's a nursery nurse in one of your staff crèches. I just thought perhaps you could *observe*? Put some feelers out, see what her reputation in the workplace is. Is she reliable? You know the sort of thing—could she make Kate—'

'*Unhappy?*' The interruption seemed a safe bet. These days his wife's happiness seemed to be Marco's main priority. Was she his? For his friend's sake, Zac hoped so.

'Exactly, be inventive.'

'I can be inventive, certainly—nursery nurse…like a nanny, right…?' Zac said slowly.

'I suppose so.'

'Leave it to me.'

'Thanks, Zac.'

'No problem. Give my love to Kate.'

Zac ended the call, a smile on his lips as he started up the almost silent engine. Kill two birds with one stone— so long as there was no sex involved he doubted Marco would care much about his methods.

He needed childcare and Marco needed a character assessment. The two needs meshed nicely.

CHAPTER TWO

'ROSE!'

Rose, who was shrugging an oversized denim jacket on as she walked along the corridor, was tempted to pretend she hadn't heard...but her conscience refused to take a day off.

'Hi, Jac,' she said as her immediate superior in the nursery, seven months pregnant, waddled towards her. If this was about an extra shift, she'd say no, though the dark shadows under Jac's eyes did make her determination waver.

The fact was, of course, that in the end she wouldn't. Rose recognised this inability to say no as one of her character flaws, she simply couldn't, and when it came to resisting a hard-luck story she was toast.

On the plus side, extra hours meant a bigger pay packet and there was no pretending that wouldn't be useful, because she no longer had the security of her small nest egg for emergencies.

Not since Dad had turned up out of the blue saying he owed some people money and they were *serious* people.

Again, even though the story was probably fiction, she couldn't take the risk. He was her dad. When had she realised that with her dad the line between fiction and fact was blurred?

Looking into his eyes before he'd buried his face in his hands in an attitude of despair, she'd seen only utter sincerity, which meant little. He was so good at rearranging the truth that she suspected he believed his own lies most of the time—but he was her dad so she could never say no.

She'd nursed her mug of tea, he'd refused to join her, and opted for the dregs of her cooking brandy while telling her she was a good girl. She had handed over her savings knowing that, despite his promise to pay her back, she wouldn't be seeing the money again.

He might have lost a little hair, but he'd not lost *it*, she had realised, watching sadly from her window as her still handsome dad had crossed the street, his slumped shoulders squaring the farther away he got and the swagger in his step getting more pronounced.

She hadn't known whether to laugh or cry as he'd morphed into a dapper, stylishly dressed figure with a spring in his step and a cheque in his pocket. Ever the prince charming when there was someone to impress—in this instance the smartly dressed woman with long legs exiting a convertible—he gallantly offered an elderly lady his arm to cross the busy road.

The tableau had stayed with her. It encapsulated her dad—he was never going to change, which left the option of *her* changing… It sounded so simple but changing the habit of a lifetime was not easy.

Her dad was the reason that she was never taken in by charismatic men. The more good-looking or charming they appeared, the wider the berth she gave them. It gave her an advantage over the women who had their hearts broken or their bank accounts emptied by good-looking charmers—for that she had her dad to thank.

There had always been a woman in his life. Some who had moved in with them during her childhood had been nice, others less so and Rose had been quite glad when they'd left. As she'd got older, and, some people said, quite pretty, there were more *others* who resented her presence.

Her dad didn't like friction in his home and had not put up any opposition to her decision to move into a bedsit at seventeen after giving up on the financially impractical idea of studying medicine her teachers had been encouraging. She'd set her sights instead on becoming a nursery nurse, funding herself by taking an extra job to supplement the bar work she'd already been doing.

A girl her age around the house made him feel old, her dad had admitted, joking with a wink that living with her old dad was cramping her style.

Living with her old dad, Rose mused, her lips twisting as the memory resurfaced, had meant that she didn't have a clue what her style was. She wasn't cynical enough to imagine that all men were toxic. The problem was how could you tell the difference?

A problem for another day, she thought as Jac reached her. The priority was to be firm. Say no for once in your life, Rose, she told herself with exasperation.

'Oh, Rose, I'm so glad I caught you. I'm sorry, but… the *boss* wants to see you in his office.'

Since they had yet to fill the post, the head of HR was standing in until they recruited a new manager for the crèche facilities.

'Now? Couldn't you just tell Mr Hewitt that I'm—'

'Oh, no, not him, *the* boss.'

Rose shook her head in confusion.

'Mr Adamos, *Zac* Adamos.'

Rose giggled. Jac was well known for her quirky sense of humour.

'No, *seriously*…?' Her soft gurgle of amusement morphed into a grunt of pain as she struggled to disentangle a flaming curl that had managed to wrap itself around the button on her blue shirt. 'Look, I really do have to get going, Jac,' she pushed out between clenched teeth as she performed the delicate operation.

When she succeeded in her task and looked up, Jac wasn't smiling. 'No, I am being *serious*.' Her voice lowered to an awed whisper. 'He has asked to see you, *by name*.' Her ponytail bobbed as she shook her head, her eyes wide as saucers. 'What have you done, Rose?'

The lingering faint flush across Rose's high curved cheeks faded as she realised this was not a gotcha joke, leaving her fair skin marble pale. She pressed a hand to her throat, able to feel the vibration of her pulse.

This, whatever *this* turned out to be, could not be good and she could not afford to lose this job.

The likes of a humble nursery nurse in one of the extremely well-staffed crèches provided for staff across the offices of Adamos Inc—a perk that was not, credit where credit was due, reserved for senior management—did not get invites to the CEO's office.

That privilege or punishment, depending on your viewpoint, was reserved for employees with impressive titles that were often not self-explanatory, but basically way above her pay grade. She frowned as she frantically trawled through any recent possible transgressions that might explain this invitation.

She came up blank, her conscience clear. She was not a rule-breaker, unless forgetting last week's contribution to the tea and biscuits kitty counted… People said nothing got past him, but Rose wasn't buying into the omnipotent rubbish.

She shrugged off the panic that had grabbed her by the throat and told herself that the explanation would be something perfectly mundane, and she was pretty sure that Zac Adamos's interest in chocolate digestives was not extensive. Now, if she'd been a six-foot blonde with endless legs it might have been different, but she definitely wasn't…and even if she had been the sort of statuesque beauty he was often seen with, it was well known that he had never dated an employee.

Though she knew several that wouldn't have minded, excluding herself, of course. She was looking for something beyond superficial attractiveness and charisma so he would never get to know about her indifference… Her cushiony lips curved into a fleeting smile of self-mockery as she thought about a world where she would get a chance to say thanks but no thanks to Zac Adamos… *That* world didn't even exist in her dreams.

No, growing up watching her father use and then discard women meant the things that she was searching for in a man were safety and solidity. Of course, if he looked nice that wouldn't be a deal breaker!

Nice was not something anyone was ever likely to call her boss. He might be respected in the business world, but she suspected that respect was based on fear, which made her despise him even though her personal contact could hardly be rated as even negligible. She had once observed him striding past her down a corridor, and once standing in a lift looking impatient as he waited for the doors to close. On that occasion she had had the opportunity to study him without fear of being caught in the act because there was no harm in looking.

'I have d-done n-nothing,' she stammered out, thinking, beyond a bit of casual ogling.

The stutter managed to cancel out any defiant confidence, making her sound guilty or pathetic instead, probably both.

Her stammer was history but in moments of stress and heightened emotion it resurfaced. 'And I c-can't afford to lose this job.'

'There are other jobs.'

'You think I'm being sacked?'

'Of course not,' Jac tacked on hastily. 'I'm just saying sometimes a change is good, a new challenge…?'

'I like it here.' If it works why change it?

She loved what she did and, while every day was different because that was the nature of working with children, there was a comforting familiarity to it, something that her life as a child had lacked.

'So do I, but I've thought about it.'

Rose's eyes flew wide. 'You'd leave?'

The older woman's lips quirked at Rose's shocked response. 'I've been here seven years now and I feel in a bit of a rut. It was the extra half-hour commute that put me off.' She patted her stomach. 'I thought when the girls started secondary school, but with this one…who knows? But nothing is stopping you—you've got no one.' Realising what she'd said, she added hastily, 'Not that you couldn't have if you wanted.'

'I've no craving for excitement or a significant other,' Rose said, thinking of the *exciting* days of arriving home from school and finding it wasn't home any more and her things haphazardly dumped in her dad's car or, more often than not, left behind. And then there were the notes she found scribbled in her dad's bold hand telling her that he was spending the weekend in Paris or wherever had taken his fancy and to be a good girl and don't answer the door to anyone and there was a tenner for a takeaway.

There wasn't aways a note.

On one no-note occasion the usual few days had stretched into ten. The memory could still shake loose the cold feeling of panic in the pit of her stomach when she began to wonder if this time he wasn't coming back, if she was alone now.

The effort of maintaining the pretence at school that everything was normal had made her feel physically ill. She'd tried to keep her head down and perfect the art of invisibility, a formula ruined after her dramatic faint in morning assembly, which might have been due to the stress or maybe the fact she'd been permanently hungry on a diet of tinned soup and baked beans.

Her dad had strolled back the next day as though he had just been to the corner shop.

'Hadn't time for a note, love. A free flight, private jet to Las Vegas, I wasn't going to say no to that, was I?'

That had been his breezy reaction to her tears of relief when he had reappeared after a ten-day absence.

He had handed her a diamond bracelet that was wildly inappropriate for a fourteen-year-old, then reclaimed it, much to her secret relief, on hearing the news that the headmistress wanted to see him the next day.

'Can't you put her off? I have sleep to catch up on. *You* breaking a rule? What have you been up to?'

'I forged your signature on my report card.'

'Oh, for heaven's sake. How hard is it to forge a signature?' he'd exclaimed, his generosity evaporating as he'd put the bracelet in his own pocket because she hadn't deserved it.

No, Rose had a very poor opinion of excitement. She was, as her dad often told her, *boring*. Frequently adding, *'I sometimes wonder if you're actually mine,'* presumably in case she hadn't got the message she was a massive disappointment to him.

'I'll miss you if you go.'

'In three years' time you probably won't be here yourself. You'll have moved on, found a gorgeous man, a beautiful thing like you...'

'I'm not looking.'

'I'd noticed,' the older woman said drily. 'It doesn't do to keep *the* man waiting, or so I've heard. Relax, I'm joking. It'll probably be an assistant or something.'

Rose's spirits lifted. Jac was right, anything to do with a lowly nursery nurse would be delegated. She didn't want to admit, even to herself, that the rush of relief she wouldn't see Zac Adamos was related to a conversation she had overheard the previous week as two women had blocked her access to a lift.

'I am quite literally shaking...my skin feels...'

Rose, wary of the flu bug going around, had taken a step backwards as the second woman had responded with a giggle.

'He's just so, so *sexy*...it's unbelievable. It hits you like a sonic boom...that mouth...mmm!'

'What wouldn't I give to work on the top floor and see him every day?'

'You'd never get any work done,' her friend had retorted as they'd wandered away.

Rose, who had identified the person with the sonic boom halfway through the conversation, now had access to the lift. She hesitated then headed for the healthy option, the stairs.

Not just for the exercise. Zac Adamos was not the healthy option. Compared to the Greek billionaire, her dad was in the minor leagues...actually probably no league at all. She'd read an article online that had called Zac Adamos a legend in his own lifetime, and if everything she'd read was half true he'd be the first to agree with this assessment. Humility and modesty were two words not associated with him.

Short of a push, nothing would have got Rose through the open door at the end of the boardroom had she not known the tall, supercilious blonde was watching. The woman had recoiled when she'd taken in the person waiting for her attention.

When it had come, the snooty smirk had been preceded by an icy, 'I think you might have the wrong floor.'

Rose, who wished she had got off on the wrong floor, had lifted her chin and given her name. She wasn't going to do meek for a fully paid-up member of the fashion police.

The woman's eyebrows had shot to her smooth hairline as she'd consulted her computer screen. '*You're* Miss Hill?'

She wouldn't give the sneering superior blonde the satisfaction of knowing that apprehension was making her knees knock.

Should I have knocked?

The thought came to her halfway through the door and caused her to stumble and lurch into the room.

Hands wide to steady herself, she managed not to fall flat on her face. The flick of the smile of relief faded before it formed as she looked across the room, a room that actually dwarfed the dimensions of the boardroom she had just walked through.

The impressive dimensions and the stunning glass wall made only a vague impression. It was the man who rose from his negligent pose behind a massive desk occupied by computer screens that dominated the space and her focus.

A big room but *not* a safe distance!

He looked impressive on a TV screen, in a Hollywood heart-throb kind of way. Rose had watched him out of idle curiosity as much as anything else—that and the fact such occasions were a rarity. He didn't court publicity, which made any interview he gave compulsive viewing—perhaps that was his intention, a variation on treat them mean, keep them keen.

From her armchair position she knew that he was possibly the most handsome man ever to draw breath. She knew that he had a way of moving that was fascinating, all restrained power and elegance. She knew about the sculpted structure of a face that was arresting from any angle, all fascinating angles and intriguing planes, a masterful straight nose, carved cheekbones, his sensually sculpted wide mouth, his glowing golden-toned olive skin that matched the rich dark hair that sprang from his broad forehead and curled into his neck.

What she hadn't known was that his sloe-dark gaze framed by long ebony lashes and set below thick straight brows could paralyse a person's faculties.

She hadn't known that his sheer masculinity, the whipcord-lean male strength of his long, lean body not disguised by the perfect tailoring, could send a quiver through a person's body until it coalesced in a warm quiver in their pelvis…

No, Rose, not a person, you. Own it—your pelvis.

It took Rose a breath-suspended moment to recognise the disturbing sensation of unfurling desire sliding through her body.

Ashamed and shocked, she shook her head to free herself from the sensual fog and, realising that her mouth was open, closed it.

Wow, that was embarrassing, she thought as she re-arranged her features into an expression of cool, polite interest. Boom! Sonic—definitely!

And she wasn't interested.

'You wanted to see me?' She tried to direct her gaze to a point over his left shoulder but that hard dark stare had a mesmeric quality... No man should have eyelashes that long.

CHAPTER THREE

AFTER ARTHUR HAD apparently lost his magic touch, Zac had been forced to personally intervene and virtually beg the outgoing nanny, who was standing, bags packed, at the door, to stay until tonight. That had not sat well with him, plus he was irritated that the information Marco had sent over had been partial at best because he apparently didn't want to prejudice Zac's judgment. For Zac this translated as 'make my life more difficult'. And as for facts being prejudicial...?

He found it easy to shift his frustrations onto the woman who already had a black mark for tardiness.

Zac didn't appreciate being kept in the dark, and as for his impartiality... He let out a measured sigh. He could not blame Marco, who didn't know Zac's plan... The additional information would have been useful as he couldn't allow just anyone into his home with access to the baby.

Sure, her work record was clean but, and it was a big but—if he'd been brought up by his own father he had wondered what man he would be now—she *had* been raised by her father. Not that he could compare a minor league conman and chancer with a brutal, violent, drug-addled character who thought the practical solution to an unwanted pregnancy was to beat up his pregnant girl-friend.

He sighed. Earlier this had seemed a win-win situation but now…?

Then she fell into the room and he discovered that once you got past the trainers, jeans that clung to long legs, and a weird baggy thing with lurid handprints all over topped by a denim jacket that was several sizes too big for her petite frame, the woman standing there was identical to her elegant twin, who he already knew was an incredibly beautiful woman.

While he had been able to acknowledge the beauty of his friend's wife, he could enjoy her company while not being attracted to her. The beautiful glowing princess he had met was a work of art with a good sense of humour had been his objective assessment.

Given they were genuinely identical, he ought to be feeling the same way now. Instead there was no objectivity to the instant and powerful physical reaction he was experiencing to this terribly dressed copy with a cloud of untamed titian hair that floated around her vivid face,

Identical but not, he mused, searching her face for some defining feature, although there was none. Perhaps it was the depth of her wide-spaced eyes, a shadow that suggested mystery that drew him in, and the way she looked up at him through her lashes…part of the indefinable additional factor that his body reacted to so spectacularly? Whatever it was, the indefinable *something* about her bypassed all logic circuits in his brain and pressed the primal button.

His shoulders lifted in a fractional shrug, a faint smile quivering along the firm sensual line of his mouth that contained self-mockery as he rose to his feet, gesturing with one long-fingered hand for her to take a seat. Sure, this was a complication, but one he was confident he could deal with.

Unlike some men he did not find the forbidden-fruit attraction an added turn-on, and he never had any problem walking away from such complications. There were plenty of women who were not already attached.

As his eyes drifted of their own accord to her truly sensational cushiony lips he found himself wondering if this woman was in a relationship, or if her attitude to sex was more *casual*, like his own.

There was something in her eyes, the suggestion of a vulnerability, that made him doubt it, though presumably Marco would know. If so, it was included in the information he had redacted so as not to bias Zac's judgment.

Rose was aware that Zac Adamos was a tall man with a lean, long-limbed body, an impressive physique that was frequently discussed in the many articles written about him. She'd always found it amusing that a piece on the financial markets had included the height—six feet four and a half—of the man whose opinion could influence these volatile monetary institutions—if he'd been a woman his age would have been added.

Only he wasn't!

As he unfurled himself from the chair, his every movement screaming graceful, restrained power, Rose felt her heart rate thicken to a dull thud, nerve endings across her skin tingled and the pull between her legs sent her into a shocked state of denial.

She hadn't taken a seat. She continued staring at him with an animal-in-the-headlights golden gaze. He found himself staring back, wondering as heat licked down his body how the pure amber of her eyes would look glazed with passion, half closed. And it took effort to get the question out of his head, not soon enough to spare him some discomfort—he was rock-hard...

Theos! Are you a man or a teenager?

Instead of walking towards her, he edged his behind onto the desk and, stretching his long legs out in front of him, waited—in part because he was aroused but mostly because people, in his experience, felt a need to fill a silence. Silence could access more information than a volley of questions.

This instance proved no exception. Words fell from her lips, lots of words but not necessarily in the right order. She had an attractive low, husky voice that had a soft, skin-tingling timbre.

'I... I'm sorry for w-wasting your time. I think there's been a mistake. I think you probably want someone else...'

'No. I want you.' It was an indulgent play on words but he could not resist it. Not the time for games, his internal voice suggested, and, judging by the expression on her face, definitely not the sort of game she played.

Rose drew a deep breath and bit her lip, unable to hide her discomfort, but at least she didn't drop her gaze, comforting herself in the knowledge that he had no idea of the shameful direction of her thoughts after her wayward brain's wilful misreading of his innocent statement...

Could words from a mouth like his be innocent?

'So, tell me, do you enjoy your work?'

He'd asked her here to check if she liked her work...? Was this some sort of box-ticking HR exercise—they chose some random employee and asked them if they were happy?

'I l-love it.'

Her voice, even rushed, was pleasant to listen to, the huskiness emphasised by the stuttering snags that he found attractive.

'You love working with children all day?'

She nodded, wondering from his tone if maybe he didn't like children. It was certainly hard to imagine him with grubby finger-marks on his pristine pale grey suit or his tie askew…from chubby toddler hands anyhow, she mused, seeing long fingers and beautifully manicured red nails removing his clothes. It was an image that made it hard to focus on his response.

'So you have no ambitions to change your job?'

He saw alarm flare in her eyes and waited for her response, distracting himself by staring at her cushiony mouth, which was another thing he had not factored into this particular equation.

It would be a betrayal to follow up—a good enough reason to exert some self-control. Friendship was a more valuable and rarer commodity than lust, even a lust that was as visceral as this, he reminded himself as his eyes drifted back to her mouth. It was a temptation that his libido escaping its leash reacted to.

He had to rein it in.

Marco would never forgive him.

The reminder was a mental version of a cold shower, helpful but not a cure.

Forget the cure, all he needed was sleep. The reason for his lack of control afforded Zac some level of comfort, but sleep deprivation was not an excuse that Marco would accept. The Crown Prince's protective instincts for his wife would almost certainly extend to her twin.

'I have been reading your file.'

Rose's eyes widened. She had a file?

'It is impressive.' And very slim, though someone whose notes sounded pompous mentioned little ambition to progress and poor leadership qualities. 'Miss Hill, are you all right with me calling you Rose?'

It would seem she didn't rate a full smile, but the lopsided half version was quite something even though the calculated charm did not warm his eyes. It clearly hadn't crossed his mind that she'd say no.

And of course she wouldn't even if she wanted to, and she did because she really *didn't* want to hear him say her name, roll it around his tongue in the way he had. She didn't want that to an extent that she recognised was totally disproportionate.

The question of *why* the sound of her name on his lips should make her skin prickle with antagonism was a question for a later date. It made as little sense as her embarrassingly visceral reaction to him. She was repelled by what he represented, a too good-looking man who possessed effortless charisma and no conscience, and, at the same time, attracted by the fact he looked like a fallen angel...if attraction was the right word for the itch under her skin.

The collision of opposites in her head was enough to give anyone a headache and she had one digging its claws into her temples at that moment.

What she needed was a couple of painkillers and a darkened room to fend off a migraine, the first in months and the last had been pretty torrid. She was too stressed to wrap up the truth as anxiety sparked defiance.

'It depends… If you're going to sack me, then no, you can't.'

He blinked and then laughed, the softening of his features as he gave vent to his amusement making him appear a lot younger. It didn't last, a moment later the hard calculating stare was back.

'Do you have a guilty conscience, Miss Hill?'

If only!

The shock of the maverick thought that popped unbidden into her head widened her eyes. But she couldn't ignore the pain stabbing at her temples, which was in danger of becoming as much of a worry as her dormant hormones springing into painful life. Perhaps the two were connected? Did physical primitive chemical responses give you a headache? Or maybe she was allergic to his overwhelming masculinity.

'I have no idea why I'm here.'

But I really wish I weren't.

She spoke so quietly that he strained to catch what she had said. 'Are you all right?'

It came less like concern and more like an impatient criticism, leaving Rose with the impression that it would be an inconvenience if she wasn't all right. It was an attitude she was familiar with; her dad had always acted as though on the rare occasions she had got ill she'd done so deliberately just to annoy him.

She lifted her chin, the irrational conviction that she would prefer to die than admit a weakness to this man rising to the surface. It would serve him right if she fainted away at his feet, though he would probably just step over her, and she had never fainted with migraine although she had thrown up. She pushed the alarming thought away.

'I'm fine.'

He shrugged and accepted her words at face value. It was possible she was always that pale or maybe she was a party animal and had a hangover from the previous night.

'I will get to the point. Firstly, I am not sacking you, secondly, I am offering you a job, though nothing of a permanent nature, more a…temporary placement.'

Her brow stayed furrowed and not just because of the throb in her temples. 'A what?'

'I have need of a nanny.'

'Aren't you a bit old?' She regretted the quip the moment it left her lips and his expression suggested he wasn't impressed. 'Sorry,' she murmured.

'I have become the guardian of a baby, a six-week-old boy… His parents are dead and the person employed to look after him is leaving.'

He watched the last remnant of the antagonism she was struggling to hide melt away. 'Oh, I am so very sorry.'

Her tender heart ached for the orphaned child. His expression did not invite sympathy but she felt it anyway, which a moment before she would have thought impossible. 'There are agencies…'

'I am aware,' he returned tersely, realising as he responded that the alternative plans he'd had in reserve to fulfil his promise to Marco should his first attempt not work would not be needed. Rose Hill had a weak spot, and he had found it: she was a bleeding heart. She was leaking empathy from every pore.

Zac felt no compunction about exploiting this weakness, and he doubted he would be the first to do so. It was not his business how many men had found their way into her bed via a hard-luck story, not that he was heading for her bed…or even his conveniently close desk, he reminded himself.

Marco would never forgive him.

'However, the fact that I am moving to Greece complicates the situation.'

'Greece!' she exclaimed, unaware of the wistful expression on her face as she immediately imagined the romance of white sand, blue sea and bluer skies, ancient history.

Zac could almost see her heart racing beneath her denim jacket. Under the layers he imagined her skin warm and smooth, only for a second but long enough to make him impatient with his lack of control and the cause of it.

'Have you ever been there?'

'No, I haven't been anywhere… I mean, I've not travelled much.' Actually, not at all, but she saw no reason to invite another sardonic brow lift.

'My present flat is not a suitable environment for a child.' That truth he had already recognised but the solution had been something to be dealt with down the line. *Would* Greece be a realistic suitable solution? he wondered. This could actually be a test run of the viability. He could stay in London during the week and commute at the weekend. After all, a young child wouldn't notice if he was there or not.

'So you are moving to Greece?' She glanced around the office. She had no idea how that would work, but his life had different rules from her own. Even so she did admire him, despite her prejudices, for being prepared to accept such a massive change to his life.

'It might not be a permanent solution but in the short term until the baby has…' he paused, trying to recall the phrase the nanny had used '…established a routine,' he offered glibly.

When lying it was always better to stick as close to the truth as possible and his solution to Marco's request had pushed his own thinking about the future along, and with those thoughts came nagging, actually *screaming* doubts.

Zac was not a man who lacked confidence or self-belief, and finding himself in a situation that he felt unqualified for on so many levels was disconcerting. Parenthood was something he had never envisaged and he felt uniquely ill equipped for the role.

Yet he had an excellent example. Kairos had been his age when he had taken on another man's son, and that man had been no friend. Had it come naturally to him or had he had to work at it? He dismissed the possibility before it had taken root in his head. Kairos had been a natural at parenting—he let his children make their own mistakes but had always been there to offer advice if they asked for it.

Zac made mistakes but he never asked for advice. Asking for help equated in Zac's head with admitting to a weakness. It was not something that the *tough one* did… Sometimes the roles assigned to children in families were hard to shrug off in adulthood.

In his case Zac hadn't tried—showing weakness in the world in which he operated was not the road to success.

'I need someone qualified to step in—'

'Why me?' she cut across him with the blunt question as she heard Jac groan in her head. She imagined her friend's reaction to her hesitation.

Don't ask why, just grab it with both hands! Travel, get paid for it, what's not to like? Out of your comfort zone? About time!

'Not that I would be the right person.'

'That's an unusual interview technique you have there.'

His drawl brought a flush to her cheeks but she didn't drop her gaze. 'It's not an interview.'

One dark brow lifted. 'Pedantic but true,' he conceded. 'But the situation does preclude a long drawn-out process and, contractually, it would simplify things. You already work for me. I don't need references or security checks.'

'I'm sorry but—'

'You have no dependents…elderly parents…?'

'My father is alive, but he isn't…he doesn't need me.' Until the next time he needs money or a bed or… He'd never find her in Greece. Ashamed of the thought, she added firmly, 'But I'm sorry, my life is here. I'm not interested in going to Greece. It's out of the question.'

He sighed. 'That is a pity—your choice, but, quite honestly, probably the right one. He's not an easy baby, he doesn't sleep… It's almost as if he knows that he's alone.'

She felt an ache in her throat as she watched him lift a hand to shade his eyes. Just because he didn't show his emotions didn't mean he didn't have them, she thought, feeling a surge of empathic warmth.

Fighting the crazy impulse to lay a hand on his shoulder, she held her ground and cleared her throat. 'He's not alone, he has you,' she husked out firmly.

'I know nothing about… I'll learn.'

'Of course you w-will,' she agreed, thinking, What next? A herd of pigs flying overhead? I feel sorry for Zac Adamos.

Zac heard the emotional catch in her voice and thought, *Gotcha.*

His hand fell away, his long elegant brown fingers briefly catching and holding her attention. When her gaze lifted he appeared sombre but composed and thankfully unaware of the distracting tactile image that had floated into her head that involved his fingers against pale skin.

'Well, thank you for your...' He paused, dragged a hand through his dark hair and added as an almost embarrassed afterthought, 'Look, it probably won't make any difference to your decision, but because of the lack of notice and upheaval I am prepared to offer an exit bonus.'

The hook was in; all he had to do was reel her in.

'It's not the money—'

He mentioned a sum that made her jaw drop.

'That is a lot of money.' And after her dad's visit she didn't even have a *little* money.

'Not to me.'

It wasn't a boast, just a statement of fact.

He watched the emotions flicker across her face and concealed his sense of triumph. She had a soft heart, he could have worked the sympathy vote, but the money had swung it. Would this count against her in Marco's eyes? He didn't see why it should. Everyone had a price.

Rose took a deep breath. 'All right, I'll do it, but for half that amount.'

He blinked. 'Pardon me?'

'It's too much.'

He fought off a smile of disbelief—she had a price, but it was relatively low. The likelihood of Marco's sister-in-law being a gold-digger seemed fairly remote. 'As you wish.'

'Greece...?' she said in a wonder-packed voice. 'I'm going to Greece.'

Her travelling had always been done from the security of her armchair with a laptop propped on her knee while she planned trips she'd never be able to afford. And even if she had, she wasn't sure she was brave enough to venture to exotic places alone. She always thought about what would go wrong. It was a mindset from her childhood when the parent child roles had been reversed—her dad hadn't thought what might go wrong and someone had to, so she had become, as her father termed it, *the voice of doom*.

'You are helping me out of a difficult situation. I'm grateful.'

Is she for real? he asked himself, watching through half-lowered lids as her golden eyes misted.

Anyone who wore their emotions so close to the surface the way she did might just as well walk around with a sign pinned to their back saying, *Take advantage of me!*

Which was exactly what he was doing.

Though in a benign way, he reminded himself, pushing away the scratch of guilt, and instantly feeling irritated that he felt the rare need to justify his actions to himself.

She swallowed a lump in her throat. It was less what he said and more what he wasn't saying that made her tender heart squeeze.

'What is the baby's name?' she asked quietly.

'Declan.'

She nodded and he watched her soft, sensual mouth quiver. 'A lovely name.'

He nodded, lowering his lids to hide the gleam of triumph in his eyes. 'Your passport is up to date?'

'Pass…oh, yes, I think so.'

'Think or know?' he cut back.

'Know.' On the receiving end of his obsidian-dark stare, she struggled to know her name, and doubts flicked through her head. There was no hint of the emotional vulnerability that had swung her decision in his face now. 'So will you…?'

'Let you know the details, yes.'

She waited but that, it seemed, was all she was getting. He seemed to have tuned her out as he retreated to the other side of the big desk, tapping something into his phone and focused on the screen.

Wondering what she had committed herself to, Rose picked up the bag that she had no memory of dropping at her feet. She turned and glanced over her shoulder, awkwardly and belatedly aware of the questions she should have asked, but it would seem that the moment to ask them had passed. He was speaking in a language that was Greek to her, and might actually have been.

In a daze she walked out of the room, her trainers squeaking on the polished wood floor of the echoey boardroom, the questions that she'd failed to ask a few moments ago buzzing in her head like a swarm of wasps.

She was already having buyer's remorse or second thoughts. She'd taken a leap in the dark and it did not feel liberating, it felt awful. It swallowed up the excitement of the chance to travel, leaving only anxiety.

Why had she said yes? OK, the money *had* been a practical factor, but turning her back on someone's need, their plea for help, even if that someone was Zac Adamos, was something her soft heart simply wouldn't allow her to do.

She tried to imagine anyone saying no to Zac Adamos and felt slightly less feeble. It had probably never happened, but she'd love to witness it when it did. She could empathise with his situation but that didn't mean that she thought he was any less of an arrogant and up-himself narcissist.

The woman with the snooty attitude and the blonde hair pretended not to see her as she walked past so Rose returned the compliment and promptly felt silly and petty, but she didn't feel up to taking the high ground.

The first loo she saw she ducked inside, glad there were no executive types to stare at her. She went over to the vanity basins, and after a face-to-face confrontation with her pale-faced, wild-haired self in the mirror she made sure not to repeat the experience as she balanced her bag on the edge of the washbasin and rummaged through the contents, which was always an adventure in itself. She gave a small grunt of triumph as she found a strip of bog-standard painkillers in one of the zipped compartments, not her prescription meds for migraine but hopefully it would fend off an attack, or at least slow down the inevitable.

Rose swallowed them without water, contemplating as she choked on them a little the result if she walked back into Zac Adamos's office and told him she'd changed her mind... Had she changed her mind?

Rose sighed. She was not a 'jump in without thinking through the consequences' sort of person. It was just so unlike her to make a decision without reading the small print.

'It's only a few weeks,' she told her reflection, then frowned as she realised she didn't know how many. 'You might enjoy it.'

She sighed and thought, And now I'm talking to myself! Not a good start. The mockery faded from her eyes as she thought of the start in life the baby had. She struggled to see Zac Adamos as a hands-on parent. The poor little scrap would probably go straight from nannies to boarding school.

Catching herself in the act of inventing a scenario that cast the tall Greek in a poor light just because she didn't like the man, Rose felt a stab of unease. She didn't normally think the worst of people, and this Greece project showed he was making an effort. It must be hard. He'd tragically lost friends and found himself with a ready-made family, and being a single parent was not easy, even for someone with limitless funds, a category her boss fell into. But, obscenely rich or not, you couldn't buy the support that came from having a partner to share parental responsibilities.

Or maybe you could? Rose was sure that any number of those leggy beauties he squired—or, more accurately, had sex with—would be happy to co-parent if it involved having a big rock on her finger.

Knowing she was being uncharitable but unable to stop the catty thoughts, Rose exited the loo, passing a couple of elegant women as she did so. They stared but she barely noticed. Her tangled thoughts left no space in her head for anything else.

CHAPTER FOUR

THE ELUSIVE SCENT—something flowery but not sweet—
lingered in the office after she had left. The attraction
was there, so he would acknowledge it.

*As if he had much option, considering he was still
semi aroused!*

Acknowledge and move on, even without Marco's red
line. Zac would never act upon it. The charming, serene
princess's twin was the sort of woman he avoided, the sort
of woman who did not consider sex a physical transaction.

He was pretty sure the redhead was into deep and mean-
ingful. It was written all over her. In short she was *exactly*
the sort of woman his mother hoped he would meet.

Having sorted out where she fitted in the scheme of
things, he felt more comfortable, his boundaries back in
place. Obviously he would need to be in her company but
only to observe...that was after all what Marco wanted.
No touching, Zac.

Thinking of his friend, he contacted Marco to give
him a progress report.

'So she'll be living under your roof? That's ideal.'

To Zac it was not. To have a woman who was the mirror image of one whose identical lips he had never fantasised about tasting, crushing, but was out of bounds was
not at all ideal in his book. Painful, yes.

'First impressions, Marco…' The impression he intended to pass on to his friend would obviously have some exclusions. Marco might not be happy if Zac included the fact that the woman he was assessing was a living, breathing threat to any man's sexual control. 'For what it's worth I don't think you have anything to worry about.'

'You don't think there's any danger to Kate? Her father came across as very plausible…'

Danger. The only person that he could see Miss Rose Hill being a danger to, other than his libido, was herself. But what did he know? Maybe it was an act, maybe she had learnt the skill of deception from her father—the negotiating her bonus down might just be a clever ruse… He had been the target of women before, perhaps it was all an act to get his attention…?

On the other hand, she might be determined *not* to be her father. Or had she inherited the flaws of her parent?

Was the fear always there in the back of her mind that she might have inherited the genetic fingerprint of her father? *No, Zac, that's you*, mocked the voice in his head.

'First impressions, Marco, I can't see inside her head, but she doesn't come across as a con artist, but then,' he conceded, 'I suppose really good ones don't.'

'Sorry if I sound—'

'Paranoid? No offence. I understand.' Except of course he didn't. He had never felt protective in that way about any woman in his life aside from his mother, not even come close, but then all the women that drifted in and out of his life could look after themselves.

Marco's tired-sounding laugh echoed down the line. 'None taken and I *am* very grateful, I don't want to risk—'

'How is Kate?'

The rest of their conversation, which Zac brought to a

close by inventing an urgent appointment, concerned the health of Marco's wife and her seeming perfection, which made Zac imagine her twin wearing the sort of priceless bling around her neck that the princess did. Rose wasn't wearing anything else except her glorious hair and the sultry smile of invitation he had not seen but had imagined curving her plump lips.

As he stood gazing out at the City panorama, the imaginary image in his head lingered.

It was totally inexplicable, not a little insane and very primal the way that woman had burrowed her way under his skin. Perhaps this was a version of love at first sight for a man who didn't fall in love—*lust* at first sight, which luckily for him didn't have the same staying power.

He remembered chastely kissing Kate Zanetti on her fragrant cheek and feeling zero desire to lay her across his desk, which was probably just as well because he was sure that if Marco had issues with Zac lusting after his sister-in-law, his wife would be a pistols-at-dawn scenario.

He valued his friendship with Marco, and it wasn't as if his friend were asking for a kidney. A few weeks of keeping his libido on a leash and his objectivity front and centre to ease Marco's fears was not a big ask. He was walking around the desk when he saw the glint of metal, a bunch of keys lying on the wooden floor, and he bent down to retrieve the object. Not his keys. Only one person in his office today would have a key ring that was attached to a knitted stuffed animal—it could have been a pig, or it might have been a horse…?

He reached out to press the button on the intercom and stopped as an image appeared of Rose Hill standing on her doorstep rummaging through her bag, and realising she'd lost her keys. It was easy to imagine the panic in her spectacular eyes. It was even easier to imagine passion, the slow burn that sparked into a full-blown conflagration. He thought about her slim, expressive hands touching… He was so absorbed by the image in his head that for a split second he forgot his pledge not to want her, but was saved from this self-indulgent torture by the sound of his PA's voice. He lifted his finger off the button he had not been aware of pressing and responded.

'No, it's fine. I'm…actually I'm leaving early.' As he made his way through the building he contacted Arthur and explained the bare bones of the situation and what arrangements he needed putting into place.

Zac could not recall entering the crèche in this or any other of the Adamos buildings. They came under the umbrella of the Adamos Trust, one of the charitable trust's less challenging projects and one he took little personal interest in. Closer to home was the adult literacy programme—one of his half-sisters was dyslexic.

The brightly painted walls and cheerful artwork on them certainly set it apart from the rest of the minimalist pale building. Long-term exposure would have given him a headache. He had just passed a particularly vibrant collage, obviously produced in-house by childish hands, when he came to a door that said *'Office'*. The upper panel was glass, the bottom urged the reader in big letters to *'Come right in'*.

One dark brow lifted as Zac read the instructions, which in his view constituted taking informality several steps too far. Was the half-open door encouragement to barge in unannounced?

Zac was about to test out the theory when the sound of a voice within made him pause.

* * *

'So? What happened?'

'I'm sorry to leave you short-handed but—'

'He sacked you!' Jac went pink. 'Why, that…piece of slime. No, I'm not standing for this. I'm going right up there to give him a piece of my mind!'

Rose was touched by this passionate, if slightly impractical, declaration of war on her behalf. 'Calm down.' She laughed, giving the older woman an affectionate hug as much as her bump allowed. 'He didn't sack me, he offered me a sort of temporary placement.'

'Oh, don't give me a scare like that…' Jac huffed out in relief, then as she pushed her owl-like glasses up her nose her brow furrowed. 'A placement?'

As Rose explained the situation, Jac's eyes went wider and wider behind the lenses of her specs. 'So you're going to Greece to look after this orphaned baby? That's so sad, not for you though, wow!' Her voice carried an even higher note of incredulity as she added, 'So now Zac Adamos is a *dad*? How is he dealing with it? Or need I ask? This is Mr Ice In His Veins.'

'Jac, that's not fair!' Rose protested, finding herself unable to appreciate the other woman's sense of humour. 'Just because someone doesn't show his feelings it doesn't mean he doesn't have any.'

'Oh, my God, Rose, why do you always think the best of people?'

'I don't…well, I know I do, but this is different. To be honest I'm really wary of working for him.'

'I can think of several people in the building who would feel differently,' the older woman suggested with a wry smile. 'So for how long are we going to be without you?'

'Actually, I'm not sure.' It would have been practical to ask but it didn't really matter. She had no ties except a father who only appeared when he wanted something.

She was a free agent, she told herself, ignoring the little ache that came with the thought. 'Until the nanny returns, I suppose.'

'But Greece and Zac Adamos…' The older woman rolled her eyes. 'If I was a few years younger…and maybe a couple of stone lighter, what wouldn't I give?'

Rose flushed, struggling to respond in the same jocular style. Her sense of humour on the subject was running low, and her laugh missed spontaneous and hit forced dead centre.

'You're welcome to him,' Zac heard her declare as he watched the speaker's mirror image shift her bag from one shoulder to the other.

'He is the last man in the world I'd be interested in!' she exclaimed.

Protesting just a little bit too much here, Rose. Anyone would think you're in denial.

Her chin lifted in response to the mocking voice in her head, then lowered from its jutting angle a moment later. She didn't *want* to find him attractive and it was true alpha males, which he undoubtedly was, did not appeal to her, at least in theory.

But she couldn't deny that walking into that office and meeting his eyes had caused her to experience the sort of skin-peeling sexual awareness she had only previously read about…and not really believed.

The worrying thing was that part of her had liked the rush of skin-tingling excitement, it had made her feel alive, but another part of her had been scared.

But then aren't you always scared, Rose?

'Don't look so worried, Jac. I doubt he even noticed I'm female.' She remembered a glitter in his dark eyes before they were shielded by his lashes and wondered…

'That's the sweet thing about you, Rose.'

Rose's smile became fixed. To her way of thinking, when people said *'sweet'* they meant *'boring'*.

'You have no idea that you're gorgeous.'

Rose's fleeting irritation became embarrassment. 'I'm excited—it's a fantastic opportunity,' she said, steering the conversation into less personal channels.

'Just be careful.'

'Careful?'

'Our boss, he's the big fish, a classic Great White, all teeth and no conscience. He can be charming, but—'

'I didn't rate his charm,' Rose cut in, her nose wrinkling as she added, 'and I may be *sweet*—' her lips moved in a moue of distaste '—but I'm not dim. I know what he is…but then who wouldn't be a bit up themselves if they looked in the mirror every day and saw that face?' An image of the fascinating angles and strong planes floated through her mind. What would it feel— She cancelled the rogue line of thought before it progressed into dangerous territory. 'But honestly, Jac, if I *was* looking, which I'm not,' she tacked on hastily.

'Why the hell not? Is it that ratbag Sutton? Oh, for goodness' sake, Rose, don't let him put you off men.'

'No, of course not.' The Andy Sutton incident was not one of the finer moments in life, but in the scheme of things it hadn't been a big enough deal to *traumatise* her. She had even managed to laugh about it with Jac the Monday after the dinner party from hell. 'He blanked me the other day, you know.'

'Rat…slime ball.'

Rose laughed. 'I opened my mouth to say hello and he walked straight past as if I wasn't there.'

'What a total...' Jac growled.

'Well, I did embarrass him—his face when he saw I was wearing jeans and a tee shirt! They were my *best* jeans, and the tee shirt did have sequins.' She gave a small gurgle of laughter, though it hadn't seemed funny at the time. 'A casual dinner, he said.' Which turned out to mean one step down from black tie—the women had all been done up to the nines in designer dresses.

'He let you make your own way home in that rain.'

'I'm a big girl, Jac, and honest it's not because of him I'm not looking. If there is someone out there for me, I'll meet him and if not?' Her slender shoulders lifted, causing the bag slung across one shoulder to slip down her arm.

'Oh, my God, you're a romantic!' Jac despaired. 'Prince Charming doesn't come knocking on your door, you have to put yourself out there. All right,' she added, folding her arms across her generous breasts. 'So what would you be looking for, should you be looking.'

'Well, not a pretty face...'

Or even a beautiful one.

She blinked. The face that floated into her head was all angles, carved planes and intriguing hollows, and the effort it took to banish it made her scowl, her annoyance aimed at herself for allowing him space in her mind for free.

'And,' she continued, retrieving her thread, 'I'd like someone who can laugh at themselves.' She arched a satiric brow and heaved her bag more firmly on her shoulder. 'Can you see the Gorgeous Great White laughing at himself? Yeah, GGW. I like it.'

Catching sight of herself in the mirror, she groaned and lifted a hand to her fiery head. 'Why didn't you tell me to run a comb through my hair before I went up—' She stopped dead, her heart throwing off an extra thud before it promptly sank into the region of her trainers—hers wasn't the only face she saw reflected there.

Her life didn't flash before her eyes but every word of the exchange did.

'I would have knocked but the instruction seemed quite clear,' the GGW said, displaying his white even teeth.

The older woman leapt as if shot. Rose flinched. The guilty looks they exchanged gave him a certain satisfaction. It was not an ego-enhancing experience to hear yourself called *a pretty face who was a bit up himself.* Or that he was the *last* man Rose would be looking for. Luckily Zac's ego was pretty robust, although had the situation been different he might have enjoyed making Rose Hill eat her words.

His smile was, Rose decided, cruel. She couldn't understand why women went for bad boys. Not that he was a boy, he was all man… While she waited for the floor to open up at her feet the word *dangerous* floated through her head.

When the floor didn't open she fought the childish urge to close her eyes and become invisible—it had worked when she was five. Jac was no help. She appeared to have been struck dumb by shock. It made Rose feel slightly better to see she wasn't the only one who became a basket around this man.

Rose took a deep breath and did the only thing possible in the circumstances—she acted as if he hadn't heard a word they'd said. There was an outside possibility he hadn't, but if he had then that was his fault for *lurking*.

'I was just explaining to Jac about my temporary place-ment.' She glanced at Jac and hesitated. Despite Jac's ad-mittedly cautious enthusiasm, she was probably thinking of the staffing headache that Rose's absence would cause when she went swanning off to Greece.

Her eyes narrowed and her chin firmed. 'I told her that you would be supplying a temp to fill in.'

Her steady golden stare challenged him to deny it. The sheer novelty of anyone attempting to manipulate him drew a grudging admiration and a grin from Zac. She had guts, he'd give her that.

'I will of course arrange a replacement, though I'm sure that our Miss Hill is irreplaceable.'

Unlike Rose, Jac didn't hear the sarcasm, but she had recovered her power of speech, and looked relieved and enthusiastic as she almost fell over herself in her eager-ness to agree and paint Rose as a cross between Super-woman and a saint.

In the periphery of his vision Zac was amused to see Rose squirming with embarrassment at having her praises sung so loudly. It would seem this twin was not into self-promotion. Not knowing Kate well enough, he didn't know if this was a shared characteristic. The whole twin thing was fascinating—if twins were raised apart, did they turn out the same?

Ironic really that, from what Marco had revealed, the adopted twin had drawn the lucky straw on the parent-ing front, a caring family who were close and supportive, whereas this twin was raised by her biological father who could hardly be considered supportive, but Zac supposed she didn't know any different.

Rose forced a smile that left her eyes suspicious and wary. Jac didn't need to advise caution with this man, she had a brain, though admittedly not one that worked too well when she shared an enclosed space with him. His sheer overpowering physicality was rapidly undoing all the good work of the painkillers.

She took some comfort from the fact that his Greek home was not going to be a shoebox size... She was going to find out first-hand how the other half lived and she was curious, but not envious. She had lived in some pretty plush places over the years, depending on her dad's fortunes, and some pretty basic places too. Given the option she would have taken plush, but it didn't always equate with happiness.

One of the worst times she remembered growing up was when they were living in a lovely house in an upmarket area. Her dad had taken off to Paris and the *colleague* who had come looking for her absent parent had called her a pretty little thing in a really creepy, sinister way. She'd not dared turn on a light every night that week because she'd seen him hanging around outside—she had hated that house.

'I was just on my way home, Mr Adamos...?' Hands stretched palm upwards in a mystified gesture, she arched a questioning brow, though she was less interested in why he was here than him leaving—fingers crossed he would take the hint.

'Of course.' Before Rose could begin to guess his intention, he reached out casually and caught her right hand, his long brown fingers curling around her wrist. The brush of his thumb against her palm sent a zigzag of sensation along her nerve endings and she forgot how to breathe.

It was a weirdly out-of-body moment as Rose watched, as though it were happening to someone else, as he placed a bunch of keys in her palm and closed her fingers over them.

'I think you'll need these.'

The contact lasted only seconds but the effect on Rose was electric. She blinked and opened her hand, knowing that she was staring at the keys like an idiot but it was better than the option of looking up at him. That was something she was delaying until her nervous system had re-established some protective boundaries.

'Oh, I didn't know that I'd...thank you.' Until she opened her mouth she wasn't sure she would sound totally sane, because what else could you call her reaction to the fleeting contact if not insane? Relieved by her steady delivery, she addressed the comment to a point over his left shoulder while convincing herself that the skin-peeling tingle was just a symptom of stress, like a headache without the pain—she already had the headache.

'Not at all.'

Rose felt some of the tension leave her shoulders when he left the room with a clipped nod of his dark head.

'Oh, my goodness. You know, Rose, he's not really so bad, is he?'

His fiercest critic was won over by one smile. Rose rolled her eyes in despair. 'I thought he was a merciless GGW?' she observed drily.

CHAPTER FIVE

'AH, MISS HILL. You are going home?'

Kill me now, Rose thought, closing her eyes and fixing an interested smile on her lips before she turned to face the tall figure who had materialised in the doorway. 'Yes…?' she said warily. He was half in and half out of the room but the disturbing skin tingling was sadly not halved.

She nodded, thinking he was not a shark and not white, he was more an olive gold, more a sleek, dangerous, unpredictable panther.

'Excellent,' he said briskly, turning his wrist to consult his wafer-thin expensive watch with narrowed eyes. She got a flash of lightly hair-roughened sinewy forearm as he appeared to make some silent calculation before fixing her with his deeply unnerving dark stare. 'I'm heading out myself, so as we're on the clock it will be simpler if I take you home and wait while you pack.'

It wasn't even couched as a suggestion! This man was utterly unbelievable.

And I am pathetic, she told herself as she *just* stopped herself nodding in agreement. The man spoke and people jumped. You could sort of see why, she conceded, studying his face. It was no hardship, but she wasn't going to be one of that number.

He took a commanding personality to the next level.

It was easy to see why people didn't question, they just went along without argument.

As he began to turn, clearly expecting her to follow, Rose, who was rarely the voice of dissent and hated confrontation, experienced an uncharacteristic surge of defiance, and along with it came a rush of resentment she hadn't even known she was nursing until it bubbled up like water under pressure to the surface.

She'd spent her life *following*, her opinion never even considered by her dad, and now she was always the one who said she didn't mind what pizza topping, what film... She told herself it didn't matter, they were inconsequential things, but it did matter.

There had to come a time to stop following and stand your ground.

You really choose your moments, Rose. She ignored the ironic voice in her head, her soft jawline firming as she pushed her hands deep in the pockets of her oversized jacket and, taking a deep breath, she dug her metaphorical heels in. Her teeth clenched. It had clearly never crossed his mind that she would not simply jump when he said jump—no please involved—or at least trot a few respectful feet behind him.

'Wait?'

He paused, turned and stepped back; sleek, exclusive and tall, he immediately dominated the room with his presence and his restless energy. Rose watched a flicker of impatience flash across his lean features but clung stubbornly to her calm defiance... Well, maybe not calm, she conceded as her heart flung itself against her ribcage. Despite her heart's contortions she felt strangely excited to be stepping outside her compliant role—*about time*, some, including Rose herself, might have said. His off-the-scale arrogance was the catalyst she had needed for this rebellion and how ironic was that!

'For you to pack,' he explained, glancing at his watch. 'You can meet the nanny. It will leave time for a handover this evening—she has agreed to stay that long.' Though it had taken the inducement of a chauffeur-driven limo to the airport and a first-class ticket to get this concession. 'Then we can leave in the morning. Arthur will go ahead.'

Her eyes had opened to their fullest extent by the time he had completed outlining this itinerary. She didn't know who Arthur was and didn't really care. It was less the arrangements and more the timescale that shocked her.

'*Tomorrow? Now?* B-but I assumed that this would be happening...' She made a fluttering gesture with her hands to indicate some vague point in the future, or at least next week.

One thick dark brow slanted. 'Is that a problem?'

'N-no.' She stopped—what was she saying? 'Actually yes, this is...too fast for me...it's happening very... very...' Hard to describe a sensation that felt like sand slipping through her fingers. She bit her lip and achieved something approaching calm as she said, 'I couldn't possibly be ready that soon.'

'We have already established you have no dependent relative. Is it a boyfriend who can't bear to let you go?' His expression made this possibility seem insultingly unlikely. 'A cat...?'

Oh, my, he had really pushed it too far. Her eyes narrowed into slits. 'I like cats but no, it isn't, and actually my personal life is none of your business.'

She fought off a laugh. He could not have looked more startled if a stray cat had turned around and told him to push off. Her amusement fizzled out fast, because the personal life she was guarding was pretty much a blank sheet, but that was a depressing thought for another time.

'Look, I appreciate that this is sudden,' he admitted, looking as if the concession hurt.

Big of you, she thought, panic colliding with resentment in her head, which ached with the sheer volume of emotions swirling inside... Hard to remember that when she had woken just this morning the only problem on her horizon had been that she'd mistakenly bought decaf coffee and that her overdraft would be nudging towards the danger red zone once she'd paid her electric bill. The bonus he'd offered, even halved, would solve all her problems.

'But the situation is urgent,' he said sombrely.

The reminder made the truculent heat fade from Rose's eyes and she felt ashamed for forgetting the reason for her trip to Greece. This was about an orphan baby, not her being forced to be decisive for once in her life.

Her internal struggle was written on her face, and she didn't have a clue she was being manipulated without any effort, which strangely left an unpleasant aftertaste in Zac's mouth. The faint scratch of guilt he felt was irrational. He hadn't lied, though in reality his situation would have warranted the odd white lie. If Rose backed out at this stage the childcare issue would be problematic. He ought to have made alternative childcare arrangements, but he rarely factored in failure, and he hadn't failed, he'd just pressed the button marked empathy plus a cash incentive—it always helped—and the rest had followed on as night followed day.

'I need time to think...'

Considering his promise to Marco, the last thing that Zac wanted was her thinking. He was impatient to fulfil his promise and get on with his life—his new life with the new responsibilities.

He had many responsibilities, the livelihoods, the future prosperity of many people rested on the decisions he made and he had never lost a night's sleep over the pressure, had never doubted his ability to come through, but this was different.

To keep a new life safe, to mould and guide it, Kairos made it look easy, but he was not his stepfather.

He was not his father either, his father who had not taken to the concept of parenthood. On discovering his very much younger girlfriend was carrying his child, giving her money for an abortion had been the sum of his paternal involvement, or *almost*. Because when he'd discovered the money intended for her abortion had been hidden away, he had tried to cause the same effect with his fists and feet.

His mother was a survivor and, despite what had happened to her when she was a teenager, an optimist.

'About what do you need to think?'

For the first time she was conscious of an accented undertone in his deep vibrant voice.

Did he make love in Greek?

The question came from nowhere and she felt her cheeks heat.

She could feel the impatience rolling off him in waves, but it wasn't a need to placate him that made her blurt out, 'Fine!' She wanted to prove to herself that she *could* step out of her comfort zone—if not now, when?

He accepted her compliance, deciding not to notice the reluctance involved, with a sharp tip of his dark head. He took a moment to say goodbye to Jac and stepped to one side for Rose to precede him through the door while she hugged her friend and said she'd see her very soon.

The touch of courtesy vanished as they stepped into the corridor—his long loping stride took no account of the difference in their inside leg measurements. Rose had to trot intermittently to keep up with him as they left the crèche and stepped into a lift that went down into the underground car park, entering an area that was reserved for people who drove shiny upper-end cars.

The one whose lights flashed as they approached was the higher end of upper, a low-slung thing as sleek as its owner. He opened the passenger door and left her to it as he walked around to the driver's side. As he did so her head turned when the corner of her eye caught two men standing by a car. One she recognised as the accountant—*Call me Andy*—who had ghosted her the previous week after the disastrous date.

As if in slow motion she saw his head turn her way. It was a reflex, no thought involved at all, when she ducked down into a crouching position behind the car.

The thinking started once she was there.

'Should I ask?'

Rose looked at the shiny handmade shoes just in front of her and thought, *Oh, someone kill me now, put me out of my misery!*

'Shall I join you?'

Oh, Rose *hated* him in that moment, hated him for having a front-row seat to her humiliation, and enjoying it.

'I take it that is the *slime ball*…?'

Things got worse—she could no longer pretend he hadn't heard every word.

'He's coming across,' Zac observed conversationally.

'Oh, God!'

'What's the problem? No possibility of misconstruing the situation, is there, you on your knees at my feet…?'

Rose, her cheeks burning bright, shot to her feet so quickly that she would have overbalanced if his hands had not cupped supportively around her elbows. There was barely a whisper of space between them and, looking at his chest, she stepped hastily back, or tried to as the grip on her elbows didn't loosen.

Rose's head tilted back to meet his dark stare. It was a dizzying experience…the lights dancing in his dark eyes had a hypnotic effect.

'Thanks, I'll take it from here.' She had to face the cringe situation. Who knew? Maybe she could extract a scrap of dignity out of it.

Not likely but possible. She had never told Jac that after the dinner party, previous to ghosting her, Andy had cornered her and suggested a threesome with one of the other dinner-party guests. A man who he declared was out of her league, who had liked her *style*…acting as if it were a compliment, not an insult! She had wanted so badly to slap his slimy smug face. Instead her stuttered response had drawn a mocking laugh from him and a *forget it* thrown over his shoulder.

'No, I don't think so. I have this one. You want to see him kick himself for not realising what he had? You want him to feel small and insignificant?'

Actually, now that he said it, that was exactly what she wanted, but it wasn't going to happen. 'Oh, God!' Her sense of impending doom increased as she heard her name being called.

'I already knew what he did. I just didn't know until I overheard your conversation that the woman they were talking about was you.'

She looked at him in horror. Greece was not far enough, she would have to move to Alaska to escape the gossip!

'So that's a yes?'

'No, it's…' She sighed and nodded, humouring him.

'Let's do it, then.'

'What?' Rose's eyes widened as one of his big hands slid to her waist, the other curved around her face, tipping it up to him. He scanned the oval of her face for a moment, his restive glance finally landing on her lips and staying there.

Rose watched him, her vision blurring as his head bent until his mouth was a whisper away from hers… Her eyelids felt weighed down, so heavy she couldn't keep her eyes more than half open as she looked up at him. Her breath held inside her chest, her heart was hammering, pounding in her ears.

Zac released her waist, his expression intent as he stroked the cushiony softness of her full lower lip with the pad of one thumb, before bending his head and tugging the same spot with his teeth, the whisper touch, the sensual slide of his firm lips across the pouting curve sending a deep trembling quiver through her body.

She leaned into the pressure as the kiss deepened and grabbed hold of his jacket to strain upwards, her senses absorbing the warmth and the hardness of his body. Flames burnt away rational thought, silencing the *This is a bad idea* as it was washed away by a dark sense of excitement exploding in her brain as she kissed him back.

Then it was over. He unwound her arms, which had crept up around his neck, and nodded over her shoulder.

Rose fell back on her heels, colour draining from her face and a moment later rising back until her cheeks burned. Mortified because she was shaking, the pulse between her legs still throbbing, her breasts tingling where they had been pressed into his chest, she resisted the impulse to touch her tingling lips. Echoes of the shocking intimacy of the moment were reverberating around her skull.

To add another layer of mortification, Zac, who was adjusting his shirt cuff, looked utterly cool.

'W-why...?' Her stuttered monosyllabic response covered most of the questions swirling around in her head.

Why had he kissed her, why had she kissed him back, why had she liked it...? Some of the answers were obvious even in her shocked state—she was no expert, but it seemed safe to assume, with her lips still tingling, that he was a good kisser.

Zac really found that stutter attractive, and with lips pumped up from the kiss, her eyes sparking, she looked—It did not matter what she looked like, he reminded himself. This was Marco's sister-in-law and as such off limits.

He had seen an opportunity and...en route to a smooth rationalisation of his actions his thoughts hit a truth roadblock. What he had seen was her mouth, the humiliation she had been trying to shrug off in her eyes, and the guy who had put it there.

He had wanted to flatten the guy right there and then. That not being an option in a civilised world, sadly, he had gone for the next best thing...give the loser a taste of his own medicine.

Zac, who considered himself a pretty good judge of character, had summed up the guy in one glance as a pretentious idiot with an inflated sense of his own importance. You could tell a lot from a glance, and when you'd heard his victim laugh about the humiliating experience—it had given meaning to the phrase *putting a brave face on it*.

And, less nobly, because he'd recognised a chance to satisfy his curiosity. Was he right to suspect there was a sizzling sensuality waiting to be coaxed into life? Turned out there was not much coaxing required.

And now he knew, which was a punishment in itself because the kiss was it. It was not going anywhere, he wouldn't allow it to. He'd lost one friend and he wasn't going to lose another. Marco would not approve of anything less than a saint for his sister-in-law and Zac was not a saint.

'I think that…what's his name…your boyfriend is realising what he has missed, which is what you wanted… no?'

Zac, on the other hand, was realising what he could not have. He continued to feel the knowledge like a nerve exposed to cold air, and he only had himself to blame. Taking responsibility didn't cool the heat inside that had nowhere to go, or answer the one question in this self-confessional mode he was dodging, namely the strength of his reaction to the sight of the man who had humiliated Rose.

'He works for you and he's not my boyfriend.' She'd been wondering how much he'd overheard and now she knew—everything!

'He will tell everyone that he saw…' Her eyes slid from his. 'And by this time tomorrow just about everyone will know. They will think…' She looked at him, suspicion beginning to dawn in her bright eyes. 'That's what you wanted, isn't it?' The *why* remained.

He gave a magnificently unconcerned shrug. 'You are making a big thing of one little kiss,' he complained, unwilling to admit that he had broken one of his own cardinal rules. Hard to take the high ground when he had indulged in the sort of behaviour he would have condemned in anyone else—workplace liaisons never ended well.

Despite multiple examples that disproved the rule, Zac clung to this belief.

'Believe me, I know, by the time you get back to work this will be yesterday's news. For the life of me,' he added in a disgruntled tone, 'I have no idea why you're so bothered about what this guy thinks, unless you were hoping to take up where you left off?'

Rose drew in a wrathful indignant breath. 'I'm not that desperate!'

'I'm glad you know your own worth.'

She looked up at him expecting to see something smug or sarcastic in his face but there wasn't. He looked...*intense...*?

'And now,' he continued, 'your accountant knows that too. The punishment fits the crime, he's humiliated.' He watched her face. 'Because on the dating food chain I come a little higher than an accountant, shallow but true,' he added before she could respond. 'You can thank me another time.' He followed up the outrageous suggestion with a throaty laugh when she hid a smile behind her hand. 'Good to know that you're not all saint. Revenge can taste very sweet, can't it?'

So did he, she thought, the taste of him still in her mouth. He'd kissed her to teach Andy a lesson, but she'd learnt one too, an important one for her self-preservation, namely she was not at all indifferent to Zac Adamos and to kiss him for real would be very dangerous.

'Shall I sack him?'

She blinked at the casual offer.

'What?'

'Sack him.'

'You can't do that.'

'I think you'll find that I can... Oh, you mean the legality? Don't worry, I'm sure he has crossed a line at some point...most people have.'

'Not me!' she snapped back huffily. 'You shouldn't judge people by your own standards.' Her eyes widened on his face in horror. 'I said that out loud, didn't I?'

'You did, but relax, and for the record I do not judge people by my own standards...most people have scruples.' He allowed his cynical gaze to move across her shocked and disapproving face. 'It gives me an advantage.'

Rose, her full lips still pursed in disapproval, had arranged herself in the cushioned leather luxury of a low-slung seat with a lot more leg room than she needed when Zac slid sinuously in.

He turned and looked at her, after a long silence finally voicing the question. 'Where do you live?'

'Oh, sorry!' She told him, expecting him to ask directions—the unfashionable backwater would not be one of his stylish haunts—but he just nodded.

'Sorry if it's out of your way,' she said stiffly as they entered the stream of bumper-to-bumper cars that he had explained away by saying *the bridge was closed*. He didn't appear to notice that she was being frosty so it seemed a wasted effort to be aloof.

She didn't ask what bridge. She found sharing the enclosed space with this man—the kiss still fresh in her mind—as mentally uncomfortable as the seat was physically comfortable. It didn't come as a shock. She had expected it. It was as if his personality was too big to fit in the small space, and she was coping, almost convincing herself that she was fine with it by the time they arrived outside her building.

She closed her eyes as he backed the long gleaming

car, too quickly for comfort, into an impossibly narrow space in front of the purpose-built and boring beige-brick three-storey building.

'I won't be long,' she promised.

He watched her struggle with the belt for a moment then leaned in and pressed a button. For a few seconds his arm confined her to her seat, not that she could have moved. He pulled away a little but before she could breathe a sigh of relief he turned his head. He was so close she could feel the warmth of his breath on her cheek and see the individual lines fanning out from the corners of his deep-set eyes. His eyes, which had been drifting across her own face, found and lingered on her mouth.

Her eyelids drifted half closed, her breath when it came was a weak breathy flutter that left her oxygen-deprived lungs hungry. Hunger was what she thought she glimpsed in his dark-sky eyes before his lashes came down and he leaned back in his own seat, pressing his head into the head rest for a moment before he turned.

'Do I not get an invite in?' He could not pass up an opportunity to see where she lived. Marco would expect no less.

There was something else besides the mockery in his voice that she chose not to investigate, instead she funnelled all her energy into forgetting that torrid moment that was probably not torrid at all. After all, he could make scratching his nose look sexy. There was no one around to witness a kiss so no reason to kiss her.

'No, I'll be quicker without an audience.'

He shrugged. 'We've got time.'

She gave a snort of disbelief. He'd changed his tune. 'Since when?'

'I've yet to meet a woman who can pack quickly.'

Her feet on the pavement after a very neat swivel, she turned back. 'You have—me,' she said with the utmost confidence.

She clenched her teeth as she heard his soft steps behind her, annoyed but not surprised. She could have asked him what part of no did he not understand but it would have been a total waste of breath.

'I don't need help or a stalker.' She pushed her way through the swing door into the communal lobby, adding, 'The lift doesn't work.' Without looking at him, she began to skip up the stairs.

Her obvious reluctance to allow him to see where she lived had sparked his interest. Was there something she was hiding?

A secret lover?

The thought left a sour taste, but she had left a sweet taste—

He pushed the hot memory away, but not soon enough to prevent the lick of heat that streaked down his front, pooling in his groin, which made it hard to tell himself how uninterested he was in how many lovers she had, secret or otherwise. He was not here to judge, he was here to observe and present facts to Marco, who could make his own judgment.

Rose was breathing hard by the time they reached her front door. He, of course, wasn't. Her hand shook slightly as she put the key in the lock. 'You can wait here,' she mumbled as the door swung in.

'Sorry, what was that?'

She turned around, exasperated, as he stepped in behind her, but the exasperation lurched towards panic. He was standing close... Her heart picked up pace as her head tilted back. She tucked a curl behind one ear and took a carefully casual step back.

'How many bedrooms do you have?'

'This is the bedroom, and living room, and kitchen,' she said defensively.

'There is no bed.'

She felt the blush run under her skin and walked across to her wardrobe. She was fine with her virgin status but she didn't want to advertise the fact by blushing when a man said bed.

All right, maybe she wasn't *that* fine. Her inexperience had become something of an encumbrance. When was the right time to own up to your inexperience? Hopefully she'd recognise the moment when it came.

Of course, she needed a potential lover first, but she could wait. The sort of real deep relationship she wanted didn't happen overnight.

'There is a bed,' she said, pretending calm. 'It pulls down from the wall. I just shift the table. Look,' she added crankily, 'do you want a lesson in how the other half lives or shall I pack?'

'It's very…neat.' It was the only positive thing he could think to say about the box-like space and he was not sure what the white walls and pale furniture said about her. All her personal effects seemed to be stowed out of sight, except the books that overflowed off some built-in shelves. He wasn't sure how interested or useful Marco might find the fact she had a weakness for thrillers and cookbooks.

Rose looked at him sharply.

Was he being sarcastic? She decided to give him the benefit of the doubt. 'It came furnished and the landlord won't let me paint anything, but it's a good location and in my price bracket, and there's no spare bedroom so my dad can't stay over.'

Her eyes widened as the last bit slipped out. This was one of the reasons her dad considered her a social liability. She'd ruined more than one of his scams by blurting out the truth at an inopportune moment and, while she was good at putting people at their ease, she was not good at being polite to men who looked at her boobs, not her face. As for when one *'important contact'* had put his hand on her knee, lucky for him she had drunk half the cup of coffee she had tipped in his lap.

'I like my own space and the alternative, on my salary, would be a flat-share. I'm too old for that.'

His eyes skimmed her smooth, youthful skin. 'Oh, yes, I can see that,' he mocked, but the joke was on him as he imagined seeing more, much more…and touching… His breathing slowed and his core temperature jumped.

The tension zinged into life out of nothing and, unable to hold his dark gaze, she looked away, a tingle under her skin.

'So do I, like space, I mean. Families can be a pain?' he probed, reminding himself belatedly of why he was here.

'Do you mind? I need to get to the…' He stepped aside to allow her access to the sliding shower-room door.

A moment later she emerged with a toilet bag and she stretched up to drag a small holdall off the top of a wardrobe. It was a big stretch and gave him an excellent view of her taut behind. She stretched a bit higher and he bit back a groan. The little sadist had to know *exactly* what that wriggle was doing to him, he decided cynically. No woman who looked like her could be oblivious to her power.

She huffed a little as she finally got a grip. 'I'll only be a minute now.'

It took actually five.

'I'm impressed, except you've forgotten your luggage.'

'No, I haven't,' she contradicted smugly, nodding to the holdall she was hugging against herself like a protective blanket.

His brows lifted. 'A woman who travels light. I'm impressed.'

She took the compliment, if that was what it was, but it wasn't actually deserved. Her wardrobe, out of necessity given the storage space, was pretty limited. Even if she had packed everything she owned she could have fitted it into one suitcase.

'We moved around a lot when I was growing up. I got used to packing.' Sometimes in the dark—a moonlight flit, her dad had called the occasions when they'd moved by cover of darkness before the landlord came knocking for his rent.

The small secret smile that tugged at her lips as she looked at him through her lashes was intriguing. 'So you are well travelled…?'

She gave a dry laugh. 'My father travelled. I stayed at home mostly.'

With her dad it was always good to have an exit strategy.

'With family…friends…?' he probed casually.

'I was not a child.' Though actually, of course, she had been.

'It sounds like your father had a high-powered job.'

Her eyes dropped. 'He is very…entrepreneurial. I might need to buy a swimsuit.'

Recognising the neat change of subject and her discomfort when it came to discussing her father, he nodded, wondering if that meant she was afraid of incriminating herself, or alternatively she was ashamed of him. 'You're good swimmer, then?'

She waited for him to follow her through the door before closing it. 'No, I stay in the shallows.'

'You're afraid of water?'

'Not at all, just of drowning.' She could feel his eyes on her as she walked to the staircase.

'You should learn to swim.'

'I had a lesson once.' Her dad had thrown her in the deep end.

Her expression was veiled but Zac sensed an untold story in her response. 'What happened?'

Rose stepped outside and walked towards the luxury designer vehicle, not the sort of transport you used if you wanted to fade into the background, but then, irrespective of his mode of transport, Zac wasn't a *fading* person.

'I didn't float,' she responded finally as she sank into the deep leather. 'But I like beaches,' she said as Zac slid in beside her, adding a defensive addendum. 'For my time off, if the sea is close enough…? I know I'm not on holiday, Mr Adamos,' she told him earnestly and tried not to inhale the clean male scent—unique and disturbing—he brought with him.

Zac's angular jaw line clenched as provocative images floated through his head, instigating a testosterone current that sent hardening heat through his body. For seconds primal instincts were in charge as he imagined in tactile detail her, sleek and wet, wading out of the waves. The images had reached the point where he had laid her down on the sand when he closed down the reel. Imagination was a great thing when you were in charge, which he told himself he was, at all times.

There was a long pause while he reached for his phone, not because he needed to use it but as a useful prop until he felt safe, conscious that any vehicle was only as safe as the person behind the wheel.

'Is it far?'

Rose waited, hoping he'd elaborate—she was naturally curious about where she would be staying—but he didn't.

She huffed out a little sigh. He still hadn't pulled away from the kerb and was looking intently at his phone. His focus made her envy his physical indifference to her presence, while she was feeling the weakening effects of being bombarded by the male magnetism that rolled off him in waves that ought, in a fair world, to be illegal.

Rose lapsed into silence, feeling the misery caused by her awareness of his sinful influence on her hormones compounded by the fact the painkillers she had taken earlier were wearing off.

Had she packed her prescription migraine meds? Rose was *almost* sure she had.

Another sigh made him turn his head to look at her pensive, pale, delicate profile. 'Is there something wrong?' he asked. Nothing that keeping her out of reach should not solve, he decided, sliding his phone into his pocket.

She shook her head, hating the breathless feeling she got when she looked at him and hoping that familiarity would breed contempt or at least immunity. If not, the next couple of weeks were going to be uncomfortable!

'You were frowning and doing a lot of sighing.'

'No, I… I'm fine.'

'That's a very aggressive *fine*.'

Rose, who had been aiming for firm, was startled. She had never been called aggressive before.

'Got a slight headache.'

He looked sceptical but didn't challenge her on it as he pulled out of the parking space.

CHAPTER SIX

IT WAS A fifteen-minute drive but a world away from her poky flat. She knew the iconic building, of course. It was hard to miss on the skyline. Occasionally she'd wondered about the people who lived there and now she knew who one of them was.

Of *course* he lived in the penthouse. She was not good with heights.

'You can open your eyes now.'

Her lips tightened at the amusement in his voice but she didn't respond until she had stepped safely out of the open doors. 'Glass, and it faces outwards. I don't like heights.' Close on the snapped comment she realised who she had aimed her snappy response at—her boss, who had already called her aggressive once.

He'd also kissed her, but not really.

'That is…'

'A conceit of the architect.'

She felt tense to be on the receiving end of his mockery, but his comment took the wind out of her sails. It wasn't until a door opened that she realised the lift had deposited her directly into his home. She was standing in a reception hall that looked large until she entered the living space.

'This is Arthur.' The man who had opened the door

looked almost as out of place in the open-plan minimalist splendour of a living area the size of a football pitch as Rose felt. She was trying hard not to stare at his characterful nose that had to have been broken multiple times.

Her eyes were drawn upwards. The ceiling was lofty and dominated by a stained-glass cupola that suffused the room with a tinted light. The rest of the decor by contrast was uniform shades of white. It crossed her mind that if someone had sat down to design a layout that was *not* child-friendly, this would be it. Open-plan with steps— just made for a small child to tumble down—designed presumably to separate the space into individual living areas. There was a great deal of dazzling glass. Even the modern sculptures were all hard edges. The scattering of art on the walls could not harm a child, just give him nightmares, or maybe that was just her? She averted her gaze from one particularly gross example with a shudder. Maybe it was meant to make a person shudder, maybe that meant it was a masterpiece, but she would not personally like it on her wall.

Struggling to adjust to the room, Rose gave her silent verdict. Impressive to look at but not exactly cosy to live in—it took more than a few bright cushions and throws to achieve that. Not that anyone's asking, she mocked herself, hoping that his Greek base would adapt more easily to child occupation. Not that she would be around when the baby became a toddler.

'Hello,' she said, wondering where this tough-looking member of the household fitted in, with his craggy face, and his track suit and trainers. She couldn't figure it out, then he smiled at her and it didn't matter. She instinctively warmed to him.

'Any questions and Arthur will know the answer, unless it is baby-orientated and then you are the expert.'

'So no pressure, then,' the other man murmured, mirroring her thoughts exactly as he exchanged a look with Rose while Zac vanished. 'This way, miss.'

'Rose,' Rose said, following him weighed down not just by the holdall slung across her shoulder but by her headache which was still in the bounds of tolerable.

If she relaxed it might go away?

She ignored the sarcastic voice of negativity in her head that pointed out this hope was an exercise of optimism over experience.

'Shall I take that?'

Relieved of the bag, which though not bulky was heavy, she gave a grateful smile, not questioning her over-my-dead-body stubborn refusal to relinquish it when Zac had made the same offer on the way up from the car park.

'Thanks.'

'I had the bed made up in this room.' He pushed open a door that led into a room that was very five-star hotel, and placed her bag on the floor beside a queen-sized bed. 'Would you like to freshen up or…?'

'No, I'd like to meet the baby?'

He nodded and waited for her to walk past him. 'The nursery is just across here. The nanny was in the adjoining room but if you leave this door open you'll still be able to hear him…plus the room is Bluetoothed for sound.'

Something in his expression made her smile and speculate. 'He has good lungs?'

'I've heard quieter Harriers. Give me a nice peaceful war zone any day.'

'Jump jets…the vertical ones…?' She threw him a

quizzical look. *'Air force?'* It would make sense. He had a definite military air about him.

He looked mock offended. 'Navy.'

Rose smiled back, wishing she could feel such an easy rapport with his boss...her boss too. 'Sorry.'

'Janet agreed to hold on until you arrived and I'll drop her at the airport on my way.'

'You are leaving?' That would mean... Rose pulled in a deep breath, mocking the thud of her traitorous heart and ignoring the quiver of illicit excitement low in her belly.

She wasn't alone. She had a baby to care for and for all she knew Zac—*Mr Adamos*, she self-corrected—having decided to keep things formal, professional, might not be spending the night alone either. There might be scarily clad supermodels drifting around the place.

One thing was certain—they definitely wouldn't be alone together!

'I'm heading out to Greece ahead to make sure everything's ready.'

'So you're a sort of...troubleshooter.'

'As good a word as any, a multitasker, that's me. It's hard for ex-servicemen to fit into civilian life. I was lucky, I've been working for Zac since I was invalided out... PTSD,' he added very matter-of-factly. 'I met him at a day centre the Adamos Foundation runs for ex-servicemen. There was a slight contretemps between a couple of guys, which I...*smoothed* over.'

He didn't detail what the smoothing had involved but Rose assumed it helped if your powers of diplomatic persuasion were backed up by muscle.

'Zac said he could do with someone like me, and it turned out he was right. OK, then,' he added in a stage whisper, 'this is the nursery.' They entered a room that was softly lit, the blinds drawn. Rose walked over to the cot. 'I'll leave you to it. Tell Janet I'm waiting when she's ready.'

'He's beautiful,' Rose whispered, looking down at the sleeping baby with a head of dark curls, his equally dark lashes resting like a fan against his flushed baby cheeks. 'Hello, Declan.'

'It's OK.' The Scottish-accented voice at her elbow was pitched at a normal volume. 'He won't wake. I know, famous last words, but really he's flat out. The poor wee thing has had a rough few days—colic, but it seems to have settled. You must be Rose. I'm Janet. Do you mind if I give you the tour straight away? My mum's had a fall and fractured her hip. She's booked into surgery later today. I want to be there when she wakes up from the anaesthetic.'

'Of course. I'm so sorry about your mum.'

The tour was speedy but comprehensive and the other woman requested her email address and sent over some detailed notes she had made, which Rose accepted with gratitude.

'I've put a routine there but basically I've been playing it by ear until he settled, poor mite. You know the story?'

Rose nodded, feeling her throat thicken. 'The basics.'

'What a start in life!'

The kitchen was last on the whirlwind tour. Gleaming and high-tech, it was gadget heaven. Janet showed Rose where the formula was and explained, as she opened the massive fridge, that Arthur cooked.

'So I've been spoilt but he's left something for you to just pop in the microwave. You're only here the one night?'

Rose nodded, relieved when she didn't immediately

regret it—fingers crossed this meant her headache was on the way out. It looked as if she could get away without taking the prescription meds, which she only resorted to when nothing else worked.

'I think so. Does Mr Adamos…do you eat with him?'

The woman laughed. 'Heavens, no, he's barely seen the baby—' her tight-lipped disapproval showed '—let alone me. He eats out most nights, treats the place like a hotel…though with you…?'

Embarrassed by the speculation in the stare, Rose gave a carefully casual shrug and didn't pretend to misunderstand what she was hinting at. 'I really don't think I'm going to get mistaken for one of his girlfriends any time soon, do you? I doubt that I'll see any more of him than you have.'

I hope, she thought fervently as she tucked her crossed fingers into her pocket, though she didn't as yet share the other woman's disapproval. People reacted to bereavement differently and the baby had to be a reminder of a loss he might still be coming to terms with.

'Sorry,' the other woman said with a grimace. 'But you're such a pretty girl.'

'Well, I don't know the man *personally*.'

Could a kiss be classed as impersonal?

'I doubt that is going to change,' the woman responded, her attitude perceptively warmer now that Rose was established as one of *the workers* and not one of the girlfriend class. 'I've barely exchanged two words with him. He hasn't been into the nursery once. He communicates via Arthur.'

Rose arranged her features into a suitably sympathetic expression while thinking that the two-word limit had not stopped the older woman passing judgment.

'People react to loss differently...' He might be dealing with grief in his own way, and that grief might involve eating out in posh restaurants with beautiful women
every night—who was she to judge?

Janet conceded this with a slightly grudging, 'You're
right, I know. It's just my friends were so excited, jealous when I got the job...but I told them the nanny never
gets the man.'

Not *this* man, Rose thought, feeling a wave of sympathy for the other woman who, despite her denial, had
obviously built a few castles in the air around her employer...something easily done.

Her own fantasies were under control and she intended
it to stay that way. An invite into his bed...she'd sooner
accept an invitation to put her hand in the fire. In the
long run it would be the less painful option, she decided,
feeling a touch more positive because she hadn't allowed
an image of his face to materialise in her head and she
hadn't thought about the animal magnetism that rolled
off him for at least five minutes.

She really hoped she would see as little of him as her
predecessor.

Rose remembered that wish when she was alone later that
evening. The apartment was so vast that it would have
been easy to forget that there was anyone else there, except the somebody was Zac Adamos and he was not so
easy to dismiss.

Up to that point there had not been too much time to
think. She had kept herself busy familiarising herself
with where the various baby essentials were kept, and
after a debate it hadn't seemed worth unpacking her own
things just for a night.

That headache that had lulled her into a false sense of security crept up on her just as the baby stirred... She sighed, as daggers stabbed her temples. The painkillers would have to wait.

Before he had left Arthur had said he'd keep Zac abreast of the arrangements and any potential issues that cropped up once he landed, but he did not foresee any problems.

On *that* count Zac had no worries, but as he sat in his book-lined, utterly silent library his focus was shot to hell! He'd not been able to work with the noise of a fretful baby and now it would seem he couldn't work without it—that really would be the supreme irony.

He was curious as to how she had calmed the child, but he had no intention of investigating. He saw no reason to revisit his decision to keep her at arm's length, preferably farther, the fact he really didn't want to proof that he needed to.

He turned back to the blank screen on his laptop, rose impetuously to his feet, changed his mind halfway to the door and, turning full circle, ended up at the built-in sliding cupboard containing some rather fine brandy... Hell, the redhead or parenthood or both is turning me to the bottle, he mocked himself as he poured a measure of the amber brandy into a glass. He held it but didn't drink, instead he found himself staring at liquid the colour of Rose's eyes.

He realised what he was doing and, choking out a snort of self-disgust, downed it in one. In the normal run of things this was a situation that would be easily remedied by scratching the itch... Sex was a great mind-clearer, not a solution available to him in this instance, so he might as well get drunk or at least get not totally sober!

Before he had time to put this plan into action there was a knock on the door.

It was no surprise to see who was standing there, it was a surprise to see how ill she looked.

'Theos!' he exclaimed, taking in her drawn ashen face, the bruised shadows under her eyes. 'You look terrible!'

Through the miasma of pain in her head Rose clutched at some bitterness. Did he think she needed telling this?

'Be fine in a minute now that I've thrown up.' Too much sharing, said her inner voice. Verbal shorthand was useful and quicker than full sentences when it took so much effort to get the words out. 'Saw a light under the door.' She was seeing lights now, ones that were not there in several colours zigzagging with dizzying intensity across her vision. It didn't distract her from the knives in her head. 'I'm s-sorry, but if you have any painkillers I forgot…' Her voice trailed away as she closed her eyes and pressed her fingers to her temples. 'Got a migraine.'

'You've got a *headache*?'

'No, I've got a bloody migraine!' She stopped and clutched her head, paying heavily for the yell as she swayed before adding in a whisper, 'Have to get back to the baby. He will need a feed.' She couldn't tell if the noise was part of the pain pounding in her skull or the baby crying. 'Can you turn the light off?' she pleaded, holding up a shaking hand to shade her eyes as she squinted up at him.

Swearing, he did just that and she sagged with relief.

'I'll call a doctor.'

'No…no… I just need a…'

He watched her sway like a sapling in the wind and then very gently crumple in slow motion. He caught her just before she reached the floor.

'Can you hear me? What do you need?'

Her head was against his chest. She squeezed her eyes closed. 'Not ambulance, painkiller and dark. I just need to close my eyes for a minute, then I can ch-check the baby.'

'I'll check the baby,' he said, sounding a lot more positive about his ability to do this than he felt. 'Piece of cake.'

'Shh!' she begged as agonising fire lit behind her eyes. 'No shouting!' she pleaded and pushed her face hard into his chest.

Startled by her action, Zac looked down at the fiery hot curls spilling down his front. She made a whimpering noise. The sound froze him to the spot as for a split second pure panic bolted through him, and something close to tenderness followed by a surge of protectiveness he refused to own.

She wanted to say, 'I'll be all right in a minute if I can just stay here.' She managed a slurred, 'Just...' Then without warning her knees sagged and gave, and she began to slide.

'Hey there, I'm up here.'

She let the hands on her waist take the strain, relieved to have the task of standing upright taken out of her hands. Her entire focus was on the hammers inside her head and the ever-tightening band across her forehead and behind her eyes. She told herself that this wouldn't last for ever, that it would go away, but it was little comfort.

She seemed oblivious when he scooped her up and carried her to her bedroom, pulling the quilt back before he laid her down. Her knees immediately came up to her chest. As he looked down at her lying there shaking, he felt something move in him...something that he refused to recognise as tenderness. He tried hard to push the feeling with no name away, but it held on tight, digging deeper until it felt like a fist in his chest, tightening… She looked so damned *fragile*. He swore.

He was not her protector, he was Marco's friend. As he wondered if he could feel any more conflicted than he did she whispered, *'Sorry,'* and he had his answer.

With a forearm pressed over her eyes she made noise that he correctly translated as a request to draw the blinds.

The darkness was bliss punctuated by pain. Rose hated feeling vulnerable, she hated asking for help with anything, but as the tears of weakness and pain began to seep through her closed eyelids she swallowed her pride and whispered, 'Shoes…' A part of her frazzled brain knew she ought not to be giving him orders, but the knowledge slipped away as she was hit by a fresh wave of agony.

She barely registered him unlace her trainers or remove the zip-up cardigan she wore over a lace-edged vest. It might have been a minute later or an hour when he urged her to swallow some water to wash down the generic painkillers he'd emptied every drawer in his own bedroom to find.

'The baby?' she fretted. The idea of abandoning Declan made her half rise before she sank back… Rose knew what it felt like to be abandoned. It gave them a connection. She had felt it the moment she saw him.

The response came, soothingly competent and calm-sounding, which he *hadn't* been when he had forced himself to walk into the nursery. Next time it would be easier—he hoped.

'I looked in on him, he was asleep.' It had come as a relief to Zac, who had built up a picture in his head of accusing baby eyes looking up at him and seeing through his pretence, seeing he was not a fit guardian.

Holding his breath, he had searched the sleeping baby's soft features, trying to see a resemblance to the parents he had lost and failing, when something had broken free inside him. Suddenly he had understood how parents gave their lives for their children.

'You go to sleep too.' Declan wasn't her child, but Rose had been willing to crawl to get to the baby. He pulled the cover up over her narrow shoulders and felt the same thing with no name move in his chest—it hurt.

If his last physical hadn't put him in the red zone of supreme fitness he might have been typing in his symptoms alongside his current Internet enquiry on migraine.

The volume of information when he had typed in his migraine query hadn't made him feel any less helpless. It was hard to pick the relevant facts out of the vast amount of information available. Helpless was something that Zac, a man of action and positivity, was not used to feeling.

There were some magic-sounding pills but as he didn't have access to them that wasn't much use. He'd rung his personal physician but had got the answer machine and an alternative number if this was an emergency. Zac had got frustrated and hung up in disgust. Should medics be allowed to have down time? At that moment he didn't think so!

'Can I do anything?' She looked so desperately ill that he struggled to believe that this was a migraine. He'd give it another thirty minutes and if she was no better he was calling an ambulance no matter what she said—not that she seemed capable of saying much.

'Distract me…' she mumbled.

He sat on the edge of the bed, his hand inches above her bright halo of hair, afraid to stroke her head in case he hurt her. Hurting a woman even accidentally was something that his entire being rejected, viscerally rejected.

'How?' Remembering her previous request, he kept his voice low.

'Talk about something nice.'

Nice... Hell, she wanted him to tell her a bedtime story! 'I don't know any stories.'

'Your Greek house, your family lived there...?'

Was she imagining a heritage that went back years? Nothing could be farther from the truth. Kairos, the man he considered his father, was a self-made man, not sentimental or resentful about his humble origins, and his mother's family had been hippies, her bohemian colourful antecedents had lived a gypsy lifestyle, colour, style, but no money.

They had both thought it odd when he took on the project of a fallen-down, derelict, formerly grand Greek stone house. What did he need a massive place in the middle of nowhere for? Was he planning to start a family? Kairos had joked.

Zac had been unable to explain even to himself. It had made him feel less sceptical when people spoke of instant connections after he experienced the strange sense of familiarity when he had stumbled on the place. The determination to bring it back to life had consumed him.

His family had speculated, the conclusions ranging from he'd lived there in a previous life—from his half-sister, deeply into crystals; he recognised a good investment—Kairos. Any financial gain had been accidental and his mother's suggestion he was looking for a baby substitute had turned out to be somewhat ironic considering he now had an actual baby.

'It's not a family home, it was a wreck that hadn't been lived in for years when I bought it…'

'Family?'

'I have a mother, a stepmother, she's Norwegian, and four stepfathers, also three half-sisters and four stepsisters,' he listed, and realised that he had gifted this woman he had known mere hours, and who he was meant to be surveying for character flaws, more personal information than he had trusted anyone with previously.

He hadn't even been aware of lowering his previously impregnable privacy barriers. How had that happened? he wondered as he watched her pale lips move in a faint smile, which he took to be a promising sign.

'So many…can I borrow one?'

He stood there in the dark and silence hearing the wistfulness in her voice. Marco or no Marco, at that moment if she hadn't drifted off to sleep he'd have told her.

Leaving her sleeping, he returned to the nursery. This time it was easier to make himself walk inside and this time when he walked to the cot he found it easier to look at the baby.

He was not asleep and his eyes were open. There was no accusation in them, just trust. Zac swallowed past the aching occlusion in his throat. They were Liam's eyes.

CHAPTER SEVEN

WHEN ROSE WOKE she didn't have a clue where she was, then suddenly it all came flooding back. She shot upright in bed, checked her head was still where it should be and sighed. Other than a muzzy feeling the pain was all gone.

Not the deep embarrassment. A second later as her thought processes cleared the embarrassment was overwhelmed by dismay! *The baby!* He had been her responsibility and she had dumped him on Zac. Gnawing worriedly on her lower lip, she slid off the bed and, not bothering to put on her shoes or run her fingers through her hair, dashed across the hallway to the nursery.

The blinds in the room were still drawn so she switched on the light and ran to the cot—the *empty* cot. Trying to stay calm, she ran towards the living area, and, exploding into the room, she stopped dead.

In a cream swivel chair Zac Adamos sat, a baby lying on his chest. The empty feed bottle on the side table spoke volumes.

They were both fast asleep.

Rose swallowed past the emotional lump in her throat. Both looked cute in *very* different ways. All right, Zac did not look cute, he looked quite unbelievably off-the-scale sexy with his tousled hair, stubble shadow emphasising the sharp angles of his face, and half-buttoned shirt revealing a slab of golden glowing skin. His relaxed sleeping face seemed younger.

Stepping over a trail of discarded ripped disposable nappies, she picked her way across the room to them. Closer, it was even more obvious that Zac, the urbane, sleek, perfectly groomed Zac, looked wrecked, admittedly a very sexy wrecked. His hair was standing up in spikes, his shirt sleeves were rolled up. Her eyes drifted as though drawn by a magnet to the section of deep toasty gold hair-roughened chest.

As she was staring his eyes opened.

'Good morning.'

She started guiltily. 'Good morning,' she whispered back, suddenly ridiculously shy. Last night they had stepped outside their designated roles and going back felt harder than it should have…

Would have helped if you'd combed your hair, Rose.

'I'm so sorry. I'm better now. I don't get them very often.'

'I am glad to hear that…' Presumably checking out her claim, he subjected her to a head-to-toe sweep, his conclusion hidden as his lash-shielded gaze was directed at the top of the sleeping baby's head.

Probably too polite to say she didn't look it, Rose decided, dragging a hand rather pointlessly through her hair. Not that so far he'd displayed much of that sort of restraint—he seemed a man who favoured calling a spade a spade, though when you were him there were no repercussions for being forthright. Nobody was going to cancel Zac Adamos and if they did, she doubted he'd care.

She watched as he shifted his position, sliding up in the chair as he flexed the fingers on the arm that was supporting the baby. 'I think my arm has gone to sleep…'

'Here, let me take him.' She bent towards him and held her arms out. As she eased the baby carefully from his chest, for a moment their eyes connected and the air buzzed with something that she refused to acknowledge as she broke the contact.

Pretending something wasn't happening got bad press but Rose was all for it. She positively embraced it!

He inhaled as she bent forward, her hair brushing his face, and Zac thought about it brushing his chest as she sat astride him. He was glad that the baby was there to bring some reality to the situation.

Lifting the baby into her arms jolted free the memory of him lifting her into his arms last night. Not much jolting was required—the memory was very close to the surface.

Equally easy to access was the strength of his arms, the warm solidity of his body something to cling to as the pain sucked her into her own private hell.

Her nostrils flared as she relived the moment minus, luckily, the pain, but with the warm male scent of him.

The blurred memories of the attack were sharpening with each passing second. She knew from experience that some would be lost for ever, but the ones that were not lost were making her squirm with embarrassment. Her boss had put her to bed, and, as if that weren't crossing enough professional boundaries, she'd asked him about his family.

He had told her.

Zac watched her settle the baby on her shoulder, his face nuzzling into her neck. She made it look so easy but he knew it was not.

'Have you been there all night?' The idea of him sleeping in a chair with the baby made emotions clutch in her chest.

'He fell asleep and I didn't want to risk waking him.'

'You fed him?'

'I would claim it was easy,' he said, levering himself into an upright position.

Rose watched, a worried corner of her brain noting the inescapable element of compulsion about her hungry scrutiny. But he made easy watching, she decided as he pressed one hand to the bottom of his spine and raised the other above his head to sinuously stretch out the kinks before he proceeded to rub a hand vigorously back and forth across his dark hair, creating a sexy mess.

Observing the effect, Rose wondered if the women he woke up with speared their perfectly manicured fingers into those ebony strands as they kissed their way down the column of his neck to his chest... Catching a sharp little breath, she applied the emergency brakes to the illicit scene playing in her head before it became personal.

'So how did you?'

'Cope...? I rang my mother, who talked me through the process. Once she had stopped laughing,' he added darkly, thinking of the conversation he'd had with his parent, trying to make himself heard above a baby's hungry screams.

This entire scene was so unimaginably impossible that Rose laughed too, then realised who she was laughing at, and stopped. The events of last night seemed to have significantly blurred the lines of their employer-employee relationship, a blurring that for her had started when he'd kissed her.

Was she imagining an intimacy that didn't exist?

'The one with four husbands?' The words were out before she could stop them. It was the sort of spontaneous stupidity that a person blurted out when they were not fully awake and their brain was still playing catch up.

'She only has one at a time and the last one appears to be a keeper,' Zac observed, watching the baby nuzzle her neck. It was an image that gave him chest pain again. The sensation was not one he embraced. 'She is a big believer in if at first you don't succeed, try, try and try some more.'

Rose, shifting her weight from one foot to the other, could only assume this family-orientated person would disapprove of a nanny literally sleeping on the job. How much influence did she have with her son…enough to get Rose sacked?

And who could blame her? Rose thought. She had not exactly covered herself in glory so far, but she really didn't want to lose this job, she decided fiercely. She didn't want to miss the chance to see Greece.

Nothing at all to do with the man who had just risen to his feet looking like a ruffled sex god.

Oh, no, Rose, nothing at all.

'I didn't mean to be… You told me about your family last night,' she finished on an awkward rush.

'Ah, your little bedtime story. Sometimes fact is stranger than fiction.'

'I don't really remember.' She wasn't sure she imagined that he relaxed slightly at her lie. 'But I do want to thank you. I'm very sorry I was such a…nuisance.'

He moved towards her at an immediate physical disadvantage due the disparity in their heights, and she felt her heart quicken. The baby on her shoulder stirred as her grip tightened slightly around his warm body.

'Hush,' she murmured, brushing his soft cheek with her lips. The baby's presence felt a protective shield, whether from his guardian's disturbing high-voltage presence or her own bewildering feelings around him. Both possibilities were equally confusing.

Her mouth ran dry as their glances connected. The contact lasted a second before he was rubbing a hand down his stubble-roughened jaw line, no doubt thinking of nothing more sexy than a shave and shower, she mocked herself. The rest was in her head. The knowledge didn't stop her tipping over into babble-inducing panic mode.

'Was your mother shocked?' *Horrified*, she tacked on silently, at the very least *not happy*. Her son demanded the extra mile from all his staff, why should the mother be any different? Though in this instance the son was being quite surprisingly understanding for a man who had spent the night in an armchair with a baby, afraid, as far as she could tell, to move a muscle. His reputation was not one of patient understanding, fair but tough.

'Less shocked, more—' He hesitated, the indent between his dark brows deepening as he recalled her comment... *'You need my help? That's a first, darling.'*

'My mother is not really shockable.'

He'd last seen her at the funeral, along with her present husband of ten years. Guy had lost more hair and the age difference was a lot less obvious. Guy was ten years older than Liam, who never got to worry about a receding hairline or hear his baby's first word.

Rose observed the fading of his half-smile and for a moment she glimpsed emotions that were more layered and complex. But before she could begin to interpret them the effective shield of his ebony lashes came down in what she understood as a 'subject closed' action, so she was surprised when he supplemented his original comment.

'She is still shaken by the death of Liam and Emma. Liam was a scholarship boy at my boarding school. Being in foster care, he used to spend holidays with us. She used to say she wished I was more like him.' Liam had always been more tactile and demonstrative than Zac was growing up.

'She struggles with unhappy endings.' Even though they were the norm in life. 'In my mother's world true love always leads to a happy ending.' The harsh cynicism in his voice made Rose wince in silent protest. She had a fondness for happy endings herself, though as yet not much first-hand experience of them. 'A prime example of stubborn optimism over experience considering her track record,' he mused.

'Is she not—' She stopped, bit her lip and apologised, cursing her runaway tongue.

'Yes, she is happy, my mother is a great believer in the power of love and an equally strong proponent of family and marriage. She believes in it so much so that…well, I have three half-sisters.'

'I know,' she began, and stopped, remembering too late she had claimed amnesia when actually she remembered every word he had said. His voice had been an anchor to cling to in a sea of pain. She smiled and lifted a hand to her head. It was so very good not to hurt.

'You still have a headache,' he accused, picking up on the gesture. She was finding it was worrying just how much he noticed.

'No, I'm fine.' She produced a slightly manic smile to prove the point and turned the subject. 'Was your father, was he her first—' Turned in the wrong direction.

It was immediately obvious even without the frost in the air that she'd hit a nerve. Her dad had once called her a social liability and he wasn't far out in this instance. 'Sorry, that was—'

'Clumsy, yes. She did *not* marry my father. He is dead.'

If she had felt bad before, now she felt mortified. 'I'm so sorry.'

He looked at her curiously. On most people's tongues the trite phrase was meaningless, but Rose meant it. Her sincerity was not in question, but his sanity was.

He had been cornered by the slickest of clever interviewers, every variation of every trick, surprise, ambush, flattery, had been tried, but he had never discussed his biological father, never revealed even a snippet of information, not even that he knew his identity. He'd never given even the smallest foothold to provide them with leverage, not even a *no comment*. To his knowledge only he, Kairos and his mother knew the man's true identity, who and what he had been.

Zac's biological father had been what *he* was never going to be, a weak, abusive bully, which was why he was never going to oblige his mother by marrying or having children. Why risk passing on his tainted genes to another generation?

This redhead, who wore her emotions so close to the surface it must *hurt*, had achieved what no experienced investigative journalist had and, with no pushing or coercion, he had voluntarily given out information.

He was stone-cold sober so he didn't even have that excuse!

Ironically the recipient was oblivious to what she had been handed, but even if she had known he was certain she would not have used it.

Or could it be an act? Just because she seemed to have dragged some hidden weakness of his own to the surface, he owed it to Marco to consider this possibility. Could she just be very good at pulling strings? His jaw flexed, the fine muscles quivered, growing taut at the idea of anyone pulling *his* strings. In his view it made sense to be wary especially of something that was too good to be true, and he could see for some Rose Hill might fill that brief—she *was* too good to be true, all warmth, sincerity, beauty, a hint of fire and blazing sensuality.

He'd see this thing through even though he suspected his report to Marco would be short and boring, but this wasn't the moment to go with his gut instincts. If he was wrong, if he made the wrong call, it was Marco and Kate who would suffer.

He knew that part of the reason Marco had tasked him with finding out if Rose was one of the good guys or her father's daughter was not just because of their friendship but because it would not have crossed his old friend's mind that Zac would be anything less than objective. Emotions wouldn't cloud his judgment.

Zac would not have questioned his ability to deliver this objectivity, even given the lust factor, *before* he saw her willing to drag herself to the baby's side when she was in agony, before she shook loose feelings that he still couldn't bring himself to acknowledge.

It would be easy for him to say case closed right now, and tell Marco you got exactly what you saw: the face of an angel with the lush lips of a sinner…missing out the part that she heated his blood like no woman he'd ever encountered.

The other option was that she was the best actress who'd never won an Award! But last night's pain had stripped away any defences she possessed, her total vulnerability exposed, and Zac had never felt so *protective*. There was a part of him that wanted to discover a dark secret, that wanted her *not* to be genuine. He'd been in her company for only a matter of hours but his gut instinct was telling him she was authentic...his gut or was that other parts of his anatomy talking?

He nodded his head in mocking gratitude. 'A lot of water under the bridge. My mother married Kairos, who is my stepfather. They co-parented me, but he's not my father, which is one of the world's most shared secrets,' he drawled.

'Not by me.'

Some of the tension that had crept into the room, fuelled by undercurrents she was aware of but didn't understand, faded at her retort. 'Good to know that my secrets are safe with you.' He hesitated a moment. 'You said it doesn't happen often?'

'No, really, it won't happen again. It's rare I have a full-blown attack like that. I usually catch it in time. There are warnings sometimes...an aura...some visual disturbances,' she explained, seeing his blank look.

'But not always a warning,' he persisted.

'I have never missed a day's work because of it.'

Zac fought the urge to correct her assumption that he was speaking as an employer, not someone who was concerned.

Why wasn't he speaking as an employer?

'I have no doubt,' he drawled. It was easy to imagine her dragging herself into work with a broken leg. She was a stubborn little thing with a martyr complex stamped into her DNA. 'I knew about migraine but I never knew it could be so incapacitating.'

She could hardly deny that, because she *had* been incapacitated. After trying to hold it together she'd just let go, and he'd been there to catch her—quite literally. Her eyes slid to his big hands and her insides quivered. Conscious of the strange ache in her chest, she remembered taking comfort in his strength, but it was the gentleness that had stayed with her.

'A lot of people have it worse.'

Remembering her lying in the foetal position, her eyes tight shut, overwhelmed with pain, Zac struggled to believe that was possible.

'I'm not sure what the schedule for today is? But if it's not too inconvenient, I could pick up my medication from my flat just in case... Is it on the way to the airport?' She waited, not looking directly at him, ready for him to tell her he'd made other arrangements—someone who wasn't likely to fall down on the job quite literally.

'A detour is no problem. It would be a lot more inconvenient if that happened again.' He might as well play the heartless employer if that was what she thought him... Besides, it was not so far from the truth. He was a good employer for practical reasons not sentiment. People who were happy in work were more productive, it was logical.

What was not logical was imagining even for a moment holding her while she slept...scooping her body against his, not in a sexual way, even though she lit fires inside him he hadn't known were there. Last night he had experienced an utterly alien need to comfort her.

The recollection was one he pushed away as he reminded himself he was a man who headed for the hills at the first sniff of neediness in a woman, a woman who wanted more than he was willing or able to give.

The baby in Rose's arms started squirming. She looked

down with a smile. His eyes were screwed up and he had shoved his fist in his mouth.

'So I still have a job?' It was only half a joke.

'Did you think otherwise?'

'You offered to sack Andy… And your reputation…' She stopped, flushing, wondering when she was going to stop putting her foot in where angels feared to tread… The mixed-up narrative in her head represented her tangled emotions.

'Please don't stop. You were just getting educational. I'd be fascinated to learn what reputation I have.'

'All right then, ruthless. I didn't say I believe them,' she added.

'Because you think the best of people?' he drawled, thinking she was the living, breathing definition of a lamb to the slaughter.

'He's waking. I need to feed him,' she said, dodging his eyes and the question as little Declan provided a god-sent distraction from a fresh surge in tension that seemed to spring into life at regular intervals when they were sharing a space. 'Come on, sweetheart, let's get you sorted,' she crooned, beginning to jiggle him in her arms. She took a step and turned back. 'What time are we leaving?'

'When you're ready.' Zac had a new and, for someone who took for granted his ability to learn new tasks easily, very real appreciation of how a baby's needs were time-consuming.

'I'll be as quick as I can,' she promised, determined to make up for last night.

She needed to show him that she really wasn't the weakest link. She'd been looking after herself most of her life—all of her life—but last night someone had been there for her. Zac had been there for her.

What would it be like to have someone there when you needed them, someone who *wanted* to be there, wanted to protect you, someone to share the good times and the bad...share a family...? Would she ever know? she wondered wistfully.

'The kitchen, it might be...sightly messy... I was looking for...things...'

It was an afterthought that mystified Rose—it was his kitchen, after all—but when she walked into the room, the tinge of something close to embarrassment made perfect sense. *Slightly* messy did not cover it. The place looked as if a bomb had hit it, cupboards and drawers open, the work surfaces cluttered with their contents.

She cleared enough of the mess to be able to prepare the baby feed, while nudging the baby in his rocker chair with her foot.

Zac made a few calls and checked his emails, and made a few Internet face-to-face calls. The last-minute nature of the Greek trip had involved his office making some major changes to his diary. The only one that he had refused to cancel was a dinner for a director who had been with the foundation since its inception and whose dedication and expertise, given freely, had gone a long way to its success. Charles deserved more than a handshake and he had plenty of gold watches.

Flying back to London for the event had seemed the only realistic solution. It was one of his team who had suggested half jokingly that he could shift the party to Greece, fly everyone out and make a weekend of it.

The idea had appealed to Zac and he had set the plan in motion.

After being holed up for an hour, when he left the room

Zac was hit by the smell of coffee and a blissful silence. He resisted the coffee aroma, sent up a prayer of thanks for the silence and headed for the shower.

Zac's dark eyes squeezed closed as he lifted his head, enjoying being pummelled by the darts of hot steamy water ironing out the kinks in his spine left by the night he'd spent afraid to move in case the baby woke.

He found his thoughts turning to Rose's relaxed competence with the baby. He doubted he would ever feel relaxed. He doubted… He pushed the thoughts away but the insecurities lingered. At least the child did not have his DNA to deal with, he just had a parent who left a lot to be desired. He would never be able to fill Liam's shoes, he knew that. The loss of his friend lay like a cold boulder in his chest. Zac was determined to do his best, whatever that turned out to be, but for the first time in his adult life self-doubt plagued him.

He deliberately let the image of Rose's face float into his head and the rest faded away. She was the biggest problem of all and one, despite everything, he would have given a lot to enjoy. The fact he was even torturing himself with the possibility said how big his problem was.

CHAPTER EIGHT

HE TURNED THE shower to cold. The icy jets only partly solved his problem, which was that he wanted something that he couldn't have... Not complicated, Zac. The control that he had grown to take for granted was being challenged because he was allowing it to be, he told himself. He had to stop indulging in fantasies and fulfil his promise to Marco and get Rose Hill out of his life and reunited with the family she appeared to long for.

Rose, the baby tucked on one hip, was talking away as though the infant could understand every word as she set about the task of untangling the straps on a baby rocking chair. She didn't immediately realise that Zac had entered the room until his shadow fell across her.

'Oh, good,' she said, focusing on the practical use he could be and not how her stomach had gone into butterfly mode. 'Could you lend a hand with this? It's got in such a tangle.' She clicked her tongue in irritation.

Before he knew what she wanted—his thought processes were a little slowed by the distraction of her behind encased in blue denim—she had got to her feet and thrust the baby at him.

'Could you? I need to use two hands.'

'What...?'

Rose watched as he looked at the baby as if it were

an unexploded bomb. 'That's right, support the head… you've done it before, yeah, that's perfect. You're a natural,' she lied.

The pat-on-the-head lie made his jaw quiver. If he could have risked taking his eyes off the baby, he would have glared at her for daring to patronise him, a circumstance that should have made him more annoyed than he was.

Zac Adamos looking *almost* vulnerable, not arrogant and in control. Who'd have thought? she mused, fighting off a smile that faded of its own accord as the word *dangerous* floated into her head.

She shivered. 'You can breathe,' she offered in a tight little voice as she bent back to her task. The task she was getting paid for. Among all this domestic familiarity, it was good to remind herself of her position here.

The baby looked up at him with what Zac imagined was disappointment… Sorry, mate, Zac thought. You did pull the short straw.

'He's not crying.'

Rose straightened up. 'I can't take the credit. Janet said he had colic, poor scrap. She had had a tough few days, but he's feeling better—aren't you?' She moved in close, pursing her lips as she threw the baby a kiss and smiled.

Zac clenched his jaw at the resultant hormone surge he had zero control over and stood rigid as she took the baby from him. Some of the tension slid from his shoulders as he was relieved of the warm bundle and she stepped away, not far enough to stop his nostrils flaring in response to the scent of her shampoo, or was it just the scent of her?

'*Janet?*' he repeated, frustration and the irritation he felt with himself putting harshness in his deep voice.

She looked surprised by the question. 'Janet, my predecessor. Oh, her mother's op went very well...' She slung him a cheery smile over her shoulder as she crouched down to clip the baby in the chair, sounding as though she expected this to be good news to him.

'How on earth do you know that?'

'She texted me a few minutes ago.'

'You appear to have bonded.'

She straightened up. Maybe he was always this grumpy in the morning? Or maybe just on a morning after he had spent the night in a chair with a baby on his knee when he might have had other plans.

Aware of a simmering tension in the room, she tilted her head to meet his hooded dark stare and felt her stomach muscles twist.

She swallowed, looked away and took longer than necessary to dab the baby's drooly rosebud mouth with a muslin square. Better to face facts. If there was tension, it was in *her*, not the room.

She was attracted to him. She knew she was being faintly ridiculous, but it had been a lot easier when she was able to balance his expertise in the kissing department when he was the shallow, selfish boss with ice in his veins, a calculator where his heart should be... Some of the stuff people said about him had to be true.

She was clinging hard to the image of a callous charmer, which was not easy after the way he had looked after her last night and then this morning with the baby... She had to get a grip!

She felt dizzy when she thought about him kissing her. She *should* have felt disgusted, it had been so calculating. Instead she felt...she wasn't going to think about what she felt because with luck it would go away like her headache. She was not going to make the situation worse by making a total fool of herself by betraying what was a belated sexual awakening. *That* would be a blow she didn't think her pride could withstand.

'Are you packed?'

'Oh, yes, things are all sorted, Janet had done most of it before she left and I didn't unpack last night.'

'You can pick up your migraine medication on the way to the airport.'

'Thanks. She says that her mum's sister is coming over from Canada.'

The relevance of this information passed him by until it dawned on him that she assumed that the previous nanny was coming back when her personal circumstances changed. He had no reason to correct her.

'Did you bring anything dressy?'

She stared at him, her smooth brow pleating at the question. 'I didn't think I'd be dressing for dinner...' Realising he might misinterpret her sarcasm, she added quickly, 'Declan is OK with informal.'

Rose extended her foot to gently rock the baby chair, smiling as the occupant began to kick his feet with uncoordinated enthusiasm.

'I just thought you might like to explore in your down time. There are some pretty nice places to eat. But no matter, you can buy what you need when you get there. Order anything you need. I've made arrangements for you to use my accounts.' When he'd made the arrangements it had seemed a good way to test her honesty or otherwise for Marco.

At what point over the last twenty-four hours had the idea stopped being a test of Rose's honesty and simply a convenience? He didn't know at what precise moment his suspicions had died a natural death, but, while she might have nothing to prove to him, Marco would no doubt be pleased when he was able to show him this further proof of her integrity.

Unless she cleaned him out and skipped the country?

Her attention swung from the baby to the man standing with his shoulders propped against the wall, his negligent stance in direct contrast to the intelligence glinting in his eyes and the air of barely suppressed energy that even a sleepless night hadn't put a dent in.

'I have everything I need,' she said, acting, to his amusement, as if he had just offered her an insult, not his trust.

'I don't need anything I can't buy myself.' Certainly not something you are paying for, she thought, before belatedly realising that she had jumped the gun. He hadn't been offering to buy *her* a wardrobe. Mortified by her error, she tacked on quickly, 'But yes, baby will need things, that will be useful. Is the house far from a town?'

'Aphrodite, my villa, is relatively remote. It is set in its own grounds, which guarantees privacy.'

Rose nodded. *She* had no concerns about isolation. She was excited about her first taste of foreign travel… and isolation had its positives. She had struggled with the decision but in the end she had not contacted her dad to tell him about her temporary move. She felt guilty but she knew that if her dad knew her place was empty, he'd offer to house-sit or, even worse, turn up in Greece and try to cadge a free bed.

'Won't the isolation make it hard for you to make your base there on a permanent basis?'

'There is such a thing as the Internet and I won't be there twenty-four-seven.'

'Obviously,' she said, even though actually it hadn't been that obvious to her. She'd be able to relax, she told herself, without his presence making her feel as though she were constantly walking a tightrope without a safety net.

'Athens is a thirty-minute helicopter transfer away and the flight into London is not exactly long haul.'

He spoke casually of helicopter transfers the way only the very rich did. 'You've thought of everything.'

She had to admire his commitment to the role that had been thrust upon him, to the extent that he was prepared to make such a major life change for the baby. But to her way of thinking interacting with Declan was more important than uprooting his life for the sake of the baby and maybe regretting the move.

Though what did she know? Maybe the timing was good and this wasn't just about the baby, maybe one of those long-legged beauties had pierced his reputedly stony heart and he'd already decided it was time for a lifestyle change?

Her lips twisted into a grimace as she masochistically dwelt on the image of his mouth losing its cynical twist and wearing an intimate smile as he looked at this faceless beauty that had captured his heart.

She pressed a hand to her stomach, and diagnosed the sensation—a touch of envy, yes, but not, obviously, of a woman who landed him.

He was easy to fancy, but living with him would be a nightmare. *Not that you're ever going to know, Rose*, mocked the voice in her head.

No, what she envied was simply the idea of being part of a family, a *real* family. In her experience people who had them didn't realise how lucky they were.

Obviously it was a plus if a child could be brought up with space and freedom to thrive, but it wasn't about where a child lived. Her eyes flickered momentarily to the drooling baby and her expression softened. What any child really needed was a family…and love.

He glanced at his phone. 'The driver is here. Tell him where to stop off and I'll see you at the airport.'

'You're not coming w—' She stopped. Obviously he wasn't coming with them and she was in danger of sounding disappointed.

'I have a few things to sign off on. I'll see you there.' His eyes went to the baby. 'I'll see you both there.' After the shortest of hesitations he reached out and touched the baby's cheek.

'So soft,' he observed, sounding startled, before seeming to realise she was watching him and dropping his hand. On anyone else she would have called the expression on his face self-conscious.

Rose had no first-hand experience to compare with, but she was assuming that the sort of luxury, every-need-attended-to service she was enjoying was not available on a typical flight.

She had not been offered a menu but she had been asked what she would like. The attendant seemed confident whatever she requested the chef would be able to provide.

Thrown, Rose had resorted to asking what the young woman would recommend.

'The lobster is—'

'Fine, I'll have it.'

'The wine list?'

'No, I'll not have…' Actually, why not? This might be her only experience of flying in a private jet, she might as well enjoy it… Also, a glass of wine might unknot the tension in her shoulders, just the one. 'You choose.'

The lobster was melt-in-the-mouth and buttery and the wine did help her relax.

The only negative of the experience was not that Zac had not joined her—a little bit of delicate probing had revealed he was sitting upfront with the pilot—but the possibility that he might suddenly appear, which stopped her relaxing *enough* to enjoy the experience fully.

She was clipping on her seat belt for landing when Zac did appear, shrugging his jacket on as he walked towards her before flopping elegantly into the seat opposite her.

'Comfortable flight?'

'I've got nothing to compare it to, but I was well looked after.'

A look of shock crossed his face. 'You've *never* flown before?'

He couldn't have sounded more shocked if she had announced that she had come from Mars. She shrugged and wondered what his reaction would be if she admitted that she'd never been outside the UK before.

'But not your first time abroad? Your father never took you with him on his travels?'

'Not for business. I was at school, we moved around the country. When he went abroad… I was old enough to look after myself.'

How old did her father consider old enough? he wondered grimly—Zac had suspicions. He found he was envying Marco his opportunity to tell the man exactly what he thought about him when he warned him off. Zac would have enjoyed some warning of his own.

'That's pretty,' he observed. The upward curve of his lips distracted from the ice in his eyes as he stretched his hand towards the amber stone she wore suspended on a gold-coloured chain around her neck.

Rose's lashes fluttered before her eyes lifted to his face. 'Oh, yes…' She caught the stone in her fist, pressing the coldness into her palm. 'It was a birthday present from my dad…' She began and stopped, her smile fading.

It was a story she had trotted out so many times that she almost believed the lie herself. She began to shake her head, then laughed, an invisible tipping point reached. She just couldn't tell the pathetic lie again.

The truth was pathetic too but at least it was the truth. What was the point of perpetuating the pretence? She wasn't a child trying to fit in with the other kids who took for granted their birthday parties and gifts, who complained about curfews and being grounded…being *cared* for, not that they realised it. But Rose did because it was something she didn't have.

'No, no, that's not true. He didn't buy it for me. I bought it myself! I saw it on a market stall and saved up. I gave the stallholder a little each week until I could buy it for myself and I told… I pretended.'

There was a silence as he stared at her. She couldn't tell what he was thinking…but then she didn't want to. She lowered her gaze to her hands clasped on her lap. She didn't want to see his embarrassment or, worse, his pity.

She pressed a clenched hand to her mouth and thought, *A bit late*, as she shook her head. Her eyes above the hand were filled with tears and she wanted to die of embarrassment.

'You have excellent taste,' Zac observed, making no reference to her massive meltdown as he took hold of the pendant between his long fingers.

Her lowered eyes lifted. She didn't know what reaction she had expected but this hadn't been it.

He leaned in slightly and Rose fought the instinct to mirror his action as her nostrils twitched to the scent of the male fragrance he used...or maybe it was just him. 'It is...' he turned the pendant over in his hand '... Victorian?'

She looked at his sleek dark head shining blue black and wondered if it was as marvellously silky as it looked. 'I don't know, I just thought it was pretty.' His eyes were on the stone and not her face. It gave Rose an opportunity to regain her composure and she was grateful for it.

'The smaller black stones around the amber are, I think, jet, though I am no expert on jewellery.'

Just how to pay for it, and not this sort of jewellery, she thought, polishing her cynicism.

'You delegate that task, do you?' She couldn't help herself or maybe she didn't try. His parting gifts to exes were the thing of legend in the Adamos building.

He let go of the pendant and pulled up straight, fixing her with a dark stare that glittered with humour.

The words *Can you see the Gorgeous Great White laughing at himself?* floated through her head... He could!

He was glad to see her biting her lip and looking guilty, not devastated. The look in her eyes as she'd told her story, the simplicity of the recounting, no play for sympathy, in fact actively rejecting sympathy, had touched him at a deep level that no one had ever reached before.

'Play nice, Rose. I was showing my sensitive side. Seriously though, I'm sorry you didn't get birthday presents...all children should,' he observed, keeping it light and hoping one day she would meet a man who would make up for all those lost birthdays... The thought of this man who would get to do this made him feel oddly dissatisfied.

'Did you?'

'Oh, yes... I still do. It doesn't matter how often I tell them I'm too old to celebrate birthdays, they keep sending me reminders of how old I am.'

'Of course, you're *never* too old to celebrate your birthday. I think everyone should have their birthday as a holiday. It should be written into law.'

He reached into his pocket, remembering the forgotten discarded home-made card that had escaped the bin. He'd stuffed it in his pocket, meaning to dispose of it. He got it out now and uncreased the folds before handing it to her.

'Oh, that's so sweet.' She looked up from the crayoned offering. 'Who is... Carla?' she asked, deciphering the lopsided name in front of the kisses.

'A niece.'

'How old is she?'

'I don't have a clue...but she can write...' he glanced at the card '...so she might be, what, five or thereabouts...?'

She laughed, assuming he was joking. 'You make fun, but it must *mean* something if you kept it.' He was not as heartless as he liked to make out.

He looked amused, a look, of course, which was very attractive on him. 'I hate to disillusion you, but I just forgot to bin it with the rest.'

Her face fell. She hated that this was something he found amusing. 'I hope you will celebrate Declan's birthday,' she said sternly, adding a self-conscious, 'Mr Adamos,' as an afterthought.

'Make it Zac. If I didn't give Declan a party with all

the bells and whistles I think his mum and dad would haunt me, *Rose*.'

She glanced from his sombre face to the sleeping baby, her heart aching when she realised she would never see any of his birthday parties. In a short space of time that little baby had burrowed his way into her heart. 'How...?' She stopped and shook her head. 'Sorry, you don't want to talk about it.'

'I haven't talked about it. The people at the funeral talked incessantly about the *tragedy*, but what they really meant was "I'm glad it's not me".'

'I suppose that's a natural reaction.'

'It's hypocrisy and—'

She watched as he clamped his white lips tight as if the physical action alone could hold the anger in. Rose was of the opinion he would be better off letting it out.

'It was a lorry,' he said abruptly. 'They were on their way from the hospital. Emma wanted to remain with the baby, but she was exhausted and parent accommodation on the SCBU was overstretched.'

'He was premature?'

He nodded. 'They never stood a chance. It went across the central reservation and hit them head-on. Dead instantly, the inquest said, like that was some sort of comfort.'

Rose didn't say anything, afraid that she would stop the flow of confidences.

'The driver had a heart attack but survived.'

'Poor man,' she exclaimed, eyes wide with horror, before catching Zac's expression and adding, 'To have to live with that knowledge must be terrible.'

'Too early for me to be philosophical. I think, to quote from the beginner's guide to bereavement and other equally useless books on the subject available, that I've moved from denial to anger.' He gave a bitter laugh. The stages of bereavement sounded so straightforward on the page of a book—in reality they were anything but.

'I've never lost anyone close,' she said quietly. Anything she said would come from a position of ignorance. 'But I'm a good listener...' The offer was there with the silent addition of no pressure.

The soft words brought his eyes to her face, her eyes wide and soft, her expression pensive as her teeth dug into her plump lower lip.

What is this? A therapy session?

His spine stiffened. For some bizarre reason he was indulging in some sort of soul-baring exercise instead of fulfilling his promise to Marco.

'I'll keep that in mind but if I feel in need of therapy I'll go *talk* to a professional.'

He saw the hurt in her eyes but didn't allow it to influence him. In his opinion if anyone needed talking therapy it was her. If she carried on leaking empathy the way she did she'd be drained dry before she was thirty.

'So your parents are alive?' he said, belatedly taking charge of the conversation.

'My dad is— Didn't I tell you this? He's alive, and I've no brothers or sisters.'

'Your mother?'

'She left...she didn't want me.' She blinked rapidly, her lashes quivering dark against her cheek, confused as to why she had told him that. She *never* volunteered information about the mother who walked away when she was a baby. 'That doesn't make me a victim,' she added quickly. 'Not all people are cut out to be parents... Oh, I didn't mean you.'

His bark of laughter dissolved some of the invisible tension that had built up. The half-smile that followed held no humour as he added in a hard voice, 'Why not? It's probably true.' His shoulders lifted in one of his inimitable shrugs. 'But I'm the only option Declan has. Let's hope I don't let him down.'

His comment opened up a range of possibilities that she had not considered. He seemed so impregnably confident that the possibility, no, *probability* that he could experience the same insecurities that anyone faced with parenting was surprising. Acknowledging he had weaknesses made things shift inside her in a way she couldn't explain even to herself.

'I'm sure every parent who brings a baby home feels the same pressure.'

Conscious of a sudden weariness, he ran a hand across his forehead almost expecting to discover lines gouged into his skin—he felt he'd aged half a lifetime in the last few weeks. 'Liam and Emma never got to bring their baby home, never got to worry.'

Her eyes misted as she leaned forward, her hands clasped tight in her lap. There were no words that would make the anger and pain she saw in his eyes go away. She wished there were. 'Life s-stinks s-sometimes!'

The hard lines on his face relaxed. If she had said the *right* thing, along the lines of *It gets better* or *Time heals* or any of the trite things that people said on such occasions he would have exploded. Instead her brutal honesty pulled him back from the brink of losing it.

'You won't get any arguments from me. You do realise that we have landed?'

Her initial thought was that he was joking, but when she turned to look out of the window her eyes flew wide.

They really were taxiing on the runway. Her face mirrored her disappointment.

'Oh, I missed it!'

He was amused. She sounded so *young*, or maybe he just felt old today.

'There's always next time.'

'The first time is special,' she said and watched his eyes darken to velvet black. Her smile died as their eyes connected and clung.

'It should be,' he agreed, wondering if hers had been, and instinctively not liking the man who had been responsible for her first sexual experience. His own was so long ago—he really was feeling every hour of his thirty-two years at the moment—he barely remembered the event, certainly not the face of the slightly older woman who had provided his carnal initiation, he just remembered her athleticism.

The flurry of activity as the doors were opened managed to shake her free of his dark stare. Even with contact broken, the feelings low in her pelvis didn't ease.

She heard him get up and move away but didn't look up. Instead she asked herself what the hell just happened as she secured Declan securely in a baby sling, which made it easier to negotiate the steps, even with a bag containing the baby essentials banging against her hip.

Arthur was on the tarmac. He waved but walked across to Zac who had disembarked ahead of her and was speaking to someone official-looking. Even from a distance it was obvious that the official was eager to please.

Waiting to be told where to go, she stood on the tarmac, which seemed to reflect the heat it had absorbed back at her. With an anxious glance at the baby, she fished in the bag for a sunhat, which she fitted carefully on a contented Declan's head. She had anointed him with sun-cream during the flight, using the spare left on her own nose—even so, she could almost hear the sound of her freckles breaking out as she stood there. Despite the precautions she was anxious to get the baby out of the sun.

She delved a second time into the bag, giving a little grunt of triumph when her fingers located what she was looking for, a cheap and cheerful plastic handheld fan, which she directed at Declan.

Allowing herself a few seconds of fan use, she directed it down her cleavage before she moved it back to Declan. Her clothes were sticking to her skin as she looked around, controlling her impatience with difficulty. After the build-up of expectation she was here, and here was not very exciting. Her emotions had dipped. One stretch of tarmac was much the same as another.

She was trying to remember how long Zac had said their transfer would be when he appeared at her side.

'How long did you say it took to—'

'The helicopter transfer takes less than thirty minutes,' came the terse-sounding response. 'Before you ask, I've checked that it's OK for babies. So this helicopter will be a first for you too, I'm assuming?'

Her lips tightened. He made her sound freakish, and there was no sign of the tentative rapport of their journey. Well, if he thought it was weird that she was a first flyer imagine what he'd make of her being a virgin. Not that she'd get to know because it was not information she was about to share with him.

'There is a large part of the population, who aren't Greek billionaires, that haven't been in a helicopter.'

He didn't comment on her spiky response beyond a sardonic look that made her feel embarrassed.

'Arthur will take you to the house. I have some business I need to attend to in Athens. I'll probably stay over.'

He delivered the information as though this were the plan all along, but it wasn't a plan at all, it was more a sticking plaster. The humiliating reality was he had to put some distance between them because he couldn't think past the sexual attraction, an attraction that seemed to divest him of his normal objectivity, and turn his iron control back on itself.

Rose just nodded, wondering what the *business's* name was, and knowing that she had no right to feel a sense of hurt that lay like a boulder in her chest.

Not that she was interested. As far as she could see they all looked pretty much identical...

Wonder if he ever gets the names mixed up?

She was not at all jealous of the identikit women.

'You all right?' Arthur sounded anxious.

Rose realised that she had been staring at the back view of Zac as he strode away, seemingly unaware of heads turning to follow the tall dynamic figure.

'Fine,' she said, painting on a cheerful smile. Zac's coldness didn't hurt her at all, why would it?

'Can I carry something that isn't alive and kicking?' Arthur gave a little wave to the baby, admitting, 'I never know what to say to children.'

'Babies are pretty uncritical,' Rose, amused by the confession, assured him. If only all men found it so easy to admit to their weaknesses, life would be much simpler, she mused, thinking of one particular man. 'If you don't mind the bag...?'

She slid the bag from her aching shoulder and handed it over, smiling her gratitude. She might travel light, but a baby did not.

Zac had walked on ahead so Rose had a grandstand view of the ripple effect of his progress—like a Mexican wave, heads turned and eyes followed him.

Rose wasn't surprised. He was very watchable, though she couldn't watch him as when she reached the concourse he had vanished. She searched for a distinctive dark head above the throng but there was no sight of him.

'This way…'

Rose nodded and followed, suspicious of something like sympathy in the older man's eyes. Was he thinking *another one…*? He must have seen it before, women falling for his boss and throwing themselves at him.

Her chin lifted. Well, she wasn't one of them, she had more pride. She was there to do a job and that was what she would do, she decided, lifting a hand to shade her eyes from the sun, which was now directly overhead.

With Arthur in charge the golf-buggy transfer to the helipad was smooth. The only hitch came when they were about to lift off. The pilot, who was speaking into his mouthpiece, turned around, hand raised, and yelled above the low-level din.

CHAPTER NINE

'An extra passenger, folks.'

That was when Rose saw the tall figure, head bent, short hair blowing wildly in the blow back from the blades as he ran towards them. The door opened, bringing a rush of air, noise and the final passenger.

It closed and he was inside, the helicopter lifting off as he was belting in.

Rose sat there, a carefully neutral smile on her lips that gave no clue to the presence of her internal turmoil. Before she'd seen him she had been feeling positive, in control, and then he'd appeared and her little bubble of calm had burst into a million pieces.

'Change of plan.'

Rose nodded, her attitude matching his casual delivery of the sparse information, and directed her gaze out of the window.

Zac's car had actually arrived when he'd asked himself why.

Why was he reluctant to ask the question, let alone answer it? He had chosen to put distance between them because he wanted her. His response to the temptation she presented implied he didn't trust himself and Zac would not admit to this sort of weakness even to himself. Such an acknowledgment would require a redrafting of…well, his life!

At that point he sent the car away and now he was sitting looking at Rose, attacked by a desire that made every inch of his skin tingle with sexual attraction…even his scalp got in the game… It was insane but it was real.

Rose had been afraid she had such high expectations that the reality would be a bit of a let-down. When she got her first glimpse of the Villa Aphrodite she knew that wasn't going to happen.

The setting alone was worth several gasps of amazement. The sprawling terracotta-roofed building, low and built around a courtyard, had a central stone tower shaded by cypresses and pine trees. It nestled into the rock above a stretch of empty glittering sand and, beyond that, the dazzling blue ocean.

But it was as the helicopter came in to land that the scale and beauty of the building were revealed.

Part golden stone, part painted classic white, and windows facing the ocean or across lush, landscaped gardens with traditional blue frames.

It seemed to be an organic part of the landscape, not something grafted on, but blending in. She gave a series of yelps and gasps of excitement as she caught a glimpse of the pool that appeared to hang in mid-air surrounded by terraces of greenery.

'There's another one, look…'

She turned and saw Zac watching her. As if he didn't know how many swimming pools or tennis courts he had…

He watched as her almost childlike enthusiasm and

spontaneous pleasure shifted into self-conscious embarrassment.

'Sorry, I...'

'Do not be sorry. I got excited when I first stumbled on this place from the air too, a wreck then, of course, but there was something about it that...' Without his being aware, his clenched hand went to his chest, pressing against the place where his heart beat as he shook his head.

The connection he obviously felt did not seem foolish to Rose. 'And you saved it?' she said, eyes sparkling. 'What a marvellous thing to do. Why was it neglected?' She could not imagine anyone not wanting to live in such a magical place.

Could there be a connection between her praise and the warm glow he was feeling? Zac dismissed the idea as absurd.

'I believe there was a family falling out that passed down through the generations, two brothers inherited, one was desperate to sell, the other refused and the place stood empty.'

'That's sad.'

It was hard to tell if she was talking about the empty home or the family dispute, but her emotions seemed genuine. She turned and caught him staring and looked self-conscious for a moment, then smiled. Her smile was genuine...she was genuine... His promise to Marco seemed more and more like a fool's errand.

'But it had a happy ending—you brought it back to life and what a beautiful place for a child to grow up.' Her smile grew tender as it was directed at the baby who had slept all the way through the transfer. 'He really is so contented…' Her lips twitched as she saw his reaction to her claim. 'When he doesn't have colic.'

She lost her fight and the laughter she had been holding in bubbled out.

Laughter at his expense had a novelty value. There had been instances he had been tempted to spout gibberish just to see how many people congratulated him on his brilliance.

The expressions flickering across her face made him think of a time-lapse film of an opening flower bud. It was just all there. She appeared to hide nothing. She possessed a rare spontaneity.

Or maybe he was seeing what he wanted to. Was he allowing his physical attraction to cloud his judgment?

He doubted that Marco would be impressed to hear him sounding more like a cheerleader than an objective observer.

'Can you imagine growing up here?' she enthused.

Zac didn't respond. His expression was opaque but she read disapproval in his shuttered eyes. Again it was less what he said and more of what he didn't say that bothered her. Rose gave a tiny sigh, exasperated by his lightning moods that made it hard to relax around him, which was maybe, she reflected, not such a bad thing. Relax too much around him and she might be in trouble.

She didn't pursue the thought as to what the trouble might involve because the pilot had set the helicopter down smoothly on a vast area of green to one side of the house. As she peered through the window she could make out massive decorative wrought-iron gates set in a stone wall that appeared to surround the house and grounds. They stood open.

'Do you own this area outside the walls too?' Her fascination for his home overcame her determination to behave more like an employee and less like an inquisitive house guest.

This place could not have been a more dramatic contrast to his London apartment, which, with its expensive neutrality, gave very little clue to the man who occupied it, other than the fact he had limitless resources, but there was none of *him* in the place, or so it seemed to Rose. But then maybe that was him, slick, and expensive?

He glanced her way before nodding and shading his eyes as he followed the direction of her gaze.

'The land goes all the way to the public road, about a mile away, and then the lower slopes of the mountain.' He nodded to the steep, densely wooded hillside.

'That is a *biggish* garden,' she said, eyes wide. 'So this is an estate?'

He shrugged casually but didn't dispute her description. 'Many hectares are forested but we have some productive olives. The family who owned it sold off sections of land over the years. I negotiated to buy some back—it is a work in progress.'

'You make your own olive oil?' She was charmed by the idea.

He laughed. 'There is a little too much for just domestic use. We supply a few outlets around the world. Artisan products have a big market these days.' He watched her looking impatiently through the window, her childlike impatience amusing him—until it annoyed him. 'They'll have finished offloading the luggage in a moment.'

'I bet you have some lovely family parties here.' She watched the shutters come down, which should have told her to back off but it only made her more curious.

'I believe they do.' Though his family had considered

him mad when he took on the task of the renovation, they were all happy enough now to spend holidays here frequently en masse.

'They?' she wondered out loud, a frown tugging at her smooth brow.

'I am a busy man. Besides,' he threw over his shoulder as he rose, 'a GGW might eat the guests.' He watched the mortified heat climb into her cheeks, and felt a scratch of guilt, but his jibe had effectively diverted her from her line of questioning.

'You heard…?'

His grin was very white. 'I appreciated the gorgeous.'

'Like you didn't know,' she muttered under her breath, her discomfort mingled with indignation because he seemed to be enjoying her embarrassment.

'Like you didn't know, Mr Adamos,' he corrected with mocking solemnity.

Arthur's arrival denied her the right of reply, which was not a bad thing because you couldn't really call your boss the things she wanted to—even if he was one!

On terra firma, Rose was immediately conscious that the air smelt different. She inhaled a few lungsful of the fragrance that the aerial view had not revealed.

'Thyme, mint, rosemary,' he said, watching her. 'They all grow wild here with a strong hint of cypress and sea salt. If you could bottle it you'd make a fortune.'

'It's beautiful,' she said, glancing across as someone slammed a Jeep door.

'The luggage,' he explained. 'There's room for you if you want a ride.'

'I'll walk, thanks.' She wanted to take it all in. 'I've been sitting down all day. I need to stretch my legs.'

He glanced down. She was wearing the baby, who

was awake and looking happy against her breasts—who wouldn't?—in the sling arrangement. 'It's a bit of a hill.' He took a deep breath. 'I'll take him.'

She swung around, the surprise in her eyes melting into approval, which he wasn't looking for, although it made sense for him to get used to the baby.

'Great. The sling is quite easy really. It'll need adjusting. You're not my size but—'

'No,' Zac interrupted the flow. There were limitations, and wearing the baby carrier was one of them. 'I'll carry him, if you trust me.'

'Of course!' she said, sounding outraged at the idea she wouldn't as she freed the baby from the baby carrier and carefully transferred him to Zac. 'You're his…' She paused. 'Are you going to adopt him?'

'Apparently that is an option. Liam will always be Declan's father.'

'Of course, but a boy needs a dad too. Your father died but he is still your father.'

Zac pulled himself back from the edge of throwing the truth back at her, revealing that, as much as he'd like to forget his father, he never could. That he'd spent his life watching for signs that he was anything like the dead man, guarding against anything resembling a paternal character trait that was hiding in his DNA, that he needed control to do that and now she was in danger of splintering it… She was pounding away at the protective wall he'd built in a way that no one had before.

He even kept his family that side of the protective wall built to shield the people he cared for, not himself.

The thoughts slid through his head, invisible behind the cold mask he wore. 'I am aware of that.'

She had hit a nerve. How, why, she had no idea.

Zac seemed deep in thought. His body language did not encourage conversation as they walked up the hill, which actually was quite steep. Breathless by the time she reached the top, she was glad he was carrying the baby.

They walked through the open gates into a cobbled courtyard filled with a succession of bubbling fountains and geometric flower beds spilling colour onto the stone. The sea, which had been to their left as they climbed the hill, was now directly in front of them, visible above the terracotta-tiled roof where the aquamarine blended seamlessly into the blue of the sky, but revealed more dramatically through a massive stone arch that acted as a portrait frame for a breathtaking view of the gardens running down to the sand and endless sea.

Enchanted, she spread her arms wide as though embracing the view. 'How do you ever leave here?' she wondered out loud.

Zac normally felt a lightening of his mood as he stepped through the gates, but on this occasion the magic failed to work. The weight that had lain across his shoulders, a burden that was not physical, did not lift as he walked into the courtyard.

But as Rose spoke and he heard the unfiltered pleasure in her voice and read the uncomplicated joy on her face he felt lighter.

Her unfeigned pleasure was contagious. She was living totally in the moment, which was a rare ability.

'I had no idea...' She looked from right to left, saw the whitewashed walls glinting in the sun, taking in the sheer size of the place. 'It's so big! Did you extend on the original building?'

'It was hard to tell how big the place was originally.

It was derelict and there were no records and the locals seem to think that the villa I rebuilt was built on the site of a previous villa that was much grander. The old land-scaped gardens, which we uncovered by accident, could have belonged to that earlier building. They were certainly very elaborate for what was an olive farm.'

'You recreated the gardens.' What she had seen of them was impressive.

'As much as possible, we kept what original features in the house there were and used reclaimed materials in the build for the most part. There are some skilled crafts-men locally. They were ingenious in recreating incomplete and damaged features.'

Rose nodded. She couldn't wait to see the interior.

'Come,' he added, glancing at her hair that blazed in the sunlight as he gestured to the building they stood in front of. 'I think we could do with some shade.'

Rose gave a self-recriminatory grimace and glanced anxiously at Declan. She had been so busy admiring the building that she had neglected her charge.

'Sorry,' she said, following him through the arch.

He paused, looking mystified. 'Why?'

'I was chattering on while the baby…his skin needs protecting.'

'The baby has barely a centimetre of skin exposed. It was your skin I was thinking about.' Almost continually. The thought of feasting his eyes on the smooth paleness, of exploring it with his fingers, tongue and mouth, feeling her skin cool or hot beneath him…had become a constant. And now the images, sparked into life by his thoughts, glutted his senses, requiring a long sense-cooling moment before he could continue speaking without betraying himself and his growing obsession.

'You are very fair. Redheads burn, don't they? You should wear a hat while you're here.'

'Yes, I suppose I should... I freckle terribly.' She touched her small straight nose and grimaced.

'I like freckles.'

Rose told herself not to be flattered. There was liking and *liking* and it was telling that the assets his dates boasted were not freckles!

Without warning he walked away. Rose started to follow, glancing around curiously as she hurried to keep him in sight. There was a lot to take in. The infinity pool below a terrace that surrounded this side of the villa took second place to the blue blaze of the shimmering sea beyond. The building itself was on three sides of where they stood. There were several arches cut into the stone smaller than the one they had entered, but beyond she had glimpses of what seemed to be a series of internal courtyards.

He led her to a doorway, not as large as the one in the outer courtyard, and swung around without warning, causing her to step back and the baby to gurgle excitedly.

CHAPTER TEN

'I LIKE YOUR stutter too.' The words emerged almost sounding as if he had spoken against his will.

Rose's mind froze at the unexpected compliment and the air of compulsion with which he delivered it.

Was there a punchline?

Was he joking?

His expression didn't suggest anything so harmless and light-hearted, but neither was there anything remotely seductive in his clenched mouth and taut, almost angry stare.

Kick-starting her brain, she followed him into the interior, finding herself standing in what seemed to be an inner hallway filled with scent from the massive terracotta bowl of rosemary in flower, the pale pastel purple of the flowers pale against the deep green of the leaves.

There were several doors leading off it, but she struggled to keep up with his low-voiced explanation or the decoration, maybe both. She simply couldn't focus so she gave up trying as he spoke about the massive arched, bleached supportive beam overhead being reclaimed from an ancient tree on the estate that had come down in a storm.

All she could think was…he *likes* my stutter.

It took her a few moments to connect the buzz of silence with the fact he was no longer speaking, which meant that she ought to be. 'It is very beautiful.'

It was. The floor underfoot was some sort of limed wood, the beams of the high ceiling exposed the dark rafters that provided a dramatic foil for rough white-washed stone, the few items of furniture were all rustic and the original artwork on the walls provided dramatic splashes of colour.

'But do you get the general layout?' He sounded impatient. 'It's quite simple if you just keep in mind that—'

'Yes,' she lied without hesitation. No way would she admit she hadn't heard a word he had said.

'So, Camille will see you to your rooms, show you the nursery facilities and, when you are ready, sit with Declan while you have dinner.'

For the first time she noticed the slim dark haired girl who was standing just behind her. 'Thank you, Camille,' she said, smiling at the girl. 'But it will be easier if I have dinner in my room. I don't like to leave Declan.'

'Camille, as I have explained, is perfectly capable of looking after a baby. We are lucky to have her to help out during the university vacation.'

The dark-haired young woman looked pleased at the compliment, and, being a female with a brain and not an overactive imagination, *she* didn't overreact and think his comment had any deep hidden message.

'I like babies when I can hand them back.'

Her English was faultless.

'As I said, Camille has six younger siblings so plenty of experience and she will be available to help out most days. Oh, and do not say bad things about the house-keeper in front of her—she is Sybil's niece.' He added a postscript in Greek, which made the brunette laugh.

'Oh, well, yes, that would be...fine, then, I think...?' Given the option of protesting further would make her look slightly unhinged, she put as good a face on the situation as possible. There was always the chance that she would be dining alone...

'Can I take him?' the young girl asked, flashing Rose a questioning look as she walked towards Zac.

Rose felt a wave of relief. It wasn't as if she'd been *dreading* stepping in close to take Declan off his guardian, but to be relieved of that moment was not something she was going to refuse.

She watched the transfer from a safe distance, if a safe distance existed when it came to Zac and his overwhelming masculinity.

She watched as his arrogant profile softened, the lines radiating from the corners of his eyes deepening as he smiled down at the baby, and Rose felt as if a hand had reached inside her chest and squeezed hard.

Common sense told her this was about hormones, and primitive urges. She wasn't going to pretend these things were not happening, but she didn't have to over-analyse them. It didn't matter how or why this was happening now, it was, and she just had to deal with it.

There was no point being defeatist. She couldn't allow this...hormone thing to ruin what could be a fantastic experience. It was pathetic, so passive.

If she was to enjoy the opportunity to appreciate her Greece stay, she needed a coping strategy. She'd tried to pretend it wasn't happening and that hadn't worked. So a new strategy, and for starters she wasn't going to over-analyse it.

Because maybe you wouldn't like the answers?

She knew a nettle would bring her out in a rash, so she

didn't touch it. It made sense not to touch Zac. Could it be that simple?

She sighed. If only... A nettle didn't have a voice that stroked the nerve endings in her skin like a caress, it didn't have a mouth... Actually the entire analogy was rubbish, whichever way you looked at it.

'Hello, baby... Oh, he's so lovely... Come on, baby Declan, let's show you your room.'

Rose waited until she saw which door the young woman was headed for then followed. She didn't look but she knew his eyes were following her, the skin on the nape of her neck tingling, the tiny hairs on her skin dancing.

The nursery suite, when they reached it, was charming. And, considering it must literally have been created overnight, remarkably well equipped—from the drawers of neatly folded baby clothes to the colourful playroom filled with toys.

It had its own little kitchen complete with some chilled wine in the fridge, which she assumed was a thoughtful addition for her, though she had to question the professionalism of sampling it in charge of a baby. She left Camille while she did a quick tour of her own section of the suite.

Her bedroom, utterly charming with a cool dark wooden floor and bleached oak furniture, was a million miles from anything she had ever lived with. No flatpack cheap and cheerful, but items with workmanship that spoke of hours and hours of the loving care and skill that went into each individual piece's creation. She walked through the open French door onto a Juliet balcony that looked directly onto the infinity pool she had spotted from the air, and the sea beyond.

If the bedroom was charming, her bathroom was genuine *wow*! The stone-lined shower had high-tech digital controls that were slightly daunting. What was tempting and not daunting was the free-standing copper bath deep enough to float in that was set beside a full-height window that overlooked the ocean.

Rose could easily imagine herself setting up residence in the bath—with that view, what would be the reason to get out? Longing to linger and maybe try out the decadent tub, she hurried back to the nursery kitchen where Camille was humming a soft melody to a heavy-eyed Declan.

She smiled and lifted a finger to her lips when she saw Rose. 'I changed him,' she whispered, adding a mouthed, Shall I put him in his crib…?

Rose nodded and felt slightly redundant. Camille seemed super-efficient. She left her to it and followed the coffee smell and poured herself a cup, then, putting her bottom onto one of the high stools that faced a small island unit, sat and waited for Camille.

She didn't have long to wait. 'He was asleep before I put him down.'

'Thanks,' Rose said, lifting her mug, and added, 'This too. Just what I was longing for.'

'No need to thank me. If I wasn't here I'd be babysitting my twin brothers who are eleven, so thank you, you have saved me!'

'What university do you go to?'

'Athens. I'm in my final year, maths, but I just got accepted at Imperial for my masters, so this job is useful.

Actually I wouldn't be going at all if it wasn't for Mr Adamos.'

'How so?'

'Well, not him personally, at least that's what he said when I thanked him, but the Adamos Foundation provides bursaries for students who have brains but no cash—that's me,' she said cheerily.

'That's fantastic. When you come to London you'll have to look me up.'

'You live in London? I'm so jealous.'

'You live here. I'm so jealous!'

They both laughed.

When Camille left it was agreed that she'd return to babysit around seven-thirty when she said dinner was served.

She actually arrived at six-thirty with a laptop and a stack of books. Rose was still in a big fluffy robe from a hamper with a pile of them in the bathroom. Her hair, half dried, hung loose and almost to her waist.

'I'm late!' she exclaimed when Camille appeared.

'No, I'm early. I'm always early,' the girl admitted. 'Can I do anything?'

'No, Declan has had his bath and feed and he's settled well. Apparently he had colic quite badly recently, so if you have any problems you will come and get me...'

'Of course, no problem, go eat, but maybe get dressed first?'

Rose laughed and whisked away to her bedroom. Picking an outfit was quite simple as there was a choice of two and the cotton sundress was creased even after she had hung it in the bathroom in the hope of getting the creases out. She was sure that she could have just asked and an iron would have appeared but the second option was fine.

The pair of wide-legged trousers had folded to almost nothing in her bag but as she laid them on the bed the silky black fabric was totally crease-free. She had brought a couple of white tee shirts to team with them in the daytime but the black boxy-shaped top, sleeveless with a simple scoop neck in the front and a deep vee in the back, was her go-to for more dressy occasions.

Under her gown she was wearing a tiny silky bra and pants. After she pulled the trousers up over her hips and fastened the zip she realised that she must have lost a few pounds since she'd last worn them, but the cut covered a multitude of sins except, in this instance, her waist. She hitched them higher but they slid down again. Even if she'd had a belt to secure them, there were no belt loops.

No point stressing, it wasn't noticeable and the top would disguise the problem—except of course it didn't. The boxy-cut top ended where the waistband of the trousers began, which was perfect but became less than perfect when she moved. Every time she did a sliver of stomach came into view, not exactly illegal or even particularly daring but tonight it made her uneasy.

Not a lot to do about that, she decided, except maybe not move... Finding the block-heeled mules she'd brought, she slipped them on, raising her height by three inches. She bent towards the mirror, to check out the make-up she had applied earlier. She had to lean in a little closer because there wasn't much of it. After a moment's reflection she added a swipe of mascara to her already dark lashes and a smudge of grey eyeshadow, and applied a second coat of gloss to her lips.

There was no time to tame her hair, so she bent forward and ran her fingers through the auburn strands before tossing it back with a drastic swoosh. She didn't want to look as if she was trying too hard, or at all really.

Looking at her reflection in the mirror, Rose laughed and thought, Not much chance of that! And trying too hard for whom? The chances were she would be eating alone and she was acting as though she were on a date! And she was getting all stomach fluttery on the off chance he'd join her.

But he hadn't said he *wouldn't* be joining her.

She looked in on the sleeping baby, his face illuminated by the night light on a dresser. The impulse to pick him up and hold him, and most likely wake him up, was hard to resist. Her smile faded as she thought of generations of nannies who cared for children, loved them and in some cases were the only parent the child knew, only to be given their marching orders when the child got too old to need a nanny.

Heartbreaking… She had only been caring for Declan for a couple of days but already she knew that it would be desperately hard to say goodbye. How soon did it take to fall in love? It was love at first sight for many mothers, and some adoptive parents too who hadn't given birth… It was as if the helplessness of a baby roused protective impulses, brought out the nurturing instincts.

Quietly leaving the room, she looked in on Camille, who was perched on one of the high stools in the kitchen, her computer and books set up on the work surface.

'Wow, you look great!' she said when she saw Rose.

Rose smiled. 'Thanks. You know where I am if you need me,' she said, which was more than she did.

As if reading her thoughts Camille ripped a page from

her notepad. 'Though this might help until you get your bearings.'

Rose took the paper and studied a detailed neat line plan of the villa.

'You will note the *"we are here"* and bingo is where you're going.'

'Oh, that is just so kind. I have the worst sense of direction,' she admitted ruefully. 'I spent half an hour trying to find a particular department store in a shopping precinct and then an hour trying to find the exit. I was too embarrassed to ask for help.'

The girl chuckled. 'See you later and don't worry about the time. I've got plenty to keep me occupied.'

Rose tried to pick out landmarks to help her remember the route as she navigated her way using the plan. When she arrived at the bingo door it was half open. She folded the plan and tucked it in the pocket of her trousers, and, taking a deep breath, she tapped on the door, called out, 'Hello,' and walked inside.

The room was empty. She told herself she was glad as her eyes moved around the room, taking in the open doors and the terrace beyond. The dark table was set for two, candles as yet unlit, and she hoped they stayed that way, in an eclectic selection of rustic holders, different sizes and textures, some glass, some wood, beautiful and also disturbingly intimate.

Her eyes centred on the wine chilling in the bucket of ice. Dutch courage or not, it was a good thing that the cork was undisturbed or she might have been tempted, because as appealing as the thought of a glass was, she was in charge of a baby.

As she walked around the room taking in all the quirky

artistic touches, it was hard to believe that the man who lived here was the same man who based himself in the soulless London flat.

The answer to the mystery was probably as simple as two different interior designers.

A noise behind her made her spin around, heart pumping. When she saw Arthur standing in the doorway the anticlimax was intense. *All pumped up and nowhere to go*, mocked the voice in her head.

'Hi there,' he said, hovering half in and half out of the room.

She painted on a bright smile. 'Are we eating together?'

He looked initially startled by the suggestion, then laughed. 'What? Oh, no, the boss sent me to apologise, he's stuck on a call. He said for you to start without him.'

'I wasn't sure he was joining me...' But the possibility had filled her stomach with butterflies...and made her add the mascara. She glanced at the empty table. 'Start what?'

'God, yes, sorry.' He entered the room and walked over to a slate-topped table, pressed a button and doors glided apart revealing shelves housing containers...quite obviously food, by the smell.

'The boss had this contraption made to order. He works some pretty unsocial hours, and eats the same way, actually sometimes forgets to eat. This saves the staff hanging around waiting. He thought you might appreciate the informality, first night and all, long journey...'

Rose received this information in silence.

Arthur was looking at her a little uncertainly, as if he was struggling to gauge her reaction. 'You tuck in.'

'Oh, I will,' she promised, floating out a brilliant and brittle smile.

When he had gone she stood there and swore. Well, she'd got what she wanted: a nice peaceful dinner with no Zac Adamos making her feel self-conscious and ill at ease. Yet at the same time there was a connection that she couldn't explain. It was as if looking at him she were looking into a mirror and seeing the things about herself she kept secret from the world...even herself...

The idea made her feel uneasy as she walked over and began to lift lids. From chilled soup to chicken in some sort of delicate sauce that smelt wonderful, it all looked delicious. She unenthusiastically ladled some soup into a dish and carried it to the table. She had lost her appetite, and her wandering glance landed on the chilling bottle.

She stood up and reached across, pulling it from the ice with a smile of defiance on her lips. Pulling the cork was less easy than she had anticipated. She struggled with it for a minute or so but when it came she got the dramatic flourish she'd wanted. It exploded like...well, like a bottle of champagne that someone had just shaken half to death.

The white tablecloth had absorbed most of the liquid but there were some small pools on the polished wood floor. She looked in the bottle and laughed as her anger drained away, leaving her feeling pretty foolish and very glad there had been no one around to witness her temper tantrum, and all that breathless anticipation that she had refused to recognise for what it was—a passing meaningless comment. With a groan she lifted the bottle to her lips and drained the last teaspoon of champagne that remained in the bottle.

Just because he said he liked my stutter! Rose closed her eyes, feeling unbelievably stupid.

CHAPTER ELEVEN

BACK IN THE NURSERY, Camille was surprised to see her so soon.

'I wasn't very hungry.'

The girl wrinkled her nose. 'What is that smell?'

'I had an incident with a glass of wine.' She tugged at her top, which was clinging unpleasantly.

'Oh, that's... She looked at Rose's face. 'So not a good evening?'

'Not so much,' Rose agreed.

'Do you want me to do anything? There's coffee on the go.'

Rose smiled her gratitude. 'No, you get off and I'll get out of these soggy things. How was Declan?'

'Great. He woke after you'd left but once I patted his back for a while he went straight back off.'

When Camille had collected her things and left Rose headed for her room, desperate to strip off and shower. She paused in the doorway of the nursery, smiling as she heard the sound of his even breathing.

She walked over to the cot and looked down at the baby-soft features, and wondered how her own mother could have walked away from her. If you couldn't trust your own mother, who could you trust? Which was one reason she was never going to put her trust in another person. If that meant she became a sad woman with a cat, so what? It was better than being rejected.

'They wouldn't have left you, never think that. Your mum and dad would have loved you. Your new dad will love you too.'

A child should always know they were loved and wanted.

Rose had reached her bedroom when she heard a soft tap on the door. Assuming that Camille had forgotten something, she swallowed her irritation and went to answer it.

She opened the door and her glance travelled upwards, stopping when it reached his face. The sensual jolt to her senses when she saw him standing there had stalled her brain, cognitive thought was not on the agenda, just shaking and feeling, feeling too much. It was a definite overload.

Zac's nostrils flared at the odour of alcohol. Realising his suspicion was correct gave him no satisfaction.

He was angry, but also felt pity, though it was hard to feel sympathy for someone who was throwing away their life. He'd known people who'd lost everything...but some came back after reaching rock bottom.

'Is Camille here?'

Rose shook her head, not trusting her vocal cords to respond.

'Then I think I'd better come in,' he said grimly.

Her chin went up. 'And I think you'd better not,' she retorted.

'Look, it's none of my business what you do to yourself but when you're in charge of a baby that is very much my business.'

She planted her hands on her hips, angling a look of

angry mystification up at him. 'What the hell are you t-talking about?'

'There's no point denying it, you reek of the stuff.'

'Reek of…?' The dots in her head suddenly connected and made crazy sense. 'You think I've been drinking?'

Her voice was so low he could barely catch the words. At least she wasn't slurring, not yet anyhow. How was he going to tell Marco? *Was* he going to tell Marco?

Where the hell did that crazy thought come from? Enabling an addict was not protecting them… Protecting. Why had that been his first instinct and since when did protecting a woman he'd known for five minutes trump the loyalty to one of his oldest friends?

'Look, there are people that can help. The first thing you have to do is accept you have a problem.'

Her eyes narrowed. 'Oh, I know I have a problem and it's six feet four and a half,' she sneered, allowing her eyes to run the head-to-toe length of his long, lean body. 'You think I'd get drunk when I'm looking after a baby! You're the one who left wine in the fridge. What do you think I am? Cancel that,' she added bitterly. 'I already know. Oh, God, I think I hate you!'

Zac's nostrils flared as he fought to contain his anger. 'Don't try and turn this around. I saw the empty bottle. I smelt the booze.'

'Of course you smelt the booze, you stupid man! The bloody bottle exploded when I tried to open it. It went everywhere. I took a champagne shower!' An expression of distaste on her face, she plucked at her wet clinging top.

'You…?' For the first time he took in her damp trousers and drenched top that lovingly outlined the hard peaks of her taut breasts. His head went back as he half smiled and gave a sigh of relief.

'How could you think I would do that? If you don't believe me, breathalyse me.'

'I don't have one on me at the moment.'

'Right, then, smell…' Grabbing his jacket, she stretched up until her forehead was level with his chin. His head bent, and a thrill of excitement shot through her as their glances connected and held.

What are you doing, Rose?

She reacted to the sliver of sanity by sinking down onto her heels and releasing his jacket, only to find her efforts countered by a strong arm that had snaked around her waist. Instead of sinking down she found her toes trailing on the ground and her upper body crushed against a chest that had no give.

'I…'

A finger hooked under her chin refused to allow her to escape his burning, stomach-melting stare.

'It's hard to tell from smell alone.'

'Well, you'll just have to t-trust me,' she responded shakily, barely able to hear her whisper above the sound of her laboured rasping inhalations.

'How about tasting you? I remember how you tasted.'

The throaty purr sent a fresh rush of debilitating weakness through her body. Her knees sagged and her clamped lips couldn't stop a lost cry of longing escaping, and then there was no escape. Her breath was mingled with his as his tongue slid into her mouth. She focused on the taste of him as their tongues collided, starting a primal chain reaction that swept her away… She gasped, feeling his hand on her breast, causing him to pull back enough to bite her lip and stare with burning eyes into her passion-flushed face.

'Do you believe I'm sober now?' she rasped, not recognising her own voice, or the deep desire to feel all of the power of his hard body, to feel him unleashed… Shiver after shiver of excitement ran through her body. For the first time in her ordered adult life, she longed to let go, to lose control.

But this was not right, this was too soon, he was not her soulmate, he was not the special someone she could trust with her life or her heart… The tipping point came when she looked up at him and knew that she wanted him more than she wanted to stay safe in her emotionally sterile bubble.

'That strip and shower… I like that idea…'

She gave a tiny mute affirmative nod of her head.

'You know I want you,' he rasped sealing their bodies thigh to thigh.

She swallowed. 'It feels that way.'

'Your skin tastes of champagne…nice…' he murmured, running his tongue along the curve of her jaw. 'But I'd prefer it tasted of me. That *I* tasted of you.'

'Oh, God!' She groaned against his mouth, the dark dirty images his words evoked making her weak with lust. 'Yes, please.'

She felt so light when he picked her up, her bones so delicate, her skin so soft, she was so fragile… But the small hands that slid down his back massaging the muscles had strength and determination he quite definitely approved of as she began to slip the buttons on his shirt, sliding her flat palm over the now damp skin of his chest and shoulders.

It was a short distance to the decadent bathroom but they were both panting like runners approaching the finishing post when he placed her on her feet. For a second her gaze was drawn past him as Rose caught sight of herself in a mirror. The person who stared back at her was a stranger. She barely recognised herself, the hectic flush of arousal on her cheeks, the incandescent glow in her eyes... She not only felt like a different person, she looked like one too.

'You're shaking.'

She nodded mutely.

The tremors that shook her began deep in her core, the waves spreading out involving every nerve ending, every inch of her skin.

He framed her face in his hands and drew back slightly. 'You're burning up.'

She was burning for him.

She nodded and sealed her fate. The need that consumed him beyond logical explanation was greater than his loyalty to a friend, greater than any other consideration at that moment.

'Then you don't need this.'

Zac held her eyes as he took the hem of her top. Not trying to escape his carnal stare, she felt more aroused than she had ever imagined possible. Rose lifted her arms and he peeled the sodden, spoiled garment over her head and dropped it on the floor.

Rose reached for her bra and unfastened the clip, letting her breasts spring free as it fell to the floor. She lifted her chin. She didn't have a clue why she wasn't self-conscious. It was as if he had awakened something in her that had lain dormant. She had never felt sexy and desirable before in this way—the idea of a man like Zac wanting her was incredibly arousing.

His eyes darkened as he stared down at the hard-peaked soft mounds. 'Perfect.' He kissed her hard on the lips before weighing one smooth rosy-tipped globe in the palm of his hand. She whimpered as he rubbed his thumb across the peak, drawing a series of low moans from her lips, before he replaced it with his lips and tongue.

She clung so hard to stop falling down that his shirt was half undone by the time his ministrations stopped. Her eyes flew wide as he dropped to his knees, then, with one hand spanning her narrow ribcage, he used his free hand to unzip her trousers and slide them down her thighs.

She was giving him the power to hurt her, and she had never imagined feeling this way, accepting the possibility was there but willing to take the risk. Maybe one day she would regret this decision but now, in this moment, she knew if she didn't take the leap into the unknown there was no question she *would* regret never knowing.

She shivered even though the wildness in her veins, the heat rising up in her, were like a furnace. He began to strip and she forgot how to breathe. He was ripping his clothes off in a frenzy of impatience, an impatience that she shared. She wanted passion to burn away all the doubts and fears that had been there all her life. She wanted to lose herself in him.

His chest was bare and he had just kicked away his trousers, naked but for the boxers that hung low on his narrow hips, inadequate to hide the strength of his arousal.

'I need…' She stopped, rose up on her toes and curved her hands around the back of Zac's head, her fingers sliding into his thick hair, her aching breasts pressed against his hair-roughened chest. Her hands slid over the smooth satiny muscles defining his shoulders, then lower to his waist.

As they kissed hungrily, teeth clashing, tongues tangling and probing, she was so focused that she didn't register the fact his hands had slid under her bottom and he had picked her up until he stepped with her into the shower enclosure and switched on the water.

The shock of the warm water pummelling her skin made her gasp as he put her on her feet, and she stood, her head back, as he dragged the pants down her legs. A second later he performed the same task for himself.

The wet, slick skin-to-skin contact drew a keening cry of pleasure from Rose's throat. She felt soft and small, feminine compared to Zac's hard masculinity. The abrasive pressure of his erection against her belly sent the ache between her legs to another level. She rubbed herself against him, the friction feeding the consuming hunger that was exploding inside her, and let his eyes devour her.

She enjoyed this wanton version of herself, she even enjoyed being shocked by it. It was wildly liberating.

His molten eyes glowed. He looked fierce and dangerous, his hair and body slicked with water as he smiled a slow wicked smile, and she felt as if her heart would stop.

She saw the soap in his hands and had no idea how it had got there. She leaned against the wall, head tilted back, an expression of rapt enjoyment on her face as the water pummelled.

He soaped her breasts, his hands massaging and stroking, driving her wild, paying special attention to her painfully erect nipples before sliding his hands lower and then dropping on his knees. The stubble on his cheek and jaw burned her inner thigh. She was floating in a mindless, sensual haze of need that infiltrated every cell of her body.

'What…?' Her eyes flew wide with protest and then

he was back, a foil packet in his hand. 'I'll keep you safe, don't worry.'

She knew what he meant but there was another sort of safe—a safe he would never give her—

She closed off the line of thought before it took her into forbidden territory—if she had regrets it would not be now.

Holding her gaze, he took her hands and pressed them to the wall of the cubicle, walking into her until their bodies collided slick skin against slick skin.

If there ever had been a moment to tell him that this was her first time it wasn't now. The possibility that he might walk away, leaving her quite broken, was not a risk she could take.

His hands cupped her buttocks. As he lifted her up his gaze was searing. 'Wrap your legs around me and hold on.'

Her head fell onto his shoulder as she did as he asked, her slim legs tight around his waist. She moaned at the hard male contact, the pressure at the apex of her legs as her sex throbbed with a need that matched his, and she moved suggestively against him following instincts as old as time, making no secret of the fact she wanted him.

An animal groan broke from the vault of his chest as Zac slid into her heat, gasping at the tightness of her as she closed around him.

Her back arched, her head falling back to expose the beautiful arc of her neck, the line between pleasure and pain blurred, and she felt a moment's panic. What if she did it wrong?

'Don't know what to…' Her voice cracked and she bit into his shoulder.

The truth came to him and the shock that reverberated through him gave way to a possessive tenderness that he had never experienced before. He had never slept with a virgin before, never felt the primal urge to be any woman's first lover.

'Relax...there are no rules except the ones we make.'

'This is...you are incredible!' She gasped, feeling the tingle of her blood as she moved to meet him, draw him deeper, his throaty voice in her ear saying words she didn't need translating, his breath on her skin. She could feel the beautiful sleek, hard muscle of him everywhere. Her nerve endings were screaming a tactile blending with the pounding thud of her tumultuous pulse. The paper-thin skin of her delicate eyelids was no protection from his hot dark gaze as he pushed her towards a goal just out of reach—then it wasn't out of reach. The breath-catching crescendo, when it hit her, was so intense she clung to him, afraid of being washed away by the tsunami of sensation as his sleek, muscular body surged powerfully against hers.

In the final moment of perfect fusion Rose called out his name in the last shuddering surge as the ecstasy hit.

She felt as though she were floating but in reality she was sinking to the floor of the shower. Their eyes sealed, they knelt, arms wrapped around each other as they fought for breath.

'Oh, God!' she said finally. 'That was...oh, God!' She wanted to laugh and cry. Instead she pushed her face into his shoulder.

'That was good sex.'

She felt tension slide into her shoulders. Was the emphasis she heard on *sex* real or imagined, and was the silent *just* she heard the addition of her own paranoia?

Rose wished it were. It was a mystery how one person could make love and the other could just have sex—

She stopped herself taking this depressing thought to the next level. She was going to get her heart broken, that was a given, but why anticipate the moment? It made much more sense to enjoy the moment that they were living.

As she disentangled herself from him and attempted to stand up, her legs folded. They were shaking, a reaction to the intensity of what they had shared.

'Are you all right?' He was on his own feet in a split second, a hand stretched out to pull her up, the other behind him to turn the water off.

She accepted it, crossing her free hand across her breasts, the display of modesty definitely a 'closing the stable door after the horse has already bolted' gesture.

'What can I say? You make me go weak at the knees.' Sometimes the truth was the best defence but not this time—she missed jokey by a country mile. It was the moment to stop digging or in this case talking...only she couldn't. 'I've never made—had sex in a shower before.' On the plus side, she closed her mouth before she could ask him if he had shower sex often.

'I am aware of that,' he responded in a voice loaded with meaning. 'A little warning upfront might have been good, do you not think?'

So he knew.

She wasn't sure how to deal with the unspoken question so she ignored it. Maybe he was actually quite glad she had dodged the issue, because though she thought he might press her, instead his glance slid from hers. Perhaps he wasn't so comfortable with discussing it either.

'Thanks,' she murmured as he draped a large bath

sheet around her. There was nothing lover-like about the gesture but it felt almost more intimate than sex. His gentleness brought a lump to her throat. She had stripped naked and not felt a scrap of self-consciousness yet having him gently pat her dry overwhelmed her with shyness. That was, she acknowledged, deeply strange.

While he covered her Zac didn't seem in any hurry to cover himself. He had a total lack of inhibitions, which was a situation she could live with. He really was beautiful, she reflected, following him with her eyes as he padded across to one of the heated ladder rails and grabbed a towel, which he looped casually around his middle, pausing to rub his forearm across the misted mirror.

She gave a helpless sigh of appreciation—every etched and carved line of his sleek muscled body was perfection. But mid appreciation she was hit by a sudden avalanche of emotions, intertwined and confusing. She had to stop thinking about it. She needed to follow his prompt and adopt Zac's attitude. It was sex, great sex, but just sex.

Except of course it wasn't, not for her. The emotions involved had been intense, scarily so. She pushed it all away, suddenly too tired to think about it. This was the new Rose who lived in the moment and extracted every last drop of living from it.

She was in her bathroom with a naked man.

What happened next?

'What happens next is we take this to the bedroom.'

Rose clamped a hand to her mouth—she'd said it out loud.

'If that is something you would like?'

'That would be nice.' *Nice, Rose! Really...?*

'Yes, I think it would be very nice too.' The fact was he could not get enough of her. She took the hand he stretched out and he pulled her towards him before scooping her up and carrying her into the bedroom, the feel of her warm, damp, soft body reawakening his hunger.

Zac knew he'd crossed a line Marco-wise but, given the same choice, he'd have done the same thing again. It was a line he'd been aching to cross since the first second he saw her. Nothing to do with logic—it was on an instinctive level.

He'd known it would be incredible…and *Theos*! It had surpassed anything he had imagined, but to realise that she had come to him a virgin! The revelation ought to have horrified him but instead it had just fed the possessiveness that she brought out in him.

He had built his life with walls of isolation that afforded him, and more importantly those he cared for, safety. For the first time those walls had taken a battering. In a matter of hours Rose Hill had done some serious damage. She'd made him think what it would be like to bring her inside his walls and keep her safe that way.

Rose's level of anticipation was off the scale as he laid her down on the bed and joined her, leaning over her, one hand braced on the headboard, the other caressing her face.

'I thought you didn't date staff.'

Zac barely heard her. He was seeing her soft lips open to him and thinking of her legs opening to him.

He kissed her as if he'd drain her before saying thickly, 'I don't. But you are not staff, you are… Rose.'

'I'm special.' She bit her lips and stopped herself adding 'not just convenient'. She didn't want to know, she just wanted this.

She just wanted him.

'I want you so much I'm sick with it,' he husked, trailing kisses up her neck until he found her mouth before pulling the billowing sheet over them and burrowing into her softness.

'This is…' He had reached midway down her belly and she had forgotten how to breathe.

His head lifted, the bands of colour along his cheekbone highlighting the razor edges. His eyes were dark and hot enough to drown in.

'You don't like it?

'I love it… I love…' She paused, her eyes squeezed tight as she said the forbidden words in her head… *I love you.* 'All of it,' she added out loud. She felt the heat of his mouth on her again and squeezed her eyes tight. 'And I like everything you do,' she declared with admirable understatement.

He encouraged her insatiable curiosity for exploring his body until it came to the point when her lips and tongue were eating into his self-control.

He took her hands, pinned them above her head and kissed her, not hard but with a debilitating tenderness that brought tears of emotion to her eyes.

'Have you any idea how many fantasies about your body I have had?'

Her breath came quick and fast, the tingle under her skin now a fire.

'Let's try slow, shall we, and see how that works out?'

Afraid to break the spell his voice had woven, she said nothing as he touched her face, one brown finger tracing a path down her jaw then across the fullness of her plump lower lip. Rose opened her mouth and caught his finger between her teeth before catching his hand and pressing his palm to her moist lips, dropping it with a low guttural moan when he covered her mouth with his. Then there were more kisses, more caresses until her senses were singing.

She opened her eyes and looked up at his dark face above her and realised that she wanted him body and soul. She wanted him with a ferocity that scared her, feeling this much scared her. Emotion thickened her throat.

'You're so beautiful,' she whispered, trailing a hand down the damp skin of his chest and across the ridges of his flat belly, loving the texture, loving... With a little shake of her head she closed the avenue of thought and allowed her hand to slide lower, watching his eyes darken as her fingers closed around his shaft.

It wasn't just her touch that was torturing him, it was her big eyes wanting him, her big eyes touching a corner of his heart that had been in cold storage. Like blood returning to a frozen extremity, the sensation was pain, pleasure.

'Slow, remember,' he whispered against her mouth as he flipped her over to switch their positions. 'I want you to enjoy this. I want this to be special...' You deserve special, he thought, reminding himself that this was all new for her. And as he dug into patience and tenderness that he'd never known he possessed, it all felt new for him too.

'You are special, Zac.' She groaned as he slid an explosive hand between her legs.

He was the pure essence of all things male. Longing had stripped her of logic and pride and she writhed beneath the delicious torture of his clever carnal caresses as he devoted attention to every inch of her body.

It was Rose who, unable to bear another moment of the delicious torture, guided him between her legs, to feel him above her, inside her. The measured power of his thrusts drove her to a place where nothing existed beyond the two of them, their mingled gasps and moans, until the climax happened and she stopped breathing, just focused on everything that was happening inside her.

During the golden glow of the aftermath she lay with her head on his chest, her limbs weighed down by a soft lethargy until, finally summoning the energy, she lifted her head.

'Slow works for me.' As she curled up into him she missed the startled look on his face before he brought his arms around her.

Zac felt the moment her breathing changed and drew back to look at her sleeping face.

Her face lit by a light set in a stone embrasure above the bed, she looked a million miles from the wanton version of Rose, the uninhibited Rose who had matched him for passion. The sleeping Rose looked vulnerable, she looked as if she could break, which he knew was a lie. The woman he had made love to had been strong and fierce.

Were there any more Roses to discover?

She wouldn't be in his life long enough for him to find out. They were sharing a moment, not a life.

He could have retreated and taken refuge in his own bed—it was his normal modus operandi. Instead Zac switched off the light. He fell asleep smelling her hair.

CHAPTER TWELVE

WHEN ZAC WOKE up in the night he reached out groggily but found the bed beside him empty. He sat bolt upright and, without thinking, threw back the covers and swung his legs over the side, and as his feet hit the floor he heard a baby noise—noise as opposed to cry.

Pulling on the boxers he had taken off before he got into bed beside her, he headed to the nursery, and found the door open, the room lit by a rotating night light that threw illuminated animal shadows on the walls and ceiling.

Rose was standing in the middle of the room singing softly to the baby in her arms. As if she sensed his presence, her head lifted, her eyes widening as she saw him. She froze, then, after a moment of standing there transfixed, she glanced down at the baby before placing a finger to her lips in warning as her gaze returned to Zac.

He watched as she went over to the cot and laid her burden down before drawing the sheet up over him, and felt something shift and tighten in his chest. For several moments Zac forgot how to breathe.

She looked up, a question appearing in her eyes as their glances connected.

There was a tense silent beat.

This is just sex, Zac reminded himself.

On this perspective-establishing thought, he heard himself blurt stupidly, 'I like your perfume.'

He watched a confused groove appear in her smooth brow, which, given he sounded like some sort of tongue-tied teenage idiot, was not to be wondered at.

'I don't wear perfume,' she whispered back, glancing over her shoulder to check he hadn't woken the baby.

He turned and walked out of the room, glad of the sense-cooling moment before Rose joined him, carefully leaving the door ajar.

'Sorry to disturb you,' she whispered, her eyelids lowering on the memory of waking to find a heavy arm thrown across her hips... She had fully anticipated him waking as she'd eased herself away but he hadn't, he'd been deep asleep.

Disturb...she had no idea. He reached out and took her arm, just because he *needed* to touch her. It seemed thin beneath the long-sleeved nightdress she had pulled on, which had in its favour a virtual transparency under certain lighting conditions.

'You should have woken me.'

She had woken up next to a beautiful man, and thought he was a dream. She'd had to touch him to make sure he was real. The kiss had not been strictly necessary but she had been unable to resist the final reality check.

'What are you smiling at?' he asked suspiciously, observing the secret curve to her beautiful mouth. 'That is a very prim nightdress.'

'I'm sure Victorian misses got involved in some kissing when nobody was looking,' she retorted naughtily.

'Only the wicked ones,' he rasped, fitting his mouth to hers. She had read his intention but she still gasped at the contact, then groaned when the pressure deepened as his tongue slipped between her parted lips.

'Checking I've not been at the cooking sherry?' she whispered against his mouth.

'You don't taste of sherry, but you don't taste of me. I think we should work on that...'

Her heart was thudding like a drum. 'I d-don't know...' she faltered.

'Oh, I know... I know many things I think a wicked lady might enjoy, and I am a very good teacher.' She raised herself on tiptoe and linked her arms around his neck. 'Am I wicked?'

'With me you are deliciously wicked.' He glanced at the door. 'Is he likely to wake again?'

'It's always a possibility with a baby.'

'Then let us not waste time,' he said, matching his suggestion with action as he scooped her up in his arms and carried her back to the bedroom and the bed.

Much later she lay with her head on his damp chest listening to his heartbeat. His fingers were tangled in her hair.

'You are a g-good teacher,' she said, lifting her face from his chest and gazing at him through her lashes before she kissed his chin and burrowed back down against him.

'I hope Declan doesn't wake now.' She yawned.

He didn't, not until the morning and by then Zac had gone.

That morning set the pattern for the next ten days. Zac spent the nights with her but was gone by the time she woke. During the day Rose cared for Declan—at least it had begun that way but for the past few days Zac had broken into his working day and appeared at unexpected moments to spend a few minutes, an hour or even two with them. She admired the effort that he was making to bond with the baby. Yesterday Declan had slept the entire time he'd been with them and she had ruefully apologised, which had made him look at her... Yes, she decided, going over the moment in her head, it had been an *odd* look.

Maybe he'd read her thoughts?

The idea worried her, as her thoughts were embarrassingly foolish, because *this* wasn't what it felt like to be part of a family, because families were for ever, and this was...*for how long?*

With an effort she pushed away the question that would have spoilt the perfect moment if she'd allowed it space in her head.

All the effort in the world couldn't mask the fact she was a mass of quivering anticipation when he came to her each night. She didn't even try. What was the point? As much as she loved her days, she lived for her nights and the trembling anticipation was part of what she lived for!

And what would it feel like when the inevitable moment arrived and Zac didn't come to her bed? Sometimes she thought it might be easier if he lost interest now. Later would involve more devastation...whereas now...

Now it would hurt like hell!

Sometimes there was no upside to a situation that you walked into with your eyes wide open...everything wide open... Well, she wouldn't be the first woman to lose her heart to Zac Adamos, but she felt a wistful envy for the woman who was the last.

Today there had been no appearance of the tall figure who was fast becoming her drug of choice. It was early evening and Rose was taking advantage of Camille's presence in the nursery to explore, when he did appear. She had headed for the beach, the sand still warm on her bare feet as she wandered along the shoreline, swinging her shoes in her hand as she waded out to meet a wave and then ran back, allowing it to chase her.

'Having fun?'

More than the top of her cut-offs got wet when she heard his voice. Studying him, she forgot to watch for a wave and it hit the backs of her legs, drenching her up to the waist.

Other than the tie that was hanging loose around his neck, he looked as though he had just stepped out of a board meeting—maybe he had. The only place they were on an equal footing was in bed. Elsewhere he was very much the boss.

'Do you ever take a holiday?' she wondered out loud.

His grin suddenly flashed and he looked a lot less boardroom and a lot more bedroom. 'If I was on holiday I'd be giving you that swimming lesson,' he remarked, taking off his jacket and slinging it one-handed over a shoulder.

'I told you, I really don't want a swimming lesson.'

'You think I'm not qualified? You don't trust me?'

Rose refused to react to the challenge in his eyes. He was treating this as a joke, which to her it wasn't.

'I know you are a very good teacher, and yes... I *do* trust you.' The realisation came with a rush of surprise.

'So are you scared?'

A lie would have worked but the truth threw him. 'I am.'

He frowned and looked as discomposed as she had

ever seen him. 'You'd be perfectly safe with me,' he protested.

'It's not about *you*.' Rose was starting to get angry. He just didn't seem to get it—so she told him. 'When I was nine my dad, who thought *he* was a great teacher, threw me in a river. He was a fan of sink or swim. I sank. I didn't just choke a bit, I nearly drowned. The doctors said that the cold helped me—my body shut down so I didn't have brain damage despite being deprived of oxygen for so long—so if it's OK with you, I'll paddle.'

'I had no idea.' That she had almost died because of the actions of a reckless man whose job it was to care for her winded him like a blow to the solar plexus.

He thought about a world without Rose Hill in it and without warning felt an emptiness rise up in him so strong that for several moments he just saw blackness.

Zac looked so shocked that she immediately felt guilty for wheeling out the old story. It was something she'd never done before, and she really wished she hadn't now. She hated sounding like a victim. She'd heard her dad do it so often. He'd never accepted responsibility in his life.

'My dad never accepted that I was in serious danger, because I suppose that would have made him responsible and that is not a role my dad feels happy playing.' Caught out in any wrongdoing, he always became the victim.

Zac's frown deepened. It would seem Rose had no illusions about her father, she knew what he was and he knew she was nothing like him, information he would have relayed to Marco had the man been able to say anything beyond a strained, *'Sorry. Later. Kate is in labour.'*

'Dad embroidered the story over the years, making it a big joke—I jumped in, I played the drama queen, and so on. So you hit a nerve. Can we talk about something else?' she asked, dropping her gaze. The pity she imagined she saw in his eyes made her feel uncomfortable. 'Did you pick up your messages? You had one from your father…' She stopped dead, realising that her awkward change of subject had left her sounding like an eavesdropper—which she was. 'The door to your study was open and the answer machine kicked in. Sorry, I shouldn't have listened, but I did.'

He arched a brow and looked amused by her faltering explanation and guilty admission. 'I had no mobile signal but he caught me later. He did mention he'd tried the landline.'

'A family party sounds lovely.'

Three weeks' time. Where will I be…?

She pushed the thought away and reminded herself that she was going to live in the moment. She flashed a covert glance up at his perfect profile and felt her tummy muscles quiver. The problem was she wanted the moment to last for ever. 'You'll be able to introduce Declan to his cousins,' she added brightly.

'I am not free.' He paused, the sea breeze ruffling his hair as he watched the animated approval fade from her face. She really didn't have a mouth made for compressing, he decided, staring at the full lush outline he had been thinking of all day. His focus had been shot to hell lately. A woman had never distracted him like this before in his life, but then he had never wanted a woman the way he wanted Rose.

'Oh, I just assumed that you'd want to introduce Declan to his family. Sorry, it's none of my business.'

He didn't contradict her. A *sensible* response to his closed expression would have been to drop the subject, but the emotions tightening like a fist in her chest would not be contained. They just spilled out.

'You have no idea how lucky you are. You have a family who love you, who want to be part of your life!' she yelled and saw the shock move across his face. 'And you push them away, at every turn you push them away!' she condemned. 'Well, fine, that's your choice, but this is about Declan and he will benefit from an extended family.' Zac's jaw had taken on an uncompromising angle, which vanished at her last quivering, 'He never needs to feel l-lonely.'

'Were you a lonely child?' he asked, things squeezing in his chest as he imagined her alone—the idea hurt.

Her eyes slid from his as she hid behind her lashes, her shrug saying, *If I have issues, they are mine*—an attitude that should have pleased him. Instead her stubborn self-reliance caused the protective walls he had spent a lifetime building around his emotions, dividing them into neat compartments, to crumble.

He wanted to share her pain, he wanted to take it away.

'You can be lonely in a room full of people.'

Zac recognised the avoidance and the truth of her words. He had frequently felt lonely in the midst of his loving, noisy family, which was in part why he avoided putting himself in that situation.

'That is not answering my question.'

'What quest—' she began, then met his look and gave a resigned sigh. 'All right, maybe, but no more than any other only child. We moved around a lot. It was hard to make friends.' She turned back to him, shading her eyes from the evening sun but unable to read his face, her efforts frustrated when he stepped in close.

She stood still, fighting the urge to put her head against his chest, craving the physical contact, the illusion of safety it offered.

Was it an illusion? she wondered, remembering her unthinking response when he had asked if she trusted him, and she did. Becoming his lover had not been a decision she had questioned, any more than she would have questioned a tidal current. The feelings he awoke in her were just as elemental and primal, but she realised that it would not have happened if she hadn't trusted him.

'I know about scars that are invisible...'

'I have no scars.'

He ignored her protest and framed her face with his big hands, capturing her eyes with his dark obsidian stare. 'Are they why I was your first lover?'

That he appeared to have tuned in on her own train of thought startled Rose. For a moment she considered denying it, instead she hid her unease behind a flippant retort.

'Well, I wasn't keeping myself pure for Mr Right.' He didn't react to her weak laughter, which trailed away in the face of his stare. 'OK, my dad is a very convincing liar.' She took a step back and his hands fell away. She immediately missed the warmth. 'So I suppose,' she conceded, 'I do have a few trust issues.'

Watching her bare toes tracing swirls in the sand, she missed the expression that spread across his face.

The implication of her words was she trusted him, the irony not lost on Zac, who had been lying, at least by omission, from the outset, and now...

Is she the only person you're lying to, Zac?

He was able to switch off the inner dialogue but not the guilt, which remained like a sour aftertaste in his mouth. He tried and failed to spin his actions. Doing it for a friend just didn't cut it, especially when that friend would definitely have issues with Zac's own interpretation of the role he had been given.

He might be selfish, actually there was no might about it, and he rarely chose the option that was not in his best interest, an acknowledgment that did not make him proud. He could keep her in ignorance and keep her here in his bed. The logic was inescapable, or it might once have seemed that way.

The simple fact was she deserved to know that she had the family she craved for. He didn't have the right to deny her that and neither did Marco.

His plan was to tell her before he reported back to Marco. He owed her that much. The sooner this farce was brought to an end, the better as far as he was concerned.

It would be a very short report, basically because there wasn't one. There was nothing to report on except to say that with Rose Hill what you saw was what you got.

His one indulgence before he came clean was seeing her in a setting he had imagined her in, no longer looking the poor twin. She deserved to have the luxury that her sister enjoyed, and tomorrow she would.

Then he would do the big reveal. He could not predict her reaction, but he was pretty sure it would involve her leaving—which he told himself was a good thing. Perhaps she'd take this new and very uncomfortable conscience he had developed away with her. What would he miss, a few extra days, even weeks of incredible sex? He knew himself well enough to know that this attraction he felt would fade, hard to justify depriving her of a future with a family.

'There is a dinner and I'd like you to be the hostess.'

She stopped digging grooves in the sand and looked up, startled.

'I'm sure Arthur is much more capable than me at the list ticking and meet-and-greet stuff. I'm quite likely to send people home with the wrong coats.'

'I think you have the wrong idea. I don't want you to *take coats*! You will be there as my hostess for the evening, and with that in mind I have had Arthur send some appropriate clothing items to our room. Hopefully there will be something you like.'

'*Our* room?'

'All right, your room.' He held up a hand and cut off further protest before she articulated it. 'Let me save you the effort: I will not take clothes from you, I have everything I need…blah…blah…' he drawled, sounding bored.

'Don't put words in my mouth.'

Zac struggled to string the words together as he stared at the lips under discussion and he wasn't thinking words!

'Tell me I am wrong, then,' he suggested. 'And in response to that I will say, no, you do not have anything suitable for a black-tie event and, secondly, it is nothing more than a uniform.'

'Meaning this is nothing more than a job?' She wished the words unsaid even before they left her lips but they seemed to have acquired a resentful will of their own.

'Now who is putting words in someone else's mouth?' he taunted, arching a satiric brow. 'I really don't get why you are being so pedantic, but for the record I am not asking Declan's nanny to be my hostess, I am asking a beautiful woman who shares my bed to be my partner for this dinner. So will you oblige me by doing this? It is a small event, twenty couples or so. I was intending to hold the reception in London, but circumstances intervened…'

So he'd had a date lined up and she was a last-minute stand-in. The possibility was not exactly ego-enhancing.

'What would I have to do?'

'Eat food, drink wine, make conversation and be agreeable. It should not be too taxing.'

Unless you were a social liability... Her dad's description of her floated into her head. She had never questioned his statement, let alone challenged it. She was ashamed that she had lacked the strength and just accepted it. It suddenly occurred to her that this was an opportunity to do just that, prove her dad wrong. He would never know but she would. Suddenly that was very important to Rose as she acknowledged a deep-buried truth, a *hurt* that she had carried.

Zac watched the emotions flicker across her face, saw the change in the tilt of her chin and the defiant resolution that put a sparkle in her eyes, and wondered about what had put it there.

His jaw tightened. It was not his business to wonder what belonged to the family she was about to gain. Before long she would be part of a royal household, protected and loved, and they were about to gain Rose, which made them the winner by any measurement he could think of in this equation.

'Fine, I'll do it, but anything I wear I'll...' Pay? Considering the sad state of her finances, that might prove difficult. 'You can take the cost out of my first pay cheque.'

'I will invoice you,' he responded seamlessly, seeing no reason to share the information that it would take more than one pay cheque to cover the cost of any of the items that he had signed off on.

'Good.'

'Excellent,' he returned, realising he had never had to

work so hard to have any woman fall in with his plans. Rose was damned hard work.

His heavy-lidded glance slid to her mouth—maybe she was worth some hard work. He pushed the thought away as with it came the temptation to ignore his conscience and keep her with him, keep Marco in the dark for a little longer.

'What exactly do I have to do at this dinner?'

'Make people feel at ease.'

What about me? Who puts me at my ease?

'How am I meant to do that?'

'People like to talk about themselves. Be interested, and...' He hesitated, the underlying amusement draining from his voice as he finished on advice he would offer few people. But then few people possessed Rose's natural warmth or her smile, and the fact she seemed utterly unaware of her power made it all the more effective. 'Be yourself, Rose.'

CHAPTER THIRTEEN

THE GUESTS, IT SEEMED, were not staying at the villa but, as Arthur explained, were being ferried in from Athens via helicopter and then flown back. Armed with the information that there were thirty guests and Camille's flattering opinion of her outfit, Rose went to join Zac, who, she had been informed, was waiting for her in the library.

She fingered the necklace that out of the selection had matched the dress she had chosen to wear, a bias-cut slip in a misty green with shoestring straps and a cowl neckline that just hinted at the swell of her breasts. If those stones had been real emeralds they would have been worth a small fortune. She wondered if people who walked around with a fortune around their necks felt nervous. But that wasn't a problem she would ever have, she reflected, smiling at the crazy thought.

She paused for a moment outside the door, telling herself that this was not about proving anything to her father or Zac or anyone else, this was about her. She was doing this for herself.

She walked in without knocking and Zac, who had been standing looking out of the window, turned around. Her breath caught in her throat as she made a rapid toe-to-head survey of his long, lean, lithe body looking utterly spectacular in a formal black-tie dress suit. He looked scarily beautiful and she had no control over her physical reaction to him. Hopefully she retained come control over her facial expression, but she doubted she did.

He had wanted the indulgence of seeing her in the sort of clothes she deserved to wear and now he was. The image of her standing there, the green dress clinging to her supple curves, the jewels around her white throat that needed no adornment, her glorious hair pinned in a loose knot at the nape of her neck, made him want to undo the pins and watch her shake it loose down her slender back.

She deserved the truth, but it would take her from him… He tried to distance himself from the internal battle raging in his head. She would hate him either way.

'You look very beautiful.'

His own voice sounded distant and stiff in Zac's ears as he pushed out the words above the flames licking through his body. Only the guilt gnawing through him stopped him from pulling those pins out of her hair and watching it slip like silk down her back.

Her skin prickled with heat, even her scalp took part in the nerve-tingling assault on her senses. She wanted to tell him how she felt. One look or word from him would have given her the courage, but his air of remoteness made her feel stupid for wanting to declare her feelings and invite rejection.

She pinned on an overbright smile. 'I'm looking forward to this evening,' she lied. She was actually wondering what she was trying to prove. This thing, whatever it was, was going to end badly—did it really matter if that end came tonight or another night? she asked herself bleakly.

When they walked into the room where a string quartet were playing and the guests, glasses in hand, chatted in front of French doors that had been flung open, all eyes turned their way.

Rose froze like someone caught in a spotlight, only moving when she felt the light comforting pressure of Zac's hand in the small of her back.

He watched proudly as she overcame her fears and gradually relaxed as she conversed with the guests, people drawn by her smile and the beauty she was unaware of. By the time they had sat down at the table for the meal she seemed totally at ease.

Except he knew she wasn't. He could see the tension in her shoulders, the tautness in the lovely line of her neck that showed the emerald choker he had noticed in an online auction and had immediately wanted to see against her glowing skin.

Rose knew it was going well and she only wished she could enjoy her success, but she didn't want to be here. She wanted to be anywhere alone with Zac... She'd always dreamed of a home of her own but now she knew that it wasn't about a place, but a person, and the person who was her home just wanted sex. He had a history of keeping everyone, even his closest family, at a distance, and despite her determination to enjoy the moments she had and extract every ounce of pleasure from being with him it was spoilt by thoughts of the future—a future that was never going to include Zac.

The effort of maintaining a front was exhausting, and by the time the only guest remaining was the guest of honour himself, who Zac personally escorted to the waiting helicopter, Rose felt drained.

'A nightcap in the library,' Zac suggested as he walked away. Something in his voice planted the conviction in her head that this would be more than a nightcap, and once the notion that this was goodbye took root, she couldn't shake it.

She walked alone to the library. She would be dignified, she had decided, she would not break down or say something stupid. While she waited, pacing the book-lined room, she caught a glass vase with her elbow. She spun and caught it before it smashed but in the process knocked against a sleeping laptop that surged into life.

Clutching the vase, she turned and her glance landed on the image and headline that appeared on the screen.

The new Princess!

Crown Prince Marco Zanetti of Renzoi married today in the island's cathedral, watched by guests including European royalty and many A-listers, including his good friend, the Greek billionaire, Zac Adamos.

Rose read the paragraph three times, her eyes moving between the new royal couple and Zac, looking urbane and utterly gorgeous…but the face that she kept going back to was that of the princess, because it was her own face. Someone else was wearing her face, a stranger was wearing her face, and Zac was there.

Zac walked into the room, saw the image on the screen and knew it was too late.

Rose, her face as pale as milk, turned when he entered.

'Who is she?'

'Your twin sister. Your father refused to take her back when your mother died, and she was adopted.'

'A sister…a twin?'

'She wanted you both, she loved you both,' Zac said, solemnly.

'My mother didn't leave me? I have a family?' Her eyes zeroed in on his face. 'And you knew?' She shook her head. 'I don't understand...' But she did. Not all of it but most of it, and she could feel the anger surging through her at the betrayal he had compounded.

Zac dragged a hand down his jaw. 'It's not what it appears.'

'Isn't it? Then what is it? You knew who I was from the start?'

His slow nod confirmed her worst fears and the sense of betrayal lodged in her chest felt like a boulder. 'You knew and you didn't tell me.' She breathed out in disbelief. 'None of this is accidental, is it? It was all some sort of set-up... What... I still don't understand, my sister is a part of this?' She felt as if she were choking on the hurt and humiliation. If her heart hadn't turned to stone it would have broken. Instead it was frozen.

'No...no. Kate was looking for you. She doesn't know that Marco, her husband, located you.'

Her sister, her twin, the one she didn't know she had, had been looking for her. Rose struggled to take in the bizarre facts.

'Look, I'm not the person who should be telling you this, but Kate was adopted. She didn't know that she had a twin, but she found a photo and—'

'What am I doing here? Why did this Marco not tell m-my *sister*?'

'Kate is pregnant and she's been unwell. Marco didn't want to upset her again, after your father—'

Her face between her hands, she let out a low keening sound. 'My dad knew... Why am I surprised? Am I the *only* person in the world who doesn't know? Unwell—you said unwell...?' She walked right up to him and grabbed the lapels of his jacket as though she'd shake the truth out him.

'Something to do with blood pressure, but she gave birth to a son yesterday. I just had a text.'

'Oh, that's…' she began releasing the fabric when she paused, her hands tightening into fists. 'You—where do you come in this…this charade? What part do you play, Zac? I take it I'm not here by accident…' Of course she wasn't. Why had she not clocked this earlier? It had never really stood up to scrutiny, but she hadn't scrutinised.

'Marco is my friend. He asked me…you understand. He wanted to know if you were like your…if you were genuine or—'

'Like my father…and you were trying to catch me out. Was sex part of the plan? Are you reporting back on that too…grading me perhaps?' she wondered with withering scorn.

He winced and opened his hands in a pacifying gesture. 'You, me, none of what happened between us was meant to—' he began urgently, only to be cut off by her yell.

'Stop…stop talking!' His agonised expression only fed her fury. She was the one who had been lied to and used, he was the one that did the lying and she had trusted him, felt safe with him.

'I finally trusted someone and it was you—you!' she repeated, her stabbing finger jabbing his chest. She caught her head in her hands…the level of her stupidity was just… 'Stupid, stupid, s-stupid!' she cried, backing away from the hand he extended towards her.

'What can I do, Rose?'

'You can get me in touch with my sister and you can whistle up one of your helicopters because I am not spending another night under this roof!' she spat at him disdainfully. 'And don't try to use Declan. It's perfectly obvious that Camille is more than capable of looking after him… You know, you made me love that little boy and I will n-never forgive you for that. At least I *can* love,' she added, looking him up and down with an expression of utter contempt. 'I don't know what your problem is, Zac, and I don't want to, but you cut yourself off, you deny yourself love…even your family you push away… One day they'll stop trying and then you'll really be alone!'

With a sob that tore his insides she turned and fled, not seeing the hand that Zac extended to her or the look of utter loss etched into his dark features.

Zac was still sitting in the chair he had slumped into when he heard the helicopter take off. Five minutes later Arthur appeared.

'She has gone?'

Zac said nothing.

The older man nodded. 'For what's it worth…my opinion…she was a keeper and you, boss, are a fool.'

The anger in Zac's eyes flared and died as Arthur held his gaze.

'Not for the first time.'

'This is different, boss.'

It was, Zac realised, because Rose had changed him… knowing and, yes, *loving* her had caused a shift in his mindset. He was not the person he had been even though he carried the same baggage. The difference was that now he knew that was *his* choice, he could have let it go, he could have lowered his protective barriers and let people in… And even if Rose wouldn't take him back, he would still do that.

Rose had woken him up.

And he had let her go!

'You're right, I am a fool.'

'That sounds like a good start.'

Rose had spent the long flight hating Zac and wanting to beg them to turn the plane around to get back to him in a miserable cycle. The inexplicable draw she felt to him was real and the farther she got away from him, the more she suffered a deep sense of deprivation.

She had been right. There were soulmates, people that you were drawn to against all logic, but she'd been wrong thinking that soulmate was a perfect partner.

The transfer was a blur and now, as she sat exhausted and dishevelled, feeling hollowed out, in an outer chamber of the palace on the island kingdom of Renzoi, she felt less scared than she would have imagined. The worst had already happened, so what was left to be afraid of?

Despite her alleged lack of fear, her knees were knocking. Rose went through all the possible outcomes that she had developed in her head—she was seeing her sister and this had been achieved in the space of twenty-four hours.

The telephone number that Arthur had given her on behalf of Zac—who at least had the sense not to try to stop her—had not put her through to some generic palace number or even the Crown Prince or one of his minions, but her sister in person.

Rose had just blurted, 'I'm your sister!' before she burst into sobs.

It would not have been surprising if her twin had hung up on her, but she hadn't, she'd stayed on the line until Rose was able to huskily continue.

As she'd listened to Rose's story she had responded with a level of anger equal to, if not exceeding, her own.

'I will kill Marco,' she declared, sounding as if she meant it. 'He has treated me like a child all the way through the pregnancy.'

Rose really didn't want Zac to get off so lightly. She had sobbed her way halfway around the world because of him and there was a massive empty space inside her that she felt would never be filled.

She had trusted him and he had betrayed her. 'But Zac—'

'Zac is a good friend and Marco took advantage, he put him, both of you, in a terrible position.' Her twin had seemed more dismissive of the part Zac played in the deception, saying that Marco had exploited the loyalty of his friend. It was a viewpoint that Rose had not previously considered.

A door opened and Rose looked up as a young man appeared, his eyes widening a little when he saw Rose, a reaction she had experienced several times since she arrived.

He introduced himself. 'I hope you had a good journey? The princess hadn't been told you had arrived. She was, er, feeding the baby,' he said, lowering his voice as though this information was sensitive. 'I have instructions to bring you right to her.'

Rose stepped with some trepidation into what was a sitting room. The moment her eyes met those of her mirror image, who had sprung to her feet, her doubts and fears melted away. They ran into each other's arms.

After the hugging and the tears came the cups of tea and the talking. There were so many things they had in common and so many experiences they yet had to share.

'So our mother died, she didn't reject me?'

'Is that what the old bastard told you?' the princess exclaimed. 'He came here and... I'm so very sorry that you were left with him. My adopted family...' She smiled. 'I can't wait for you to meet them.'

'I always wanted a family and I thought... I won't see Declan again!' Rose wailed.

Slowly the whole story emerged, relayed in shaky fits and starts as she was gently encouraged to get it all out by her sympathetic audience.

The exchange was interrupted when a tall, extremely handsome man appeared.

The prince addressed Rose, not his wife.

'I must apologise. My only defence is my intentions were good, but,' he added quickly in response to the snort from his wife, 'I have been told that I am guilty of infantilising grown women who are able to make their own choices.' He flashed a look at his wife, who Rose could see was fighting off a smile. 'Is that not right?'

There was another snort but Rose could tell her twin's anger was feigned now. 'Do not think you are forgiven yet.'

'You will let me know when I can stop grovelling?' He halted at the arrival of another snort and moved swiftly on. 'Zac is here. He is asking to see Rose. I told him—I told him that it was not my decision to make.'

This time Kate did not hide her grin. 'You're learning.' She turned to her twin. 'So will you see him?'

Rose's heart was hammering a frantic tattoo as it tried to climb out of her chest. 'No...yes...maybe... I think...'

She gazed around the room on the point of tipping over into panic when her twin clasped her arm, pulling her into a hug, and took the decision out of her hands. 'Tell him to come up, Marco,' she said quietly.

'I doubt I could stop him if I tried.'

'Rose, I'll leave. Later you can meet your nephew and his big sister.'

Left alone, Rose began to pace, wringing her hands. Zac was here…why? What did that mean? The door opened and she stopped, her eyes drinking him in… From the beginnings of a beard on his jaw, it would appear he had not shaved since she last saw him, the haggard look around his gorgeous eyes suggested he hadn't had much sleep either, but then that made two of them.

'Thank you for seeing me,' he said, devouring her with his dark-ringed eyes.

Rose didn't say anything. She couldn't. Her throat was clogged with emotion.

'Will you allow me to…? Oh, to hell with this, I'll just say it.' He gave a fatalistic laugh and rushed into impetuous, passionate speech. 'You said I denied myself love, kept myself apart, and it is true I do that. I… I never wanted to hurt anyone…' She could not maintain her frosty stance in the face of his obvious anguish. The tortured expression in his dark eyes tore at her tender heart.

'Tell me, Zac,' she said softly. Whatever he was holding inside was eating him up.

'You know that Kairos, my mother's first husband, raised me. He has been good to me, more so than people understand. My father died of a drug overdose—he was a dealer and an abuser. When my mother, who was sixteen when she was with him, didn't have an abortion as he instructed, he tried to beat the baby, me, out of her… It didn't work and he was sent to prison for the assault, where another inmate stabbed him. When he was in the hospital wing he acquired drugs and overdosed.

'*That* is my heritage, that is the child that Kairos welcomed into his home. I even look like him, apparently, so my mother has to see her abuser every time—'

His voice cracked and she rushed to him, wrapping her arms around him as she buried her face against his chest. 'Your mother sees the son she loves, that is obvious from what you have said. She knows, your stepfather knows, that you are not responsible for your father's actions any more than I am responsible for mine.' She lifted her face to his. 'Unless you think I am?'

'Of course I don't!' he exclaimed, sounding offended by the suggestion as he framed her face between his big hands.

She smiled up at him. 'Exactly.'

'It's not the same. My father was violent, *vile*. If I hurt someone that I cared for…? That I loved…'

His naked fear was out there in the open and her heart ached for the secret dread he had kept inside.

'But you won't,' she said with utmost confidence. 'You are not a predator, you are the opposite. Please don't deny yourself love, Zac. I don't mean me…that is, I *do* love you, but I understand if you can't love me back,' she said, doing what she knew was a feeble job of sounding OK with the situation. 'There will be someone else and—'

'You love me?'

Her eyes slid from his so she missed the fire that lit them. 'Well, I would have thought it was obvious, but as you are being honest so will I. Yes, I'm crazy mad in love with you—'

She got no farther as he rained kisses on her face before claiming her lips and kissing her deeply, soul deep.

'I love you, Rose. The darkness I have carried inside me, you have shone a cleansing light on it. I swear I will never hurt you.'

'I have always felt safe with you, Zac,' she said, stroking his stubble-roughened cheek lovingly.

'You will want children. When I see you with Declan… I never thought I'd father a child, but a child with you…?'

She smiled, more happy than she had ever imagined she could be. 'Don't you think we should get married first?'

He drew back in mock shock, his eyes smiling down at her. 'Did you just propose to me?'

'I rather think I did.'

'Then, my dearest love, my only love, the answer is yes!'

* * * * *

COMING SOON!

We really hope you enjoyed reading this book. If you're looking for more romance be sure to head to the shops when new books are available on

Thursday 28th September

MILLS & BOON

MILLS & BOON®

Coming next month

REDEEMED BY MY
FORBIDDEN HOUSEKEEPER
Heidi Rice

My taste buds were already dancing a jig as Jessie uncovered the feast she had prepared for me.

But as my gaze devoured her lean frame disguised in the baggy T-shirt and scuffed jeans she always wore, and I noticed the flushed dewy skin of her face devoid of makeup as she straightened and grinned at me, the swell of something hot and fluid blossomed in my groin. *Again*.

The irritation twisted into resentment in my gut.

Somehow, the housekeeper I didn't even like had begun to captivate me. I was actually beginning to look forward to seeing her each day, anticipating her arrival like a lovesick teenager.

"I'm sick of always eating vegetables," I added, knowing that my anger had nothing to do with her choice of menu and everything to do with the fact I could not act on my attraction to her, even if I had wanted to.

I did not sleep with my employees. Even ones that fascinated and—*damn it*—excited me.

Continue reading
REDEEMED BY MY
FORBIDDEN HOUSEKEEPER
Heidi Rice

Available next month
www.millsandboon.co.uk

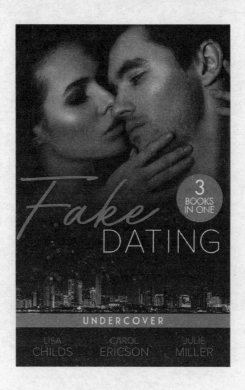

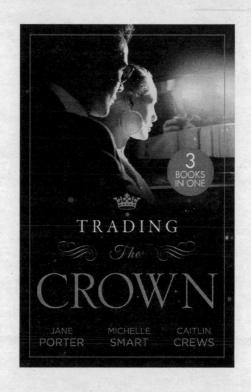

LET'S TALK

Romance

For exclusive extracts, competitions and special offers, find us online:

- **f** MillsandBoon
- **𝕏** @MillsandBoon
- **◉** @MillsandBoonUK
- **♪** @MillsandBoonUK

Get in touch on 01413 063 232